Maggie Ryan
Volume Two

By

Joan Leslie Klengler

Copyright 2011 All Rights Reserved

ISBN-13: 978-1461116110

ISBN-10: 1461116112

II

Many Thanks

To readers of Maggie Ryan Volume One for returning to read the end of Maggie's story.

And special thanks to Restless Globetrotter Jason Rogers for the cover photo. On his journey through the U.S., Jason found himself on a beach in Menominee MI. He took the photo, I found it on my internet search for a true depiction of the beauty of the place where Maggie lived and he was kind enough to allow me to use it.

You can see his work at :

http://www.flickr.com/photos/restlessglobetrotter/

IV

1

Book Four - Maggie and Joseph

More people than will admit it believe in love at first sight. And some of those believe that there is just one person who is meant to be your true love and that you know it the instant you see that person.

People who pride themselves on possessing logic and reason dismiss this kind of thinking even while their own actions make liars of them.

Chapter 1

Joseph Dodge came to Maggie with the horses and it happened like this.

He was a man raised in violence, but one who laid a gentle hand on everything he touched, his guitar, horses, women. There would be no mistaking his heritage. His skin shone like copper, his eyes as black as water at the bottom of a well, and as fathomless. Hair as black as his eyes fell past his shoulders, tied back with a strip of leather when he was working.

The broad planes of his face, high cheekbones, a handsome face, close to beautiful despite the scar than ran down its right side, from just below the cheekbone to his jaw. A thin scar, made by a knife, the skin there a shade lighter than the rest of his face. A thin scar, but the cut had been deep enough that, when he smiled, his mouth lifted only on its opposite side.

He had fought only one man in his life and that man had been his father. Still there was a quiet strength about him that had made fighting unnecessary. He never raised his voice, spoke so softly in fact that people leaned in to hear what he had to say because he commanded respect without asking for it.

He was just under 6 feet tall, lean and hard from his work. He had been a logger, but preferred the company of horses so he had left his home and looked for a place where he could raise and train and ride them. He worked for a variety of people and at last came to a farm on Hoffman K Lane outside Daggett Michigan, the home of an elderly couple named John and Ida Nash. In their younger days, they had raised and trained horses and still had 4 fine quarter horses left of their herd, a young mare and 3 geldings, all bred on their farm.

Advancing age had forced them to ride less, but they would not give up their horses though they had little money to spare. Joseph worked there for room and board, riding the horses, teaching the Nash grandchildren to ride, driving Mrs. Nash to town for groceries and in general doing whatever needed doing on the place.

In January 1975, about the time that Maggie gave birth to her daughter Megan, John Nash had a stroke, not a bad one as strokes go, but enough that it was soon clear that he would have to give up riding altogether and sell the horses.

Joseph Dodge had begun to think of their place as home although he knew in his heart that he would always be the one to move on when circumstances of other people changed, unless he got a real job and made enough money to buy a place of his own.

For now, he had only a meticulously cared for truck, a mid sized mutt named Moses, who rode beside him in the truck's cab, accompanying Joseph wherever he went, and a battered guitar case that held a guitar that he loved second only to Moses.

For their part, the Nashs hated to see him go as much as they hated to let go of their horses.

The first people to come wanted only one horse, a riding horse for their daughter. They favored the mare, but Ida could not bear to separate her from the gelding that had been her companion since birth. So she turned them down and waited.

It was winter and not so many people were looking for horses. But in mid February, Dan Ryan drove into their yard and told them he was looking for horses. John Nash, leaning on his cane, took Dan along to the barn. John could see that Dan knew little about horses.

"Who'll be riding?" he asked.

"My wife" then "Well, I'm not sure. This is a surprise for her. Perhaps she'll just want to watch them."

John Nash wondered how the man could know so little about his own wife. "Where will you keep them? Do you live in the country?"

"No, I bought a farm, 80 acres along the river. There's a good barn and corral. The people who sold me the place are horse people."

"You'll be moving?" John asked, wondering how a man who knew so little about his wife, or horses, would fare in the country, where the woman you lived with and the horses under your care, made up so much of day to day existence.

"No, not me. Not us. The horses will live at the farm. We have a house in town."

John could see that Dan had given this little thought. "Who'll take care of the horses, if you're not living there? Because it's best if someone lives on the land and looks after them. If you only have someone in once or twice a day, things can go wrong with horses fast. They're fine in the morning and then by afternoon, you'll come and find one colicking."

Dan had no idea what Mr. Nash was talking about. Babies colicked, didn't they? "I guess I could hire someone to live on the place. There's a little house on the land."

"Well, now, I've got a man. He trained these horses, taught all of my grandchildren to ride and once these horses are gone, I'll have to let him go. He's a good man."

"Would he be interested in the job?"

"Perhaps he would. You can talk to him. Just one thing, you have anything against Indians?"

Dan had never met an Indian, though the Reservation wasn't far away. But he said truthfully "No."

"Joseph Dodge is his name. Off the Menominee Reservation. Has a gift with the horses. You have kids?"

"Two boys and a girl."

"Then you should think about taking all 4 of the horses. He can teach the kids to ride. It's a good life for kids."

"This is really for my wife."

"At least 2 horses then. One for your wife, one for Joseph, if he's to teach her to ride. Here he is." John pointed his cane at an old truck turning into the drive.

The man who got out of the truck was younger than Dan had expected. A scar ran down one side of his face and Dan tried not to look at the scar when they shook hands.

Joseph began to tell Dan about each of the horses, age, conformation, things that Dan barely followed, but that helped him to make up his mind that Joseph Dodge knew what he was talking about. "Your wife, has she ridden much?"

"Never."

Joseph asked no questions about that, just said "Take the mare for her then. She's a good, gentle girl. I'll take the gelding that's paired up with her for myself, if that's alright. Do you have children?"

"Three"

"You should really take them all then, if you have the space. They might take to riding one day given the chance."

Dan bought all 4 of the horses, also John Nash's trailer, tack and grooming tools. He gave the directions to Joseph Dodge and agreed to meet him at the farm 2 days later.

When Dan arrived on the scheduled date, Joseph was there ahead of him. Before he unloaded the horses, Joseph inspected everything, Dan following behind as he pronounced the barn and stalls sound, corral fencing safe and the ground having good footing and drainage. He tested the waterers and troughs. "Someone really liked horses here. See, these heaters are to keep ice from forming on the water. It's important that the horses drink a lot of water, especially in winter or they can colic."

He even climbed up to the second story and confirmed that the barn roof was solid, no leaks. "We can get a good supply of hay in here without worrying about it getting damp and moldy. Do you buy from a feed supply store or from a local farmer?"

Dan shrugged. "I never needed to buy hay before."

"I brought enough to make the transition so if you'd like, I'll ask around, try to get the best price and order a supply."

Dan agreed.

"As soon as the trails are good, not icy, I'll ride the fence line and make sure it's all secure. It looks pretty, but the weather is rough on wooden fences."

He unloaded the horses then, bringing them off the trailer without effort while Dan stood out of the way, intimidated by their size and the noise they made as they came down the ramp. Joseph took off halters and turned them into the corral, then threw down the hay.

When he finished, Dan said "I'd like to bring my wife out tomorrow. What time would be good for you?"

"It's your place. You pick the time."

"Actually, it's my wife's place. She just doesn't know it yet. Would 10 be alright?"

"Ten's fine. Horses get up early. I'll be done with chores by then."

After Dan drove away, Joseph got his guitar and his suitcases and he and Moses went to check out the house. It was small, the furnishings well worn, but comfortable. He was happy to see a fireplace in the living room. It looked sound and he made a note to see if there was a supply of wood in any of the outbuildings.

The bathroom had a clawfoot tub but no shower. He found bed linens and towels in the hall closet and made up the bed in the larger of the 2 bedrooms, mainly because it looked out at the barn and corral, easier to hear if any of the horses needed his attention in the night.

The kitchen cupboards held assorted mismatched dishes and pots and pans, all serviceable. The gas range and refrigerator were equally old but in working order.

Off the kitchen was a service porch with a relatively new washer and dryer, gas furnace and hot water heater. It would make a good mud room, a place for boots and barn clothes.

Moses followed him from room to room. "What do you think, Boy? Does it feel like a home?" Moses grunted and got comfortable on the bed. "Little early for a nap, Buddy. We need to get some food."

Moses sighed and followed him to the truck. Joseph had

taken Mrs. Nash shopping in Menominee so he knew where to find the grocery store. He stocked up and that night, after he'd seen to the horses and eaten a solitary dinner, he and Moses settled on the couch in front of the little black and white T V. There were no books so he'd have to go to the library and get a card.

He took a bath in the big tub and lay awake in bed for a long time wondering about the woman whose husband would surprise her with a horse farm.

Chapter 2

It had been Maggie's intention to get the boys off to school, but she had been up with Megan and was just too weary. Dan brought them in to say good bye before they left, then stayed behind instead of leaving for the office.

Maggie felt the need to apologize. "I'm sorry, I meant to get up but I'm so tired all the time. Don't you have to get to work?"

"Not today. I thought we'd take a ride."

She looked at him. "A ride?"

"Yes. Come on. Get dressed."

After some cajoling, she agreed and came down and ate a little breakfast. Then she nursed Megan, handed her over to Hannah and let Dan pull her along to the hall to get her coat.

"Not that one, honey. Something warmer. And boots."

"Why? There's a heater in the car."

"Maybe we'll want to stop somewhere." She went along, but with the lack of enthusiasm that had characterized her since she had learned of her pregnancy.

Dan had been so worried about the change in her that he had gone to see her doctor who had told him it wasn't uncommon for new mothers to be depressed.

Dan protested. "It's not like Maggie. She was never depressed before, not with either of the boys."

"What was different this time?"

"She was ready to start her last year of college when she found out about it."

"She can go back and finish. Has she talked about that?"

"No. I tried to talk to her about it, but she refused."

"Well, perhaps you need to help her find a new interest."

Out of that conversation had grown Dan's determination to give Maggie that new interest, something that would bring her back. On his own, he would never have thought of horses, but one night just after Megan's birth, he came upon her in the living room, watching a show on horses on the public television station. Her face was alight with interest for the first time in months. She looked up at him and actually smiled. "They're beautiful, aren't they?"

The next day he had gone to see a realtor he knew. Dan was a logical man and he knew that horses needed land and the land needed to be close enough to home for Maggie to drive there and back.

The realtor said "Strange time of the year to be looking for a horse farm, but you are in luck. A family from Chicago bought a place on River Road. 80 acres with 1500 feet of river frontage. The house isn't much, but you won't be living there. They put up a new barn and an indoor arena, fenced the whole place with that expensive white wooden fence that horse people love, even though it's a nightmare to maintain in this climate. Then they decided it was too far from Chicago and put it up for sale. It's on the market for $120,000 but they'll take less."

Dan said "No, I'll take it. I don't want to quibble back and forth. I want a 30 day escrow, shorter if you can swing it. I'll pay cash, you handle the paperwork."

16

"Don't you even want to see it?"

"I trust you. Oh, and put everything in Maggie's name."

On the drive out River Road, Maggie was silent, staring out the car windows at the snowy woods that lined the road, dense trees thinning occasionally for homes that grew farther apart as they left the city behind.

When he turned in at the drive leading to the farm, Maggie spoke for the first time since they'd left home. "What is this place?"

"It's your place, Maggie. Come and see your horses."

The lack of emotion that had characterized her face for months was replaced by astonishment. "What are you talking about, Dan?"

"Remember the night you were watching that show on horses? You looked happy. I thought this would make you happy. Was I wrong?"

She shook her head, as though to clear it. "I don't know what to say. I don't know anything about horses. What am I supposed to do with them? Who's going to take care of them?"

Joseph Dodge was nowhere in sight but his truck was there, parked in the driveway next to the house.

"I hired a man to live here and take care of the horses and the place. He worked for the man I bought the horses from. He seems dependable, seems to know a lot about horses. That's his truck so he must be around somewhere. So, do you want to come and meet your horses?"

She nodded and, without waiting for him to come around to open the door for her, got out of the car and they walked over to the corral where all 4 of the horses had come to the fence to see who the newcomers were.

Maggie took off her gloves and began to stroke their faces, to talk to them, telling them how very beautiful they were. Without looking at Dan, she said "Are they really mine?"

"It's all yours Maggie, the farm, the horses, all yours."

Joseph Dodge had been about to come out of the barn to greet Mr. and Mrs. Ryan when Maggie pulled off her gloves in the bitter cold to touch the horses. He waited then, wanting her to have this moment to herself. He stood just inside the shadow of the barn, watching Maggie with the horses.

Dan quickly tired of watching Maggie ooh and ah and told her he was going to look around the property. She smiled absently in his direction and went back to stroking the horses.

What may have seemed to some a rash act, going out to buy a farm and 4 horses on the basis of such a little thing, Maggie's momentary spark of interest while watching horses on T.V., was actually based upon a skill that Dan seemed to have been born with, one that assured his success as a lawyer, one honed to perfection over the years.

Dan had the ability to read a situation and to know what was needed to influence the outcome, what steps he would need to take to resolve it to his satisfaction. It was why he was so often on the winning side. Still, he knew equally well when he was not, and then he settled things early so that, even when he lost, he somehow seemed to win.

It was his very success, as much as his love for Maggie, that had made it so hard for him to watch her slip away into long silences and tears, and not to be able to bring her back.

He also knew there was no real downside to the horse farm. If it didn't work out, if she had no interest, or lost interest after a short time, they could always sell the place at a nice profit once the weather turned warm.

Maggie spent a very long time that morning making the acquaintance of her horses, but Joseph continued to wait. Like all good horsemen, patience was a part of his make up. When he decided the time was right, he came out of the barn, into the corral and walked toward her.

She saw him first just as an outline against the darkness of the barn, but before he had taken the first step toward her, she saw him clearly, with a shock of recognition although she knew they had never met, never even passed each other in a crowd.

For his part, Joseph saw her eyes widen, and thought 'she feels it too, this knowledge of each other'. There had been women in his life, but he'd never found what he was looking for until this moment when he found it in the wife of another man.

Would anyone watching them have seen it? Would Dan, if he'd been there, instead of exploring the woods leading down to the river?

Joseph said "Mrs. Ryan, I'm Joseph Dodge. Your husband hired me to live here and take care of your horses."

Maggie put out her hand and said "I'm Maggie, Mr. Dodge."

"You need to put on your gloves before your fingers get frostbite."

"I wanted to feel the horses with my skin, not through the gloves."

"I know, but do you see how your fingers are starting to react to the cold?" He was still holding her hand in his and he turned it against his palm to show her.

She had to take her hand away to put on her gloves. She was thinking about what excuse she might use to put her hand back in his when she realized he had said something and she hadn't heard him. "I'm sorry?"

"Will you be wanting to learn to ride?"

She hadn't considered it until he asked but answered

immediately. "I will but I suppose we'll have to wait for Spring." Her voice full of disappointment.

He smiled, the one sided smile that she would come to know and love, that she already knew and loved. "You don't know your own farm. Can you climb this fence?"

She nodded and put her foot on the lower rail and swung a leg over. He reached up and caught her around the waist and swung her easily to the ground on his side of the fence.

"You did that well. Mounting a horse is kind of like that." He let go of her, and, as she followed him through the corral, the horses fell in behind them, as though they were being led on ropes.

"This is your barn, there are some nice big stalls inside, but I like giving the horses the option of going in and out. There's shelter if they want it. Most of the time, they'll be outside here, with snow on their backs."

"Don't they get cold?"

"They're young and tough. If we baby them, they'll start to have all kinds of problems. If the wind picks up, they'll head inside to get out of it. Otherwise, like I said, they'll choose the outdoors."

On the far side of the barn was another building, just as big as the barn. Joseph opened the gate and put up a hand which halted the horses, while he and Maggie went out of the corral. He closed the gate and the horses waited, looking after them.

"What is it?"

"Riding arena. A big one." He flipped on lights. "The footing is as good as you'll see in a place where they hold horse shows. There's room for jumps if you ever want to try your hand at that."

"I've never even ridden."

"You move like a horsewoman, natural grace. I think you'll be good at it. So, if you like, we can start lessons in here during the winter and go out on the trail when the weather clears, and the trails are safe."

"Okay."

"When would you like to start?"

"Soon. Tomorrow?"

"Sure. We can start tomorrow. Do you have some good boots?"

She looked down and he said "Not those kind of boots. You need some good, safe riding boots, a good heel, not too high, support for your ankles. You should wear something warm. We'll be out of the wind and the weather, but it's cold in here, no way to heat a space this big. Wear layers, none of those big padded down jackets, they'll hamper your movement. There's a good tack store up near Escanaba where you can get the boots and some winter breeches."

He walked around her appraisingly and she said "What?"

"The mare takes Ida Nash's saddle. Just seeing whether it'll be a good fit for you. I think it will."

She heard Dan calling her name. She called back "We're in here."

A minute later, he joined them. "It looks like there's a place for a dock down on the water. It's probably stored in one of the outbuildings for the winter." Then he looked around. "I guess this is your riding arena. Looks like you could put on a horse show in here."

"I'm starting lessons tomorrow. We have to drive up to Escanaba."

"What's up there?"

"A place to buy my riding clothes. Joseph told me what to get."

"Are you sure you want to start so soon?"

She nodded. Dan thought she was close to jumping up and down like a little girl would so he said "We should get going then, if we want to get home in time for dinner. Joseph, you'll be careful with her, right?" Dan put an arm around her shoulders and she resisted the urge to shrug it off.

"I'll keep her safe." As they walked away, he called after her "Maggie, get a helmet too. Not a show helmet, a real one,"

When they got to the car, she said "Dan, wait here. I just have to run back for a second."

When she got back to the fence, Joseph was inside the corral with the horses.

"I don't even know their names" she explained.

"The mare is Sugar. She's yours for sure. This boy" he indicated a rangy black gelding "is Beauty. The smaller chestnut is Hank and the one with the star is Rio."

She repeated all of their names then said "We didn't pick a time."

"Anytime is good. I'm not going anywhere."

"Ten. I'll be here at 10."

She ran to the car without looking back at him. She could feel him watching her.

In bed, that night, she remembered the first touch of their fingers and the way it had felt when he'd reached up and put his hands on her to lift her down from the fence. She flushed all over with the memory of how much she'd wanted to lean against him, feel his warmth all down the length of her body.

Chapter 3

On the day of her first riding lesson, Maggie came down to breakfast with the family. Dan saw it as a sign of good times to come. She had given up family breakfasts early in her pregnancy, due to morning sickness, and had never come back, skipping breakfast altogether unless Hannah forced tea and toast on her while she sat nursing Megan.

Declan said "Those are funny clothes."

Maggie laughed and the boys looked at her and then at each other. It had been so long since she laughed. "They're riding clothes. Mommy is going to learn to ride a horse."

"Can I come and watch?"

"Not today, Deco, you have school. Maybe after I've been riding awhile."

After breakfast, Maggie finished dressing. Over her turtleneck and breeches, she layered several long sleeved tops as Joseph had recommended and last, the jacket she'd bought in Escanaba, fitted, not bulky, made to hold in warmth.

On the drive to the farm, she was so warm, she had to turn off the car heater. She pulled her car in behind his truck and saw him coming out of the house with the dog at his side.
They walked toward each other and she bent down to pet the dog. "What's his name?"

"Moses."

"Is Moses coming along to watch me?"

"Sure, unless it makes you nervous."

"As long as he doesn't laugh at me."

"You'll be fine, Maggie."

As they walked to the indoor arena, Joseph explained what he had planned. He would work from the ground while she would be horseback on Sugar. "She's a real gentle mare, easy gaits, natural rate. That just means when you establish her speed, she'll stay with it till you ask for a change. I saddled her for you today but, as a rule, I'd like you to groom and tack her up yourself. It will strengthen the bond between you."

He showed her how to mount and had her mount and

dismount several times, including on what he called the off side, explaining that you never knew when you might have to do that in a bad place on the trail. "I train horses to accept mounting and dismounting from both sides so she'll stand quiet."

He started her on the longe line, walking her around the arena, first in one direction, then the other, as she got the feel of the mare. "Maggie, sit back on your seat bones. Good. Now let your body follow her motion. That's right. Real relaxed. Very pretty." He unclipped the longe line.

She looked down at him. "Are you sure I'm ready?"

"You're ready. You're just going to be walking here, and I'll be walking alongside you the whole time."

She had felt relaxed from the start, working with Joseph, and was sorry when he told her it had been enough for one day. "When can we do it again?"

"Tomorrow morning. We can work every day, as often as you like."

He showed her how to lead Sugar back to the barn and tie her.

Then they unsaddled and groomed the mare, working together. When they had finished and turned her out with the other horses, he asked Maggie if she'd like something warm to drink before she left.

She followed him to the house and he said "You haven't seen the house yet. Why don't you look around while I fix us something."

She left him in the kitchen and walked through the rooms, accompanied by Moses. When she came to the bedroom that was his, she ran her hand over the bedspread and touched the pillow. As she turned to leave, she saw the guitar case.

When she got back to the kitchen, he was pouring hot chocolate into 2 mugs. She sat down and he sat across from her. "You play the guitar."

"I play a little. Piano too, when there's one to play."

"Where did you learn?"

"Reservation school. My mama encouraged it. She told me I could play football if I learned music too." He smiled at some memory.

30

She asked him to tell her more about horses and he obliged. She just wanted to listen to the cadence of his voice, the rhythm and intonation so different from her own, from anyone she'd ever heard.

Finally, she forced herself away, not wanting to leave, but thinking I have to go home sometime. I can't stay here forever.

He walked to the car with her and said "So, tomorrow then."

And she said, "Yes, tomorrow" looking in the rear view mirror at him until she turned onto the road and couldn't see him anymore.

Chapter 4

Every morning after that, Maggie woke early. She got Megan up, nursed her, bathed her, rocked her and cuddled her, even holding onto her while she ate her own breakfast, yoghurt, fruit, tea and toast. She had this breakfast in the dining room with Dan and the boys, and expressed great interest in everything that Colin and Declan had to say about school, sports, and their friends.

Dan was enormously pleased at how well his plan had paid off. The horses had brought Maggie back from her depression.

When he drove the boys to school, they said "Mama's happy again" and he was even more pleased.

As soon as Dan and the boys left, Maggie pumped breast milk for Hannah to give to Megan by bottle, and then, wifely and motherly duties satisfied, she dressed for riding and drove to the farm.

As soon as she left the River Road and turned onto the long drive leading to the farmhouse, she felt that she was crossing a line that divided her life. On one side, she was Dan's wife, and the mother of Colin, Declan and Megan. On the other side lived Maggie, a person separate from everyone else in the world but Joseph Dodge.

By the time she arrived, his chores were finished and he was waiting for her. Their routine was to groom and tack the horses together, working side by side in the barn, their breath and the breath of the horses cloudy and warm against the cold air.

When they finished riding, unsaddling and grooming, it was their routine, unspoken after the first day, to go to the house for coffee or hot chocolate to warm up. They sat across from each other, sometimes talking, sometimes silent, but always comfortable. One morning, in the second week of her lessons, they were sitting just that way, when Maggie looked down and saw that her breast had leaked milk, leaving a round wet spot over her heart. She pressed a napkin to the spot, embarrassed.

She began to wean Megan then, though Dan watched the process with disapproval, finally commenting that it seemed too soon. "My breasts are sore" she said in explanation. But it freed her to lengthen the time she spent at the farm each day.

At first, she had arrived by 10 and left by 1. When she began to linger, they added lunch to their routine. Some days, she arrived with sandwiches and salads from a shop on the Square near her home. Other days, she arrived empty handed and he fixed them something, often leftovers from his dinner of the night before.

After lunch, they cleaned up the kitchen and then she accompanied him on his rounds of chores, helping wherever she could.

But then she had to rush to be home before Dan which she always tried to do to avoid his saying that she spent too much time away.

She always rode Sugar, while Joseph alternated among the 3 geldings to give them all equal time and exercise. They had begun riding together in the arena the first week in March and now March was drawing to a close, but the trails remained icy. Joseph promised her that soon it would begin to thaw, and once that happened, they could start riding on the trails.

He wanted to ride the fence line to be sure everything was secure, before the weather turned enough to allow the horses access to the pastures. And he felt that it would be a good way for her to get a real feel for riding in the open. "Checking fences is slow work. We'll probably have to break trail in some places. By the time real good weather comes, you'll have enough hours in the saddle to start doing some trotting on the trails and after that, we'll see about teaching you to lope."

Maggie was already longing to be out of the arena. One day she told him "I love being on Sugar, but riding around in circles is getting old."

"What kind of music do you like, Maggie?"

"That's a strange segue. Why do you want to know?"

"Just tell me."

"I like some classical, but mostly I like rock music, basically I like anything I can dance to."

When he finished the afternoon chores, he drove into Menominee to shop for groceries. When he finished, he took the bags back to the truck. When he didn't get in, Moses gave him a "What gives?" look. "Just have an errand to run, Boy, then we'll go home." Moses sighed and settled down to wait.

Joseph walked down to the K Mart at the other end of the shopping center. He found a decent tape player and then selected some tapes that he thought she might like. The next day when she arrived, he had set up the tape player in the arena.

When he turned it on, she laughed. "Are we going to dance?"

"In a manner of speaking. We're going to let the horses do the dancing. It'll be a little more fun for you than riding in circles. Take a look at the tapes. If you don't like them, tell me what you do like and I'll get more when I go shopping."

They worked that day, and the days after that, on riding patterns and exercises to the music.

The week after Joseph brought out the tape player, Maggie arrived for her lesson early. "I brought a tape. It's one of my favorites. A lot of the music is slow but we can listen while we ride, right? We don't have to ride in time to the music."

"Whatever you like, Mrs. Ryan."

"Don't call me that."

"Why not?"

"I'm Maggie. For you, I'm Maggie." What she thought but didn't say, was that she didn't want Joseph to think of her as Dan's wife.

Joseph looked at her for so long that she felt her face growing hot, flushed, but she held his gaze. Then he said "Maggie." He held out his hand for the tape. He looked at it. "Neal Diamond's Greatest Hits."

"Do you know his music?"

"I do." He read the song titles to himself. "There's one here that you can ride to. Are you ready to lope?"

"You tell me. Am I ready?"

"You are. Come on."

When they had saddled and walked into the arena, he stood back and watched Maggie mount up. He stayed on the ground, keeping Beauty by his side. He went and put the tape in and started it, finding the song he wanted.

Before he pushed play, he told her what he wanted her to do. "Sugar is trained to lope when you kiss to her. You don't need to cue her with your legs or anything. Just kiss. Sit back, relax, keep your reins at that length, that's good, not too long or too short. You don't want to catch her in the mouth and pull her down to a trot. Are you ready to try?"

Maggie took a deep breath and nodded.

Joseph smiled. "When the music starts, kiss to her." He pushed play and watched.

Maggie had a certain natural gift for riding, but Joseph could see that she was nervous. He turned down the volume. "Listen to the rhythm of this song. Now follow Sugar's movement with your pelvis. Relax, Maggie. Ride her like you're making love. Stop thinking about it. Just go with your feelings."

He watched as Maggie began to relax, as Sugar, sensing her relax, picked up a gentle little rocking horse lope, a slow, graceful gait. He watched as Maggie and Sugar fell into perfect synch.

When the song ended, she continued to ride, calling out to

him "Again, please, Joseph. Can we do it again?"

He replayed the song, able to watch her without coaching, without speaking. He felt an ache inside at how beautiful they were together, Maggie and Sugar, their breath making white clouds in the cold air.

When the song ended, Maggie slowed Sugar to a walk and rode to where Joseph stood with Beauty. "Can we ride together, to that song?"

For answer, he rewound to the beginning of the song, pushed play and swung into the saddle. They circled the arena at a slow lope, side by side, close enough to feel each other's warmth.

They continued to ride after the song ended and another song began.

As they walked the horses back to the barn to unsaddle, Maggie said "You picked the most perfect song in the world to teach me to lope. Who would ever think that Holly Holy would be the exact right tempo for riding a horse?"

When they finished caring for the horses, Maggie said "You

can go ahead to the house. I'll be right in."

She went back to the arena and got the tape player and tapes.

She came in through the mud room and took off her boots and heavy jacket and came into the kitchen in her stocking feet. She put the tape player on the counter and found a tape by Gordon Lightfoot. She turned it on, the volume low and said "I'm freezing."

"Are you starving?"

"That too. Are you making lunch? Can I help?"

"Almost ready. It's clam chowder."

She saw that he was holding a bottle of Bud. She took the bottle from his hand and took a drink, gave it back to him and watched as he put his lips to the place where her mouth had been.

He handed the bottle back to her while he filled bowls with the chowder.

She finished the beer and went to the refrigerator and got two more bottles and sat down at the table.

He sat across from her and watched while she tasted the chowder.

"It's so good. Did you make it?"

He nodded. "My mom's recipie. No potatoes allowed. You like it?"

"It's wonderful. I can't cook at all. If it weren't for Hannah, we'd all starve at my house." She wished at once that she could take back the words. She never wanted to remind him that she had a husband, children, a life outside of the time she was here with him.

In early April, there was a thaw that lasted and on the third day, Joseph had the horses saddled when she arrived in the morning. "What's this? I thought I was supposed to saddle my own horse."

"First day on the trail. I wanted us to get an early start."

They rode along the driveway toward River Road, on the pasture side of the fence, Moses walking alongside, occasionally running ahead and then back to them, Joseph in the lead on Beauty, whom he pronounced the calmest of the 3 geldings, "in case we meet up with any wildlife."

"Like what?"

"Deer, a bear, never know around here."

She listened to the calm in his voice and thought that with him in front of her, she wouldn't even be afraid if they did meet a bear. "Will Moses be okay if we meet a deer or something?"

"Sure. He knows not to chase the wildlife."

Just before River Road, he turned Beauty and they followed the fence. "If you see anything I miss, a broken board, anything like that, you just give a holler. We'll need to mark where it is so I can come back later and fix it."

They had been out about 20 minutes when Joseph pointed to a break in the fence. "There's the first one." He stopped Beauty and Sugar stopped behind him. He studied the fence. "It's not bad. I think I can put that back together without a new piece of wood." He rode on.

There were no other problems with the fence until just before the end of the open pasture. Maggie spotted this one. "Joseph, the fence is kind of sagging right there."

"It looks like I'll need to shore up that post. It's too cold to cement it. I'll shore it up with rock till it warms up a little."

Where Maggie's land turned along the bend of the road, the trees started. They hadn't ridden far when Joseph halted the horses again. "The woods are pretty deep here. I don't see an easy way through. We'll turn back."

"Didn't you say we could break trail?"

"I did, but not at this time of year. There's still a lot of unmelted snow and ice in under the trees where the sun can't get to melt it. And a lot of dead branches that could snap off over our heads. Breaking trail is a job for warmer weather. Don't worry, I'll take you along when it's time."

"What are we going to do now?"

"Turn around and start back. It'll be lunch time by the time we get there. After lunch, I'll come back and fix those bad places in the fence."

"Can't I come along and help?"

"If you'd like. We'll take the truck and drive along the road, work from that side. We'd take the horses if all I needed was a hammer and nails, but you remember that sagging post?" She nodded. "We'll need a shovel and some rock for that."

They rode on and after a bit she asked "How will you find the places we need to fix?"

"I marked them, in my head. Old Indian trick." The corner of his mouth turned up in a smile.

She smiled back at him. "Really, can you do that?"

"Nah, I just looked around at the terrain, spotted some things to use as landmarks." But she wasn't sure he hadn't been telling the truth the first time.

They took care of the horses and went in to lunch. She heated soup while he made toasted cheese sandwiches. They were silent while they ate, but when they finished, she said "Tomorrow's Saturday. What do you do all weekend?"

"Take care of the horses, clean up the house, laundry. Maybe make something special for dinner, read, listen to music. Pretty dull around here on weekends. What about you?"

"Saturdays we take the boys to the Y. There are a lot of kid activities and they swim. I just started back in playing racquetball, then I sauna and have a massage. The guy who gives the massages is blind. It happened in Viet Nam. His wife works there too. They're my friends. Actually, they're why I went to college."

"When did you finish college?"

"I didn't. This was supposed to be my last year."

"Why did you quit?"

"I had Megan, my baby."

"That's right. You were nursing when you first came here."

"You knew that? You saw me the day my milk soaked through my shirt."

"She's old enough to be weaned?"

"I started weaning her the day after my shirt got wet."

"Why?"

"Dan said she was too young but I told him my breasts were sore. I was already pumping breast milk to cover the time I was here riding. But I couldn't pump enough to feed her all through the day and I wanted to be here." She almost added 'with you'.

"Will you go back to school?"

"No. I found something better."

He stood up. "We should get started on that fence if we're going to finish today."

She followed him out to the tool shed and watched while he selected what he needed, then she helped him carry things to the truck. After that, he looked around until he found some good sized rocks and he lifted those into the truck bed. Then they got in, with Moses between them, and drove out and along the road until he said "There" and pulled onto the shoulder.

Maggie had seen nothing to identify the spot, but he was right and she held the boards in place while he hammered in nails and tested it to be sure it would hold.

The second place required more work. She watched Joseph dig around the post and then place the rocks to secure it.

On the way back to the house, he said "I'll ride out along the road past here tomorrow and check out the fence from this side, since we can't access it from your land because of the woods."

"Couldn't you wait till Monday? Then we can do it together."

"It'll be longer than today. It's pretty cold work."

"I'll be fine, really."

"Okay then. Monday's lesson is riding along the side of the road, looking at more fence."

While they were seeing to the horses, he said "I've been thinking it might be a good idea to fence off some of this pasture to keep the horses from getting back there in those deep woods. No telling what they might run into if they wander off. There's going to be a lot of heavy vegetation under the trees that could hide some bad holes and in the summer there'll be ground bees. It's up to you though. It wouldn't be cheap. I'm guessing you don't want to do it cheap and use barbed wire."

"No, no barbed wire. But you're right. I think we should do that."

"You okay it, I'll get the supplies. I can do most of the work myself, but I'll need some help with the posts. Not from you either. It's hard work. I'm sure there's some kid around here who can use a little extra money. We can work weekends when school's out. Finish before we turn the horses out for Spring. And it won't interfere with your lessons."

On her way home that afternoon, Maggie stopped at the lumber yard and set up an account for Joseph to buy whatever he needed for the farm. At dinner, she told Dan that they'd be getting some bills for supplies that Joseph would need to cross fence the pastures to keep the horses out of the woods.

"You seem to be taking quite an interest in running that place. What are you going to do when you go back to school and don't have the time?"

She didn't tell him that she wouldn't be going back, just said "September's a long way off. No need to plan that far ahead."

Chapter 5

On Saturday, Dan took Maggie to dinner at Red and Ed's Supper Club. It was a busy night and they waited at the bar a long time for their table. Maggie had stopped drinking with her pregnancy and while she was nursing, but when Red Bradley, who was behind the bar that night, asked her what she'd like, she ordered a martini and when she finished that one, she ordered another.

She felt lightheaded on the way to their table, but it passed when she started to eat. Dan suggested a good Cabernet and they finished the bottle.

When they got home, she looked in on Megan and the boys. By the time she had bathed, she thought Dan would be asleep, but when she got into bed, he reached for her. She pulled away. "What's wrong?"

"It's too soon."

"Maggie, Megan is almost 4 months old. It's been a long time."

She sat up and turned on the bedside table light. "I don't

want any more children."

"We'll be careful."

"You said that before. I wanted to get my tubes tied when Megan was born and you said I was too emotional to make such a complicated decision. I'm not going to take any more chances, Dan."

"You're refusing to sleep with me?"

"No, I'm refusing to have sex with you until I know we won't make any more mistakes."

"Are you saying that Megan was a mistake?"

"Don't twist my words. I'm not going to get into that argument with you. If you don't want me to have my tubes tied, then you do something. Have a vasectomy."

"Are you serious?"

"I mean it, Dan."

"You'd ask me to do that?"

"Aren't 3 children enough?"

"I'll think about it, really, I will."

He reached for her again, but she said "Don't touch me."

"Maggie, I know how difficult it was for you, getting pregnant when you didn't plan it, having to miss a year of school. But you can go back to school. Everything is going to be fine now. I missed you so much. You won't get pregnant again. I promise you."

She got up then, and walked to Megan's room. It had been a guest room and, in addition to the crib, there was a double bed. She tiptoed in so as not to wake the baby, and got under the covers and lay awake in the dark, thinking that, even if there were no chance of her getting pregnant, she didn't want to sleep with Dan any more. Wondering how she was going to manage that, knowing it wasn't possible to refuse him forever.

Chapter 6

It had become a tradition for Maggie's parents to have dinner at the Ryans on Sunday evening. The day after Maggie slept in the guest room for the first time, when she saw Maeve and Patrick, Maggie remembered back in the day when her mother had banished her father to the sewing room. Still she never felt there was any common meeting ground between her mother and herself, felt no desire to confide in her mother or seek her counsel.

Patrick noted that Dan was quieter than usual, and that he refilled his wine glass more than was ordinary.

His grandsons, Colin and Declan, had a great deal to say about school, friends and sports. Maeve, although she appeared impartial to the casual observer, doted on Declan, something that Patrick could see because he was no casual observer. He knew it was because Declan looked like Robbie, or perhaps it appeared as if he did, because he had Robbie's sweet manner.

Most striking to Patrick however, was the change in Maggie, who was suddenly lively and cheerful in a way she hadn't been since she had learned of her pregnancy with Megan. As

Hannah served dessert, he leaned toward her and said "So sweetheart, how're the riding lessons coming along?"

Now her face truly lit up. "Oh, Da, it's wonderful. Sugar, that's my mare, is so beautiful. At first, we rode in the arena for weeks and weeks till I told Joseph I was tired of just riding in circles so he asked me what kind of music I liked, and the next day we had music, a tape player, so we could ride to the music, like dancing, he said."

Patrick exchanged a glance with Maeve, who hadn't missed a word, in spite of the other conversations going on around them. Maggie would have gone on, but Patrick put a hand on her arm and interrupted. "Darling, let's go up and take a look at my baby granddaughter, shall we?"

On the way up the stairs, she took up her story again. "We finally went out on the trail, riding the fence line, looking for breaks, and we found two and I helped Joseph make the repairs. When it gets warmer, we're going to ride in the woods and break some trails."

By then, they were at the nursery and went in to find Megan awake and cooing happily to herself. Patrick reached down and picked her up and cooed back at her. She smiled in delight and he rocked her in his arms while he and Maggie stood together.

Maggie continued on. "Oh, Da, you have to meet him. I'll bring him to Kelly's one day or better yet, you can come out to the farm. You haven't been there yet. You can see the horses."

Patrick continued to rock Megan but turned his attention to Maggie. "This has surely been a good thing for you. It's brought you back to life. But, Maggie, don't speak of these things to Dan, or where he can hear you. It's written all over your face, the way you feel about this man."

"Joseph, his name is Joseph."

"And Joseph, how does he feel about you? Do you know?"

"The same, I think." Then, after a minute, "I know he does."

He nodded down at Megan. "She looks like you."

"Does she?" Maggie asked, but he could see her thoughts were elsewhere.

In the car on the way home, Maeve said "Well, we're in for it now."

"It seems so."

Is there anything to be done about it?"

Patrick shook his head. "It's a done deal, my girl. Maggie has found her one true love."

"Is she in his bed already?"

"Not yet, Maeve, but she will be.

"Ah, poor Dan."

Patrick said "Save your pity. I should never have let her marry him. But she was so sure it was for the best."

"Because of the baby, I suppose" she mused.

"You knew? Of course you did. And the father?"

"Oh, no doubt Colin is Michael's baby. Dan wouldn't have touched her before he married her. Patrick, do you suppose

Dan knows?"

"About the baby? Hard to say. Smarter men than Dan Ryan have fooled themselves when they were hopelessly in love. My fear is the danger to Maggie if he should find out about what's going on now. And how can he not, she's already crazy in love. She won't even try to hide it."

"I don't see Dan as violent, but vindictive, that he would be."

Chapter 7

Patrick was the first person Maggie could talk to about Joseph.

For his part, Joseph had no one to talk to but Moses. If he had, he would have talked of Maggie Ryan. He would have said that her eyes were the deepest blue he'd ever seen, that her smile made him want to smile, that her presence in his kitchen was a gift and he wished for excuses not to wash the cup she drank from so that he could place his mouth where her mouth had been. He delighted in watching her on horseback.

And at night, in his bed, he longed for her, dreamed of her, knowing that the fact that she was another man's wife made what he wanted wrong, but already beyond caring that it was wrong, beyond pity even for that poor man who would lose Maggie Ryan.

Chapter 8

When Maggie got to the farm on Monday, Joseph had driven into the pasture where the woods began and was unloading fencing supplies from the truck. She went out to help him. "You got an early start."

"Found a helper too. Boy from the farm across the road. He'll work cheap, mainly he just wants a horse to ride. They don't keep horses over there. I'll make a start afternoons when you and I are through for the day, and he'll work all day Saturday and Sunday. He'd be willing to work after school, but he has his own chores to do for his dad."

"Maybe I could help on the weekdays after we ride."

"This ground is still pretty frozen. I'm thinking of building a small fire at each place where we need a post. It'll make the digging easier. With these cold nights, if we wait for a real thaw, we won't finish in time. At this time of year, as long as there's no wind, we won't have to worry about the fire getting out of control."

All that week, Maggie and Joseph rode for 2 hours in the morning, ate lunch and then went out to the pasture to work on the fence. By Friday, they had dug and placed posts across almost half the field. They were finishing up when Maggie looked up from her work and saw a boy walking toward them.

He looked to be 16 or so, with curly blond hair and a shy smile, about her height and of average size, except that, even in his winter clothes, she could see that he had the strong arms and legs of a boy who has been doing manual labor all his life.

For just a minute, she thought of Michael, of how he'd changed physically after he began to work construction for the Richards brothers. It was like comparing Dan, who sat behind a desk, and got his exercise on the golf course, and Joseph, who worked outside training and riding horses, and fixing everything that needed fixing.

When the boy reached them, he said "Hi, Mr. Dodge", smiling shyly in Maggie's direction.

"Hi, Chuck. And it's Joseph, I thought we agreed on that. Chuck Schmitt, this is Maggie Ryan, the lady who owns this place."

"Hello, Mrs. Ryan. This is really a nice place. You've got some nice horses too."

"Thank you, Chuck. And it's Maggie, please. Have you had a chance to ride yet?"

"Not yet. It looks like you guys have done all the work."

Joseph smiled. "Maggie's been working me really hard all week. But there's still plenty for us to do this weekend."

Chuck said "Don't worry. Mrs. Ryan, Maggie. We'll get the rest of those posts in real quick."

She leaned toward him, as though to tell a secret. "Don't you let Joseph do nothing but work all weekend. The two of you take the horses out for a ride."

Chuck hung around and helped them to put away the tools. Then the three of them went to the house and sat at the table drinking hot chocolate. Maggie learned that Chuck was an only child, his parents having married when they were older. He was 16 and wasn't sure he wanted to farm when he finished high school. "My parents have made a real good living off the farm. They run a dairy herd and grow their own hay, with enough left over to sell. And they've got some row crops too. But it's hard work, not that I'm complaining, but with animals, you're real tied down. I'd like to go to college, probably just the Center to start."

"That's where I went" Maggie said.

"What did you study?"

"This and that, a little psychology, philosophy, history. I thought about going to law school, but I didn't finish college."

"Why'd you quit?"

"I had a baby."

"But you could go back. Are you going to?"

"I don't know. I don't think so. I like the farm, the horses. I like being here all day."

"But you don't live here."

"No, I live in town."

"Your husband, he's that lawyer, right?"

"That he is."

"Is that why you wanted to be a lawyer?"

"No. That was something I wanted when I was younger."

"Sorry, I ask too many questions. I'd like to be a writer." He looked self conscious when he said it.

Maggie said "That's wonderful, Chuck. What a great ambition. Make sure you never let anybody tell you that you can't do it."

Joseph had been quiet, listening to them talk. Chuck suddenly seemed aware of that and apologized for taking up their time. But Maggie assured him it had been a pleasure and then he said good bye.

After he'd left, she said "He seems like a really nice boy, Joseph. I'm glad you found him to help out. And I'm glad he'll have an opportunity to ride since he likes it so much. Make sure you both take the time. I meant that. We don't have to hurry with the fence."

"Maybe when we finish the fence, we could find some other

little chores for him to do. That way, he could keep riding. Once he starts, it would be too bad if he had to give it up. And you've got the 4 horses to exercise."

"It's fine with me, Joseph."

"He and I will make some real progress tomorrow."

That reminded Maggie that it was Friday and she wouldn't be back to the farm until Monday. She felt her old depression creeping up on her, and Joseph sensed it. "What's wrong, Maggie?"

" I hate the weekends. I hate not being able to come here."

"Maggie. We have 5 days out of 7. We shouldn't be greedy. Many people have less."

When she came back on Monday, a long section of fence had already been completed. Each day, she and Joseph did a little more, and then on the weekend, Joseph and Chuck did more, so that by the first really warm weather, in May, the fence was complete.

Maggie and Joseph invited Chuck to come over after school

on Friday to celebrate and they turned the horses into the pasture, and watched them for awhile, then went inside, and made a feast out of Joseph's leftovers and took all the food outside and sat on the porch steps and ate, looking out to where the horses were exploring their new place, tentatively at first, and then, with increasing spirit, until they were running and playing like foals.

Chapter 9

June. Glorious warm summer that arrived early. The boys were out of school, but fortunately for Maggie, involved with their own friends, and with Day Camp.

Maggie still spent the early morning with Megan, but then handed her over to Hannah, who was happy to spend her day with the baby, almost as happy, it seemed, as Maggie was to spend her day with Joseph. Dan appeared oblivious to the routines of his wife and his housekeeper, so things hummed along without incident, without questions.

One morning in the second week of June, Joseph cut their ride short due to an unexpected early onset of oppressive heat. "When you combine the temperature and the humidity readings, and the figure is this high, it's not good to work the horses long or hard."

They hosed all 4 horses down and then watched them find places in the shade under the trees. Maggie and Joseph went into the kitchen for cold drinks, but found the kitchen already uncomfortably warm before noon. She mopped her forehead with a paper napkin.

He said "You should go home. Your place is on the Bay. It's bound to be cooler there."

But instead of agreeing, Maggie got an aha look on her face. He watched it appear and waited to see what she would say. "Come on."

"Where?"

"Just come on. You too, Moses." When they got outside, she said "You drive."

"Where?"

"Head for Menominee and I'll give you directions when we get there."

Initially, Moses sat between them in the truck cab, but eventually, he crawled over Maggie's lap to hang his head out of the window, pushing her toward the middle, next to Joseph.

She took him into Marinette over the Interstate Bridge, avoiding First Street and the Ryan house, although when they crossed the Bridge, she could look to the right and see the Law

Office of Daniel Ryan. They went through downtown and continued on Main Street until they got near Kelly's. "This is Menekaunee. I grew up here. Turn down this street, I'll show you our house and the beach." When they got to Red Arrow, there weren't so many people and they got out and let Moses run ahead to a place in the sand. Maggie took off her shoes and they sat down. "I think it's at least 10 degrees cooler here by the water than it is on the farm."

"So this is Menekaunee. Do you know that this is the place where my people come from? The Menominee tribe settled here, at the mouth of the River in the 1600's, maybe earlier."

"I never knew that. My people came here from Ireland, but a lot later, 1933. So, in a way, we come from the same place. See that pier? My father took me fishing there when I was a little girl. Now we take my kids fishing." She stood. "Come on. I'm going to take you to meet my Da."

When they got to Kellys, she said "We can bring Moses in and put him in the back room."

But he said, "No, it's cool here. We're in the shade and there's a breeze. He'll be good with all the windows open on the truck." Still Maggie went in and came back with a bowl of water for Moses. Then they went in through the back door.

The regulars were playing cards and greeted her as though they saw her every day. She introduced them to Joseph and they were polite, betrayed no curiosity, and went back to their game.

When she and Joseph came into the bar room, it was quiet, dark and cool. There were a few customers, no one Maggie knew, and Patrick was behind the bar. She and Joseph sat down side by side at the end of the bar and waited for Patrick to come over.

"Da, this is Joseph Dodge. Joseph, this is my father, Patrick Kelly."

Joseph stood and held his hand out across the bar "Sir."

"Nice to meet you, Joseph. Must be hot out on the farm today."

"Yes, sir, it is. We gave the horses a bath and left them sleeping under the trees. Maggie wanted to come and show me Menekaunee."

"And Da, guess what, Joseph's people are from here, since at least the 1600's."

"You don't say. Well, that calls for a drink. Bud okay?"

"Yes, sir."

Patrick came back with 3 bottles of Bud and said "To the tribes – both the Menominee and the Irish." They clinked bottles and drank.

Patrick and Joseph talked – about the early settlement of Menekaunee, then what it had been like for Joseph growing up on the Reservation, which Patrick confessed to never having visited. Maggie looked from one of them to the other, delighted and breathless, until, too soon, Joseph said "We should be getting back. I have to see to the horses and Maggie will need to be getting home."

Moses was asleep on the front seat. He greeted them and sat in Maggie's lap on the drive back to the farm.

"Your father's a good man. You're very close to him."

"Me and my Da. It's always been that way. My Ma and I are

always rubbing each other the wrong way. Except for the times when one of the men does something careless or unthinking. Then she looks at me like another woman, like we see things clearly, things the men don't understand. Even when I was really young, she'd look at me that way."

Joseph glanced at her, then back at the road. She seemed lost in some memory. He didn't question, but after a minute, she went on. "I was 15 the summer that my brother Robbie's girlfriend got pregnant. I was there when he told my Ma. He didn't really seem to know what it was going to mean to him, how it was going to change everything. My Ma and I, we looked at each other, and we knew."

She was quiet again, far away. "The baby was born dead. And then he died. My brother. Robbie. He was the favorite. Of all of us, but especially my Ma. He was killed in a hunting accident." There were tears on her face but she didn't make a sound.

Joseph reached across the seat and put his hand over hers. She closed her fingers around his and held on all the way back to the farm.

******

That night, Maeve and Patrick sat on the porch after dinner to catch the breeze off the Bay.

"Maggie came by the bar today."

"Did she? Any special reason?"

"She brought along her man, Joseph Dodge."

Patrick could feel Maeve looking at him even without turning his head to see.

"And?"

"He's a fine man, quiet, strong. You can see he's worked all his life."

"I'm sure. And Maggie? Will anyone who sees them together know that she's smitten?"

"Even more than that. She adores him and he feels the same."

"Did they say?"

"No need. It's plain as day."

"No good can come from this."

"One good, anyway. Maggie will know what it is to love and be loved in a way most people only dream."

"She'll pay dearly for her love before it's done."

"Perhaps it will be worth the price."

"You always loved her too dearly to see the consequences of the things she does." She watched his face. "Don't deny it Patrick. It's the truth."

"I wouldn't lie to you, my love. But there's no way around this. It's done. Dan Ryan set it all in motion years ago when he determined to have Maggie at any cost."

Chapter 10

Maggie learned the story of Joseph's scars because of the mosquitoes, although she would have learned of them sooner or later anyway.

They had finished their ride and their lunch and as usual, Maggie had lingered through the early afternoon, sitting next to Joseph on the porch, on chairs he'd found in one of the sheds where lawn furniture and an old barbeque were kept.

She slapped her arm in annoyance for perhaps the third time, and said "Look. I'm all covered with welts. We'll have to sit inside."

Joseph said "I've been thinking, we could screen this porch in. It would make it nice to sit outside."

"You could sleep out here too, Joseph, when it's hot. My Da screened our porch in when I was little, and that's what we did."

When she left the farm that afternoon, Maggie stopped at the lumbar yard. That evening, after dinner, she called Joseph and told him to get whatever he needed whenever he wanted to start work.

Joseph picked up the supplies early Saturday morning and started work. Since it was the weekend, he did not expect Maggie. It was hot and he stripped off his shirt and tied a bandana around his head to stop the sweat from running into his eyes.

Maggie drove her own car to the Y, finished her racquetball game and cut short her massage and left the boys with Dan, with the excuse that she had errands to run. In reality, she wanted to see Joseph for once on a Saturday.

She left the Y and drove out the River Road.

He was nowhere in sight when she arrived, but his truck was there. She parked behind it and went looking. When she found him, sawing wood for the screens, he was facing away from her. He seemed not to have heard her car, or her footsteps, but he heard the sound of her breath drawn in sharply, and he turned and reached for his shirt, pulling it on. He gestured to his work. "Just about finished with the screens for one side of the porch."

"Can I help?"

"I'm ready for a break. How about some lemonade?"

She thought about following him inside, but instead she sat down on the front steps to wait. Moses ambled over and lay down beside her, resting his head in her lap.

She stroked his fur and thought of what she'd seen, before Joseph had pulled on his shirt. His back criss-crossed with scars.

From inside, she heard the crack of ice cubes being taken from the tray. Then he shouldered the screen door open and came through with a glass in either hand.

She took a glass from him and he sat next to her. "You like my dog?"

She swallowed past the lump in her throat, forced back tears, forced a light tone into her voice. "I do. I think he likes me too."

"Seems like he does." He glanced at her, then looked away, across the yard toward the barn where the horses were standing together, half asleep in the heat of the day. "My father was a mean person through and through. Not a drinker although maybe drink would have softened him. He considered himself a religious man, not tribal religion though. He kept a long birch rod. He used it to discipline my brother and me."

"Couldn't your mother do something?"

"I don't blame her. She was afraid of him. We all were. One day when I was 15, I came home from football practice. My mom was on the floor. She tried to get between my dad and my brother and he knocked her down. That's the only time I saw him physically abuse her, although maybe he did all along and I didn't know it.

I jumped him from behind and he threw me off and turned on me and his knife was in his hand, just like that." Joseph snapped his fingers. "That's how fast it happened. I didn't even feel it but then there was a lot of blood and my mom was screaming at him. She said ' Go away and never come back here.' He started to say something but she looked at him and said 'If you don't go now, I'll find a way to kill you one day'. He turned around and walked out."

"Did he ever come back?"

Joseph shook his head. "Haven't seen him since that day. Do you want to know why I never got it fixed?"

She touched the scar. "No. Its just part of your face, part of who you are, like your eyes or your mouth."

He touched where her fingers had rested the moment before. "It is part of who I am. Sometimes I think I wouldn't know who I was without it. When somebody beats you, it either breaks you or makes you stronger. It broke my brother. He was the oldest so maybe he felt he should have been able to protect us."

"But it made you stronger."

He shrugged. "Maybe."

They sat side by side on the porch without speaking for a long time after that until Maggie saw by the light that she would have to leave or explain why her errands had taken the whole afternoon.

A few days later, over dinner, Dan said to Maggie "Why do you suppose Joseph never got that scar fixed? Money I suppose, or rather the lack of it."

Maggie said without thinking "It's part of who he is."

Dan looked uncomprehending. "It makes him look a little dangerous, don't you think? He probably doesn't have to worry about getting into fights."

"You think it makes him look dangerous?"

"You don't?"

"He's not a dangerous man."

"Of course not. I only meant that someone who doesn't know him might see him that way."

Maggie came close to telling Dan about the kind of man that Joseph was, the way she saw him, just because she loved to talk about him so, to hear the sound of his name on her lips.

She realized what a foolish and dangerous thing that would be, and still, she had to force herself to remain silent. That night, when she came out of her bath, and stood before the mirror, brushing her hair, alone, she said his name, said Joseph, first in a whisper and then out loud, watching her face as she said it, to see if what her father had told her was true.

And she saw that it was, she saw that when she said his name, anyone would see that she loved him.

Chapter 11

It was June when Maggie won a battle she had no idea she was engaged in and one that, had she known, she would have had no desire to win. She had come home one afternoon flushed, sweaty and happy from a day of riding to find Dan home early from work. He hugged her hello, then pulled back. "You reek of horse."

"There's no better smell than the smell of horses."

"How about some soap and water and perfume? Why don't you bathe and change and we'll go out to dinner? Maybe the Flying Dutchman."

"With the boys? They were at camp all day, they'll fall asleep with their heads in their plates."

"No, I thought just us for a change."

Maggie went upstairs and rushed through her bath and dressed in a hurry, trying as she always seemed to these days to avoid any opportunity for intimacy with her husband. She had slept in Megan's room since that night in April, but knew she couldn't continue to do that forever.

She could tell at once that there was some reason for this seemingly casual and unplanned evening out. Her apprehension grew during their silent drive to The Dome. They were seated at a table overlooking the water, almost finished with their first glass of wine when Dan said suddenly "You won, Maggie."

"What did I win?"

"I had the vasectomy. No more children, accidental or otherwise, just as you wanted. Now you can come back to our bed. It's been long enough."

She was silent for so long that he said "Maggie?"

"You did this without telling me? When?"

"Last week. It was a simple procedure. Nothing to it really."

But she could see that he didn't feel that way at all and she felt a rush of something like regret for having forced him to do something he hadn't wanted to do. Something he had believed would bring her back to him. She supposed in a sense it would because she had no choice now.

Finally, she said "But there's still a risk of pregnancy for some time after it's done, isn't there? We'll need to wait until the doctor says it's safe." And so she gained a short reprieve.

When she did go back to her husband's bed, she felt as though she were being unfaithful. In keeping her marriage vows, she was breaking some unspoken vow to the man she truly loved. That somehow seemed a greater sin than adultery.

She and Joseph had not made love, had not kissed and had barely touched. She wondered often how that could be, as much as she wanted him and as much as she knew he wanted her. But still they walked and talked, rode their horses together, sat across the lunch table from each other, sat side by side on the porch through the long afternoons of summer.

Now that school was out, Chuck was with them often. He came to help with chores and stayed to ride and to visit, and then, abruptly, as if sensing something between them, he would make some excuse and be gone.

There were a string of days at the end of June that seemed more like the tail end of summer, too hot to move, too hot to take the horses out but still, on the first of those days, Maggie came to the farm though it was far more comfortable in the

Ryan house on the Bay.

Joseph was already finished caring for the horses when she drove in. He met her on the porch. "Too hot to ride today, Maggie."

"That's for sure. Let's go see my daddy."

"Are you sure you ought to be seen hanging around with me?"

"Oh, I'm very sure. Actually, I don't care. I've got an idea. How does Moses feel about boats?"

"He's ridden in canoes."

"This will be a little bigger."

"What are you up to?"

"Joseph, will you follow me wherever I take you?"

"I will." He said it without hesitation.

She drove. When they got to Kelly's, Patrick greeted them.

"Too hot to ride, am I right?"

"You are, Da. "Where's the Maeve?"

"Your Ma or the boat?" He teased.

"The boat."

"She's down at the dock, gassed up and ready to go."

"Can we take her out?"

"Sure you may. You haven't forgotten how to handle her, have you? It's been awhile." He took a key off the ring and put it in her hand.

Maggie kissed his cheek. "I was raised on that boat, Da. I haven't forgotten."

From Kellly's, Maggie dragged Joseph and Moses down the block to the liquor store, where she bought a Styrofoam cooler, two bags of ice, a 6 pack of Bud, a loaf of rye bread and a roll of paper towels. From there she drove to Pedersen's Fish House and bought 6 smoked chubs.

After that, she drove to the Menekaunee Harbor and parked next to the dock. They went aboard with Moses and their purchases. The Maeve was an old fishing boat, but was so well cared for she looked new. She had a small cabin with life vests stowed under the bench seats, but none of the amenities of the Maggie Ryan. Maggie's father had taught her to handle the boat when she was a little girl and, as she'd assured him, she hadn't forgotten anything.

Once they had left the dock, and the mouth of the Menominee River, and were in the Bay, Maggie pushed the speed up, staying along the Wisconsin shoreline. Joseph called to her over the noise of the engine. "Are you sure you know what you're doing?"

She laughed. "You said you'd follow me wherever I took you." Her hair blew wild around her face. "I've been taking this boat out since I was a little girl. Haven't you ever been out on the Bay before?"

"I've been pretty much on rivers my whole life, a few little lakes, nothing this big."

"But you can swim, right? In case we capsize or something" she teased.

She pointed out landmarks as they went. The Pine Beach Club where all the really rich people had their cottages, and just past that, U W – Marinette, then the Dome.

"Where are we going?"

"A place I know. I was only there once in the winter and I always wanted to go back."

Eventually, by following the shore, she found the entrance, but she throttled back and cut the engine and he helped her drop the anchor outside the little harbor. Still, they could see over the reeds into an inlet where there were boats, most old and abandoned looking, although there were a few that looked to still be in use. "This is the old Peshtigo Boat Harbor. I guess that means there's a new Peshtigo Boat Harbor somewhere, but I don't know where. A friend brought me here one day a long time ago. We came by land though, in a car. It was winter." She seemed to be remembering and he waited for her to go on. But when she spoke, she just said "I'm so hungry, aren't you?"

She took the fish out of the cooler and opened the paper, laying it on the bench next to her. "I didn't think to bring a knife or anything, but I'm pretty good at this with my fingers, if you don't mind."

"I don't mind." He watched her take the fish between her hands, and open it from the underside, fanning it out, then taking the bones in her fingers and removing them in one piece.

While she worked, he opened the rye bread and 2 bottles of beer. She boned all 6 fish, then said "I think I got all the bones, but it's hard to tell, so be a little careful. We have to eat with our hands too. We're going to need those paper towels."

They ate the fish, cold, salty, smoky, with the rye bread to balance the oil. They washed it down with cold beer. Maggie fed pieces of her fish to Moses. When they finished, Maggie said "We're a mess, Joseph. It's a good thing there's all this water around us to wash our hands."

He leaned over the side and wet the paper towel. They used it to wipe their hands and faces. He leaned toward her and wiped her mouth, thinking to kiss it, but the sound of a boat engine caused him to sit back.

It was a small outboard and the man in it called out a greeting, just a hello until he got closer and said "Maggie Kelly, is that you?"

Maggie looked closer. "Bud Taylor. What are you doing so far from Menekaunee?"

He drifted closer. "Just a little fishing. How about yourself? Taking your dad's boat for a spin instead of that fine big cruiser of yours?"

"That boat's too big. I prefer the Maeve. Bud, this is my friend Joseph."

Bud raised a hand in greeting. "How's your Dad doing? I heard he retired from the ore boats."

"I'm happy to say he did. He's good. You should stop in at the bar and see him."

"I'll do that. Well, nice to have met you Joseph. Maggie, stay happy now." Then he waved and maneuvered away from them before putting on enough speed to take him around a turn and out of their sight.

The almost kiss was a chance that had passed for that afternoon. They stowed their garbage in the cooler, and got underway, heading back to Menekaunee.

On the drive back to the farm, they were quiet. When she stopped the car behind his truck, he opened the door and Moses jumped out and ran toward the house. She turned toward him, hoping he would kiss her then. But he said "Thank you, Maggie. It seems I can't go wrong in following you. I need to take care of the horses and you need to go home." He walked away from the car toward the barn.

Chapter 12

When she got home, the house was in an uproar. Declan ran to meet her. "We're going on the boat, Mom, you have to get ready."

There were duffels bags piled next to the front door. Hannah came down the stairs with a suitcase and then Dan came from behind her and said "Here, let me take that, it's heavy."

Maggie said "What's going on?"

Dan said "I'm taking a week off. It's almost the 4th of July. We're all going over to Door County on the boat, Hannah included. She can help you with Megan so you can enjoy yourself."

"It'll be awfully crowded on the boat for a week."

"I booked rooms. It was too short a notice for the White Gull, but there's that little motel right by the beach. I was able to get adjoining rooms, one for us, one for Hannah and Megan and one for the boys."

"I can't just leave. What about the horses?"

"Isn't that why we have Joseph? I packed you some things, but you'll probably want to go up and look around, see if I missed anything. Where have you been all day anyway? You're close to sunburned."

"I took Daddy's boat out."

"By yourself?"

He sounded surprised and she said "Yes, just me." The first of many lies to come.

Maggie climbed the stairs, thinking a week, I can't do this for a week, without seeing him. She called the farm, watching and listening to be sure Dan didn't come upstairs while she was on the phone, but it rang and rang with no answer.

Dan was calling, "Maggie, come on. We want to get over there before dark."

They put in at Fish Creek a little before 7, checked into the motel and left the bags to be unpacked later and walked over to a favorite restaurant for dinner. The meal was festive enough that the rest of them didn't seem to notice Maggie's silence. She looked for any opportunity to call Joseph, but there was none.

Everyone agreed it had been a long day, especially for the children. The boys got themselves into bed and Maggie got Megan ready to put down for the night while Hannah showered. When she came in, Dan was reading in bed. "This is going to be a nice change. I needed to get out of that office for awhile and with the holiday, there's nothing much happening that needs my attention. Except maybe you. Come here, honey."

Maggie thought of telling Dan she was too tired. But then she thought, just get it over with. Maybe if I do that, he'll leave me alone for a few nights. Dan was a considerate lover, and would always think of her satisfaction before his own, so she began by feigning excitement. But then, she closed her eyes and began to think of Joseph, began to imagine that it was his hands touching her, his body against hers and she came wildly, biting down to stop from calling his name out loud.

The next day, after a morning at the beach, they went to a pizza place for lunch. They were sitting at a table outside, and the boys and Hannah were engaged in a conversation of their own, when Dan said to Maggie "It's the strangest thing. Your hired man called me earlier this week."

"Joseph" she said.

""What?"

"Joseph. His name is Joseph."

"Yes, I know his name."

"You called him my hired man."

"Well, he is your hired man. Anyway, he called and told me he doesn't need the wages I've been paying him. He's training horses and giving riding lessons on the weekends. He says being able to live at the house is payment enough for the work he does. Is he still doing the work to your satisfaction? I mean, working on the side wasn't part of the deal."

"No, he does everything. More than he has to do. I didn't know he was working weekends besides."

"It's up to you Maggie. He's your hired help. If he starts to slack off, you can always let him go."

After lunch, Dan agreed to take the boys for a water skiing

lesson. Hannah said she would put Megan down for a nap and do some reading in her room and Maggie begged off the water skiing with the excuse that she had a headache from too much sun.

She went to the office and got enough change for a lot of phone calls, not wanting to have a call to the farm show up on the motel bill. Then she walked to a pay phone away from the noise of the beach. The first time she tried, there was no answer.

But the second time, he picked up after 3 rings. "Joseph, it's Maggie."

"Where are you?"

"Fish Creek. When I got home yesterday, Dan had made plans to take a week off and bring us all over here for the 4th. I tried to call you before we left but you didn't answer."

"I was probably out with the horses. Are you alright?"

"Joseph, why did you tell Dan you didn't want any more pay for your work?"

"He told you. I suppose I knew he would although I hoped he wouldn't."

"Why? Why are you doing extra work on the weekends?"

"Because, Maggie, I couldn't keep taking his money, loving you the way I do."

"Do you? Do you love me? Because I love you, from the first minute I saw you, I knew. Sometimes I think I must have loved you always, even before I knew you. But I don't want you to work like that."

"Maggie, the weekends here are long, so long, the work helps fill them up. And Chuck comes to help out, just for the privilege of riding the horses. Don't worry, I won't neglect your horses or your place."

"I know you won't. That's not why I don't want you to have to work. Anyway, what will you do when winter comes and you can't work with people's horses?"

"I already lined up some jobs for end of summer and fall, helping with haying. I figure to earn enough to take me through the winter that way. Maggie, listen to me. I can justify to myself living in this house that your husband's money paid for because it's your place and I work it for you. Maybe that's just a rationalization because if I give it up, I'll have to move on and leave you behind and I can't do that. So this is the way it has to be. Are you alright over there?"

"No. No, I'm not. When I'm with him, not because I want to be, but because I have to be, I close my eyes and pretend it's you. When we get back, I'll drive there, to you, as soon as I can. Joseph, I love you so much I could die from it."

"Don't die, Maggie. Just come back."

Maggie didn't call him again that week. But she said to herself over and over 'He loves me." And every time she said it, she smiled. The children found friends to play with, and Maggie and Dan spent days on the beach and evenings with friends from Menominee who were in Fish Creek for the holiday. After an evening with the Ryans, their friends said to each other, "Maggie certainly is looking happy these days."

They went to the White Gull Inn's famous fish boil and Maggie thought she would have to tell Joseph all about that when she saw him. They dined on people's boats and in restaurants and watched the fireworks and finally, it was over and they went home.

Chapter 13

By the time they docked the boat and drove home, it was so late that Maggie could think of no plausible excuse for going out to the farm. She sang softly to herself while she unpacked and sang some more while she soaked in the tub. When she came to bed, she told Dan she was too tired for sex, and for once, it was true.

She woke up later than usual, and by the time she came downstairs, Hannah had gotten Megan up and bathed and fed her. Colin was heading down the block to play ball with friends. Dan was lingering over coffee at the dining room table, dressed in slacks and a polo shirt.

"Aren't you going to be late?"

"I thought I might drive out to the farm with you, take a look around. I haven't seen the place since the first day I brought you there. We can take Declan and Megan along. He wants to see the horses."

Maggie felt physically sick on the drive and even worse when she saw Joseph in the corral. She hated having him see her as Dan's wife, as a mother. She hated Dan for coming along.

Dan took Declan straight over to meet Joseph, while Maggie got Megan out of the car. In all the days and nights since they'd talked on the phone, she had seen herself running to him. Now she came slowly, holding the baby, watching as Joseph introduced Deco to the horses, thinking now he would no longer see her as the woman who could be his lover.

But as she watched him, he looked at her, and he smiled in a way that made her face flush warmly and she smiled back until Dan turned to look at her, a questioning look, as if some truth had just dawned and she thought for the first time 'Careful, be careful, don't let it show.'

She came up to the fence and stood next to Dan and endured it as he put an arm around her shoulders, a little demonstration of ownership, she thought, suddenly wondering if he had planned it all, the seemingly spontaneous visit to the farm along with the children to demonstrate to Joseph that she was spoken for.

She wanted so badly to step away from Dan, to put distance between them but knew it would be a mistake, would perhaps open some dialogue between them when they were alone again. Still, how long must she stand like this, in the circle of his husbandly arm?

Declan said "Joseph says there's a river. Can we go and see it?"

Maggie said quickly "You take him, Dan. I don't want to take Megan. There are too many mosquitoes down by the water. Besides I want to take a look at my horses. I feel as though I've been away for weeks and weeks."

She watched them until they disappeared into the trees, then turned back to Joseph who was still on the other side of the fence. He reached out and laid his hand on her face and she turned her face into his hand and kissed his palm. His hand was work roughened and he smelled of the horses.

When she looked up at him, he said "She's beautiful, Maggie. She looks like you. She has your eyes and your smile." As he spoke, Megan's face broke into a wide and sunny smile and she held her arms out to him. "Can I hold her?" Maggie lifted the baby over the fence into his arms where she settled against him and put one little hand on his cheek. "Your boy is a great kid. Maybe we want to turn him into a rider. He seems to have inherited your love of horses."

"Would you like to teach him?"

"I would if he wants to learn. You could bring him along mornings."

As he and Declan came back from the river and crossed the yard, Dan saw the picture they made, his wife and her hired man holding Megan who fitted perfectly into his arms.

He stopped and studied them and Declan ran ahead, reaching them first. By the time Dan got there, Declan turned to him and said "Daddy, Joseph is going to teach me to ride a horse, that one." He pointed to a black horse that looked frighteningly large to Dan.

"I don't think that's such a good idea, Deco." Then, to Joseph, "Isn't he a little young?"

"No, sir, Mr. Ryan. I've started kids on horseback a lot younger than him. The earlier they get started, the less fear they develop."

"Still, that horse is really too big for him."

"This horse Beauty is a fine horse to start him on. Mostly the bigger horses are calmer, quieter and this one is especially so. Deco, do you want to sit on him and get the feel of it?"

Declan allowed himself to be lifted onto Beauty's back and Joseph led the horse in a circle in the corral first in one direction, then the other, with Declan holding onto the mane.

When they were out of earshot, Dan turned on Maggie. "Don't you think you should have discussed this with me before putting the idea in Declan's head?"

"It was your idea to bring him out to see the horses, Dan. Now he's taken to them. He's old enough to learn and we'll keep him safe." Maggie felt an inner satisfaction knowing that, whatever Dan had hoped for in coming to the farm with her, bringing along the children, had turned itself back on him.

Before Dan could say anything more, she called to Joseph, "We'll need to get him a helmet before we start."

Joseph called back "I think there's a kid's saddle in the tack room. I used it on Beauty when I taught the littlest of the Nash grandchildren to ride." He lifted Declan off Beauty and Joseph, Maggie and Declan went to look at the saddle, with Dan trailing behind.

Joseph found it, confirmed that it was in good condition and took it back out to the corral along with a saddle pad and tried it on Beauty. "It's a good fit for the horse. Declan, come over here and let's see if it fits you as well." In a minute, Declan was aboard and Joseph confirmed that it was a good size for the boy.

As they were leaving, Joseph reminded Maggie to get a helmet and boots for Declan. Declan talked of nothing but the horses on the way to the tack shop and on the way home. He refused to remove the riding helmet even at dinner.

"You look pretty stupid" Colin said.

Maggie, wondering if Colin felt left out, asked "Colin, would you be interested in learning to ride? We have enough horses."

But Colin made a face. "No, thanks. I'm not interested in hanging out with my mother. I've got better things to do."

Maggie couldn't tell whether he was truly uninterested, or if he felt slighted so she persisted. "If you change your mind, you've only to tell me. We would love to have you along. It would be fun."

He seemed to soften then and came to give her a hug,

something he hadn't done in a very long time.

The remainder of summer, Declan went with Maggie to the farm 3 mornings each week and took lessons. He would have done more, but Dan insisted that he balance his summer activities and continue to see his friends. His lessons began in the arena, but after the first week, the 3 of them began to ride on the trails, Joseph in the lead on Rio or Hank, then Declan on big Beauty and Maggie on her mare Sugar. When he finished chores early, Chuck came along.

By the second week, Declan announced that he wanted to get levis and a denim shirt like Joseph's to ride in.

On the 2 mornings a week that Declan did not come with her, Maggie and Joseph were sometimes alone, and sometimes accompanied by Chuck. Maggie sensed that Joseph was not looking to be alone with her and she took his lead. She was strangely at peace with the situation as it stood, satisfied to see him, talk with him, watch him, knowing that the day would come when it would all change. Their time together was coming, as surely as the winter, and until then, their self imposed celibacy served only to intensify their passion for each other.

Chapter 14

In September, the boys went back to school and Declan's riding lessons on weekday mornings ended. Chuck was back in school as well, so Maggie and Joseph now had their weekday mornings to themselves again.

Between Declan's riding lessons and the heat, they had barely made a start breaking trail through the woods over the summer so when Joseph asked her if she'd like to do some hard work before the weather turned, Maggie was quick to agree.

When Joseph and Chuck had put up the fence separating the pasture from the woods, they had installed a gate. Maggie's first lesson in breaking trail was how to open the gate, ride through and close it behind her, all from the back of her horse. Joseph's advice was "Sugar already knows how to do this, so just don't get in her way by over steering."

It was a lesson quickly learned, thanks to Sugar's prior training. Joseph had outfitted both of them with work gloves before they left the corral and Maggie soon understood why.

Joseph rode ahead of Maggie. "Hank's done a good bit of this, so just follow his lead."

They made their way in among the trees along what looked to be a trail, the horses stepping over downed branches. But soon, they reached what appeared to be a dead end, overgrown with vegetation and small saplings. Still Joseph pushed forward, breaking through the underbrush which gave way easily, and snapping off enough small branches to clear a way. Several times, he warned Maggie to watch her head as a branch swung back toward her. She caught the ones she could and broke them off the way that Joseph showed her.

The day was cool and overcast, a precursor of Fall. But after several hours of working their way through the woods, Maggie was sweating inside her shirt. Still, they made some progress and continued to push forward in the days to come until they had established a fairly good trail along one side of the woods, not far inside the treeline.

In the second week, they began to circle around, reversing direction. "What we're doing here looks random" he explained, "but when we're done we'll have a nice little riding trail that'll feel as though we're riding for miles, all just inside your woods."

"Do you hunt, Joseph?"

"No, never liked the idea even of sighting on a deer. My dad tried to get my brother and me interested, but neither one of us took to it."

"I'd like to post this land No Hunting before the deer season."

"You won't be too popular with some of the locals, but it's your land. We'll get some signs and ride out and put them all along the road on both sides. The sooner, the better."

"You remember that I told you my brother was killed in a hunting accident."

"I'm sorry, Maggie. That's an awful thing."

"My mother wished me dead in his place."

Joseph stopped his horse and nudged him closer to Maggie's horse, until they were flank to flank. He didn't say any words of comfort like 'I'm sure she didn't mean it' or 'People can be hurtful when bad things happen.' He just reached for her hand and pressed it to his lips. The touch of his mouth on her fingers flooded her with feelings, desire, love, wonder, all in equal parts. She would have dismounted and pulled him down with her had he not said softly, without letting go of her hand, his breath on her fingers as he spoke, "Someone's coming."

She had heard nothing, but in the next moment, there was the sound of a horse nearing them, and then Chuck broke through the vegetation they had just begun to clear, riding Rio. "I thought you could use some help. The more we get open before the snow, the less you'll have to do come spring."

"That's right" Joseph said. He had moved Hank away, letting go of Maggie's hand just before Chuck appeared. "No school today?"

"Half day for teacher conferences. I figured I might be able to catch up with you before you finished for the day."

With the 3 of them riding, they finished the 2nd loop, but deferred starting the 3rd section. Joseph was now working at various farms, bringing in the hay, not just on weekends, but on weekday afternoons as well.

On the way back, he told Chuck that they were posting No Hunting Signs on Maggie's land.

Chucks face turned solemn. "There are guys around here who might give you some trouble about that, Maggie. They started up with my dad years back when we posted our land."

"What happened?"

"They came around trying to bully him, but he came out with his shotgun and told them to go somewhere else."

"They backed down?"

"Yeah, there were plenty of other places to hunt, County land, and private land where the owners are only here in the summer. But seems like every year more people are posting, so you be careful. I'll help you get the signs up though. The earlier, the better. And, Joseph, you should keep Moses inside or close by you once the season starts. Keep the horses close to the barn too, not out in the pasture."

When they got back, they saw to the horses, then the 3 of them had a quick lunch together, before Joseph headed over to a farm down the road to work. Chuck went back to his dad's place to do afternoon chores and Maggie stayed behind at the farm, and washed the lunch dishes and visited with Moses.

When she finished, she picked up her purse to leave, then put it down again and walked from the kitchen ,down the hall and stood in the doorway of Joseph's bedroom. Moses trotted behind her, looking up at her questioningly.

She went inside, and turned back the covers, sat down on the edge of the bed and took off her boots. Then she lay down, in the place where he would lie at night. She turned over on her stomach and pressed her face into the pillow, into the sheets, seeking his scent. Then she put her hand between her legs and touched herself, In her mind, she saw his face, felt his hands, until she came, She stayed there until her breathing quieted. Then she stood up and remade the bed, put her boots on, said good bye to Moses and went out to her car and drove home.

That night when Joseph turned down the covers, he drew in his breath, looked around him, thinking surely she would be there. But he was alone. At first, he thought it was his imagination, conjuring her up out of his desire. He lay down and, as she had done, he turned over and pressed his face to the sheets. Then he knew it was not his imagination, that she had been there before him. Her fragrance had been left behind for him.

Chapter 15

It was that second week in September that Maggie noticed that Declan was unusually quiet at dinner. "What's wrong, Deco?"

"I miss riding. Why can't I take more lessons?"

"You have school now, Honey."

"I could go on weekends."

"Right now, Joseph is working on the weekends. But the haying will be done soon. Maybe we can ask him if you could ride on Saturday mornings."

Deco's face lit up, but Dan said "He has other activities planned on Saturdays. He's not going to just quit everything else. Anyway, it will be too cold to ride before long. If you're still interested next summer, we'll see."

Maggie watched Deco's face crumple up, close to tears. "We'll be riding in the arena in the cold weather. It's not as much fun as the trail, but it's better than not riding at all."

"What about swimming? And Basketball?"

"Maybe he prefers horseback riding."

"I do. I'd rather ride horses with mom and Joseph than swim or play stupid basketball."

"Deco, this discussion is between your mother and me."

Colin, who had been looking from one of them to the other, said suddenly "What's the difference. He already knows how to swim and if he'd rather ride a horse than play basketball, why shouldn't he? He's not very good at basketball anyway."

"Yeah, Dad, I'm not. I really stink at basketball. I'll never be tall enough to get on a team anyway. Come on, Dad, please."

Colin joined in. "Yeah, come on, Dad, please."

Maggie, unable to resist, joined in "Yeah, come on Dad, please, please, please."

Hannah, who was clearing plates, winked at Maggie and said "Yeah, Dad, come on, please, please let this kid ride a horse."

Dan smiled, a good guy giving in kind of smile that Maggie knew he didn't mean. "Alright, I'm outnumbered. You can take a lesson on Saturday morning. One lesson a week. But that's it. No riding on Sundays or you and your mother will never be home."

Then, to Maggie, once the boys' attention was elsewhere, "Why are you so sure that Joseph is going to want to spend his Saturday morning giving Deco riding lessons? Doesn't he do enough all week? Doesn't he have any life of his own? A girlfriend, maybe some nice Indian maiden on the reservation?"

Maggie felt a little sick, just at the thought of Joseph with someone. "It's just a couple of hours in the morning. He has all the rest of the weekend to see whomever he likes."

"Do you know if he does see anyone? Has he ever talked to you about it?" He seemed to be enjoying the effect his words were having, or maybe it was her imagination.

"There's no reason he'd talk to me about it."

"I thought the two of you were pretty close. You spend a lot of time with him. I think he sees you more than I do."

"Don't be silly. We're just working with the horses, that's all." Her face felt hot and she forced herself to meet his eyes. Lie number 2.

"It really must get lonely for him out there. He's a young man, right around your age, isn't he?"

"I don't know how old he is." Thinking, I really don't. I wonder when his birthday is. Thinking, I'll have to ask him.

"We could introduce him to somebody, but I don't really know anybody who'd be interested in a penniless Indian working as a hired farm hand, do you? "

She knew that he was goading her and she was biting down hard to keep control. She thought that if he didn't stop soon, if he went any further, she would begin to scream at him, began to scream in front of her children, scream "Me, I'm interested. He's all I want. I'd trade this house, and the boat and everything else you've ever given me, just to be with him. I'd get down on my knees and thank God if I could live with him in that little farmhouse and never ever again have to go to the country club or anyplace like it, if I could just stay there with him for the rest of my life then I'd die happy."

Dan stopped, mercifully, suddenly he just stopped. Maybe he saw something in her face, in her eyes and realized he was going too far. "You go ahead and check with him then and see if he wants to spend his Saturday mornings giving riding lessons to my son."

Glad of an excuse to call him, to hear his voice, Maggie called Joseph after dinner. She waited until Dan and the boys were in the living room in front of the T V and then she used the kitchen phone, the one with a cord long enough so that she could stand and see into the living room while she talked. Hannah was at the sink, washing dishes, her back to Maggie.

Maggie spoke softly, her lips against the receiver. "Joseph? Are you busy?"

"No."

"I'm calling to ask a favor. Deco misses riding so much. We wondered if you would be willing to have us come out on Saturday mornings to ride, once you're done with the hay, if you don't have something else you'd rather be doing."

"We'll be done with the hay next week, Maggie. There's just the one farm left. You know there's nothing I'd rather be doing."

"That's good. That's good to hear. So, not this Saturday, but the next. We should still be able to go out on the trail a little longer."

"Sure, till we get the ice and snow, as long as the boy is warm enough."

Maggie glanced at Hannah who continued to rinse the dishes and put them into the drainer. "What are you doing?"

"Playing the guitar a little. Singing out loud, making Moses howl."

Maggie laughed and Hannah looked over her shoulder, then began to run water out of the sink. "Well, then, I'll let you get back to it. I'll see you in the morning."

He said good night and Maggie hung up, but instead of going to the living room, she sat down at the kitchen table. Hannah came over and sat down with her.

"How long have we known each other, Hannah?"

"Sixteen years" Hannah said without hesitation.

"Maybe I shouldn't ask this and you can tell me it's none of my damn business if you'd like, but isn't there anybody in your life except this family? Because I've never known you to go out with anyone, or take a vacation. And Hannah, this family isn't worth that kind of loyalty. You're a really pretty woman. Haven't you ever been in love?"

Hannah looked at her steadily. "This is for you only to know, Maggie."

Maggie nodded, a promise to keep whatever Hannah told her a secret between them.

"I've been in love with one man in my life and that man was Daniel Ryan Sr. I came to this house in 1942 when Michael was born. I was 18 and I had been in this country 9 years then. My English in those days was not so good. My accent was much heavier than it is now. This country was at war with the country where I was born. You can imagine."

Maggie nodded. She could imagine.

The Ryans were very good to me. I loved them both, you

understand. You knew Elly. Anyone would love her. But after I'd been here awhile, it was Mr. Ryan that I loved. Not in the way I loved her. Then Erin was born. I loved helping to raise those babies. His babies. Don't misunderstand. He never looked at me in that way. He only loved her. But I was content to live under his roof, see him every day, although it was not always so easy to see him with her.

When she became ill, God forgive me, I began to think that perhaps when she died, he would turn to me. But, you see, he could not live without her. I could not have comforted him. After that, I thought I would have to go away, have to live my own life at last. Then Dan asked me to stay and take care of Erin and the house and I was happy to do that because I found I didn't want to leave. I'd stayed here too long, you see.

Then you came here to live and had your babies and so here we are. Now I stay here for you, Maggie, for you, and Colin, and Declan and Megan. Not for him." She lifted her chin in the direction of the living room. "I've been honest with you, Maggie. It's the first time in my life that I've spoken of these things out loud. He's not a bad man, your husband. But not the man for you. I see that. I've always seen it. But it wasn't my place to say it, although sometimes I wish I had told you that right at the start, when Michael was still here." She lowered her voice and leaned toward Maggie. "The man you spoke to just now, Joseph, I know from your voice that you love him. Be careful what you give away in front of Dan. I'm always here for you." She touched Maggie's hand and then she stood up and left the kitchen.

Deco came in then. "Did you talk to Joseph?"

"Yes, I did. And we can begin one week from Saturday."

"One more whole week."

"You know how to make it seem shorter? Just say only one more week instead."

Maggie lay awake in bed that night listening to Dan breathing. She realized that, if Hannah had seen the way she felt about Joseph, then surely Dan had. She had been careless, hadn't even tried to hide her true feelings.

For the first time, she wondered what she expected to happen. Did she think that Dan would graciously allow her to have an affair? Perhaps he would, if she were discreet, and if he were sure it didn't really mean anything to her.

But she was quite sure that he already knew, or at least suspected, that her feelings for Joseph ran deep and would not burn themselves out if he simply allowed her to take Joseph as a lover. And she herself wanted more than that, wanted a life with Joseph.

Perhaps Dan would kill her, or Joseph, or both of them but she thought not. He was too restrained, too conventional, too protective of his place in their small society. He would never allow himself to act out of passion. He would consider the consequences, which would include disgrace to himself and the children, and punishment. Even a wealthy lawyer would go to prison for murdering his adulterous wife.

That left divorce. The thought of facing Dan and telling him she wanted a divorce left her weak with fear. She would gladly give up everything, the house, the boat, all of it. But she knew with certainty that he would never allow her to have the children. He would find a way to take them from her, probably quite easily, if she left him for her lover.

At that moment, Maggie determined that she had no choice but to go along as they had been. She would be more careful about showing her feelings and perhaps Dan would be happy to keep up the façade of a happy family. Eventually, she knew that she and Joseph would be lovers and where that would lead, she was unable to imagine. She would have to face whatever it was when the time came. For now, she knew only that she could not live without Joseph, no matter what the cost.

Chapter 16

They began the Saturday riding at the end of September, continued through October, still able to ride the trails into early November. Then, as hunting season approached, the first snow and ice blanketed the trails and they moved their rides into the arena. As they had in the spring, they played music while they rode, and with 3 of them working, they rode patterns and made a game of it.

On weekdays, Maggie and Joseph also rode in the arena, then had lunch and lingered together in the kitchen until he sent her on her way. Physically, he maintained a careful distance from her, as he came to know her in other ways. It began when he told her one day that he wanted to know all about her.

She laughed. "You'll be sorry you asked. It's such a boring life I've led."

"Tell me anyway. Tell me every boring thing about your life."

"Once when I was little, I got my mother's wedding dress out of the trunk where she'd packed it away in tissue and I put it on and went outside to play. She caught me."

"Were you punished?"

"I fell down and skinned my knees, and I was yelled at, until my Da came home and took me fishing on the pier."

"Your face lights up when you talk about your father."

"My favorite parent. He was always there for me. Until he had to go away and work on the ore boats summers. Till then, we went out on the boat all the time, and fishing, and to the beach. Then he was just gone. I think I was about 8 the first year he worked on the lakes. He just retired from it a few years ago. Winters I went from school straight to the bar and did my homework there till we could walk home together."

"Did you have a first love?"

"I did. Don was his name. He was a hood in a black leather jacket, with long sideburns. He hung out at a store across from the high school where we weren't supposed to go. He smoked cigarettes and he had a bad reputation, which was pretty undeserved. He was really a good guy. He tried to protect my reputation by only seeing me where he thought no one would see us together. But my Da found out and told me he wanted me to stop seeing Don because I would get a reputation."

"And you did stop?"

"I did. Then I met Michael, Michael Ryan."

"Michael Ryan."

"Michael is Dan's baby brother. I guess you would call us high school sweethearts."

She stopped talking then, lost in the past and he waited for her to come back. "You wanted to know everything about me. Are you sure?"

Joseph nodded.

"Michael and I were in love, the way you're in love in high school for the first time and you think it will last forever, but it never does. When he went away for college, it seemed he had forgotten me. And Dan was right there, always making me feel better. I got mixed up then. I thought maybe I loved Dan. He loved me. He wanted to marry me. I was 17 and I was still in high school." She began to tell it very fast, to get it out before she changed her mind.

"I told Dan to let me tell Michael, but Dan talked to him first. When I found Michael, he was so upset. He told me he had never stopped loving me, it was just that college was so hard for him. He was failing all his subjects and he didn't want to go back. I said 'Michael why didn't you tell me?' I guess he thought I wouldn't understand or that I'd be disappointed in him. Instead of talking, we made love. It wasn't the first time, just so you don't think I'm trying to sound innocent. I knew for sure then that I didn't love Dan. I thought everything would be alright. But Michael left. He went away and we couldn't find him.

I was pregnant and I had never slept with Dan. That's the truth, Joseph. Do you believe me?" He nodded and she went on. "So I married Dan and I let him think Colin is his. Do you think I'm a terrible person? Do you think this isn't who I thought Maggie was?"

"I don't think that, Maggie."

"Then I had Declan and I went back to college and I met a boy named Paul who was my best friend and I was a little bit in love with him, but nothing ever happened. He went away and I had just one year of college left and I said to Dan 'we have to be so careful that I don't get pregnant' and right after that I got pregnant. I couldn't take the pill and I counted on Dan, so I guess it's my fault. But Joseph, I think he made me pregnant on purpose because he thought I was slipping away from him. And I was, I was slipping away."

She realized that she was crying and Joseph pulled her out of her chair and into his lap and he held her while she cried.

She said "Then I met you and I knew. I knew the first time I saw you. I said this is the person I love."

"Maggie, Maggie. I looked for you my whole damn life and when I found you, I thought it didn't even matter to me that you were another man's wife. But now I know you and your children and it's not so easy. Do you understand why I haven't taken you into my bed even though I want you more than I've ever wanted anything?"

Maggie shook her head and smiled through her tears. "No, I don't understand. I'm crazy with wanting you and it's only because you seem so in control of everything that I've just followed your lead. But I'm just waiting and waiting, knowing I can't wait much longer."

"It's because I don't just want you for now, I want you for life.

And, Maggie, you may think sometimes that you don't need your children, that you would be willing to give them up to have me but you'd be wrong. Your children are part of you, part of who you are. If you lost them because of me, there would always be something missing from your life. I don't believe that you would blame me or stop loving me because I think that what we have for each other is not so easy to lose. But you would not be happy in the way I want you to be happy."

"The morning that Dan and Declan and Megan came here with me, I knew that he had planned it, wanting to make you see me as his wife, as the mother of his children. It was as though he were putting a kind of brand on me, a stamp of ownership. I felt sick all the way here, thinking you would look at me differently. When you smiled at me, when you took Megan and held her, I thought it's fine, he still sees me as the woman he loves. But now it seems as though Dan's won after all."

"He's won nothing, Maggie. But you give so much away with your face and your voice. It's not just me that sees your love. We don't want to give him a reason to try to take your children away from you."

"He would do that, and if he tried, he would succeed. He's an attorney, you know, a very good one, and he knows everyone, all of the judges, everyone who has influence and money and power. If I leave him, I will lose my children."

"You're their mother, and a good mother. I've seen you with Deco and Megan."

"I'm not a good mother at all, Joseph. I get bored with them and go off and leave them all the time, first when I went to college and now with you and the horses."

"That doesn't make you a bad mother. I know you love them."

"Maybe more than I thought I did. You make me see that."

"Don't the courts generally think that children are better off with their mother, especially young children?"

"I don't know, maybe, I've never thought about it before. I don't even know anybody who's been involved in a custody fight. Our friends are the kind of people who don't get divorces. They just have affairs."

"Are you starting to understand now? Do you want us to be like those people? In some sense, it might seem easier for us to become lovers and go on as we are. If we're careful, we might even get away with it. You keep your children, and your fine house and everything else that goes along with being Mrs. Ryan. I get to keep what, for me, is a very comfortable place. The work isn't hard. I'm doing what I want to do, working with the horses. And I have you. But not really, I don't really have you. Because every night you go back to your own home and you sleep with your husband. And in the end, we're diminished by it, because we're hiding what we are to each other."

"Do you think it matters to me, having a big house, having the things that go along with being Mrs. Dan Ryan? Because I don't come from that. You saw the place I grew up. You know money doesn't mean anything to me."

"You are used to a certain kind of life, Maggie. That will all change if you're with me. I have no money, no property. I will work for you and I will take care of you, you and your children, but it will not be the same for you or for them as it is now. You'll be making a choice not only for yourself but for your children."

"You must know I'd trade everything I have to be with you. And my children would learn to do with less. But have you thought about what all of this means for you? Do you really want me enough to take on 3 children who aren't your's?"

"They're your children, Maggie. So, yes, I'll take them along with you and I'll love them too. Although they might not be so happy, at least at first. We'll be asking a lot of them. They'll be losing the only home they've ever known and the only father they've ever known. It will be hard for them to go to a new place."

"We could stay here. This is my place, my land."

"Ah, Maggie, it all seems so simple to you. But I told you once, your husband's money bought this place. Even if he gave it to you without a fight, how could we stay here? It would be as though he owned us both. There's a place over by the Wolf River. I always thought I'd settle there some day. A few acres of land and a cabin. One of my uncles owns it and he'd be happy to sell it now that he doesn't get around well. It's a place to begin."

"How far? How far from here?"

"A few hours."

"So far. Dan won't accept that, to have the children where he can't see them every day. There must be another way."

It tore something inside him to see her face fill with fear and uncertainty because of a choice he would force on her. So he began to give in to her, because he loved her, and because he couldn't be the one to cause her pain when all he wanted was to see her happy. He ssh'd her and kissed her tears and told her they could wait and talk more and perhaps they would find a way to make things work out and she believed him because she wanted to, and because she was so afraid of facing Dan and telling him the truth.

Chapter 17

Maggie wanted Joseph as her lover. She wanted more than that, but, at least for now, she would have settled for that much, just to continue to see him every day but Sunday, and how she hated Sundays now. How they dragged on, those endless Sundays, beginning with Mass that Dan insisted they continue to attend as a family, Maggie mouthing prayers and thinking carnal thoughts and knowing that Dan was plotting strategies for his cases, and the boys were probably thinking of school friends or sports. Declan, certainly, was dreaming of horses.

An early lunch before a long afternoon in front of the TV, some football game in the background, while they read the Sunday papers, and the boys, restless and bored already with winter, prowling around until Dan said sharply "Find something to do" and they wandered off to their rooms, or played cards or games until Maggie's parents arrived for dinner. Maggie looked for opportunities to talk to her father alone, but there were none.

And then, at last, it was Monday and she could breathe again, could see the boys off to school, care for Meagan and hand her off to Hannah, thinking such a terrible mother to be so impatient to be away from her baby. But laughing out loud as she drove to the farm, running to meet him wherever he was when she arrived, on the porch, looking for her car, or in the corral with the horses.

If the trails were not icy, they could still ride outside, unless a bitter cold wind drove them into the arena. Maggie no longer minded the arena. Maggie no longer minded being anywhere that Joseph was.

It was increasingly difficult not to touch each other, to sit across the table from each other in the warm kitchen after their ride, to maintain distance. But if they closed the distance, they would not stop. Maggie was reaching the point at which she would have promised him anything if he would make love to her. Even her fear of bringing everything crashing down around them once she faced Dan with the truth would not have stopped her. She lay awake at night rehearsing the words.

One night, she stood in the doorway of the den where Dan was working at the desk on some case, and she actually began. "Dan" she said, but he answered her without looking up.

"Can it wait, Maggie? I've got a trial starting in 2 days" and as much as she felt like a coward, she was glad of the reprieve.

Two days later, at the beginning of deer season, the phone rang just as they sat down to dinner. Hannah answered in the kitchen and even before she called Maggie, Maggie was half out of her chair, an icy dread in her chest, her stomach turning over. She stumbled walking to the kitchen, and saw Dan standing up, reaching out to help her, but she put up a hand to stop him.

"Maggie? Is that you?" She recognized his voice even though he didn't sound like himself.

"What is it, Chuck? Tell me."

"Something happened."

"Tell me" her voice unnaturally high, loud enough that she saw the faces of her family turn to look at her from where they sat around the table.

"I went over to Black's place to help with the milking late afternoon today. I was on my way back in the pick up when I saw a truck pulled over by your woods and there were some hunters there. I slowed down, thinking I'd talk to them, tell them they couldn't hunt there, but there were 4 or 5 of them so I thought I should maybe just go home and call and report them to the Sheriff."

Maggie's knees were giving out. She leaned into the wall and slid down until she was sitting on the floor. She was too afraid of what was coming next to ask him to hurry and tell her so she waited.

"They were standing around in a circle and then I saw a man on the ground, and they were kicking him. And it was Joseph." Chuck was crying, she could hear it, he wasn't even trying to hide it and still she couldn't ask. "When I saw that, I didn't think, I drove the truck at them and they jumped out of the way. I got out and I started hollering at them and I guess they got scared, although I don't know why because there were 4 or 5 of them and one of me, but maybe they didn't know I was alone. They ran to their truck and they drove away. I'm sorry, Maggie, it was so fast, I couldn't get their license number or anything."

Finally, she had to ask. She had to know, didn't she? "Joseph?"

"Oh God, Maggie, he was beat up so bad, I thought I might

have to leave him there and go for help. But I was able to get him in the truck. I guess I shouldn't have moved him, but I was afraid to leave him."

"He's alive?" She could hear herself, she sounded like a crazy woman, scared, and crying and laughing at the same time because he wasn't dead.

"Yeah. We're at the hospital. The doctor's in with him. He didn't want to even come here but I could see he had to so I just didn't listen to him. And he kept saying 'Don't tell Maggie' but I called anyway. What should I do?"

"Stay with him. I'm coming there."

She was aware that Dan was standing there, looking at her. He reached down and helped her up and she went past him to the closet and got her coat. "What happened? Where are you going?"

She saw her purse, but couldn't find her keys. "Where are they?"

Dan said "Who?"

"My keys, I can't find my keys."

Dan said again "What happened?"

She turned her purse upside down and watched as everything in it cascaded to the floor, saw the keys there amid all of the other things she carried everywhere with her and snatched them up. She was almost at the door when his voice stopped her. "Maggie?"

"Some hunters beat Joseph so badly that he's in the hospital. He'd probably be dead if Chuck hadn't come along. Thank God he had milking over at the Black's farm today. I've got to get to the hospital."

"I'll come with you. You're too upset to drive."

"No, no. If you want to do something, call the Sheriff and report this. Use some of that legal influence that you have in this town to find the people who did this and put them in jail."

She heard him say Maggie again, but she went out the door and slammed it behind her and ran to the car before he could follow her. She should have been stopped for speeding and running red lights between her house and the hospital, but it seemed as though this was a night when the police weren't around when they were needed.

When she got to the hospital, she realized she had no idea where to find him. The woman behind the reception desk smiled at her and said "Mrs. Ryan? May I help you?"

Maggie couldn't place her. Was this someone she knew? "I'm looking for someone who was brought in a little while ago. He was beaten. His name is Joseph Dodge."

The woman said "They're in the E. R. Go straight back through those double doors and ask one of the nurses."

Maggie pushed through the double doors but there was no one around. She went past the nurses station and began looking into the rooms on either side of the hall. A young woman who appeared to be in labor and her frightened looking young husband were in one, the next was empty. As she approached the third, a nurse came around the corner and said "May I help you?"

"Yes. I'm looking for someone. Joseph Dodge. He was beaten."

"If you could just wait here" the nurse began, but Maggie said "No, I can't wait here. I have to see him now."

"The doctor is with him. He'll come out and talk to you in a few minutes. Are you a relative?"

"Yes, no, he works for me. He doesn't have any family here."

"Well, if you'll just sit down…"

Maggie was about to argue when she saw Chuck coming down the hall. She left the nurse and went to him. "Where is he? That woman won't let me see him. He's alright, isn't he?"

"He's hurt pretty bad, Maggie. It's going to be hard for you to see him."

"I don't care. Where is he?"

"Come on. They probably won't let us in till the doctor's done, but we can wait right outside." She let him lead her around a corner to where they could sit down outside the room where Joseph was.

"Where's Moses? He wasn't with Joseph when it happened,

was he?"

"No. He's up at the house. Joseph told me a little. He heard gunshots in the woods. So he left Moses in the house and put the horses inside the barn, then he went out to investigate and that's when it happened."

"But he's going to be alright? It's not anything serious, right?"

"I don't know, Maggie."

The doctor came out at last. He was young and Maggie didn't know him. He introduced himself as Doctor O'Brien. He had been on call for emergencies that night, in fact he had been called in for a baby that was arriving early when Joseph had been brought in.

"Please, is he going to be alright?"

"Well, he's lucky that Mr. Schmitt here came along when he did. He has a non-displaced fracture of the shoulder, some broken ribs, probable bruising to at least one kidney and a concussion, multiple contusions and lacerations. He's going to be in a lot of pain. He's also a very stubborn man. He doesn't want to stay here overnight, so why don't you see if you can convince him it's necessary. We want to monitor the head injury."

"Can I see him now?"

"Yes, of course, but you should be prepared. He looks pretty bad. Are you going to be alirght?"

"Of course I am."

Chuck said "Maggie, while you see him, I'm going to call my dad, let him know where I am with his truck. Then I'll be back."

Maggie went into the room. Joseph was just a still form under white sheets. His eyes were closed, but he opened them when she got close. "He called you even after I told him not to."

Maggie bent close, touched his face. "How did you think you were going to keep this a secret? You think I wouldn't have noticed?"

"Are you here to take me home?"

She kissed his cheek. "You have to stay here tonight. You

have a concussion. But if you're very, very good, maybe they'll let me take you home tomorrow."

"Mrs. Dodge?"

Maggie was focused on Joseph, touching his face, his shoulder, his arm, as though to reassure herself that he was really there. But she glanced away from him when the doctor spoke, looked around the room, seeing only the 3 of them there. "Mrs. Ryan. Maggie Ryan."

Dr. O'Brien seemed embarrassed by his mistake. "I'm sorry, I just assumed…" But he saw that she was smiling, that she looked pleased at his assumption that she was the patient's wife.

"Yes, Mrs. Ryan, well, as I said, we're going to watch the head injury closely tonight and then, if Mr. Dodge still insists, you can take him home tomorrow. There are a couple of things we should discuss." He gestured toward the door.

Maggie leaned back down to Joseph. "I'll be right back." She followed Dr. O'Brien into the hallway.

"Mr. Dodge really should stay here for a few days, but he

seemed to be very concerned about the expense."

"Please be sure that the bills come to me. I'll stop at the business office tomorrow before we leave to make the arrangements. And I'd rather Mr. Dodge didn't know that. He manages my horse farm. He was hurt protecting my property."

"He's not going to be able to work for awhile and he really needs someone to stay with him, at least for a few days."

"I'll take care of that."

"Well, then, if you'll excuse me, I've got another patient to check on, but I'll look back in on Mr. Dodge in a little while."

Maggie was about to go back into the room when Chuck came down the hall. "Did you reach your dad?"

"Yeah. He said to tell you we'll help you out. He thinks it might be the same guys that gave us a bad time. He was heading out to feed your horses and check on things as soon as we hung up."

"Chuck, I have a favor to ask you. Joseph insists on going

home tomorrow, but he can't be on his own for awhile. I can stay days, but I wondered if it would be okay with your dad if you stayed over nights? Unless you think there's some danger of those guys coming back."

"I don't think they'll be back, Maggie. They're cowards. I didn't recognize them, but they don't know that. I'm sure it'll be fine with my dad."

"If it's not, you just tell me and I'll find somebody."

"You don't want a stranger taking care of your place. And Joseph wouldn't like it either. My dad and I can help you with the horses and whatever else needs doing. But it's going to be a long day for you. I'll have to get home and help with the milking before school mornings, and again after school before I can come over."

"I can handle it. There isn't so much to do now that it's winter. It's just mucking and feeding. If we don't get them all ridden every day, they'll be fine. Most people don't ride all winter. And Chuck, I'll pay you for all the work."

"We're not going to take money for helping a neighbor."

"If I had to hire somebody from outside, I'd pay them. You can put the money away for college. I want to get back to him now."

"I need to get home." He started away then turned back. "Do you want me to go to the house and get Moses? He's probably pretty upset alone without Joseph. I could take him home with me overnight and bring him back in the morning before school."

"Thank you, Chuck. I don't know what we would have done without you." She reached out and pulled him to her in a long hug. "You saved his life. I'll never forget that." When she let him go, she saw that he was blushing. She watched him walk away then went back in to Joseph.

His eyes were closed, but he opened them as she got to the bed. "Moses is alone at the house."

"Chuck is going to get him right now and take him home for the night. And Chuck's dad fed the horses."

"I'm sorry, Maggie."

"Why are you sorry?"

"I should have called the sheriff. But I'm used to handling things on my own. It was a mistake. Now I'm no use to you. I should probably take off, go stay with my mom till I'm back on my feet."

Maggie sat carefully on the edge of the bed. A feeling of loss swept over her at the thought of being without him. "Please tell me that you don't want to do that. Please tell me that you only said it because you're too proud to let me take care of you. And, Joseph, please do not think about leaving me. Not now. Not ever."

"No, I don't want to leave you. But I can't stay here and do nothing. I'll come back as soon as I'm better."

"No. You can't go. I won't let you. Chuck and I will take care of things and you'll be better before you know it and everything will be fine."

Gently, not wanting to hurt him, she kissed his mouth. It was the first time and she was filled, not with passion, but with a love so intense that it made her afraid. The door opened then, and a nurse came in. "Mrs. Dodge" she said "I'm sorry to interrupt but I have to check on your husband now. If you could step outside for a minute."

Without correcting her, Maggie said "It's okay. I have to leave now, but I'll be back first thing in the morning."

She went to the nurses' station and gave the charge nurse her phone number and asked to be called if there was any change, then she walked to the car to drive home. While she had been in the hospital, it had begun to snow. She realized then for the first time that she had left home wearing a pair of thin ballet slippers that she wore around the house. By the time she got to the car, her feet were soaked and icy cold.

When she stopped for the red light at the intersection just past the hospital, the car hit a slippery patch and without warning, spun 360 degrees. The street was absolutely deserted. After that, she drove slowly, creeping over the light accumulation of snow that could hide another patch of ice until she turned into her own driveway.

There was a light in the hall, but the house was otherwise dark and quiet. Then Hannah appeared in the dining room doorway and beckoned Maggie toward her. Maggie followed her into the kitchen. "Your feet are soaked."

"I know. It started to snow."

"Give me your shoes." Hannah took them and disappeared into the laundry room. When she came back, she was carrying a pair of heavy socks. She handed them to Maggie who sat down at the kitchen table and put them on.

By the time she finished, Hannah had put 2 mugs of hot tea on the table. She went to the cupboard, got down a bottle of brandy and poured a generous portion into each of the mugs. "This'll warm you and help you sleep. How is he? I assume not critical or you wouldn't be here."

"Oh, Hannah, not critical, but hurt so badly. Still he insists on going home tomorrow. He actually wanted to leave and go to his mother's until he's better but I told him he couldn't."

"What are you going to do?"

"Chuck, the boy from the farm across the way, he and his father, are going to help me. I'm going to stay out there during the day and Chuck will take over after chores and stay the night. Between the 3 of us, we can take care of the horses and the place."

"Dan won't like this."

"Probably not. Has he gone to bed?"

"He's in the den. After you left, I put the kids to bed, then I went to see if he needed anything. He was supposed to be working on a case. But he was drinking, Maggie."

"He didn't come out when I got home."

"Probably better. Why don't you go to bed? You can tell him your plan in the morning."

Maggie finished her tea and brandy, thanked Hannah and started across the hall to the stairs. She saw that Dan was standing in the doorway of the den, looking at her. She felt a chill of apprehension.

"Is he going to live?"

She bit back a bitter response. "Yes. He'll be fine."

"Is he going to be able to work?"

"Work? That's what you're worried about? Whether he'll be able to work?"

"He's your employee. Somebody has to manage the place."

"The neighbors and I are working it out."

"The neighbors and you? You're going to do the work?"

"I can take care of the horses."

"Don't be ridiculous. We'll give him a generous final paycheck and you can hire someone else. You're certainly not going to have him lying around while you do all the work."

"He was injured protecting my land."

"He should have called the sheriff, let him handle it. He made a mistake. No reason we all have to pay for it."

Maggie's voice was steely. "It's my place and this is my decision, Dan. I'll handle the work out there in the daytime and Chuck will handle the nights. Joseph will be back on his feet in a few weeks and everything will be back to normal."

"You aren't up to this."

"You don't know me at all." Thinking, I shouldn't have said

that.

"Maggie, I've been living with you for 13 years. I know you better than you think I do."

She felt an unspoken threat somewhere in those words. But he turned abruptly and reentered the den and she took advantage of his absence from the doorway to get up the stairs and into bed.

Chapter 18

Maggie woke when the alarm rang at 4:30. She had only 4 hours sleep, but was instantly wide awake and saw that Dan had not come to bed at all.

She showered and dressed and went down the steps as quietly as she could. Hannah was in the kitchen. "Why are you up so early?"

"I knew you'd want to get an early start. And I knew you wouldn't eat if I didn't force you." She handed Maggie a foil wrapped package and a thermos. "It's just a bacon and egg sandwich and a thermos of hot coffee, but it'll hold you. Be sure to remember to eat it."

"You'll get the boys to school and take care of Megan?"

"Do you have to ask?"

"Thank you Hannah. Is he still in the den? Because he never came to bed last night."

"He is. Once I get the boys off, I'll wake him with some hot coffee and get him going. He has a trial, you know."

"No, I didn't know." Maggie wondered how many other things about her husband she didn't know, but she had no time to think about it now.

As she left, Hannah said "When you get out to the farm, check and see if you need any groceries. You can call me and I'll pick up what you need at Angeli's and meet you at the hospital with it."

"Hannah, you're wonderful. I didn't think about that at all."

By the time she got on the road, the plows were out, and the River Road was clear. As she neared the turn to Chuck's farm, she saw him standing at the drive with Moses. She pulled over, slid across the seat and opened the passenger door. "Aren't you freezing out here?"

"Nah. I'm dressed warm. I'm just back from milking at the Blacks and I thought I'd watch for you. Do you want to take the dog with you?"

"Yes" and she called "Moses, come on." He jumped onto the seat and greeted her with kisses. "I'll feed the horses and see to things at the house, then I'm going to the hospital to get Joseph."

"Okay. After school, I have to milk again, but then I'll be over. Listen, Maggie, when I picked up Moses last night, I left my dad's hunting rifle at your place, just in case. Do you know how to shoot a rifle?"

"Sure I do. My dad taught all of us when we were kids. My brothers used to hunt, till the accident with Robbie. Do you think we might need a rifle?"

"Better safe than sorry."

"Is your dad okay with you staying the nights?"

"Yeah. He's the one who thought of the rifle. But he said we should call the Sheriff if anything happens and not try to handle it on our own."

"Your father's a wise man. You need to get ready for school. I'll see you later."

The plow had cleared the road, but Maggie's driveway was covered with a good amount of snow. She drove slowly, not wanting to get stuck there. Just before the house, she turned the car around so that it was facing toward the road. She parked and went along to the barn, Moses dancing alongside her.

She fed the horses and checked the waterers to be sure they were ice free, then she and Moses went to the house.
She looked around. Joseph had apparently been doing household chores when he heard the gunshots and went to investigate. The bed was stripped and there was laundry in the washer. She started the washer and then found clean sheets in the hall closet and made up the bed. The house was clean. She looked at Moses and said "Your daddy is such a good housekeeper." He wagged his tail happily as if to agree.

She was about to check the refrigerator to see what groceries they might need when she saw the shopping list on the table. She had never seen his handwriting before. The list was short – milk, eggs, butter, bread – and there was a pencil beside the paper as though he'd been interrupted. She held the list in her hand and then she sat down at the table and began to cry for the first time since she'd heard the news the night before.

She pictured him sitting here, making his shopping list, planning to take Moses and drive to town, then coming back to fix himself a dinner that he would eat alone. She couldn't seem to stop crying, but finally she realized she had to get to the hospital and that made it easier.

She washed her face with cold water and called Hannah and told her what she needed from Angeli's. "Hannah, could you get some things that you think I might make a few dinners out of, nothing fancy. Maybe some spaghetti and sauce." Her voice trailed off as she tried to think of what she could cook.

Hannah said "I'll bring you some things out of the freezer. Like you say, nothing fancy, just some dinners I prepared ahead. The portions will be large, because it's enough to feed all of us and it'll just be the 2 of you, so you'll have to divide them up. But it's all stuff you can heat up in the oven. You have enough to do out there without worrying about cooking. Did you eat? Don't answer. I know you didn't. Do it now or you never will."

As she thanked Hannah, Maggie found herself close to tears again. She had to pull herself together or she wouldn't be any use to Joseph at all. She sat at the table and ate the sandwich and drank the coffee from the thermos.

When she got up to leave, Moses followed her to the door. She considered taking him along, but decided it was too cold to leave him in the car. "You wait here, Honey. You can be the welcoming committee." She watched him until he turned and wentn to the bedroom and curled up on the bed.

The car slewed a couple of times between the house and the River Road, but she made it without getting stuck.

She went to the business office first and took care of the bill, then to Joseph's room where she found him sitting on the edge of the bed, already dressed. He tried to refuse the wheelchair, but the nurse insisted it was hospital policy. Maggie saw that it diminished him in his own eyes to be treated like an invalid, but there was nothing she could say or do to make it easier for him.

Once he was in the car, she explained that Hannah was coming with groceries. He nodded, always a quiet man, but more so now than she'd ever known him to be.
She was relieved when Hannah pulled into the parking lot and found an empty space next to Maggie's car.

She left Joseph sitting in the passenger seat and went to where Hannah was unloading bags. When Megan saw Maggie, she held out her arms and called "Mama" and Maggie hugged her. When she tried to let go, Megan kept her arms around Maggie's neck. Maggie got her out of the car and held her in one arm while she helped Hannah transfer the groceries to Maggie's car.

In the process, she introduced Joseph to Hannah. "Joseph, this is Hannah. You're going to be thanking her a lot one of these days when we run out of the food she fixed, and you have to eat my cooking."

"Hello, Hannah. Is she really a bad cook?"

"I couldn't say. She's never cooked for as long as I've known her."

Megan saw Joseph then and held her arms out. Joseph said "You can give her to me while you load the groceries."

Maggie put Megan into Joseph's lap carefully, afraid of hurting him, but he took her easily, cradling her with his good arm. As she'd done the first time he'd held her, Megan rested her hand on Joseph's cheek which caused him to smile again.

When they finished, Megan fussed at being taken out of Joseph's lap, but Hannah quieted her and settled her back in her car. "You'll be late tonight?" she asked Maggie.

"Yes. Chuck has to help with milking at one of the neighbors, before he and his dad do their own. Do you think you can keep everybody settled down?" Both she and Hannah knew she meant Dan.

"I'll do my best, Maggie. If there's a problem, I'll give you a call out at the farm. Don't worry."

On the drive out River Road, Joseph was silent. She risked a glance at him and saw that his eyes were closed, head against the backrest. He stayed that way until she had parked, and come around and opened the passenger door. "Joseph?" He opened his eyes and started to get out of the car. She saw him wince with pain and she said "Hold onto me."

They made their way up the steps and into the house, like an elderly couple she thought. Maybe someday, we'll be like this, helping each other along, barely able to walk, but the thought inspired no fear in her.

Moses waited to greet Joseph, but did so quietly, as though sensing something wrong. He trailed along behind them, as they walked to the bedroom. Once Joseph was sitting on the side of the bed, she bent toward him, thinking to help get him undressed and into bed. He looked at her with a great sadness. "This isn't the way it should be. I always want to be the one to take care of you."

She knelt in front of him and looked up into his face. "Oh, Joseph, that's not the way it is when people love. They take care of each other." She took off his shoes, then stood and unbuttoned his shirt and helped him take it off, conscious of the broken shoulder, the tension in his face giving away the pain he tried to hide from her.

He wasn't wearing a tee shirt so now she saw for the first time some of the injuries inflicted on him. She forced back tears, forced lightness into her voice. "Where are your pajamas?"

"Never wear them."

"Well, you need to put on something."

"There are some sweat pants and sweat shirts in that drawer."

But when she tried to get the shirt over his head, she realized he wouldn't be able to raise his arm so she went to the closet and found a clean flannel work shirt and helped him on with that.

When she picked up the sweat pants, he took them from her. "I can get these on by myself."

She flushed and nodded. "I'll get the groceries in and come back to check on you."

He was under the covers when she came back, Moses curled up next to him.

"Are you hungry?"

"Maybe later."

"Do you want a pain pill?"

"No. I don't like the way they make me feel. I'd rather have the pain."

"Is there anything I can do?"

"Can you lie down with me?"

Her answer was to take off her shoes and get under the covers on the other side from Moses. Careful not to hurt him, she moved closer, until she was lying against him. "Is this alright?"

"This is more than alright."

She lay still, feeling his body growing warm against hers, listening as his breathing smoothed, becoming deep and even. He was asleep and by turning her head just a little she could study his profile. In a little while, she fell asleep too.

She woke when he moved away from her, his breath catching in his throat as he sat up.

"What's wrong?"

"Nothing, I have to piss."

"Let me help you."

He began to laugh, then winced in pain. "God, Maggie, please don't make me laugh. My ribs are broken."

"At least, let me help you to the bathroom."

"Stay there. Keep my bed warm."

When he came back, she lifted the covers for him. "Are you hungry?"

"A little."

She got up. "I'll fix us something. It's after 2."

She heated soup, found a tray and brought 2 bowls back to the bed. They sat up against the pillows side by side and ate.

"Can you sleep some more?"

"I think so. I don't know why I'm so tired."

"I'll clean up the kitchen and take care of the horses."

When she left the house, the temperature had dropped and the day was gray and gloomy, threatening more snow. By the time she'd fed the horses, her fingers felt frozen inside her gloves and once back in the house, she stepped out of her boots and dropped her jacket, thankful to be where it was warm.

Joseph and Moses were asleep. She got out one of Hannah's frozen dinners – Ham and Scalloped Potatoes, the label said – and put it into the oven and watched the news on T.V.

It was after 7 when Chuck arrived with apologies. While they were talking, Joseph hobbled into the kitchen and insisted he could eat dinner with them at the table. When they finished,

Chuck insisted on cleaning up so that she could get home.

Joseph was still sitting at the table but when she told him she'd help him back to bed, he said "I need a bath." Before she could offer to help, he said "I can manage. Chuck's here if I need anything." She wanted to kiss him good bye but felt self conscious with Chuck at the sink, doing the dishes. She contented herself with touching his hand.

She let herself out. Chuck had cleared the driveway.

When she got home, the children were in bed and Dan was closeted in the den. Hannah met her in the hall. "He said I should tell you not to disturb him. He's busy with the trial preparation."

Maggie, expecting a scene over her late homecoming, was grateful for the reprieve and went upstairs and fell into bed exhausted. When her alarm rang at 4:30, Dan was asleep next to her, so she took clean clothes and went down the hall to the guest bathroom to bathe and dress.

When she left, no one was up, not even Hannah.

Chapter 19

The second day varied little from the first. She saw Chuck off, took care of the horses and looked in on Joseph who was sleeping restlessly. She sat in the kitchen, drinking coffee until she heard him stirring. Before she could get up, he was in the hall. "No, I don't need any help" he said and went on to the bathroom.

When he came back, he sat at the table with her and she fixed him hot cereal and tea, then she insisted he go back to bed. When she had washed the dishes, she went in to him, and without being asked, got under the covers and moved beside him.

She had thought he was asleep, but then he began to talk and he told her what had happened. He told it dispassionately, without emphasis. It had been mid afternoon. He was starting the laundry when he heard gunshots echoing out of the woods. He left Moses in the house and went out and shut the horses in the barn. He didn't think to call the Sheriff or to take a rifle with him although there was one in a gun cabinet in the living room.

He walked along the road, thinking it would be safer than

being in among the trees where he might be mistaken for a deer, drawing gunfire. He saw their pick up truck, pulled off onto the shoulder. They weren't far from the road, just inside the tree line. He had called out "This is private land. It's posted" pointing to one of the signs they'd nailed up.

"They were all pretty young, and there was one who seemed to be the leader. They all looked at him to do the talking. He said 'Hey there Chief. It's Deer Season. You're probably not from around here so you don't realize that it's not friendly to deny people the right to hunt.' I told him he could hunt anywhere he wanted, just not on this land. Then he said 'Why don't you just get your ass back to the Reservation where it belongs.'

They all looked at each other then and they jumped me. And that was it. Till Chuck came along and they took off. It was like I was a kid again, with my dad. I've never been a fighting man. I've known a lot who are, whose idea of fun on a Saturday night is to have some beers and shoot some pool and look for an excuse to get into a brawl in a bar, or outside in the parking lot when the bars close.

Maybe it's because of the way I grew up, but I never wanted any part of that. Still, I always thought if I had to, I could defend myself."

"I'm sure you could, just not against 5 armed men. That only happens in the movies, not real life."

"I know you're right, Maggie, but it doesn't make me feel any better."

"I want to find out who they are and make them pay."

"You forget that, Maggie. If you do, you'll bring more trouble down on all of us. Chuck's right. They're cowards. They were seen so they won't come back here. They'll try it somewhere else and maybe someday they'll come up against the wrong person and get paid back that way. Or maybe they won't but it doesn't matter to us. It's done."

That night, she had dinner ready when Chuck arrived, but didn't stay to eat with them, so she was able to see her children before bed. After Megan and the boys were settled, she was getting ready for bed herself when Dan came in. "So how long is this schedule going to go on?"

"Just a few more days. He'll be back on his feet and won't need anyone to take care of him."

"So you think you might be able to spend Thanksgiving with your family?"

"Oh my God, I forgot all about Thanksgiving."

"Yes, I guess you did. Your mom wants to have the whole family at their place this year, your brothers and their wives and kids and us, of course, including Hannah."

"That'll be a nice change for Hannah, not having to do all the cooking."

"Does that mean we'll be seeing you there?"

"Of course." She ignored the sarcastic cast to his voice and went on brushing her hair.

To change the subject, she asked "How's the trial going?"

"Oh, you're aware that I'm in trial. That's a surprise. I thought your only concern these days was your hired man's state of health."

"Dan, I'm tired. I have to get up at 4:30 again tomorrow. I don't want to argue."

"Are you complaining about the long hours, the work? Because I seem to recall it was your idea."

"I'm not complaining. I just want to get some sleep."

"Of course. Well, I'll leave you to it. I have some work to do."

Maggie breathed a silent Thank God as he left the room.

Chapter 20

They came back on day 3, in spite of everyone's assurances that they wouldn't. It was late afternoon, getting dark already and Chuck wasn't due for another hour. Joseph had been sleeping on and off all afternoon. He had seemed to be in more pain than the previous two days, and Maggie had finally convinced him to take a pain pill.

She was watching him sleep when she heard the truck. It was a diesel and noisy. She got up and looked through the window, but it was unfamiliar. She went into the living room and picked up the fine hunting rifle with the scope that Chuck's father had loaned her. She told Moses to wait and she stepped out onto the porch, closing the door behind her.

She could just see 3 people in the truck's cab and 2 riding in the bed. The 2 in the bed jumped to the ground, and the driver got out and walked closer to the porch. He hadn't seen her yet, standing as she was in the shadows. He called out "Hey Chief, how come those No Hunting signs aren't down?"

Maggie stepped forward to where they could see her. She raised the rifle to her shoulder, and settled it comfortably, the way her Da had taught her. Then she said "Those signs stay up. There's no hunting allowed here."

The driver looked at the two behind him and gave a short laugh. "You folks just aren't very hospitable, are you?"

"I'm Maggie Ryan. You get the hell off my place now. If you ever set foot on my land again, or if you ever hurt any of mine, I'll hunt you down and I'll shoot your ass, and nobody will prosecute me because I'm married to Dan Ryan and he knows every judge in the County."

The driver looked a little uncertain, but appeared determined to play tough guy for his friends. He took a step forward. Maggie sighted about a foot to the left of his head, away from the barn where the horses were, and just slightly down so that, hopefully, the bullet would hit the ground, then she fired. She heard the whine of the bullet as it passed his head, and the thwack as it buried itself in the ground.

"You crazy psycho bitch." But he threw it back as he and his friends ran for the truck. The truck's rear end slewed as he spun it around and headed down the driveway. The door opened behind her as the truck disappeared and Joseph said "Maggie, what the hell is going on? Did you just shoot that rifle?"

"Yeah, Honey, I did. Come on, let's get inside. You're in your stocking feet."

"So are you." Maggie looked down and realized that she was, and that her feet were freezing.

Before they could close the door, Chuck was crossing the yard at a run. They let him in. He looked at the rifle in Maggie's hand. "What's going on here?"

"That's what I want to know" Joseph said.

"I was walking up the drive when I saw this truck coming. It was those same guys and when they passed me, the driver rolled down his window and yelled "Watch out, Buddy. There's a crazy bitch shooting a rifle back there."

"The good news is he didn't recognize you." Maggie laughed.

Joseph reached out and pulled her to him with his good arm. "What did you do?"

"Nothing" she said innocently.

"Maggie?"

"I threatened to kill them if they set foot on my land again and then I told them I had connections so I wouldn't even be prosecuted."

Chuck reached out a hand and carefully took the rifle from Maggie. "I don't think they'll be back."

The three of them looked at each other and began to laugh. Joseph laughed in spite of the pain caused by his broken ribs.

Maggie got home in time for dinner with the family that night. She thought it best not to mention to Dan the reappearance of Joseph's assailants or the fact that she'd fired a rifle at them.

When she came in to say good night to Colin and Declan, Declan beckoned her closer so that he could whisper. "Mom, where is Joseph going to have Thanksgiving dinner?"

"I don't know, Honey."

"Maybe we could ask him to come to Grama's."

"I don't know if that's such a good idea. He won't know anybody there."

"He knows you and me. I miss him."

"Would you like to go out with me to see him? There's no school next week."

"Can I see the horses too?"

"Sure. But we can't ride, you understand. Joseph got hurt so he has to rest."

"That's okay."

The weekend passed uneventfully. Chuck was finished at Black's farm so he was able to give her more help.

Joseph was improving more quickly than she had thought possible, or he was attempting to make her believe he was. On Saturday, he came out to the corral while she was feeding horses. He walked slowly but unassisted and hung around to watch her, even suggesting that he could help her.

"Sure, you just go ahead and do some heavy lifting with that shoulder. Then you'll displace the fracture and need surgery and be laid up all winter."

"For such a pretty little thing, you can be very scary."

"Get back in the house and rest. I'll be in as soon as I'm finished." But she was smiling when she said it, delighted to see that his mood was lighter than it had been since the incident.

She was finishing up when Chuck came down the driveway. "You should have waited for me to do that."

"You men are all alike. Joseph was just out here wanting to help."

"He's feeling better. That's good."

"My little boy wanted to know if we could invite Joseph to Thanksgiving dinner at my parent's house. I thought it might not be a good idea."

"Yeah, the way you two look at each other, everybody would know right away, how you feel, I mean."

"Is it pretty obvious?"

"I spend a lot of time with both of you so maybe I'd notice

more than somebody else would."

"How does that make you feel about me?"

"What do you mean?"

"I'm married. I have children."

"I guess we can't help who we fall in love with. If you and Joseph had met a long time ago, you'd be married to each other and that's the way it should be. But you met later and so you fell in love then. It wouldn't have mattered when you met. It would have turned out the same. I'm not very good about explaining what I mean."

"I think you're awfully good at it. I couldn't have explained it better myself."

"So as far as Thanksgiving goes, my folks already told me to ask Joseph to have dinner with us. I just wanted to check with you first and see if it was okay."

"That's very nice, Chuck. It'll make it easier for me to get through the day knowing he's not alone out here."

"I wish…"

"What?"

"I wish you could be with us. You and Joseph together. Your kids too."

"My boy, Declan, he asked me if he could come out and see Joseph. I'm bringing him with me on Monday. There's no school. I guess I'll bring Megan along too. She always wants Joseph to hold her when she sees him."

"Joseph's a good man. I know he likes your kids too."

Joseph accepted Chuck's Thanksgiving invitation without hesitation, as though knowing it would make the holiday easier for Maggie. He told Chuck "I think you can start spending your nights at home again. I'm getting around by myself. And you" he said to Maggie "need to spend tomorrow with your family. Speaking of which, you should get home now."

Maggie felt a pang at his words and he seemed to sense it, because he walked with her to the door, leaving Chuck in the living room. "You know how good it's been having you here all day every day. But it's costing you at home. You want to keep the peace there. I know you're afraid, but the day is coming when we're going to have to face him. We can't keep on as we are. If I hadn't been hurt, we would have crossed the line by now." He pulled her close and held her so that she could feel his heart beating. "You know it's true, Maggie."

She did know. She thought of little else. She thought of ways to make the break with Dan. But none of them would work, of that she was sure. In the end, it would come to an impossible choice, A little longer, she thought, just a little longer, to go on as they were.

Chapter 21

On Monday, after breakfast, she bundled Megan up for the trip to the farm. Declan was jumping around in excitement. Dan had left early for Court and Hannah was cleaning up in the kitchen.

Colin was lingering at the table and Maggie was struck with the idea to ask him to come along with them. He'd never been to the farm, never met Joseph. But when she suggested that he go along, he said sullenly "Why would I want to go along and meet some dumb Indian who works for you?"

She took a deep breath before answering. "He's not dumb, Colin. Why would you think that?"

"He works on a horse farm. He's uneducated. He doesn't have his own place or any money."

"Why would you say these things? You don't know him or anything about him."

"Dad says he's just a penniless drifter off the Reservation."

Maggie was so stunned to hear that Dan had made any

comments about Joseph that she didn't immediately grasp what his comments had been. "Who was your father talking to?"

"Me."

"You?" But before Colin could answer, Declan ran to his mother, saying "Come on, Mom, let's go. Megan's getting all hot and fussy and besides, it's getting late."

Maggie was forced to let the subject drop for the time being, but she continued to think about it on the drive.

When they arrived, she saw that Joseph was on the porch. Declan didn't wait for her to get Megan out of the car, but ran directly to Joseph. By the time she got there, she saw that Declan was handing a small package to Joseph. "I made it in school, for you. We had to make something for Thanksgiving and the teacher told us all about how the pilgrims and the Indians celebrated the first Thanksgiving together, so I thought it would be really good if I made it for you."

"Thank you, Declan. I think it's the first time I've ever gotten a gift for Thanksgiving. Can I open it now?"

Declan nodded. As soon as Joseph began to unwrap the paper, Declan began to explain the gift. "See, there's a ring for your keys and a little pouch for your money and it fastens on your belt so you can always find it. See, that little loop goes on your belt."

"No one has ever made me a gift before." Joseph took the key ring he carried out of his pocket, and transferred the keys to the one Deco had made, took the change from his pocket and put it into the pouch and then unbuckled his belt and slipped the loop onto the belt. "This is really great."

Deco, big smile on his face, said "See, the key ring part unclips so you don't have to take the whole thing off your belt to get the keys, like when you drive the truck."

"I'll use it every day, Deco. Thank you."

"Can we go and see the horses now?"

"Sure, we can. Will your sister be warm enough? It' pretty cold out there."

Deco looked at Maggie. "Mom, is it too cold for Megan?"

"No. She's bundled up." Maggie trailed along behind Joseph and Deco, watching Deco try to match his steps to Joseph's, feeling warm contentment that she knew was only temporary, wishing this whole small world they had created could last more than just a few hours.

Joseph took Deco into the corral so he could pet all of the horses, but especially Beauty. Finally, he said "Why don't we go inside and warm up, have some hot chocolate, then we can come back out and maybe your mom and I can lift you up and you can have a little ride around the corral."

They came in through the mud room, leaving their boots just inside the door and went into the warm kitchen, where they sat around the table in their stocking feet while Joseph heated milk. When he had poured the chocolate and sat down, Megan immediately held her arms out to him. He lifted her and she settled happily against him. Deco told Joseph about his school and Joseph paid attention to him when he talked, not, Maggie thought, like most adults who nod and say 'uh huh' their mind somewhere else while children are telling some story.

Maggie was feeling pleasantly warm and sleepy, watching Joseph with her children, when Deco suddenly said "My brother's a jerk."

"Why?" Joseph asked.

Maggie wanted to turn this conversation in a different direction but before she could, Deco said "Because Mom asked him if he wanted to come along and he said he didn't want to meet a dumb Indian. Then mom got mad and said you aren't dumb and where did he hear such a thing."

"Deco?" Maggie said softly and watched his face as he realized he had told Joseph something he shouldn't have.

"I'm sorry."

Joseph said, without hesitation, "Nothing to be sorry for, Deco. Didn't you want to go out and take a little ride around the corral?"

"Can we still do that?"

"Why not?"

"You're not mad at me?"

"Why would I be mad at you?"

"For what I said. I don't think you're dumb."

"I know you don't. And I'm not mad at you. Come on."

Joseph put Megan back into Maggie's lap and bent close to whisper in her ear. "Don't look like that."

"Like what?"

"Like all the fun went out of the day." Deco was already in the mud room putting on his boots and Joseph took advantage of the moment to kiss the top of Maggie's head. "I've never met Colin, but he's older than Deco. You'd have to expect him to feel threatened by somebody who takes his mother away so much of the time."

When they got outside, Maggie gave Megan to Joseph to hold while she haltered Beauty and then, before he could protest, she swung Declan up and onto Beauty's back, took the rope and began to lead the horse around inside the corral. When they passed close to Joseph, she said "I've been lifting him all my life and you aren't supposed to because of your shoulder so stop giving me that look."

When Declan finished his ride, Joseph asked Maggie if they could stay for lunch and she happily agreed. Joseph and Declan got the food ready while Maggie changed and fed Megan and put her down for a nap. The three of them sat around the table eating tuna salad on toast.

"This is the best lunch I've ever had" Declan declared "but, Mom, don't tell Hannah cause her feelings might be hurt."

In the car on the way home, he said "I wish we lived at the farm with Joseph."

Without thinking, Maggie responded "From your lips to God's ear."

"What does that mean?"

"It's an old Irish saying. It means something like sending God a message that you want something and God hears and makes it come true. Don't tell anybody I said it and don't go home and tell anyone that you wish we lived at the farm."

"But you do too, right, Mom?"

Maggie's eyes burned with unshed tears. Declan reached out

and patted Maggie's arm. "Don't cry, Mom. It'll be alright." Then he repeated "From your lips to God's ear."

Chapter 22

For Maggie, Thanksgiving was a family nightmare. Nine adults crowded around her mother's kitchen table while the children were set up at two smaller tables. The food was plentiful and everyone talked about how delicious everything was and that was no doubt true. But Maggie had to chew and chew and drink glass after glass of water to force it down.

Dan drank too much and he wasn't alone, both of her brothers matched him drink for drink. Maggie limited herself to a glass of wine so that she could drive home. It was no sacrifice. After several hours of people shouting to be heard over the noise of screaming children and the football game blaring on T.V., her head was throbbing with pain.

She lost herself in a little fantasy in which she and Joseph, Declan, Megan, and even Colin were sitting around the kitchen table out at the farm, having a turkey dinner of their own, with candles on the table and a fire in the fireplace, maybe some quiet music in the background, Moses asleep under the table. And after they finished eating, they would all bundle up and walk out and feed carrots and apples to the horses. Then, after dessert, the children would fall asleep, and she and Joseph would sit in front of the fire with their arms around each other.

She started when she felt a touch on her shoulder and heard a voice at her ear. "Maggie, darling, you look like you're in pain. Would a bit of fresh air help?"

Bless her father for knowing her so well. He helped her into her coat and boots and they walked down to the beach, cold and deserted, ice already pushing up against the shoreline. "Do you want to talk?"

"I do. Do you want to hear?"

He nodded and waited.

"Joseph and I love each other. He feels that we have to go to Dan and tell him the truth and then I'll be free to leave Dan, and we'll take the children and go away somewhere to live."

"It's what you want?"

"Yes, it is. But he doesn't understand Dan. Dan will never let me take the children."

"Far more than that. Dan will not give you up easily."

"He'll have to when he sees the way things are."

"Dan knew the way things were when he married you. He knew it was Michael you loved, but it didn't stop him from taking what he wanted."

"That was a long time ago. Perhaps he isn't so happy with the bargain he made when he married me. I haven't been a good wife. And once he has to face that I don't love him, why would he still want me?"

Why indeed? Patrick thought. Because he's not one to give up what he considers belongs to him. Patrick didn't tell Maggie that. It would only frighten her and he couldn't bear to do that. So he said "It's true that he can't force you to stay with him. But you're right. He won't give up the children without a fight."

"I'm afraid. Afraid it's a fight I can't win. He has everything, all of the power, all of the money."

"Still you are the mother. Judges most often feel young children should be with their mother."

"That's what Joseph believes. But even if I win, I don't feel right about moving away where the children can't see their father every day."

"You don't have to leave. There's your place. You could live there."

"Joseph is too proud for that. Dan's money bought that place. So even though it's mine in name, he feels it gives Dan some kind of ownership over us."

"Yes, Joseph would feel that way. It's admirable, that kind of pride, but it can cost a great deal. It would make things easier for you if you stayed. A judge might give you custody but set some boundary on how far away you can take the children."

"Could they do that?"

"I'm not a lawyer, Darling, but your husband is. You can be sure he will have the advantage over you. You're right about that much."

"What am I going to do? I'm afraid to tell Dan, but Joseph won't do things any other way."

"What other way is there if you love each other? Neither of

you would be satisfied with having an affair while you remain Dan's wife."

"That's what Joseph said."

"Are you telling me that you would settle for less than being Joseph's wife?"

" I would do anything to have him."

"Would you give up the children?"

"No. Sometimes when I'm feeling crazy with loving him I think I could even do that, but I couldn't, not really. And it's Joseph that made me see that, that I could never be happy without them."

"Ah, Maggie. You're the child I love the best of them all so I know something about that. You're going to have a very bad time of it. Dan is not a kind man. Perhaps he appears to be but that's because you've never crossed him. Of course, I'm being unfair. What husband would be kind if he lost his wife to another man? Don't act rashly. Think long and hard and take no chances. Don't give Dan any excuse to put you in the wrong."

"Joseph said that too, or something very much like it."

"He's a wise man, your Joseph. I know you belong with him. I know there's no hope for it. You can always come to me, you know. Even though I don't know what it is I can do to help." And he held her close for a minute, then they turned and walked back to the house where Maggie had grown up.

Chapter 23

The week after Thanksgiving, Maggie decided that Joseph was well enough to get along without her for one day. As she was leaving the farm on Monday, she told him. "I have to go down to Green Bay tomorrow to see a friend. Will you be okay on your own?"

"I'll manage."

"Promise me you won't do any heavy work."

"I promise. Call me when you get back if you can. Just let me know that you're back safe."

She moved close to him, took off her glove to touch his face, kissed his mouth lightly, barely a touch, still careful not to hurt him.

First thing Tuesday morning, she drove to Dr. O'Brien's office to keep an appointment she'd made the week before. He seemed surprised to see her. "Mrs. Ryan? My nurse said I had a new patient. Are you here to see me about Mr. Dodge?"

"No, I'm here for myself, as a patient."

"How is Mr. Dodge doing? He should have been in for a follow up by now."

"He's very stubborn about seeing doctors. I'll see that he makes an appointment. But he seems to be recovering very well."

"That's good to hear. What can I do for you?"

"I'd like to get a prescription for birth control pills."

"Don't you have a family doctor?"

"I'd like a doctor of my own. I thought of you. You took good care of Joseph."

"Fine. I'd like to take a history, do an examination, before prescribing anything."

"Of course."

He called the nurse in, and went out while Maggie disrobed and put on a gown. After the exam, Maggie dressed and waited for him to return. When he came in, he said "Well, your health seems fine. I'll write you a prescription. May I ask, what method of birth control you've been using?"

"I was on the pill, but I stopped taking it because we wanted another baby. After Megan was born, we used condoms, but I'd like something more reliable for the long term." Maggie listened to the lies fall from her lips, thinking she could probably lie as convincingly to Dan when the time came.

She had the prescription filled and, on her way out of the drugstore, put the first pill in her mouth and swallowed it with water from the drinking fountain. Then she got into the car and drove to Green Bay.

When she got there, she stopped at a pay phone, and read the yellow pages until she found what she was looking for. She knew the city fairly well, found a parking place and walked down the block to the music store. There were a lot of pianos on the showroom floor and she browsed among them until a salesman approached her. "May I help you?"

"I'd like to buy a piano."

"Do you play?"

"No, it's a gift."

"Were you interested in a Grand or a Baby Grand?"

"I'm afraid we don't have room."

"We have some lovely uprights. What brand were you considering?"

"I'm afraid I don't know anything about pianos. Perhaps you could help me. I'd like the best one you have and I'd like it delivered for Christmas."

Once Maggie had made a selection, she asked the salesman if he could schedule the delivery for the morning of Christmas Eve.

"I'm terribly sorry. We're closed on both the 24th and 25th."

"I'd be willing to pay extra for delivery on that day. It could be early in the morning, so your help would be back in plenty of time to celebrate with their families."

"Is it a local delivery?"

"No, it's in Upper Michigan, just over the Wisconsin border. It's only about 60 miles."

"I really don't know."

"Could you just ask your deliverymen? Please? I'll pay double whatever they usually charge."

Once it had been ascertained that the deliverymen were happy to earn twice their usual pay, and the arrangements had been made, Maggie drove back to Menominee. It was just after 3 and Dan's car was at the office when she drove by, so instead of driving home, Maggie took the Hattie Street Bridge and headed out River Road to the farm.

Joseph's truck was in the driveway. When she got to the door, she heard music. Joseph was playing the guitar. She stood on the porch in the cold, listening, hating to interrupt, but as she hesitated, the door opened, and Joseph was standing in front of her. But the music continued. "This is a nice surprise. You're already back from Green Bay? How was your visit?"

"It was a wonderful visit. What's going on?"

"Come in out of the cold and see." He led the way to the living room. Chuck was sitting in a chair, cradling Joseph's guitar.

Chuck smiled at her, a big beaming smile. "Joseph is teaching me to play the guitar."

"You sound good. I thought it was him playing."

Chuck's smiled widened.

"I didn't know you had a guitar."

"I don't. This is Joseph's guitar. I figure I can pick up some money helping some of the neighbors with their milking and such till I save enough to buy one of my own."

Maggie stayed a bit and listened and watched. Mostly she watched Joseph, who appeared to be so focused on his teaching that he didn't see her watching him. Then she said she'd better get home and would let herself out. Moses accompanied her to the door like a good host.

When she got home, she went upstairs to change clothes and called the music store in Green Bay. The salesman remembered her. She asked him to select the best acoustic guitar in the store and deliver it along with the piano on December 24.

Chapter 24

Each day when Maggie covertly swallowed one of the pills from the round white container hidden at the bottom of her purse, she experienced a thrill of anticipation. Each day she counted as one step closer to the day she would make love with Joseph.

Every weekday morning, she drove to the farm, found Joseph wherever he might be waiting and watching for her arrival, still in the kitchen if she was early enough, or out with the horses if she couldn't get away as soon as she liked.

He was obedient to the orders of Dr. O'Brien, still not riding or doing heavy lifting, but he was once again feeding horses and mucking, although Maggie tried to do at least half the work. As far as grooming went, they agreed they were fighting a losing battle against the thick, furry winter coats that had transformed all four horses into wooly mammoths.

Three or four days a week, Maggie would saddle one of the four horses and ride around the inside arena, then trade off and ride another, just to have the feel of a horse under her.

The mornings passed that way, the two of them working side

by side, in the cold, Moses running around in the snow. Then, morning chores behind them, they went inside, shedding boots, coats, hats and gloves and sitting in the kitchen in their stocking feet while coffee, or chocolate heated on the stove.

Maggie thought, if only this could be my life, this routine that some people would find monotonous or dull, but which filled her with lazy contentment.

They talked of nothing special, the horses, the cold, watching each other, smiling, but careful, careful not to come too close, knowing how quickly they could get lost in their passion for each other.

At first, they waited for Joseph to heal from his injuries, but as he did, they waited, each for their different reasons. He waited because he wanted her to make the break from her husband before he took her as his own.

Although she wanted that as well, she understood more than he did, that it would not be so simple as her telling Dan the truth. She knew that Dan would not give up his wife and children, that he would do what he could to keep her, and when he realized that he could not, he would use all of his formidable weapons against her.

She knew this was a fight she was unlikely to win and so she would put it off as long as possible, hoping, she supposed, that some outside force would magically free her, intact and with her children still hers.

Unlike Joseph, who seemed content just to be with her, look at her, hear her voice, Maggie was on fire for him. She was sure that, if he had not been so badly hurt, she would by now have forced the issue, made it impossible for him to say no to her. She would have taken off her clothes, stood naked before him, gotten into his bed and put his hands on her body.

But he was still healing so she took her pills and counted the days, thinking that by the New Year, she would make him her lover and then somehow she would find a way to face Dan, win the fight and have it all.

Chapter 25

By December 22, school had recessed for the holidays and Maggie asked the boys at breakfast if they wanted to go along with her to the farm that morning. Declan nodded and said yes through a mouthful of toast, while Colin predictably refused, looking to his father for approval.

In response Dan said "Well, then, why don't you come along with me to the office for the morning. We're going to close up at noon for the rest of the week, and we can go to Mickey Lu's for lunch." Colin gave Declan a look as if he'd somehow gotten the better of the deal, but Declan just went on eating his breakfast.

Joseph was outside with the horses when they arrived and, before Maggie could intervene, he swung Deco up on Beauty's back for a ride around the corral. "You are so bad" she chided him. "Do you want to separate that shoulder and end up back in the hospital?"

"It's better. Really" he insisted.

But when it came time to get Deco down, Maggie handed Megan to Joseph and she helped Deco to dismount. Once they had given the horses some extra rations of grain and apples, they went to the house. Before he opened the door, Joseph made Maggie and Declan close their eyes and hold onto him while they walked to the living room.

Maggie knew what the surprise was before she opened her eyes. The fragrance of evergreen filled the house.

Deco said "A Christmas tree. Look, Mom, Joseph got a tree. Did you cut it down yourself?"

"I did, but don't tell your Mom. It came out of her woods."

"Can we help decorate it?"

" I was hoping you'd come by to do that today. Why don't we start now and then we can have some lunch."

The ornaments were still in their packages and Maggie felt near tears at the picture of Joseph shopping alone for Christmas lights and decorations. She sat with Megan in her lap and let Joseph and Deco work on the tree together. It was a small tree, but bushy and full. The lights were multi colored and when they finished, it looked very much like the kind of Christmas tree that sat in its corner in the Kelly's living room every holiday season, and nothing like the tree that Dan had delivered to the house because it was too big to carry on top of their car.

At the Ryan's, the decorations had been collected over the years by Dan's parents and Maggie was always afraid that she or one of the children would break some priceless piece, although she knew that Dan would probably not have cared if they had. The tree was simply a back drop for one or more Christmas parties that the Ryan's hosted during the holidays – one for people from the legal community, fellow lawyers and judges, another for family friends, and, of course, one for family, family being Maggie's family, her parents, brothers and sisters in law and their children since Michael was, as far as they knew, still in Oregon and Erin, unmarried, had moved East and seldom visited.

"What do you think, Mom?" Declan interrupted her reverie.

"It's a beautiful tree."

"I think so too. I like it better than ours at home." Then, to Joseph, " Did you really cut it down in the woods?"

"I really did. Do you think your Mom is mad at me for doing

that without asking her? I can't tell."

Declan came over to stand in front of Maggie, studying her face. After a minute, he said "No. She's not mad. See, she's got that little smile she gets when she's real happy."

Joseph said "Yes, she does. Is everyone ready for lunch?"

They trooped to the kitchen where Maggie saw a cast iron kettle already simmering on the back burner.

"I made clam chowder. I hope everybody likes it."

"Deco" Maggie asked "Do we all like clam chowder?"

"We all do. Except Megan, cause she's still too little."

"Maybe she can have a taste" Maggie said. And once they were settled around the table, she took a small spoonful, blew on it till it was not too hot, and let Megan sample it. Megan made a little face, but then reached for the spoon and put it back in her mouth.

They all laughed and Deco said "Even Megan likes it."

Joseph took Megan while Maggie washed the lunch dishes then they all went back to the living room and sat around the tree. Joseph had laid a fire in the fireplace and now he lit it.

Megan fell asleep in Maggie's lap while Deco and Joseph talked about horses. Joseph said "The horse is a prey animal. Do you know what that means?" Deco shook his head, intent on Joseph. "It means he is hunted by animals called predators. Man is the greatest predator in nature. That's why it's a miraculous thing that a horse will let you ride him."

The more Joseph told him about horses, the more questions Deco asked. Joseph's answers were patient and detailed. Maggie was lulled by the sound of his voice into forgetting time completely. She hadn't realized how late it was until there was a knock at the door and Joseph said "That'll be Chuck for his guitar lesson. He's out of school this week so he comes by before the afternoon milking."

"We should head home" Maggie said reluctantly. They were getting into their coats and boots when Joseph came back with Chuck.

Joseph handed the guitar to Chuck and told him to tune it up while he walked Maggie to the car. Once Declan and Megan were settled, Joseph and Maggie stood outside the car, close together. It had turned bitter cold. "I should probably stay home tomorrow and I won't be able to get away on Christmas Day, but I'd like to come out Christmas Eve morning. Is that okay?"

"You don't need to ask."

"Early. I'll be here early. I'll help you feed the horses."

He took her fingers in his and kissed them. "Put on your gloves. You'll get frostbite."

When they got home, Dan was having a cocktail in the living room. "Want one of these?"

"What are you drinking?"

"Whiskey sour."

"Sure. Just let me get Megan settled. Lot's of ice, please" she threw back over her shoulder as she left the room.

Hannah met her in the hall and took Megan. "Let me help you. You were gone a long time today." She raised her chin in the direction of the living room. "That's not his first, not his second either. He asked me what I thought you did out there every day."

"I had the children with me. What does he think I'd be doing?"

"I guess he didn't just mean today." She said it in a warning way.

"Thanks, Hannah. Where's Colin?"

"In his room. Sometimes I think he'd like to get closer to you, but he's so defensive of his father."

Since Hannah had Megan, Maggie climbed the stairs and knocked on Colin's door. There was no answer, so after a minute, she opened the door a little. "Colin?"

"Yes?"

"May I come in?"

"Sure."

The room was dark and Maggie turned on a light. Colin was sitting on the bed.

"Did you have fun at dad's office today?"

"Yeah. I think I want to be a lawyer."

"Well, that would be good. Your grandfather was a lawyer, and your father, and even I thought about going to law school."

"You still could, if you didn't spend so much time out at the farm."

"Yes, I could. But it would be a little harder for me. There's no law school near here, you know. I couldn't drive back and forth every day."

"I never thought of that. We went to Mickey Lu's. What did you have for lunch?"

"Clam chowder, even Megan tried a little."

"Oh, yeah. Did she like it?"

"She made a face, but then she grabbed the spoon and had some more, so I guess she did." Maggie took advantage of the relative friendliness of the exchange to sit down next to him and put her arm around his shoulders. She thought he might shrug her off, but he didn't. " Why don't you come downstairs with me? It's almost dinner time."

They walked down the stairs side by side and into the living room where Colin joined Declan on the floor in front of the TV and Maggie picked up her sweating cocktail glass and sat in her own chair by the fire, rather than on the couch next to Dan.

He put down the paper he was holding, but, she could tell, not reading. "What do you do out there every day, Maggie?"

"Work with the horses." She stared into the fire, refusing to meet his eyes that were suddenly probing. Now would be the time, she thought, if the children weren't here.

But later, after dinner, when the children weren't there, having gone up to bed, there was a surly tone to Dan's voice. He had continued to drink throughout dinner and carried another glass of whiskey back to the living room after they had finished. No, she thought, now's not the time.

Chapter 26

The next day, Dan slept in. Maggie had been asleep when he came to bed and she was up before him, having breakfast with the children. When he finally came downstairs, it was clear that he was hung over and she told the children to keep the noise to a minimum. Finally, they announced that they were going down the block to play with friends, where they could be as noisy as they wanted to.

Maggie hung out in the kitchen with Hannah, helping with advance preparations for the Christmas Eve dinner that would be just for them, and the Christmas Day dinner, with Maggie's entire family in attendance. Maggie thought that Thanksgiving had been bad enough, now the festivities would be here, in her own home, and the only tolerable thing about the entire day would be that her father would be here and perhaps they would have an opportunity to talk.

Dinner that night was an improvement over the night before. Dan appeared chastened and apologized to her. "I'm sorry, Maggie. I don't know what got into me. Actually, I guess I do, it was too much to drink, no denying that. Curse of the Irish" he said with a weak laugh.

Maggie, in the meantime, spent the evening wondering how to break the news that she was going out to the farm for a few hours early on Christmas Eve morning, and finally went to bed without saying anything, thinking perhaps she could just slip out unquestioned early, leaving Hannah to care for Megan. But, what, she thought, if Dan decided to drive out there himself.

She was saved from an awkward situation when the phone woke them early. It turned out to be the wife of a colleague and old friend of Dan's who had suffered a mild heart attack the night before. She knew it was a terrible imposition to ask on what was practically Christmas, but was there any way that Dan could come by the hospital for a few hours. Their own children were so busy with their own lives that they weren't even getting there until the next day. "Can you imagine" she said tearfully. "Not only is it Christmas, but their own father could have died and still they can't be bothered to try to get here sooner."

Dan reassured her that they had probably tried, but it was impossible to get a flight this late and said that, of course, he would come by the hospital right after breakfast and stay a few hours to cheer up his old friend.

Still, it took him an impossibly long time to shave and shower and have breakfast so that by the time he pulled out of the driveway, Maggie had to race to get to the farm in time to meet the delivery truck.

As it was, she saw the truck turning into the driveway as she rounded the last curve before her property. She blew her horn to get the driver's attention and finally he slowed and she pulled up alongside him, leaning across the seat to roll down the passenger side window. "It's a surprise, so I'd like to go in first."

He nodded and she pulled ahead of him and parked behind Joseph's truck. Joseph came out of the barn and looked at the parade pulling into the yard. "What's going on?" he called to Maggie.

"Christmas. Come on in. I'll help you finish up the horses in a bit."

"No, it's okay. I'm done out here. You said you were going to be early and I didn't know how long you could stay so I got started before breakfast. Maggie, what's the truck doing here?"

The driver had gotten out of the truck and was looking at the steps up to the front porch. Then he got out a tape measure and measured the front door. "Lucky" he said. "You've got just enough clearance." Then he turned to the men with him. "Okay, let's get this thing unloaded. I want to get back on the road before the weather changes and we get snowed in up here in the middle of nowhere."

Maggie went and stood next to Joseph. "Don't say anything. I was lucky to get them to drive up here today."

He watched as the men unloaded the piano that was swathed in quilted padding, loaded it onto a dolly and began to truck it toward the porch. When they got to the steps, they huddled among themselves and then began bumping it up, one riser at a time, until it was on the porch. "Lady" the driver called "You want to go in ahead and show us where you want it."

But Maggie shook her head. "Ask him where he wants it."

She expected an argument, but Joseph looked as though he'd been struck dumb. Then he said "The living room, on the wall away from the fireplace. We're going to have to move some furniture."

"Well, hurry up" the driver said "we don't have all day."

Maggie and Joseph ran ahead and between the two of them shifted a couple of large chairs over to the fireplace. Maggie said innocently "Those chairs look much better by the fireplace."

Joseph gave her a long, level look. "I'll talk to you when we're alone."

Once the piano was in place, the two helpers unwrapped it from its padding while the driver went to get the piano bench. He sat down and tuned the piano while Maggie offered coffee to everyone.

Joseph just stood and watched until they packed up to leave, then he pulled out his wallet and tipped them.

As they went out the door, Maggie remembered "Oh, wait. Where's the other gift?"

"Oh, yeah" the driver went to the truck and came back with the guitar case.

Maggie carried the case carefully into the living room. Joseph was standing where she'd left him, near the piano.

"Okay, tell me."

"Remember, when I first met you and you said you played the guitar and the piano too, if there was one around to play. So now there's one around to play."

"And what's that?"

"That's Chuck's Christmas gift. It's a guitar."

"I figured it was when I saw the case. Maggie, you're too generous."

But she could tell there was something more bothering him. "Tell me."

"This is what scares me about you, about you and me, Maggie. You're just so used to having money, being able to buy whatever you want. If you're going to be with me, it won't be like that. Do you understand that? We'll be poor people, Maggie. You're husband was right. I'm penniless. I don't have an education or a career. I never wanted one before. I was content to drift around, working with horses. I used to think 'one of these days, I'll have to settle down and get a real job or I'll never have a place of my own.' But I never did. There didn't seem to be any hurry. And now here I am, I love a woman who's used to having everything, a woman with 3 children to take care of, and I want to be able to do that. I think we can do it, but it has to be us who are doing it. We can't live off your husband's money, even if he was willing to help you, which I'm pretty sure he won't be."

"I know." But she was suddenly ashamed, because the truth was, she hadn't really thought about it at all. She had somehow envisioned them living together just the way they did when she was here at the farm, even though he had told her they couldn't because although it was her place in name, it had been bought with her husband's money.

"Do you know, Maggie? Really? Because you have to think about it and be sure."

"I don't have to think about it. I'm more sure of this than I've ever been of anything in my life. It's the first time I've really known what I want. And money's not important to me, really it isn't. I just wanted to get you something that you would have for years, for all your life, and every time you would sit down to play, you'd think of me."

"I don't need reminders. I never stop thinking about you. When I'm here alone, when I'm feeding horses, and mowing grass, whatever I'm doing. When I'm in town shopping, I think 'maybe she'll come into the store and I can smile at her across the aisle, knowing that in a few hours, she'll be with me again.'"

She crossed the space between them, just two short steps and she was in the circle of his arms, leaning into him, raising her face to be kissed. But he maintained that careful posture he had adopted in the days since he'd begun to recover from the beating. "We can't go on as though this is going to be our life. We have to tell your husband but before that, we need to know where we're going. If Keshena is too far away, then we'll find a place near here."

"There's this place. It's mine. Wait, please, listen to me. I know you don't want to stay here because it was bought with Dan's money. But we could sell it and buy another place."

"Maggie, how would that change anything? In the end, it would still be Dan's money, once removed. I want you to keep this place. You can find a tenant for it. Maybe someday one of your children will want it. We'll find a new place, one that's really ours. But to do that, I'm going to have to find work, real work, not just seasonal things like haying, and training other people's horses. Once I do that, we can look for a place."

"Can we have a place in the country so there's room for the horses?"

"We can."

"Can we still keep the horses?"

"I won't make you give up everything, Maggie."

He sounded infinitely sad when he said that and Maggie took his face in her hands. "I would give up everything for you."

He put his hand to her lips. "God, Maggie, don't say that."

But she didn't take it back, only kissed his hand, although it was the first time she realized that he, too, was afraid of the consequences of their love.

"Come here" he said, taking her hand and leading her to the little Christmas tree. She saw that he had turned on the tree lights, although they were dimmed even by the weak winter sun that came in through the windows.

He bent down and took a small package from beneath the tree and put it in her hands. She opened the wrapping paper, careful not to tear it and lifted the cover from the box. Inside was a locket made of wood, some smooth and beautifully colored wood, polished by hand and adorned with two tiny interlocking horses, running together, carved into the wood, deeply enough so that years of touching them would not obliterate their figures.

To most people, it would appear to be a single entity, but Maggie saw at once that it could be opened. Joseph watched as it came to her how to turn the pieces. When she did, she saw that he had carved inside the words All My Love Forever, the letters so tiny that she wondered how he'd done it.

She turned and lifted her hair so that he could fasten it around her neck. Then she turned back and kissed his mouth. She thought later that if Chuck hadn't chosen that moment to knock on the door, then the day that she and Joseph made love for the first time would have been Christmas Eve morning. But it would be a little longer still.

They broke apart and Joseph went to open the door. Chuck

had brought a gift he'd made for Maggie, a fine small saddle bag on which he'd done the leather work, imprinting a horse to resemble Maggie's mare Sugar and above it the words Maggie and Sugar. She hugged him in thanks, not trusting her voice to thank him.

When she gave him the guitar, it was his turn to hug her. Then he sat and opened the case carefully, took the guitar out and cradled it in his arms. Joseph helped him to tune it, then Maggie sat and listened to the two of them play a duet of guitar and piano on Christmas Eve morning. She thought she'd never had a more perfect Christmas.

Maggie took her locket off only to bathe. Without thinking or being aware of it, she rested her fingers on it often. When Dan noticed it one day, and he noticed little during that time other than the fact that Maggie had slipped away from him as he had always feared she would, she told him she had bought it at an art fair in Door County the summer before. Dan knew then that there was nothing that he could buy her, nothing that he could offer her that she wouldn't have traded in a heartbeat to live her life with Joseph Dodge, a poor man with nothing but an old truck and a guitar. A man with everything because he had Maggie.

When one day, many years later, the leather thong that held the locket around her neck broke, Maggie cried as though her heart would break, and then went out and bought a fine gold chain for it.

Chapter 27

It had become a tradition for the Kellys and the Ryans to attend midnight mass on Christmas Eve and that year was no exception. All 3 of the children slept through the service, Megan in Maggie's lap and Declan and Colin leaning against her, one on each side. Maggie was awake, but dreaming herself somewhere else.

Joseph, unable to sleep, put a tape of Erik Satie's Gymnopedies into the tape player, and sat at the piano, listening, rewinding and playing along. Moses, watched for awhile, then yawned and went to sleep under the piano, next to Joseph's feet.

On Christmas morning, Maggie and Dan were awakened early by Colin and Declan for the unwrapping of presents. It wasn't until they had almost finished that Maggie realized that, for the first time in their marriage, she and Dan had no gifts for each other.

By 3, the family began to arrive, Sean and Annie and their 4 children, followed by Connor and Paula and their 2, then Patrick and Maeve. Maggie had taken refuge in the kitchen on the pretext of helping Hannah, the two of them sipping good, strong whiskey on the rocks, and tasting the food they were preparing, while they worked. More and more, Maggie found herself seeking Hannah's company, finding solace in the fact that Hannah knew her true feelings. She didn't yet talk about Joseph to Hannah, but knowing that she could made her happy.

When she was finally forced to join the family in the living room for cocktails before dinner, she noticed at once that Dan had clearly started drinking before anyone else had. His eyes had a glazed, not quite there look, and his hand on the glass trembled. In the general uproar of a family gathering that included 9 children, no one else seemed to notice. Everyone, in fact, looked and sounded as though they were on their second or third drink, which Maggie attributed to their strong desire to appear to be having a wonderful time, whether or not they actually were.

When her eyes reached her father, she saw that he had seen it all, Dan's drinking and the family's somewhat forced heartiness. She made her way across the living room to where he stood and went up on tiptoe to kiss his cheek. "Merry Christmas, Daddy."

Several years earlier, the adults had agreed among themselves not to exchange gifts but to limit the giving of presents to the children. The suggestion had come from Maeve who had told Patrick privately that she felt that the others were uncomfortable because of the income disparity between the Ryans and the rest of the family. Maggie and her father, however, had continued to privately give each other some small token without letting anyone else know.

Once they assured themselves that their temporary absence wouldn't be noticed, they walked together into the hallway. Patrick's dress overcoat was folded on a chair near the front door. He reached inside and drew out a small flat package that he put into Maggie's hand. For her part, she opened the closet door, and took a package from her coat pocket and gave it to him. As always, they opened the gifts at the same time. Maggie's gift was a pair of fine leather riding gloves, while Patrick's was a warm, soft scarf that matched his overcoat. She draped it around his neck. "Be sure you wear it every day, not just when you wear your dress coat."

"Will those gloves keep your hands warm enough for riding?"

"They will. They're perfect. Joseph has been telling me I need a pair of good riding gloves to really have a feel of the reins."

"Is the locket a gift from him?"

"No one else seemed to notice."

"And does it hold a picture?"

"Ah, you can see it opens. I could too, but most people wouldn't." She separated the pieces so that he could read the inscription.

"What will you say if Dan asks where it came from?"

"Oh, this, I bought it at an art fair last summer when we were over in Fish Creek. I just found it at the bottom of my jewelry box and started to wear it because it has horses on it, you see."

"I see. Yes, it suits you. The craftsmanship is beautiful. He could make jewelry for a living."

"We will need to make a living."

"It's definite then?"

"It is. I just don't know how I'm going to tell Dan."

"Choose your time carefully, and your words as well."

"I will." She would have said more, but Hannah appeared in the dining room doorway.

"Do you want to ask everyone to sit down to dinner or should I?"

As he watched her walk away from him to tell everyone that dinner was ready, he felt a strong and terrible fear for his daughter. It made his mouth go dry and his heart race. He wanted to talk to her, to warn her although he knew it would change nothing. For the remainder of that Christmas day, he had no opportunity to speak to her alone.

The dinner was a great success and everyone was back in the living room, enjoying an after dinner drink, while the children, tired out from the long day and excitement, quieted down.

Maggie excused herself to help Hannah with the clean up, and when Maeve offered her assistance, Maggie suggested that she spend the time with the grandchildren instead.

As soon as she and Hannah were alone in the kitchen, Maggie

dialed the farm's number and stood where she could look through the dining room and see the family in the living room beyond. Hannah began to run the dish water. Then, as if that wasn't enough to give Maggie privacy, she turned on the radio on the counter next to the sink and sang softly along as she began to wash the dishes.

He answered on the second ring, just said "Hello?" and she leaned against the wall, suddenly warm and soft with desire for him.

"It's me. What are you doing?"

"I'm playing the piano. It reminds me to think about you" he teased "in case I forget."

"What are you playing?"

"I'm working through some pieces that I think you'd like. Maybe by the time I see you again, I'll be able to play them for you."

"What did you do for dinner?"

"I was invited to the Schmitt's. She's a good cook."

"Turkey?"

"Yes, same as Thanksgiving. You?"

"Ham. It's always ham on Christmas, turkey on Thanksgiving."

"They asked me to give you Christmas greetings. They thought it was wonderful of you to buy Chuck the guitar, but too generous. I told them it's just the way you are and there's nothing we can do about it."

As Maggie watched, Dan got up and started across the living room, in the direction of the kitchen. Not ready to hang up yet, she said "It's so good to talk to you, Connie. Maybe I can come down there for a visit one of these days."

Dan walked past her. He took a bottle of Glen Livet from the cabinet and poured himself a drink, then held the bottle up in a questioning fashion. Maggie shook her head no and he poured a little more in his glass. On his way back to the living room, he said "Tell Connie I said hello."

Once Dan was back in his chair, she said to Joseph "I'm sorry. The whole family's here. They've been here all day. I don't think they're ever going home."

"Your father's with you then."

"Yes, he is. He gave me a pair of riding gloves, just the kind you thought I should have."

"He's very observant."

"He is. He thinks you're a fine craftsman. No one else even noticed my locket. I don't know when I'll be able to get away. This whole next week between now and New Year's, Dan closes the office."

"It's alright, Maggie. Have you thought about talking to him?"

"I think about it all the time. My father says I need to choose the time carefully, and the words too."

"It's not something you should do alone. Together would be better."

"No. You've got to let me find a way to do this. I know you're afraid of what he'll do, but he won't hurt me, not physically."

She saw that Connor and Annie were gathering up their half asleep children. "Joseph, I've got to hang up. I'll be there when I can, as soon as I can. I love you." She hung up without waiting for his response, knowing what it would be.

Chapter 28

For Maggie, the week between Christmas and New Year's was close to intolerable. Each day, Dan planned some outing to keep the family together. The day after Christmas, it was a drive up to the County for ice fishing, followed by dinner at Shaeffer's. The next day, a trip down to Green Bay for a production of The Nutcracker.

When they returned from Green Bay, Dan suddenly announced that he wanted to have several couples whom he described as their closest friends over for dinner on Tuesday night. Maggie argued that it was short notice and not fair to Hannah, but he turned on her with a sudden surprising anger. "You've had things your own way long enough. For once, you can be supportive of something I want."

Maggie, sensing the danger in allowing this to turn into an argument, acquiesced quickly and went to make the calls to the people he had chosen as their closest friends. They were people she had known since Dan had first begun to take her with him to the Country Club, when she was still a high school girl. Back then, they had all seemed incredibly sophisticated. Now, from the vantage point of years of social contact, she had few illusions left. Most of them drank too much, most of them cheated. But then, she realized she was no longer in a position to judge anyone in that regard. And somehow, she no longer felt the age gap between herself and them that she had been so aware of when she was 17. Somehow, even though they'd all gotten older, she had caught up with them. She was surprised to find that everyone accepted her invitation without hesitation. She would have thought at least some of them would already have had plans.

At least, the dinner party was an excuse to spend less time with Dan. She busied herself with helping Hannah with the menu and shopping, the flowers and food preparation. Although Dan held it together well during the day when he was with the children, she found that at night, after dinner, he had continued to lose himself in the bottle, often disappearing into the den, leaving her to sit alone in the living room, with a book after the children were in bed. She alternated between worrying about what was happening to him and being grateful that the drinking had caused him to have no interest in her physically. She was generally asleep before he came to bed, and some nights, he slept in the den, or passed out there, as she woke up alone in the morning.

Somewhere inside herself, she knew that his drinking had to do with her, and every day that he failed to confront her, saving her the agony of having either to lie, or to finally admit the truth to him, no matter what the consequences, was a reprieve.

It snowed on the day of the party, just enough to further enhance the beauty of the Ryan's home, light from the tall windows spilling warmly onto the fresh white that covered the front yard.

Dan had only one drink before the first of the guests arrived and he looked very handsome, very distinguished, dressed in one of the expensive suits generally reserved for court, or evenings out.

Maggie rarely shopped for clothes, so wore a dress she'd worn repeatedly for special occasions. When she came downstairs, expecting him to compliment her, he said "For God sakes, Maggie. You'd think we were paupers. How many times do I have to see you in that old thing? It's either ratty old riding clothes or jeans and, now, when you have a chance to dress up, that's what you pick." Before she could answer, he stepped closer and reached out toward the locket around her neck. She stepped back before he could touch it and he looked at her strangely. "Where did this come from?"

The lie that she'd rehearsed so often fell from her lips sounding like gospel truth. "I bought it at that art fair last summer in Door County."

"It seems like a strange thing to wear when you're dressed up. Don't you have any nice jewelry? What about that necklace I bought for your birthday?"

She was saved from answering by the doorbell. Hannah came from the kitchen, but Dan waved her back and took Maggie's arm. "Let's greet our guests. We can discuss your jewelry and your wardrobe later."

Maggie supposed that most people would have considered the evening a success. The guests all arrived within a few minutes of each other, and everyone admired the Christmas tree and settled comfortably in the living room to enjoy cocktails before dinner. There was a fire in the fireplace and the entire scene reflected back from the French Doors that led to the terrace beyond, as though in a mirror.

Hannah had prepared and served a particularly lovely meal and they lingered around the table in the kind of companionable conversation shared by people who've known each other their entire lives, and who share unquestioned values.

Maggie smiled until her face ached and watched Dan pour himself enough after dinner drinks to have put most men under the table. It was almost impressive how coherent he sounded, how charming he remained.

Several couples excused themselves around 11. Several others remained until after one a.m., but finally, Maggie and Dan were standing in the open front door, waving as the last of them drove away. Maggie felt chilled enough for her teeth to chatter, but Dan's face appeared flushed and shiny with sweat.

Dan closed the front door and draped his arm around Maggie's shoulders. "Alone at last. It was a nice party, don't you think?"

Maggie moved out from under his arm and started for the stairs. "Very nice, but I'm so tired I can hardly stand up."

"You can sleep in tomorrow."

Afterward, Maggie wasn't sure why she said something that she knew would be inflammatory to him. "I thought I'd go out to the farm tomorrow. I haven't been there all week. I'd like to go and check on the horses."

"Why do you need to check on the horses? I mean isn't that why we hired the Noble Savage?"

"What?"

"The Noble Savage, the Indian, the guy who won't take my money. Why is that, Maggie? I mean, he works for you, but he doesn't let me pay him."

"I think he feels that the room and board is enough pay for what he does."

"Well, it is a pretty cushy life for him, isn't it? Just hanging out, tending to your horses."

"He takes care of the place. There's a lot of work."

He took a step toward her. "Yes, I'm sure he works very hard. I'm not really very interested in talking about him any more tonight. Let's go up to bed."

She turned without waiting for him and started up the steps, sensing him closing the distance between them. She got to the top of the stairs before he caught up, putting his arm around her shoulders again. Oh please God, she thought, not tonight. I can't do this.

But if she refused, would he go back to the topic of Joseph, begin to question her? How long could she lie and lie? Still, her fear of what would come from her confession kept her silent.

Inside their bedroom, he bent to kiss her and the sour taste of alcohol on his breath almost gagged her. "Dan, just a minute, I have to go to the bathroom." She expected an argument, but got none.

She lingered as long as she could. Undressing, putting on a nightgown, taking off her make up, brushing her teeth. When she returned to the bedroom, he had passed out on her side of the bed, fully dressed, still wearing his shoes. She left him that way, afraid of waking him. She got in on his side of the bed, and lay rigid and still, as close to the edge of the mattress as she could until she fell asleep.

When she awakened, it was past 10 a.m., and the bed was empty. She put on a robe and went downstairs. Dan was drinking coffee in the dining room. The boys were nowhere in sight and Megan was in the kitchen with Hannah.

She poured herself a cup of coffee and sat down across from him.

He looked pale, but otherwise seemed remarkably unscathed by the night before. He took another swallow of coffee. "Maggie, I just wanted to say I'm sorry about last night. I was pretty drunk. I may have said some things I shouldn't have."

"It's alright" she lied.

"I got a call this morning from Pat." Pat was the wife of Dan's colleague Lewis who had suffered a heart attack the week before. Maggie waited. "Lewis needs heart surgery. They're taking him over to Mayo Clinic. She hates to impose, but she wondered if I could see my way clear to go along with them. I know it's terrible timing, but there isn't anyone else. Their kids, I don't know what's wrong with them. They can't be there. She's so scared, Maggie. I couldn't say no."

Maggie, feeling like the worst sort of hypocrite, said "Of course you have to go."

"Tonight is New Year's Eve. But they're going to be running all kinds of tests on him and then the surgery could be as early as tomorrow or the day after. I could try to get back right after the surgery, but I just can't say. I wouldn't want to leave her all alone over there till we know he's going to be okay."

"Of course, you have to stay with them. We didn't have any special plans for New Years anyway. Are they flying over or driving?"

"They're transporting him by ambulance this afternoon. She's going along with him. I thought I'd drive over. We'll probably need a car while we're there."

"What time do you have to leave?"

"By 2, I thought. I made a reservation at the Marriott."

After lunch, Dan spent some time with the boys, apologizing for missing New Years with them. When he left, Maggie stood in the driveway, holding Megan, bundled up against the cold while the boys hugged their dad good-bye. Then she put Megan in the stroller and walked down First Street and back, feeling elated and warm even as the temperature dropped. The boys ran ahead, pelting each other with snowballs.

Maggie, Hannah and the children ate dinner at the kitchen table. Already as they were clearing the table, she expressed concern to Hannah about how late it was getting with no call from Dan, but Hannah reminded her that it was at least a 6 hour drive.

Finally, while they were watching the New Year's Eve festivities from Times Square on television, the phone rang and it was Dan, telling her he had arrived safely and checked into his hotel. He had spoken to Pat and was meeting her at the hospital first thing in the morning. She told him to let her know as soon as there was any news.

Maggie and Hannah put the children to bed.

Maggie packed a few things into an overnight bag and took a bath. She thought of calling him, but decided against it. When she was ready to leave, she knocked on Hannah's door. It was late, but Hannah was sitting up in a chair by the window, with a book in her lap. It appeared to Maggie that Hannah had been waiting for her knock.

"Would you take care of the children for me, for tonight and tomorrow, maybe tomorrow night too?"

"If he calls, I can let you know so that you can call him back. But what do you want me to tell the children about where you are?"

"Tell them I went down to visit my friend in Green Bay for a day or so. I'm sorry to ask you to lie for me."

"I don't mind lying for you. I guess that makes both of us immoral. But somehow, I don't feel that way."

"Thank you, Hannah."

As she turned to go, Hannah said "Maggie, be careful. You'll want to be the one to tell him when the time is right."

Chapter 29

It began to snow as she drove and the car fishtailed a little on the turns on River Road. When she turned in at the gate, she turned off her headlights, and turned off the ignition and let the slight downward slope of the drive carry the car to a place out of sight of the road.

The house door was locked, and she used the key on her ring. Moses padded into the hall to greet her. She hadn't worried that he would bark. He knew her step and her scent well enough by now. She left her boots, her coat and gloves on the floor just inside the front door.

In the hall outside his bedroom, she took off the rest of her clothes and then she crossed the room to stand beside his bed. She heard the furnace click on, but the air was cold against her bare flesh. There was just enough moonlight for her to see that he was awake, but believed himself to be dreaming until she put her hand against his face, against his mouth. Then he lifted the covers and drew her in, his skin burning against hers.

"How is it that you're here in the middle of the night?" he whispered.

In answer, she put her mouth on his and there were no more questions, no more words, not even words of their love for each other. There was only feeling as they began to learn each other's bodies after months of waiting and wanting. Together they threw off the covers so that they could look at each other, every curve, every line silvered by the moonlight, the chill night air not just forgotten, but changed, warmed by the heat rising off them.

He laid her down on her back, kissed her everywhere while she opened to him like a flower opens to the sun after months of hiding beneath the snow and it was how she felt, but even more, as though she'd been buried alive for years under a weight of feeling nothing. She had forgotten what it was like to feel this way, or maybe she'd never known.

For his part, Joseph had never known a woman in the way that Maggie let him know her. She held back nothing, gave herself completely, wrapped him in her arms and legs, bound him against her as though they were surrounded by a silken cocoon.

It might have lasted minutes, or hours, he would never know afterwards, but something happened for each of them that had never happened before. They came at the same instant, with the same intensity, looking straight into each other's eyes when it happened.

They stayed as they were, his weight covering her, still inside her. They slept, or perhaps only drifted in a dreamlike state, until desire began to intrude on their state of intense and lazy satisfaction. Then they made love again.

It was only after this second time, as the first light began to creep in at the windows, that Joseph gave voice to what he knew he should have said the moment he'd realized that she was really there, and not just a dream that he'd dreamed night after night. "Maggie, perhaps we'll want a baby one day, but we can't take this kind of chance now." He could not say the words 'not while you're still his wife'.

"I started taking the pill last month. We're safe." There was reassurance in the words, but at the same time, he felt as though it were a cheat. He did not want to be safe. He wanted her to be free, so that the two of them together could be reckless if they chose to be. It was not what he wanted for them, a life of hiding their feelings for each other, living in the shadow of her husband. It had bothered him from the beginning, the thought of her going home to Dan Ryan night after night, but he had taught himself to never think of her in her other life, just as when he drove into town for something, he was careful never to drive by the Ryan house.

But he didn't share those thoughts with her, not that day. She was so happy, happy that they had had this night, and now the whole day, and another night. "Please" she implored him "let's not talk about any of that now. I know we'll have to face it soon enough, but how many times like this will we have, times when I don't have to look at the clock."

He wanted to answer her "A whole lifetime, once we face Dan Ryan and he lets you go." But he understood that things would not be that easy. In Dan Ryan's place, Joseph knew that he would do anything to keep her. So for that day at least, he acquiesced and they talked of nothing at all except their love for each other.

They got up and dressed and went out to care for the horses, then came back in and cooked breakfast together, he in jeans and bare feet and Maggie in one of his flannel work shirts. They took their food to the living room where Joseph built a fire and they ate a picnic breakfast. Then he played the Satie pieces for her while she sat beside him on the piano bench watching his hands move over the keys in the same gentle way they moved over her body.

They went back to bed and made love and slept and got up and filled the old claw foot bathtub with hot water and got in together and washed each other.

In the late afternoon, he offered to go out and feed the horses so that she could stay in and keep the bed warm, but she couldn't stand to be away from him so they pitched hay and checked waterers and mucked the stalls and turn outs together.

The phone was ringing when they came back inside. He answered and then handed the phone to her. It was Hannah.

"It's alright" she said at once. "He just called and I told him that you had gone down to spend some time with one of your friends in Green Bay. He didn't even ask who it was, just asked when you'd be back and I told him I wasn't sure. He said if you called, I should let you know that the surgery went well but Pat asked if he could stay till Lewis is out of ICU. He thought that would probably be day after tomorrow so he should be back late afternoon Saturday. If anything changes, I'll let you know."

Maggie thanked her and hung up. "I can stay tonight and tomorrow night too, if you want me. He's staying over in

Rochester till Saturday. His friend came through the surgery okay."

"That's good. That the friend is going to get better."

She went to where he stood at the counter, setting out food to prepare for dinner, and put her arms around him. "What can I do to help?"

"Get us a glass of wine. Watch me cook."

There was a bottle of Cabernet on the counter. She found two wine glasses on a shelf and poured, brought a glass to him. He took it from her and said "Sit down. You're too much of a distraction when you stand that close."

She smiled at that, and sat at the table, taking a sip of the wine, watching as he seasoned salmon steaks and placed them on a baking sheet. Then he washed potatoes and rubbed them with shortening and cut an acorn squash in half, scooped out the seeds and filled the inside with brown sugar. He put the potatoes and squash into the oven and put the fish back into the refrigerator. "The fish won't take so long to bake" he explained. Then he came and sat at the table across from her.

"How did you know I like Eric Satie?"

"I didn't. But I know you, Maggie."

"Yes, you do. Do you want me to tell you why I came to you before I told Dan about us?"

"I think I know. You're afraid he'll try to hold onto you and when he realizes that he can't, you're afraid that he'll try to take the children from you."

"I'll find a way. I will. I just need a little time to think about how to do it. Tell me about the cabin in Keshena, the place your uncle might sell us."

"It's in the woods, but there's a few acres cleared where we could put up a barn and a corral for the horses. It's a log cabin, not fancy, you understand, but at least there's indoor plumbing and electricity and a furnace. A lot of those places aren't meant to be lived in year round. There's a bedroom downstairs, and a sleeping loft upstairs."

"That would be nice for the kids. We could divide it in two so Megan could have her own space, separate from the boys."

Joseph heard it in her voice, a wish that things could be that way, not a certainty that they would be, and he said, trying to make it real for her, "We'll do that. The ceiling slopes, but there are big windows at each end. It would make 2 nice bedrooms."

"Is there a fireplace?"

"Sure, a big one, made out of river rocks."

"That sounds nice, just like the fireplace in my Mom and Da's house."

"The downstairs is mostly one big room with a kitchen along one side. The stove and refrigerator are pretty old. We'll probably have to replace them one of these days. And there's no washer and dryer."

"That's okay. I'll bet there's a Laundromat in town."

"I'll get us a washer and dryer. We can put them outside in the shed."

"Is there a screened in porch? Cause that would make it nice in the summer. We could sleep there when it's hot."

"The porch goes around 2 sides of the cabin. It's a deep porch. There's a hammock out there that we can sleep in. But we'll have to screen it ourselves."

"I can help you do the screens. I helped my Dad when he screened in our porch."

He felt a hot rush of tears as he listened to her planning, and he covered it by getting up to put the fish into the oven. When he sat down again, he had decided.

"I'd like to take you to Keshena tomorrow, as long as we have the whole day."

"What will we do there? Can we see the cabin?"

"We can see the cabin. We'll get the key from my mother."

"Am I going to meet your mother?"

"I told her about you. She would like to know you."

"What did you tell her?"

"Everything about you."

"She knows about him, about my children? What must she think of me?"

"She doesn't apply moral judgments to things she believes were fated to happen."

"That's what she believes?"

"Yes. Do you want to go?"

"Yes, I do. When will we leave?"

"Early. I'm going to call Chuck to see if he can tend the horses while we're gone. We won't get back until late."

Once the arrangements had been made with Chuck, they had dinner. After they did the dishes, they went outside and did a bed check of the horses.

They went to bed before 9, and did not make love. He turned on his side and drew her in against him, her back to him, and they lay still, feeling each other breathe until they slept. Sometime in the middle of the night, she woke as he shifted his weight against her, and she turned to face him and they made love then, long and slow love, in the darkest part of the night. Moses slept on at the foot of the bed undisturbed.

Chapter 30

Chuck arrived to take care of the horses as they were leaving the house, just after 6 a.m. If he was surprised to see Maggie, he didn't let on. He did suggest that they might want to put her car in the garage. "No point in coming back to a dead battery in this cold" was his rationale. "If you give me the keys, I can do it for you. I'll leave the keys on the kitchen table." She thanked him and got into the truck cab. Moses walked across her lap to sit next to the window, pushing Maggie to the middle of the seat, next to Joseph.

As Joseph started the truck, Chuck came over to the driver's side and Joseph rolled down the window. Chuck said "Stay as late as you like. I'll take care of the evening feeding and if I don't see the truck at bedtime, I'll check on them again then." Maggie turned and looked back as they drove away. Chuck waved and then turned toward the barn.

They stopped for breakfast at a coffee shop in Shawano. While they drank coffee and waited for their food, Joseph said "My mother's name is Marina. She owns the general store on the Reservation. By the time we get there, she'll be open for the day. It won't be busy this early so we can visit without too many interruptions."

"Will I meet your brother?"

"I don't know if he'll be around. Sometimes he is and he helps her out at the store. Other times, he just takes off."

"I'm nervous."

"You don't need to be." The food came then and they ate in silence.

After Shawano, it was only a short drive to where they were going. The store sat at a crossroads. It was a log building, with a long porch out front on which there was an old fashioned coke machine. The only other vehicle was a Chevrolet Bel Air. It looked just like Michael's, only it was yellow and white.

"Where does she live?" Maggie asked him.

"Here. The house is attached to the back of the store. It's where I grew up."

He came around and opened the door for her, helped her out of the truck and whistled to Moses to follow them. Their boots made a loud thunk as they climbed the three broad stairs and crossed the porch to the front door where a sign said "We Are Open. Please Come In." It was hand lettered on a square of cardboard. When Joseph pushed the door open, a bell jangled.

A woman came from behind the counter to meet them. She was shorter than Maggie. At first Maggie had an impression of plumpness, but then she realized it was only because the woman's face was very round. Below that, her body was slender. She was dressed in jeans, a man's flannel shirt and boots. Her hair was long and worn in a long thick braid that hung down her back. She looked very young, leading Maggie to believe that this was not Joseph's mother, but perhaps someone who worked for her.

But then the woman opened her arms and Maggie thought 'oh, it is his mother' and she began to step aside to allow Marina to hug Joseph, but Marina gathered both of them into her embrace at once. Maggie allowed herself to be held, breathing in the smell of laundry soap in the flannel shirt, the fragrance of shampoo in Marina's shiny black hair. Maggie had an instant sensation of being cared for, almost the way she felt when her father held her like that.

Marina let them go then and they followed her to the counter.

Joseph and Maggie sat down side by side and Marina went behind the counter and got down 3 cups and poured coffee, then came and sat with them. "Welcome, Maggie. When Joseph told me you were Irish, I pictured red hair."

"My mother has the red hair. I take after my father. Didn't he describe me?"

"He just said that you were very beautiful, in every way, not only physically." Maggie flushed, but Marina went on, seemingly not noticing. "I'd like you to tell me about yourself. I know how he sees you, but I'd like to hear how you see yourself, how you see him." She indicated Joseph with a nod of her head. "Joseph, you should stay and listen, see how well you know her."

They sat through the morning, Maggie talking, Joseph listening, Marina asking an occasional question, but silent for the most part, observing everything. They were interrupted three times by customers, all of whom Marina brought over and to all of whom Marina introduced Maggie as "This is Joseph's Maggie."

Finally she said, "Let's go in the back and have some lunch. Then I imagine you'd like to go over to the cabin." Maggie offered to help Marina with lunch and Marina accepted, giving Maggie bread to toast, and lettuce to wash, while she took bowls from the refrigerator, egg salad and tuna salad that she had prepared before they arrived. She made sandwiches and set them out on plates and opened 3 bottles of Budweiser from the refrigerator and asked Maggie if she wanted a glass. She seemed pleased when Maggie declined and drank from the bottle.

When the bell rang from the store, Joseph went out to wait on the customer while Maggie and Marina sat at the table. In his absence, Marina said in a low voice "I believe you are the one that Joseph has been waiting for his whole life. It will be very difficult for the two of you. There will be a lot of pain, but it won't matter. Once you saw each other, it was too late to change anything. So no matter what the price, you'll pay it. I'm not telling you this to frighten you, Maggie. If I could take away any unhappiness from you, I would. If I could bless you with a long and happy life together, I would. No matter what happens, I will always be here for both of you." She stood up and came to where Maggie sat. She bent down and put her arms around Maggie and held her.

Maggie had a sure sense that everything that Marina had said was true. She clung to Marina. Then she whispered "Does

Joseph know? Does he understand? Sometimes I think he believes it will be easy, that we'll get everything we want."

"Joseph knows. He thinks it will be easier for you if he lets you believe that everything will be fine. No matter what happens, Maggie, you and Joseph will always love each other. It will carry you through."

They heard Joseph's step and broke apart as he came into the kitchen. "Mom, can we get the key. I thought after we see the cabin, I'd take Maggie over to the Wolf River to meet some people, maybe dance a little, have a fish fry for dinner. Can you meet us there later?"

"I'll see how things go here. Friday's busy. Lots of people get paid today so they'll be in to shop. When do you have to head back?"

"No later than 9. It'll take us a couple of hours to make the drive."

They walked outside together and they hugged good-bye and Maggie turned and watched Marina through the truck window until she went back inside the store.

The cabin was down a gravel road, off the county highway and Maggie would always remember her first sight of it, sitting on a little rise above the Wolf River, in a stand of trees. Moses ran around the yard while Maggie and Joseph went up the steps to the porch. Before they went inside, they walked around the corner and looked at the whole of the porch and he showed her the hooks in the ceiling where the hammock hung in the summer.

Inside, it was as Joseph had described it, but there was something more. To Maggie, who had never felt at home in the Ryan house, this small cabin felt like home at once. She walked ahead of Joseph, looked at the fireplace, the kitchen wall, with it's ancient gas cook stove and old fashioned refrigerator, the pots hanging from a rack over the stove, the dishes and glasses lined up on open shelves above the wooden counter.

She went through a door into a little hall leading to the bedroom, where windows on two sides looked out at the woods. There was a double bed with a cedar chest at its foot, and an old pine dresser. The closet was fragrant with the smell of the cedar that lined it.

From there, she walked back to the little hallway and into the bathroom. It was big enough for a bedroom, and she guessed that perhaps it had been once, before there had been indoor plumbing here. Just like at her farm, there was an oversize claw foot bathtub. The toilet had a tank hanging on the wall above the seat, with a brass pull chain and the sink looked like a small kitchen sink, instead of a wash basin. There was no linen closet, just open shelves that held towels.

Joseph followed behind, watching her. She went up the steps to the loft which was a big space, almost as big as the room below, but with a railing on one side that looked down into the living room area. There were windows at each end, and the sloping roof was made of wood.

There were four double beds, two on each wall, with dressers in between. Maggie said "Can we make love here?"

Joseph said "Pick a bed." The furnace had been turned off for the winter, and the water as well, the pipes drained so they wouldn't freeze and burst. They took blankets from one of the other beds and added them to the covers on the bed Maggie selected, then undressed, shivering, and dove under the covers, coming together laughing, their laughter almost instantly silenced by kisses.

Afterwards, they slept, Moses curled against Maggie.

When they woke, Maggie said "I have to pee. Do I have to go outside in the snow?"

"There's an outhouse back there in the trees."

"Really? Can't we turn on the water and warm some on the stove so I can wash up before we go wherever we're going for dinner?"

"You're not much for roughing it, are you? Alright. Stay in bed and keep warm. Let me see what I can do."

"Hurry" she called after him. "I really have to pee."

She lay in the darkening late afternoon, listening to the sounds of him moving around downstairs. Then he came back. "Alright, you've got a flush toilet and I'm heating a pan of water for you. But we'll have to make sure the pipes are drained before we leave. I turned on the furnace. There's enough propane in the tank, but it won't get real warm for awhile."

Maggie draped a blanket around herself and went to the

bathroom. She was standing in front of the sink, looking at herself and thinking she looked awfully happy for a freezing person, when he knocked.

"Here's your hot water." He poured the panful into the sink and added a little cold, got a towel from the shelf and watched her wash.

When she finished, she said "You can wash too if you don't mind using my water."

"I don't mind. I shut off the water already. By the time we finish dressing and get ready to leave, we should be okay. Otherwise, I'll be paying the plumber."

As they locked the door behind them and walked to the truck, Maggie turned to look back at the cabin. She felt a sense of loss at leaving that place, but said nothing, not wanting to make Joseph feel sad. In the truck, she said "Where are we going?"

"Wolf River Tavern. It's a local hang out, nothing fancy. But you can dance to the juke box and they serve a good fish fry. There'll be a lot of people I know there on a Friday so you'll get looked over pretty good. No one will mean anything by it, they'll just be wanting to know you."

The parking lot was almost full, but they found a place near the door. "What about Moses? We can't leave him out in the cold."

"He can come in and stay in the back room. I know the owner."

Inside, it was hot, crowded and smoky. There was a smell of fish frying and the juke box was loud. Joseph, Maggie and Moses made their way through the crowd, straight to the end of the bar where the bartender waved at Joseph and agreed that Moses could hang out in back. They went back there with him and settled him down with a bowl of water. The owner got down a box of dog biscuits and put two next to the water bowl.

When they got back to the bar, Joseph introduced Maggie. "Maggie, this is my friend Jake Boland. Jake, this is Maggie Ryan."

Jake shook her hand. "Happy to meet you Maggie. What are you drinking?"

They ordered Budweiser and went to sit in a booth along one wall. It was a big room, bigger than Kelly's but for Maggie it had that good bar room feeling that she'd always felt at home in.

After they finished one beer, and ordered another, Joseph said "Come on" and led her over to the juke box. He made his selections and said "You like to dance, right?"

She shook her head. Roy Orbison came on singing Dream Baby and she and Joseph danced together for the first time.

"You're a good dancer, Joseph" she called to him over the music. "I didn't know you could dance."

As he swung her out and away from him and then pulled her in close again, he smiled and said "Oh, there are a lot of things you don't know about me."

They danced again before people started coming up to them to be introduced to Maggie and she then became aware for the first time that Joseph had been right. A lot of people were looking her over, not in an unfriendly way, but with undisguised curiosity.

She met so many people, she couldn't keep all of their names straight, until a chubby very young looking man with Marina's round face, very black eyes and a long buzz haircut came up and hugged Joseph. "About time you came back home. Cousin."

Joseph said "Will, this is Maggie. Maggie, my cousin Will. It's his dad that owns the cabin."

Will hugged Maggie as though they were old friends. "You and Joseph looking for a place to buy around here? The cabin would be great for you."

"We might be" she said.

"Would you dance with me?" Will asked.

Joseph smiled and said "He's a very good dancer. He dances at the Pow Wow's."

She danced two dances with Will Dodge and he was a very good dancer indeed. He selected the songs, each of which he told her was his favorite. Nutbush City Limits and Get Out of Denver both by Bob Seger. She was sweating and flushed when they finished and she saw that Joseph was watching them, with a big smile on his face.

When Will brought her back to where Joseph was waiting, he said "If I couldn't tell that she was crazy about you, Cousin, I'd ask her to run off with me. You're a lucky man."

After that, they ate fish fries and drank more beer and danced to some slow songs, then gathered up Moses, and drove the truck through the frosty cold night, back to the farm on River Road.

When they drove into the yard a little after midnight, the horses were silent snow covered shapes, sleeping standing together in a group of four. There was still hay on the ground around them.

They undressed and fell into bed, asleep in each other's arms in minutes, attended by Moses, who snored quietly against Joseph's back.

Maggie woke to weak winter sunlight. Joseph and Moses were not in bed. She got up and looked through the window at the two of them inside the corral. Then she hurried to get dressed to go out and help, but before she finished, she heard the door open and shut and then Joseph was back, the dog just behind him, smelling of cold, his muzzle wet with snow.

"Why are you dressed?"

"I was coming out to help. Why didn't you wake me?"

"We were up late. You needed to sleep. You have to go home today."

Maggie sat down on the edge of the bed. "Not for awhile."

"It would be better if you're there when he gets home."

"But I don't have to leave yet. We have a little time."

"Just a little." He bent to kiss her and she pulled him down beside her.

They undressed and got back under the covers and made love. She held his face between her hands. ."We have to make it last. It has to last until Monday."

"Maggie, we won't have times like these until we tell him, until you make the break from him. We'll just have a few hours in the mornings, and you'll always wonder when he's going to find out. An affair behind his back isn't what either of us want."

"I'm going to find a way, I promise you. And in the meantime, we'll have these hours, and in between, I'll think about you all the time."

After he'd sent her on her way that day, he realized the essential unfairness of forcing her into a confrontation with Dan Ryan now. It wasn't just the two of them involved. It was her children, 3 children to provide for. Before he could ask her to give up everything she had to be with him, he had to be able to take care of all of them. He lay awake late into the night, thinking of how he could best do that.

Chapter 31

Maggie left the farm, her head full of thoughts of Joseph and the last three days. But as she drove into town, and got closer to the Ryan house, which is how she had begun to think of it, not as home, but as the Ryan house, her apprehension grew. She was suddenly convinced that Dan hadn't really gone to Rochester at all. There had been no call from a friend. He had followed her and watched her and knew everything and now he would be waiting to confront her. She felt sick to her stomach at the thought, and was relieved when she saw the empty driveway. Relieved, but unconvinced that her fears were groundless.

The door opened before she was out of the car and Declan came running to meet her, flinging himself into her arms, intensifying her guilt. She had hardly thought of him, of any of them, since leaving on Wednesday night while they slept. She hugged him tight to her and saw Hannah in the doorway holding Megan. Megan's arms were held out to Maggie. "Come on" she whispered to Declan "Megan wants a hug too."

Still he clung to her as she held Megan and looked around for Colin. Hannah, anticipating said "Colin is down the block at his friend's house for the afternoon."

"Is he upset?"

"A bit. But don't feel too badly, it's mostly his father he missed. Well, that didn't come out right."

"No, I'm sure its true, Hannah. Any word from Dan?"

"Nothing since you and I spoke last. Do you want me to keep these two busy while you get bathed and changed?"

"Thanks. Deco, Honey Mom's going to get bathed and dressed. I'll be right back."

He let her go reluctantly and as she started up the stairs, Hannah said "Better give me your clothes to wash." Maggie was suddenly aware of the smell of Joseph in everything she wore, everything in her overnight bag.

She hurried her bath, put on a sweater and a pair of slacks instead of jeans, thinking that would please Dan. She felt a sudden inclination to try to make things go as smoothly as possible.

When she heard a step outside the bedroom door, her stomach tensed, but there was a knock, Dan wouldn't knock, she thought, and then Hannah opened the door and said "I just came up for your laundry." She gathered it up and left and Maggie remained in front of the dressing table, brushing her hair, thinking how it had never crossed her mind in the last three days that she would have to face Dan, and tell greater and more convincing lies than any she'd ever told in her life. Well, I'm a good liar, she thought, when I need to be.

She went downstairs then, noticing that it was after three, and still no sign of Dan. The later it got, the better she felt. Surely if he hadn't really gone to Rochester, if he'd been following her around, he'd have been home by now.

Hannah, knowing Maggie well, brought her a strong whiskey sour on the rocks and Maggie sat and sipped her drink and watched the television with Declan beside her, not really seeing the show. Megan dozed in her lap. It seemed like any ordinary Saturday afternoon, the hours ticking away until Hannah would tell her dinner was ready.

Dan arrived just past 4, and Colin came in with him. "Look who I found" Dan said.

"How long have you been outside?" Maggie asked, seeing how red Colin's cheeks were.

"Awhile. I was waiting for Dad."

"You could have waited for him in here with us."

"I wanted to talk to him alone" Colin said. His tone seemed accusatory.

Did you? And about what? Maggie wanted to say, but she held back the words, thinking they sounded guilty somehow, as though she had something to hide; thinking, but, of course she did have something to hide, a lot to hide.

She realized that she should get up from the sofa and go to Dan, kiss him hello, it must have seemed strange to him that she remained seated.

But then he came over, saying "Don't disturb her by getting up" indicating Megan who continued to sleep in Maggie's lap.

"How is Lewis doing?"

"Remarkably well. He can probably come home next week.

Pat's talking about having us over to dinner to thank us for being supportive."

"Well, it was all you. I didn't do anything."

"You graciously gave up our New Year's Eve and New Year's Day, so I think she feels she owes you thanks as well. But I told her there was no rush, with him still recovering."

"Of course. How was Rochester?"

"Cold. Speaking of which, I'm going to the kitchen for a drink. Would you like a refill?"

"Yes, please."

"When I come back, you can tell me all about your visit in Green Bay."

Maggie was grateful that his back was to her as she was sure something must have shown in her face. Then she saw that Colin was watching her. He's too young, she thought, too young to read anything in her expression. She forced herself to smile at him and he looked away. She remembered her brother Robbie all those years ago telling her about their mother and the priest. What was his name, that priest? She'd thought she would always remember, but couldn't.

Dan came back then and sat down on her other side. So there she was, Dan on one side, Declan on the other, Megan heavy in her lap and Colin, watching her again. Dan handed her the drink and she took a long swallow and gave it back to him to put on the end table.

"So, how are Connie and Dave?"

"Dave?" Maggie said uncomprehendingly.

"Well, when Hannah said you went down to Green Bay for a visit, I assumed it was Connie you went to see. Isn't her husband's name Dave?"

"Oh, not that Connie. Not high school Connie." Never high school Connie, she thought, high school Connie whom Dan knew. "Connie from the Center. I don't know if you ever met her."

"No, I don't think I have met her. Is she married?"

"Divorced. No children."

"So, just the girls. Was it fun? Did you go out anywhere?"

"No, just hung out at her place, ordered in pizza and Chinese food and caught up."

"When did you get back?"

"Early today."

"Three days of catching up? I didn't know you were that close. I mean, she's never been up here to visit, has she?"

"No. I guess that's why we had so much to talk about."

Hannah appeared then to tell them dinner was ready. Maggie forced down her dinner, asking Declan and Colin about what they'd been doing while she was gone, listening hard to their replies to cut off her own thoughts.

After dinner, they sat in the living room and read until bedtime.

And finally, there was no way to avoid it. She was alone in their bedroom with Dan and he said "I really missed you, Maggie."

She smiled and said "I missed you too" thinking how am I going to do this, thinking this man is my husband but if I do this, I am cheating on the man I love, but not seeing any way around it.

But when they lay down together, Dan seemed desperate, somehow. She had been struck from her wedding night, and throughout her marriage, by his experience, his adeptness in the bedroom. Until she had met Joseph, Dan had always satisfied her, even though she had never felt real passion for him. This night was different. He held onto her like a drowning man, his caresses clumsy, and ultimately, he had turned away from her with a mumbled "I'm sorry, Maggie. Maybe I drank too much" although they both knew that he had had less to drink that night than on many other nights.

Maggie was simply relieved to have been granted this great favor. She was so grateful that he was unable to make love to her that she almost put her arms around him to comfort him, but was stopped by a fear that perhaps it would arouse him. So she said, as kindly as she knew how "It's alright, Dan. It happens to everyone. It will be fine."

After he had gone to sleep, or pretended to, it occurred to her that he was now 57 years old and perhaps at his age this was not uncommon.

After that night, he didn't try again for a very long time, which suited her well. Nor did he raise the topic of her visit to Green Bay and so she drifted into a certain complacency, although she knew things couldn't go on this way indefinitely. Joseph would not accept this kind of a life, and the longer she was with him, the more she longed to be with him openly and all of the time.

Chapter 32

On the Monday following the trip with Maggie to Keshena, Joseph spent the morning with her, then told her he had business in town. He kissed the disappointment from her face and told her he would see her early the next day.

He had gone through the classified ads in the Sunday paper and had found few jobs that would pay good money. He then went to the phone book and looked up the local companies that he knew would pay good wages. There were paper mills in Marinette, Menominee and Peshtigo. There was Marinette Marine where they built boats for the navy. And there was Lloyd's Furniture Factory in Menominee. He started with the mills, but none of them were hiring and the reception at the first two, in Menominee and Peshtigo was not encouraging.

At Scott Paper Company in Marinette, however, the personnel manager was kinder and told him that there were no openings at the time, but that there might be in the Spring. He asked Joseph if he had any personal references in the area. Joseph would never have used Maggie Ryan's name, and, in fact, hesitated to use the name of anyone he knew, but in desperation, he mentioned that he had worked for John and Ida Nash. The personnel manager, whose name was Mr.

Baker said "John Nash worked here for many years. His son John Jr. works here now. Do you know him?"

"Yes, sir. I taught his children to ride."

"Well, Joseph, you come back and see me in the Spring, mid April. Be sure to mention John's name when you make the appointment. I may be able to find something for you."

Marinette Marine had no Personnel Manager. The owner himself talked to Joseph and he was curt. It was hard to tell if he was that way in general or just disliked Indians. He said he only hired men who were experienced at boat building and Joseph wasn't.

The last stop at Lloyds was equally discouraging with no openings and none expected. "We pay pretty well, so there's not much turnover" the man in Personnel told him.

Joseph got home close to dinner time. He changed clothes and took care of the horses and fixed himself dinner. He knew he could find work in Keshena but then he thought about Maggie telling him that Dan would never let her take the children so far away that he couldn't see them every day. And he understood that. You can't take everything away from a man, his wife and his children.

When Maggie came on Tuesday, she had expected him to raise the topic of confronting Dan. When he didn't, she thought of bringing it up, then decided to leave it alone for now. What could it hurt if they just had this time together and put off reality for a little while longer?

And so it went, through the rest of January and February. Their mornings were divided between riding the horses, in the arena in bad weather, and on the trails as the thaw set in, and making love in Joseph's warm bed, then eating lunch together before she had to leave.

They had developed an unspoken agreement to take care, to be sure that she didn't become so lost in him that she stayed away from the Ryan house too long. There was no point in arousing suspicion. Although it was more and more difficult for both of them, trying to live a whole life in a few hours, and then getting through all of the hours apart, they knew the time would come when that would change.

On Saturday mornings, Maggie brought Deco out for his riding lessons. And so they had a few extra hours together, although not alone.

Then one afternoon in early March, Maggie had a dizzy spell while she was coming down the stairs. Fortunately Hannah was walking with her, and caught her, or Maggie would have fallen. She tried to deny the cause, but when it happened again the next day, and the day after that, she went to see Dr. O'Brien.

"Mrs. Ryan, your blood pressure is seriously elevated. We're going to have to take you off the pill."

She had known what he was going to say, but still she said "No. There must be something we can do."

"Have you had this problem before? When you were on the pill, I mean."

"Yes" she admitted, and when he looked surprised that she hadn't told him when she had first come to him for the prescription, she went on "but I thought I was going to be fine this time. That it was just a transitory thing."

"With your history, we just can't take a chance. What about a diaphragm?"

"How reliable is that?"

"Quite reliable if you use it properly."

Maggie went from the doctor's office to the pharmacy. Then she drove to the farm. Joseph was surprised to see her so late in the day. He asked her what was wrong. She never considered not telling him. She lied to so many people in her life but never to him. The honesty between them was part of who they were to each other.

"I had to stop taking the pill today. It makes my blood pressure go up. Don't look scared. It's alright now. The doctor gave me a diaphragm." She unsealed the bag from the pharmacy and took out the case, opened it and showed him. Then she took the round cylinder of birth control pills and went to the sink and flushed them down the drain and threw away the container.

"Is it reliable?"

"Quite reliable if you use it properly. That's what Dr. O'Brien said." She turned to him with a smile. "Shall we try it?"

"It's getting late."

"I can be late for once." She took his hand and they walked to the bedroom. When they were undressed, she said "I have to put this in now. Once you touch me, I'll forget everything."

"Can I watch you?"

"Sure you can." She went into the bathroom and coated the diaphragm with the spermacide. Then she put one foot up on edge of the tub, but it was too high and she almost lost her balance. "This isn't real romantic, is it?"

"It's romantic enough." He closed the lid on the toilet seat. "Try that."

When she had put the diaphragm in and checked to be sure it was in place, as Dr. O'Brien had explained, she washed her hands and turned to Joseph. "Do you still want to make love?"

For answer, he put his arms around her and lifted her, so that her feet were just off the floor, and carried her to the bed, where he dropped her onto her back and then laid down on top of her. "I love you, Maggie, more than I thought it was possible to love anybody."

"I love you, Joseph, so much that I would die without you."

"Never say that."

"It's true." She would have said more, but he kissed her to stop the words.

Afterwards she said "Was it different with the diaphragm?"

"No. For you?"

"Not really."

They lay quiet in each other's arms and it was nice, to be together that way. But it was time, he thought, to tell her the way things were. She had been honest about the pill and he needed to match that honesty. "Maggie, there's something you need to know. I've been around to all of the good places to work here, the places that pay well, looking for a job."

"You didn't tell me."

"I'm telling you now. I would have told you sooner if there'd been anything to tell, but none of them are hiring now. The Personnel Manager at Scott Paper Mill told me to come back and see him in April. He might have something then. But I'm going to put the word out at all of the farms around here that

I'll do plowing and planting, milking and whatever else needs doing. It's time, Maggie. The time is coming when we have to stop hiding here and face Dan. And for that, we'll need an income. We'll need to be able to show that we can take care of the children."

Her first thought was the loss of their mornings together, but then she realized that she would be trading those few hours for a life with him. "I can get a job" she said, thinking Dan would laugh at me if I said that.

Joseph kissed her forehead and said "Let's hope you won't have to do that."

In April, Joseph went back to see Mr. Baker at the Paper Mill who told him he was sorry, but they had actually had to cut back on hiring due to the economy. He went around to all of the local companies, but it was the same everywhere.

Maggie missed her first period in May. She rested her hands on her still flat stomach and knew. She knew that she and Joseph would have a baby and because of that, the life of dreams and deception that they had been living was over. There would be real life now and the only thing that wouldn't change would be their love for each other.

Chapter 33

She told Joseph without waiting to miss another period. She didn't need a trip to the doctor to know. She watched his face when she said "I'm going to have a baby" and saw that his first expression was elation, delight, and only when he had time to think what it meant was there a shadow there, and it was just a small one.

"Are you afraid of what it means?" she asked.

"Only for you. But it's long past the time we should have told him so perhaps fate intervened. That's what my mother would believe."

"I'll tell him tonight."

"I won't let you do this alone."

"You have to let me. It would be so much worse for him to hear it from us together." She remembered saying those same words years before, thinking that in some ways her life seemed to be repeating itself.

"I don't know him, but it could be dangerous for you. Do you really think I'd send you alone into something that could hurt you?"

"He doesn't own a gun and he's a man who believes in the law. He won't hurt me physically." But, she thought, he can find other ways to hurt me. "I have no choices left, Joseph."

"What are you going to tell him?"

"That I'm leaving him, that I want a divorce. I don't think I should tell him about the baby, not yet."

"What do you think he'll do?"

"I think he'll be hurt and angry and that he'll use the children against me. But when he sees he has no choice, he'll let go."

And so he agreed to let her do this her way, but from the moment he watched her car disappear down the driveway, he felt such a deep foreboding that he forced himself through the ritual of caring for the horses and then went inside and sat alone in the dark, with Moses beside him, waiting, thinking 'What have I done?' Half a dozen times he got up and took his keys, but stopped at the door, thinking 'Will this only make things worse?', cursing himself for his indecision.

Maggie was relieved to find herself home before Dan. The boys were down the block playing with friends. Megan was toddling around the kitchen after Hannah and came to Maggie and put up her arms to be held. "Hi, Mama."

"Hi, Sweetie." Maggie kissed her and Megan rested her head against Maggie's shoulder. "You're getting almost too heavy to carry."

Hannah looked at Maggie. "What's wrong?"

"I'm pregnant."

Hannah sat down. "What are you going to do?"

"I'm going to tell Dan I'm leaving him. Would you keep the children with you while I talk to him, no matter what?"

Hannah nodded. Then she said "Don't be afraid. I'll be here, close by. If you need me, you call my name." Before Maggie could reassure her that everything would be fine, Hannah said "That's his car. I'll watch for the boys and bring them into the kitchen when they get home."

Maggie went and stood in the hall. When Dan came through

the door, she saw by his face that her own expression must have given something away because, before she could say anything, he said "Are you waiting for me?"

She nodded. "There's something I have to tell you."

"Shall we go in here?" He gestured toward the den and stood aside to let her go in first. "Is Hannah caring for the children?" She nodded again and he said "For God sake's Maggie, find your voice."

Just say it, she thought, he already knows, just say the words. He sat down at his desk and turned the chair to face her. She had thought she would stand but found suddenly that her legs felt too weak to support her so she backed up until she felt the soft cushions of the leather love seat behind her and then she sat down heavily. She took a breath and then said it. "I'm leaving."

He looked at her questioningly. "Leaving?"

"Leaving" she repeated.

"What do you mean?"

"Dan, I have to go. Please understand."

"Understand? Understand what?"

She thought 'Is he just going to repeat everything I say?' "I have to tell you…"

"Stop now" he interrupted "before you say too much, before you say something you can't take back."

"No. I can't stop."

But he wouldn't let her get the words out. "Whatever it is, I don't care. I don't want to know. You'll tell me nothing. We'll just go on as we are. I've been more than reasonable with you. All I ask is that you be discreet. Don't do anything that causes talk, that disgraces the family. You can have everything you want."

"No. I can't go on like this. I love him."

"You only think you do. You'll get over it."

"I won't. Dan, I'm sorry, so very sorry."

He looked at her, looked closely, and she felt the first stirring of fear. "No, you're not. You're not sorry, but you will be. You'll be sorrier than you can imagine."

He looked away from her, and when he looked back, his composure had dropped back into place like a mask, hiding whatever he was really feeling. "I'm going to give you a chance, one more chance to keep everything, your lover, your children, this home."

"Why would you be willing to do such a thing?"

"Because I want you, Maggie. I always have, since the first time I saw you. I have no pride left where you're concerned. So, you see, nothing needs to change."

"Everything has to change now Dan. I can't live with you anymore." Once she started to tell it, she couldn't stop herself. The words poured out of her. "I have to live with him all of the time. I love him so much I would die without him."

"Shut up."

"No, I won't. I've lied for so long. I love him."

He stood and came toward her. She lifted her face. She started to stand. He slapped her in the face so hard that she sat back down heavily, thrown against the back of the loveseat. He raised his hand to slap her again and she told him. "I'm pregnant."

His arm dropped to his side. He turned his back on her and walked to his chair. He sat for a minute with his head in his hands. He said "I'm sorry. I shouldn't have done that."

When she didn't answer, he said "Why, Maggie? Why were you so careless?" But he didn't really want an answer. She could see that. "Now, of course, you will have to leave. I can't have you parading all around town with your belly getting bigger and bigger. There's no way you can pass off your half breed bastard as my baby. Everyone would know."

Maggie felt a sense of something like relief sweep over her. In spite of his words, words she would have taken offense at under other circumstances, she was grateful because now she could leave. She could stop lying and leave.

He went on, almost as though he were talking to himself. "You should pack your things and go right away. We'll tell the children that you're ill, that you need a rest."

"Wait" she said. "No, the children come with me."

He looked at her as if she had lost her mind. "With you? Don't be ridiculous. You aren't in any position to take care of 3 children. You can't stay in town. You'll have to go away. He has no job, no money. He isn't even going to be able to take care of you."

"No, no, we'll manage. We'll work. We'll make a home."

But he was shaking his head, smiling as though at an amusing child.

She said "You can't take my children away from me."

Now that he realized how completely he'd lost her, he could afford to be cruel. "But of course I can. This is the best place for them. You can't just drag 3 children out of here in an old pick up truck and go where? To the Reservation? Is that what you were thinking? No, wait. I'm guessing you didn't think about any of this, did you? You were too busy spreading your legs for your lover, too busy getting pregnant. Just like you did with Michael. You look surprised, Maggie. Did you think I didn't know from the beginning? I never cared though. Colin is my son in every way that matters." And it was as though, like her, once he started talking, he couldn't stop. "I'll tell you something else, Maggie. I knew where Michael was. I knew all along. He wasn't hard to find. He probably wanted to be found."

"Why didn't you tell me?"

"You were better off without him, Maggie. He left you. He should have known you were pregnant. If he had loved you the way that I did, he would never have left."

"You should have given us the choice, Dan."

"I did what was best for everybody. Just like I'm going to do now. Unless...."

"What?"

"What if I were to give you a choice? A choice to keep the children?"

"What? What do you want me to do?"

"Get rid of this baby. You can just get rid of this baby, and we'll pretend none of this happened. I'll even let you keep your lover, as long as you want him."

"You're crazy."

"No, Maggie, I am not crazy. I'm practical. The children need their mother, I understand that. And you, although God knows you're not much of a mother, you seem to love them. So just do this one thing and you can have it all." He looked pleased with himself, the way he looked when he hit upon a particularly good strategy for one of his cases, as though he'd solved a problem.

When she stood up and walked to the door without responding, he looked surprised. "Where are you going?"

"To pack."

"You're really leaving?"

She nodded. As she opened the door, he said "Maggie, just your clothes. That's all you can take out of this house. Nothing else in this house is yours. Do you understand?"

When she said nothing, he said "I'll send Hannah up to help you while I talk to the children. And Maggie, try not to get hysterical. It will upset the children if you start crying and carrying on. I'm just going to tell them that you're going away for a little rest. That way, if you tire of him and find that poverty isn't to your liking, you can come back home. If, on the other hand, this is what you really want, they will have had a chance to adjust to your absence before they find out it's permanent. If you're reasonable tonight, I'll consider allowing you to have visitation rights."

As she went up the stairs, she thought that he was right about one thing, she couldn't cry. If she started, she would never be able to stop. She was pulling the suitcases out of the back of the closet when Hannah came in. "What in hell is he doing to you?"

"He's throwing me out of the house. He's telling the children I'm going away for a rest. He offered to let me stay if I have an abortion. He's taking the children away from me, but if I go quietly, he'll consider letting me see them." She was surprised to find that she could tell Hannah all of this without crying.

"Dear God, he is a monster."

"No, no he's not. He's a man whose wife has cheated on him

and is carrying the baby of another man. Joseph told me long ago we should go to Dan and tell him I was leaving. He wanted to do that before we ever became lovers. If we had, then I could have gotten a divorce and had a chance to fight for custody. It will be so much harder now."

They began to pack Maggie's clothes. She took her underwear, and the clothes she wore every day. She left behind all of the dresses that she had worn on special occasions over the years. She took from her jewelry box the locket from Michael and the letter from Paul. She took off her engagement ring and her wedding ring and put them into the box. She wore the locket from Joseph and a pair of pierced gold hoop earrings that she never took off.

When they had finished, they went downstairs together. The house was quiet. Maggie saw that Dan was sitting in the living room with Megan in his lap. Colin was standing by the French doors, looking out at the bay. When Deco saw her, he ran to her and put his arms around her. "Dad says you're sick, that you have to go away for a little while."

Maggie forced a smile. "Just a little while."

"I want to go with you."

"You can't, Honey."

She felt the tremble as he started to cry. She held him tighter. How was she supposed to do this?

Dan stood up and said "Declan, let your mother hug Megan good bye. She has to go."

Megan came into her arms and clung, laughing into Maggie's face, too young to understand what was happening. Maggie smiled back and kissed her.

Dan said "Colin, come over here and say good bye to your mother."

Maggie saw that Colin stood rigid, and she saw him shake his head no, not trusting his voice. She went to him, still holding Megan, but when she touched him with her free hand, he flinched away from her. "I love you, Colin." He didn't respond.

When Dan took Megan from Maggie, Megan began to cry. Maggie turned and began to walk out of the living room. Deco ran after her. She saw that Hannah had taken the suitcases out and put them into Maggie's car. When she got to the door, she dropped to one knee and pulled Deco close to her. She whispered to him. "Deco, I love you. I'll see you again soon. Please don't be sad."

Then Dan was there. He reached down and pulled her up. His touch was almost tender. He said to Deco "Let your mother go now. This is not easy for her either."

She went through the door. At first, she thought she wouldn't look back, that it would only make things worse. But just before she opened the car door, she turned to look anyway and saw that the front door was closed.

Chapter 34

Joseph was outside, standing at the gate, when she drove up. She stopped the car and he got in. "What happened?"

"I'll tell you when we get inside the house. I can't tell you here."

She pulled in behind his truck and got out. She knew he had seen the suitcases on the back seat. He carried in two of them and she took the third. Moses greeted her with a worried whine as though he knew something was wrong.

"Can we please go and lay on the bed while I tell you?" When they got to the bedroom, she said "Don't turn on the light."

She told him everything. She was pretty sure she hadn't left anything out. After that, she cried and at first, she was crying so hard that she didn't realize that he was crying too. He said "I've cost you everything you love."

She sat up and turned on the light so that he could see her face when she told him. "Never say that. Never think it. I love you. That will never change. It's just the way things are."

"You shouldn't have to pay like this for loving me."

"What are we going to do now?"

"I can find work in Keshena and we can live at the cabin, but if it's better that we stay here, I'll find some way to make a living so you can be close by the children. We'll need a lawyer."

"We can't stay here. Dan made that clear. If I disgrace the family, he'll see to it that I don't even get visitation. So we should go. Once we're there, we can think about what to do."

Over the next few days, they took care of business. Chuck and his father agreed to take care of the farm. Joseph called his uncle who told him they could rent the cabin until they decided if they wanted to buy it. Joseph arranged with a neighbor close by in Keshena to board the horses until he could put up a fence.

Maggie hired a truck to move the piano. Everything else they left behind.

Within 3 days of her confrontation with Dan, Maggie locked the farmhouse door and put the key into Chuck's hand.

Chuck hugged her close and started to shake Joseph's hand, but then hugged him as well. Maggie said "The taxes and insurance are paid up till the end of the year. Once winter comes, you can shut off the water and drain the pipes.. Let us know if you need anything."

At just past 10 a.m., they turned out of the gate onto River Road, pulling the trailer with all 4 horses. Maggie sat in the middle, next to Joseph, and Moses sat next to the passenger window, looking back.

When they got to Keshena, they went straight to the neighbor, who greeted Maggie as though he's known her as long as he'd known Joseph. They turned the horses into the pasture next to the barn and he told Maggie to come over anytime she wanted to ride or visit her horses.

They drove to the cabin and unpacked, hanging their clothes side by side in the closet. Joseph opened the windows to air the place out, and Maggie put clean sheets on the bed. They made a shopping list together and drove to Marina's store to shop.

When she saw them, Marina came from behind the counter. She hugged Maggie first, then Joseph. She laid her hand on

Maggie's stomach and said "It's a boy. My first grandchild. Have you chosen a name?"

Maggie said "It's so soon."

Marina said "It will help decide who he becomes."

Maggie looked at Joseph. "I'd like to name him Gabriel."

"Now that we've named my grandson, come and sit down, the both of you." When they were seated, she went on "I hope you won't think I'm meddling, but when I knew you were coming, I called Jim." When Maggie looked questioning, she said "He's my brother. He's a captain with the Tribal Police. He needs a deputy. He'd just as soon that be you." She looked at Joseph, then she looked at Maggie. "Can you be a policeman's wife?"

"I don't know. It's a dangerous job, isn't it?"

"Maybe a little more than some jobs. But not so bad as it would be in a big city. Anyway, you can probably get killed easier logging, or doing half a dozen other jobs."

"Doesn't he need some kind of training?" she asked Marina.

"He needs to be able to shoot a gun, drive a cruiser, keep his temper and command respect. The first two he learned from his uncle when he was fifteen. The last two he's always been able to do."

Maggie looked at Joseph. "Would you want to do that?"

"It's a good living. It's a steady job."

"I'd like to work too. Is there some job I could do?"

Marina seemed to have been busy. "The librarian over at Shawano could use an assistant. 9 to 3."

"It's kind of fortunate that there just happen to be these job openings right now." Maggie said.

Joseph smiled at his mother. "The librarian over at Shawano is my mother's cousin."

"Well, she does need the help. The pay won't be much, so it's not like they're lined up for the job."

So it was that Maggie's new life began. She thought that it was an amazing thing how you could go on living, how you could learn to accept anything when you had no choice. It was the way she imagined it would be if a doctor told you that you had a terminal illness. At first, you would think ' how can I possibly wake up tomorrow, and get out of bed, and go through the day knowing this.' But then, you got up and you had breakfast, and you were able to talk and even laugh and life went on somehow.

Joseph's tan summer uniforms hung in the closet next to her clothes. They got up early and had breakfast together before he left for his shift that was 6 a.m. to 6 p.m. 4 days on, then 4 days off. Sometimes, in the morning, after he left, she would go to the closet and run her hands over the uniforms.

Maggie drove the 10 miles to Shawano and worked in the small library. She found it pleasant, being surrounded by books, meeting the people who came and went, restocking shelves and checking out books for people.

At 3 o'clock, she would go home and wait for Joseph. While she waited, she would do whatever chores needed doing, cleaning up, laundry, starting dinner.

On Joseph's days off, they worked on the horse fence together and talked about screening in the porch once they were finished with the fence.

Maggie had no morning sickness at all. The local doctor pronounced her fit and healthy enough to continue riding horses.

They found a canoe in a shed behind the cabin and began to paddle on the Wolf River.

When they first got to Keshena, she would try to call the Ryan house. She always waited till she thought Dan would have left for work. But no matter when she called, it seemed he always answered the phone. When she heard his voice, she hung up. But the third time she called, before she could hang up, he said "Maggie?" She didn't answer, just waited to see what he would say.

"Don't do this, Maggie. You'll just upset the boys. If you keep it up, I'll change the number."

Maggie had spoken to her father before they made the move to Keshena and he promised that he and Maeve would look in on her children often. They did that, and called every few days with updates. After Dan's warning, she contented herself with this second hand news.

The darkest time had been the day that Maggie and Joseph went to see a lawyer about divorce and custody. Maggie had been honest with him about her situation. What else could she do? He had not been encouraging.

"I know of your husband, professionally that is. He's extremely successful and he's well connected. He seems to have the upper hand here for reasons I don't have to enumerate.

The one thing on your side, of course, is that the courts are often sympathetic to the mother, particularly when there are young children. Your children, I assume, are close to you, would express a desire to be with you?"

"My son Declan would, and my little girl Megan. The oldest boy, Colin, is very close to his father."

"Perhaps something could be worked out. Is there any chance that your husband would be willing to share custody, allow the younger boy and the girl to live with you, the oldest boy to stay with him. Do you think he might be willing to consider that kind of arrangement?"

Maggie shook her head. "I don't know what he would agree

to, or if he'd agree to anything."

"May I be blunt with you?"

Maggie nodded.

"Your position is not a strong one. I think it would be best to avoid a courtroom battle. Do you want me to contact your husband? Make overtures?"

Maggie and Joseph looked at each other. Joseph said "Yes, I think you should."

The lawyer was young, and he was not unsympathetic. He gave them a break on his fees and while Maggie was working out payment arrangements with the attorney's secretary, he took Joseph aside. "Does she realize that her chances are not good? Unless, of course, her husband is willing to go along with some arrangement. And I'm guessing from your situation, and from what I know of Dan Ryan, that he's not likely to be cooperative."

"I don't want to take away all of her hope. Why don't you see what you can do? If the news is very bad, please talk to me first."

Chapter 35

Maggie and Joseph had been in Keshena just over a month. It was a Tuesday and Joseph was off work. Maggie was working Saturday that week so that she could help finish the horse fence. Joseph had hurried the work as much as possible because he thought that it would be good for Maggie to have the horses home where she could see them all of the time.

They had been working side by side in the heat and she was about to go in to get them some cold lemonade when she heard the sound of a car coming on the gravel drive. She stopped and shaded her eyes and saw that it was her father's car. "Joseph" she called.

He put down his tools and came to stand beside her. Patrick parked the car and got out. Maeve got out her side. The back door opened and Declan launched himself out of the car and into Maggie's arms. Maeve lifted Megan out and came over. Megan reached for Joseph and touched his face the way she always did.

It was happy chaos for the first few minutes with everyone kissing and hugging and crying. Finally, Declan let go of his mother, and reached out to hug Joseph. Joseph handed

Megan to Maggie.

When things settled down, Declan asked "Where are the horses? Where's Beauty?"

Joseph said "They're at the neighbor's place until we get this fence finished. By the next time you visit, they'll be here at home. You can take a ride."

They sat on the porch and drank lemonade, Megan in her mother's lap and Declan sitting between Maggie and Joseph. Later, they walked down to the River and Joseph told Declan maybe they could take the canoe out one day soon.

The day passed all too quickly and finally, Patrick said "We'd best be on our way."

Declan said "I want to stay. I want to come here and live with you and Joseph. I'm going to tell Dad."

Maggie bent down, close to his face. "Declan, you can't do that. You can't even tell your father that you were here. Do you understand? Your Grandpa and Grandma would be in terrible trouble if you did. You wouldn't be able to come and see us again."

Declan hugged her. "Grandma said that's why we couldn't tell Colin that we were coming. That he would tell Dad."

When the children were in the car, before Patrick and Maeve got in, Maggie said "You have to be careful, both of you. I don't want Dan to make trouble for you."

Maeve pulled Maggie tight against her. Maggie couldn't remember her mother ever holding her like that. "Fuck Dan Ryan" Maeve said.

Chapter 36

Joseph finished the horse fence by hanging the gate on the last of his 4 days off, just after the visit from Patrick, Maeve and the children. He decided to go over and pick up the horses, thinking that having them waiting when Maggie got home from work would cheer her. He was already out the door, keys in hand, when the phone rang. He debated letting it go, but then he thought it could be Maggie so he went back inside and answered.

It was the young lawyer, whose name was Matt McCarthy. "I've had a response from Mr. Ryan to my suggestion that he consider some kind of shared custody arrangement. I'm afraid I don't have good news for you."

"He refused to consider it."

"That's about the extent of it. He wasn't amenable to any kind of scheduled visitation either."

"Where do we go from here?"

"I suppose the next logical step would be for Mrs. Ryan to file for divorce. That would get the custody issue before the court. It's really the only way, given Mr. Ryan's refusal to consider any kind of informal agreement. If you decide to go that way, we'll need to retain an attorney in Michigan to prepare and file the papers and make court appearances. I can act as a liason if you'd like me to or you can deal directly with the lawyer up there. There's really no need for you to pay two attorneys."

"What do you think the chances are that the court will approve some kind of shared custody?" There was a long silence and that was an answer in itself. Joseph had only asked because he had hoped that his pessimism came from a lack of knowledge of the law. "There isn't a lot of hope, is there?"

"I'm sorry. There are probably some more liberal jurisdictions where this kind of situation wouldn't be such a problem. You're best bet is to keep trying to reach some kind of accommodation with Mr. Ryan. Otherwise, the best you can hope for is unsupervised visitation. Does Mrs. Ryan know any attorneys in Menominee who are particularly good at family law?"

"I don't know. Probably."

"Would you like to tell her or would it be easier coming from me?"

"I'll talk to her. I assume we can count on you if we need any help?"

"Anything I can do, of course.

Joseph went ahead and drove over to the neighbor's and trailered the horses home. He had run a water line and set up a trough. He thought that before winter, it would be nice to have a heater to keep the ice off the water so the horses would drink enough to avoid colic. They should build a shelter too, nothing fancy, no big barn. These horses had always preferred to stand outside in the snow, but he wanted them to have a place to go to get out of the wind and rain.

Moses accompanied him, happy to have Joseph around. The dog had been used to being with him all of the time. Now he was alone on days when Joseph was on duty and Maggie was at work. But once she came home, he attached himself to her side, no matter what she was doing. She had considered coming home to get him when she had errands to run, but most days it was too hot and humid for him to wait in the car so she explained to him that it was more comfortable for him in the cabin. When she talked to him, Moses sat looking up into her face, and when she was done, he often gave a satisfied little grunt, as though he had understood whatever she said.

Joseph had laid in a supply of hay in the shed the day before, and he had just finished throwing the afternoon feeding to the horses, when Moses gave an excited little bark and ran toward the drive. "How is it you always hear her car before I do?" he asked, and Moses looked at him as if it was obvious that, being a dog, he had the better hearing.

Maggie parked alongside the truck to which the trailer was still attached. She ran to meet him by the new corral gate. "We've got our horses back." She looked so happy that he hated even more having to tell her what Matt McCarthy had said. He hugged her hello, trying to think of a way to soften the news without being entirely dishonest.

"Maybe we can take a ride tomorrow after work. Oh, no, you're back on duty."

"I'll be here by 6:30. It'll stay light till almost 9. We can do that and have dinner late. Would you like that?"

"Yes." She was smiling again. "I'm all hot and sticky. I want a bath. Will you come and wash my back? I might let you take liberties."

He followed her inside, started the water running into the tub and watched her undress and drop her clothes into the hamper. "Look" she said. She passed a hand over her stomach. "I'm starting to show."

He looked and saw that there was a roundness to her, sure that it must not have been there the day before because he noticed everything about her. He put his hand on her warm skin, then he knelt in front of her and kissed her belly. "Hello, Gabriel" he said.

She rested her hand on the top of his head. "Would you like to get in the tub with me? You're all hot and sticky too."

He stood and she unbuttoned his shirt, opened his jeans, pulled them down to where they met his boots. Then she said "I'm too tired to deal with the boots. I'm starting without you." She stepped into the tub, sat down and then lay back, letting her hair hang over the back of the tub, watching him take off his boots, awkwardly, standing first on one foot, then the other.

After he was undressed, he stepped in and sat facing her. "It's a good thing it's a big tub" she said. "Pretty soon, I'll be so huge you'll have to squeeze in if we want to take a bath together."

After they washed, they stood and toweled each other dry, then she took his hand and led him to the bed. When they were lying side by side, he felt suddenly that it would be a lie of sorts to make love without telling her about his talk with the lawyer. "Maggie, Matt McCarthy called today."

"Ssh. I know. I mean I knew there was something. I just didn't know what. Your face is so easy to read. We'll talk about it afterwards." Then she rolled on top of him and sat up, straddling him. She made love to him, falling forward against him finally, covering his face with her kisses. "I'd like to stay right here, just like this. Am I too heavy?"

"Just a little" he teased, holding her when she tried to move off him.

She rested her head against his chest. "You can tell me now."

He'd expected tears, but when he finished, she just said "Are you hungry?"

He thought that they should talk about it but he had nothing to offer her, nothing that would make her feel better so he just said "Are you?"

"Yes." She got up and put on a pair of panties and one of his tee shirts. He pulled on shorts and a shirt and followed her to the kitchen. She was already looking through the refrigerator, taking things out. "We have cold chicken. Where did this potato salad come from?"

"I made it this morning while you were at work. I thought it would go with the chicken. It's too hot to cook."

"You even put hard boiled eggs on top." She looked like she was going to cry, but she ducked back into the fridge and opened the crisper. "I'll make a green salad." Her voice was muffled.

He came up behind her and put his arms around her. She straightened up and leaned back against him and they stood together in the rush of cold air until he said "We're wasting electricity."

She turned and wrapped her arms around him while he closed the refrigerator door. Then he held her tightly, feeling her body shake with sobs. Finally, she took a breath and said "I'm sorry."

"Why, honey?"

"For falling apart. None of this is surprising. I knew it would be this way. I knew he'd never agree to anything."

"It's not over, Maggie. We'll just have to fight now."

"We don't have much of a chance, do we?"

"Don't say that. Even if it takes awhile, even if he never gives in, the kids are getting older. They'll speak up. They'll let everyone know they want to be with you."

"Declan will, won't he, Joseph? Colin never will, but Declan will."

"Colin will come around."

"But Megan, she's so little. I'm afraid she'll forget me."

"No, that won't happen. Your mother and father and Hannah will never let her forget you. And no matter what Dan says, when we go to court and the judge sees how much you love them, he won't keep them away from you."

She heard the words that he spoke and she understood the words he couldn't say. She knew how much he wanted to tell her that the children would come to live with them and that he didn't say that because he would never lie to her.

She lifted the tee shirt and used it to wipe her face. "Okay, I'm going to make a salad now. Will you make the dressing?"

When they sat down to eat dinner, she said "Look, we can see the horses. We can watch them while we eat. I like that."

He agreed, but he was looking at her, wishing that the happiness they had found together wasn't weighted with sorrow at what it had cost them.

Chapter 37

Maggie had hoped that her parents could bring Declan and Megan to visit again in July, but when she called to ask, Patrick told her that when they had gone by to see if the children could spend a day or two with their grandparents, Dan said maybe in August. He had decided to take the children on a vacation. They were going over to Mackinaw Island and from there, they planned to drive up into Canada. Hannah was going along to take care of Megan so that he and the boys could do some hiking and fishing.

Joseph checked the balance in the savings account and, although it was low, he decided to go ahead with his plan to screen in the porch. He knew that Maggie would like to eat outside and to sleep there on hot nights, but the mosquitoes made it impossible. On the first of his next 4 day off stretch, he drove to the lumbar yard and picked up the supplies. When she came home from work, he had already begun the framing.

She came up the porch steps, smiling and his spirits lifted at the sight. "I'd better watch what I wish for" she said. "All I have to do is say one little thing and you go out and get it for me."

If only that were true, he thought. If only it were that easy. But he smiled back and said "Go check out that hammock. Do you think it's big enough for both of us? I think it'll be okay for naps. But if we're going to sleep out here, we should get some kind of a real bed."

"How soon can we sleep out here?"

"I have 3 more days off. I might be able to finish before I go back on duty."

"I can help. Just let me change clothes."

She came back in less than 5 minutes in shorts and a tee shirt and he resisted the urge to pull her down in the hammock and put her to work instead. They worked until almost 7 and, while he cleaned up and put away the tools, Maggie drove into town to pick up a pizza for dinner.

As promised, he finished up on his last afternoon off in time to drive in and buy a screen door. They worked by the porch light, hanging the door and that night they slept together in the hammock, listening to the night sounds from the woods, the rustle and occasional low nickers from the horses, the sound of water from the River running over the rocks.

In the morning, she said "You were right. We need a bed out here. My back is broken."

He took his lunch break at his mother's store. "Maggie and I screened in the porch. It's nice for sleeping but we need to get a bed for out there. We tried sleeping in the hammock."

"The hammock might work for one person, but two of you? And one of the two pregnant? Why don't you take that rollaway I've got in the back? You can bring it back here in the winter when you're done with it for the season."

"You sure?"

"What do I need it for? I'm not expecting company. Tell you what, help me get it in the back of my truck and I'll run it out to your place this afternoon. I haven't had a visit with Maggie in awhile."

"Who's going to watch the store?"

"That useless boy who comes around to help me out. He'll be okay if it doesn't get too busy."

So it was that Marina drove in just after Maggie got home

from work. Maggie was always happy to see her. They were comfortable together and Maggie felt as though she could tell Marina almost anything. The rollaway wasn't heavy and between the two of them, they got it out of the truck and up the porch steps. "Where do you want it?" Marina asked.

"Over there so we can see the River from the bed."

They pushed the bed to where Maggie indicated and opened it. Maggie got sheets, a blanket and bed cover to make it up while Marina got them glasses of iced tea.

Then they sat side by side on the made up bed, leaning back against the wall, with their legs sticking out in front of them, looking through the screen at the Wolf River.

"It's nice here" Marina said. "Do you like it?"

"I do. Sometimes I miss my farm but I think it's mostly because that's where I first met Joseph."

"Yes and when you were there, you could go home to your kids at night."

"You're always honest, Marina."

"No reason to be otherwise. It's not right, what that man is doing, keeping you from your children."

"I guess a lot of people would say I'm getting what I deserve."

"People are real quick to pass judgment as long as it's on somebody else. You and Joseph were meant to be together. No way around that once you saw each other. If things were all neat and tidy in life, you would have met each other first and you would have made all your babies together. But life's real messy most of the time. It's not much comfort right now, but some day everything is going to be the way it should be. I know that. Don't look so happy, Maggie. I also know that it will be a long time coming. You're going to have to be real strong and real brave to get through it. Just always remember what I told you today. Joseph will wait for you. I see you coming back here someday."

Maggie wanted to say 'I'm here, right here. I'm not going anywhere.' But there was no denying the fear that rose up inside her as she listened to Marina. Marina who saw things that no one else could see. Maggie forced herself to focus on one thing. In the end, everything would be the way it should be.

Chapter 38

Maeve and Patrick were able to bring Declan and Megan to see Maggie and Joseph just once more that summer before school started. They saddled up three of the horses and rode around the property slowly, Deco on Beauty, Joseph on Hank, and Maggie on Sugar. Megan held her arms out to Joseph and Patrick lifted her up in front of Joseph so that she could have a little ride as well.

They had lunch on the screened porch and then Joseph took Deco for a ride in the canoe while Maggie visited with her parents and played with Megan on the porch.

At 4, Maggie said "Maybe you could stay for dinner?"

Patrick said "I'm sorry, Honey, but you know it's a couple of hours drive. As it is, Dan will be pacing back and forth in the driveway when we get there, wanting to know where we've been so long."

"What will you tell him?"

"That we had a long drive up in the County to visit the waterfalls, had a picnic, didn't realize how late it was getting to be."

"How is Colin? Still angry at me? Or doesn't he talk about me at all?"

"He doesn't say much. I think he's very divided. He loves you, Maggie. He's just confused. What's going on with the case? Have you found a lawyer?"

"We have. It's Jimmy Faller. Do you know him?"

"I know of him. He's a pretty good lawyer. Honest. No friend of Dan Ryan."

"I suppose that's why he took our case. He wasn't very optimistic but he said he'd do his best for us. He filed and served divorce papers. Dan filed an answer. He's contesting the divorce."

"What does he hope is going to happen?"

"I honestly don't know. I think he's just trying to drag it out. Jimmy thinks that Dan will delay as long as he can so that I'll have to go into court when I'm really far along. I'm already showing so it's just a matter of degree. I can't hide the pregnancy."

Their parting was more difficult than it had been after the first visit. Both Declan and Megan cried, and then Maggie joined in, even though she knew she shouldn't make things worse. When the car turned the curve in the drive and was lost to sight, she leaned against Joseph and cried some more. She remembered what Marina had told her, and the cold dread rose up in her, so that she clung to Joseph even more tightly.

After that day, Maggie and Joseph stayed busy. On Joseph's days off, they filled their time with riding the horses. They took the canoe out. Evenings, he played the piano as she sat beside him on the bench, resting against him.

She taught him bridge, and they played two handed.

Maggie woke often in the middle of the night, panicked until she heard him breathing, felt him lying next to her, then she pushed herself even more closely against him, waiting for the pounding of her heart to slow and quiet.

Once school started, Maeve and Patrick were no longer able to bring Declan and Megan to visit. Declan was in school weekdays and on weekends, Dan kept the children busy.

Maeve and Patrick saw them every Sunday as the family dinners continued as they always had.

In October, Jimmy called to tell them there was a hearing scheduled in family court for the next week. He had debated for a long time as to the wisdom of Joseph appearing there with Maggie, but in the end, decided it would be best. There was no way to deny the relationship, and if he didn't appear, it might look as though it was a casual adulterous affair. As things turned out, it wouldn't have mattered. Maggie knew it as soon as they walked into the courtroom. There was a palpable sense of hostility that she knew was not imagined.

The family law judge was Adam Nance. He was a long time friend of the Ryan family. He and his wife had often had dinner with Maggie and Dan. He looked at her with undisguised contempt. She was 5 months pregnant. She was conscious of Joseph, uncomfortable in a suit, with his hair tied back on his neck. She saw the two of them as they appeared to Adam Nance. She knew there was no chance, none at all.

The only unexpected part of the entire proceeding came when Judge Nance questioned Dan as to his reasons for contesting the divorce. It was clear that Judge Nance could not understand why Dan was not anxious to be rid of this embarrassment. Surely he didn't want to retain her as his wife?

Dan was uncharacteristically unable to express himself. At last, Judge Nance made his preliminary ruling from the bench. He asked Dan to consider withdrawing his papers and allowing the divorce to proceed uncontested.

He granted temporary custody to Dan. He gave good reasons. The children were living in the home where they'd always lived. The oldest children were attending school where they'd always attended school. They were all healthy and happy. It would be disastrous to uproot them.

He felt that it would not be in the children's best interest to have visitation with their mother at this time. They would be confused and upset by her condition. He would reconsider the ruling in 6 months when Mrs. Ryan was no longer pregnant. He said the word with distaste.

If Dan were to allow the divorce to proceed uncontested, once the divorce was final, and Mrs. Ryan had married the father of her child, then she could come back into court to ask for modification of the ruling.

When they were outside in the hall, Maggie asked Jimmy over and over "How can he do that? He can't, can he? He has to let me see my children, doesn't he? Is there some way to appeal?"

Jimmy promised her that he would look into it, do further research, that he would continue to talk to Dan's attorney, try to make him see reason.

Neither Joseph nor Maggie said anything for the first part of the drive home but she sat pressed against him and she kept her hand on his leg as if to reassure herself that he was really there. At last she said "I'm not surprised, are you? About the way it turned out." Her voice was so calm. When he didn't answer, she looked at him and saw that he was crying.

"No, no, oh please no, Joseph, don't. I can't stand it. Stop. Stop driving."

He pulled onto the shoulder and turned the key in the ignition. It was quiet. He turned toward her and she pulled him against her. She wiped his face with her hands. He caught her hands in his and put them to his mouth, kissing her fingers. "Maggie, Maggie. I'm so sorry."

"Never say that to me. Never. It's like saying you're sorry we met, sorry that we're having a baby."

"You know that's not why I'm sorry."

"I know" she said. "I know. But you mustn't be sorry. It's alright to be sad. We'll both be sad sometimes, but we won't ever be sorry."

Chapter 39

One week to the day after the court hearing, the phone rang in the cabin just as Maggie came in from work.

She thought it might be Joseph, calling from patrol to see if she needed anything. It wasn't.

"Maggie, it's Dan." She didn't think to ask where he'd gotten the number.

"Yes?"

"I've decided that you should see the children. You'll have to come here, of course."

"There? To the house, you mean?"

"No. You could see them at your parents' house. I think Saturday afternoons would be best."

"Every Saturday? I could see them every Saturday?"

"Yes. I realize it will be a long drive for you, but you understand I won't let them come there."

"No, it's alright. It's not that far. Can I come this Saturday?"

"Yes. But Maggie, it's just for you. I don't want him there. Do you understand?"

"I understand."

"If he drives you, he'll have to wait for you somewhere else."

"How long? How long can I see them?"

"Let's say from 2 to 4. That seems fair, doesn't it?"

No, she thought, but she said "Yes, it's fair."

"Alright then. Why don't you call your parents and tell them."

"Yes, I will. Dan, the judge said no visitation."

"He'll go along if I agree to it. I thought we'd see how it goes and if there are no problems, we can go back to court for a modification of the order."

"Why? Why did you change your mind?"

"Thank Hannah. She told me that in trying to hurt you, I was really hurting the children." Then abruptly, as though he regretted having told her, he said "I'll have the children at your parent's house at 2 on Saturday. Please let me know if for any reason you can't make it." He hung up before she could even say thank you.

When Joseph got home, she told him. The only part she hated to tell him was the part about him not being able to be there. But he only kissed her and said "I'm off on Saturday. I'll drive you."

When the day came, they left early. Maggie thought they could stop and have lunch at Mickey Lu's, but when they got there, she was too excited to eat. Joseph dropped her off at 1:30. "I'll come back at 4:30. That way, he'll have come and gone."

"Where will you go?"

"I'll take a drive. Maybe stop in at Kelly's."

Maeve was at home but Patrick wasn't. "Where's Daddy?"

"He's at the bar. Once Dan drops off the children, I'll leave so that you can have the time just for you."

"Thanks, Mama."

"You're looking good. Big already. Sure it's not twins?"

"No twins. Joseph's mother says it's a boy."

"Does she see the future?"

"I think she does."

"Are you feeling well?"

"It's the easiest pregnancy I've ever had."

"Still working?"

"Yeah, but Joseph wants me to stop pretty soon. He doesn't want me driving once it gets icy."

"There's a car. I think he's early." Maeve stood and looked through the window. "It's them. Have a good visit."

Maggie hugged her mother. "Joseph said he'd drop by

Kelly's. You can visit with him."

Maggie went to the door to meet them. Megan ran to her mother and Maggie picked her up. Megan hugged her. Then Declan was there, his arms around her. She looked over Declan's head to Colin, who held back, standing next to his father. "Won't you come and give me a hug" she asked?

She saw that Dan gave him a little push forward. He said "I'll see you at 4." Then he turned and went back to the car.

"Colin" Declan said "give Mom a hug."

Colin held her briefly, then moved away. He went to the T.V. and turned it on. She wanted to say 'please don't do that' but she could sense his anger so she thought go slow, give him time.

She sat down on the sofa. Megan stayed in her lap and Declan sat beside her. "Tell me about you, all about what you've been doing, about school, everything." She meant it for both of the boys, but only Declan answered.

He talked a long time, and Maggie simply drank it in, all his news, his excitement at sharing it with her. Finally, he said

"Colin, tell Mom what you've been doing."

In all that time, Colin had been focused resolutely on whatever had been on the T V. Now he turned and looked directly at Maggie. "You're pregnant."

"Yes. Your father didn't tell you?"

"No."

Maggie thought that Dan should have prepared him, but then maybe he wouldn't have come, maybe she wouldn't have had the chance to see him at all. And why, after all, should Dan make it easier for her?

"You're going to have a baby brother, in February. Maybe he'll have the same birthday as you."

"He's no brother of mine."

"Don't say that" Declan said. "Don't make Mom feel bad."

"Why not? She should feel bad. She did a bad thing."

"No." Deco sounded close to tears.

"Yes, yes she did. She left us. She just walked out and left us." His voice was cold. He sounded, she thought, just like Dan.

"No. It wasn't like that at all." She tried to think of a way to explain it to him.

"No? Well, you're not living at home with us, are you? You're living on the Reservation with him. So I'd say that you left us."

"Colin, please. I've missed you so."

"I'm going to wait for Dad outside." He put on his coat.

She got up, holding Megan and tried to stop him, but he shrugged her off and slammed out the door.

She saw that Declan was crying so she went back to the sofa and put her arm around him. When Megan saw that he was crying, she started to cry. Dear God, she thought, Dan probably knew this would happen, knew it would be a disaster. Now he could say he had tried and he had even more evidence for the judge, even more reason not to allow her even this little bit of time.

She saw that it was almost 3:30. How could the time have gone so quickly? "Deco, please don't cry. If your father sees you and Megan crying, he'll never let you come back to see me. Do you understand? He'll say it isn't good for you, that it's too upsetting. You do want to see me, don't you?"

"He shouldn't have talked to you that way."

"He's hurt. He can't help it. But I still have you and Megan. Come on. Let's wash faces. Let's see if Grama has something to drink in the kitchen. So Daddy will see it was a good visit and we can do it again next week, okay?"

When Dan arrived at 4, Maggie saw him stop to talk to Colin, then Colin went and sat in the car while Dan came to the door. Declan greeted him with a big smile. Dan said "How did it go?"

"It went great. I told Mom all about school and everything. Megan mostly napped on Mom's lap."

"Would you like to see your Mom again next Saturday?"

"Yes" Deco said.

"Alright then. Take your sister and go wait for me in the car."

Deco turned and hugged Maggie. "See you next Saturday."

"Next Saturday." Maggie repeated. She hugged and kissed Megan and kept smiling, not wanting any upset.

When the kids were in the car, Dan said "Colin doesn't want to see you again. Maybe he'll come around in time, but I don't think we should push it, do you?"

"No, it wouldn't do any good."

"I guess it is a lot to expect him to understand, your pregnancy and all of it. He feels that you abandoned him."

"Yes, I can see that he would think that."

"Well, you seem to have kept your end of the bargain so we'll see you next weekend."

Maggie walked outside and watched the car pull away, watched Deco wave at her from the car window.

She sat down on the steps and waited for Joseph.

Every Saturday after that, Maggie made the trip from Keshena to Menekaunee. On his days off, Joseph drove her. As winter came on, and as her pregnancy advanced, Marina drove her, at Joseph's insistence, not wanting her alone on the road.

Colin never came along to see her.

The weather held and the roads were clear, all except one Saturday in November when Maggie woke to that absolute silence that meant only one thing. She didn't even need to get out of bed and look out the window. It was as though they were cut off from the rest of the world, wrapped in layers and layers of cotton. "Wake up, Joseph" she said. "We're snowed in."

She called Dan to tell him it was still snowing and they wouldn't be plowed out in time to come. He let her talk to Deco and Megan.

Other than that, they never missed a Saturday.

Chapter 40

What would have driven most people apart only pulled Maggie and Joseph closer to each other. They kept to themselves, wanting only to be together while they waited for their baby. They rode their horses on the trails and along the county road until there was too much ice and snow. By that time, they had finished building a sturdy enclosure big enough to shelter all four horses.

By then, too, they had stored the canoe in the shed and taken down the screens from the porch, returning the roll away bed to Marina.

Joseph had laid in a supply of wood so that they could have a fire in the fireplace every night. On days that Joseph was on duty, Maggie had dinner ready when he got home. On his days off, he cooked.

They sat or lay together on the sofa, reading, dozing in each other's arms. And always, at night, in bed, Joseph cradled Maggie in his arms, and she felt safe, sheltered, listening to the wind, thinking she wouldn't be able to sleep, but then sleep would overtake her and when she woke again, there would be that thin pale winter sunlight, made warmer looking because it came in through the cheerful yellow curtains at their bedroom windows..

On the Saturday before Thanksgiving, Maggie waved good bye to Deco and Megan as Dan drove them away from her and went back inside to wait for Joseph. When he arrived, Maeve was with him. As they got ready to leave, Maeve said "I'm having the Thanksgiving dinner here this year. Sean and Annie and their brood will be here, and Connor and Paula and their kids. Would you two like to join us?"

"Oh, Ma, thank you, but we already have plans. We're going to be with Joseph's mother."

"Well, maybe Christmas then." She hugged them both, Maggie first, then Joseph.

When they were in the car, Maggie said "You must have really charmed my mother today."

"Maybe she's just getting to know me."

Maggie gave a little gasp, then when Joseph looked alarmed, she laughed. "It's just the baby. He's really very active."

"He's in a hurry to be born, in a hurry to know you."

The rest of the way home Maggie thought about that. For weeks now, there had been no activity in the divorce case. She had almost forgotten about it in her euphoria over being able to see her children every week. She watched Joseph's profile as he drove. He glanced at her and smiled, and she moved closer, close enough to feel the warmth of his leg against hers.

On Monday morning, she called her attorney. She had thought about asking Dan directly, but she was afraid of upsetting the precarious balance between them. If she made him angry, he might decide to rescind her visitation. When Jimmy came on the line, she said "What's going on with the divorce?"

"Nothing. Your husband hasn't withdrawn his papers contesting. We can ask for a hearing date and force the issue if you'd like. But I got the impression you were hoping that if we gave him some time, he'd eventually just agree to the divorce. It's looking like things could work out that way, given the fact that he's allowing visitation."

"I'd like you to contact Dan's attorney and see if we can't

move things along now."

"It might be better if you talk to Dan yourself. I wouldn't ordinarily advise that but he gave in on the visitation when he didn't have to. He might be more willing to listen to you than to an attorney."

"I thought about that, Jimmy, but I'm afraid that if I upset him on the divorce issue, he'll change his mind about letting me see the kids. If you could just talk to his attorney, but be real careful."

"Has something changed?"

"My baby is due in February. I hoped that Joseph and I could be married by then. And once we're married, then maybe we'll have a better chance to get custody, or at least to see the children more."

He called her that afternoon to tell her that Dan's attorney was out of town for the entire week and promised to follow up and get back to her after Thanksgiving.

For Maggie, Thanksgiving had always been a family holiday. It was, for Marina as well, but Marina's definition of family was far broader than the Kelly's or the Ryan's. The parking area at the store was already full when Joseph and Maggie arrived with Moses.

Maggie and Joseph had baked pies the night before, 2 pumpkin and 2 pecan. "Why so many" she'd asked? Joseph had smiled and said "You'll see" and now she did.

"I didn't know your family was so big."

"It's not. But my Mom makes sure that everybody who doesn't have family to go to on holidays comes here."

Inside, the long counter was covered with platters and bowls, casseroles and roasting pans. It was the biggest pot luck Maggie had seen since those long ago suppers in the church basement.

Maggie had already met some of the people, others she met for the first time that day.

Joseph's cousin Will hugged her carefully. "I brought my tape player. Maybe you can dance with me later. You can still dance, can't you?"

She laughed. "I'm not so graceful, but I can still dance." She saw Joseph hugging a man who looked very much like him. "Will, is that Joseph's brother?"

Will nodded. "That's Thomas. You haven't met him yet?" Then before she could answer, he said "Yeah, probably not. He just got back in town."

"They look so much alike."

"Just on the outside, Maggie. Inside they couldn't be more different. Thomas's pretty messed up. He does okay for awhile, then he just goes off the tracks. It's really tough on Marina."

"I guess I should go meet him. He's Joseph's brother. But don't forget, you're going to dance with the big fat pregnant lady later on."

Will's laughter followed her to where Joseph stood with his brother. When she got there, Joseph reached out and drew her into the circle of his arm. "Thomas, this is Maggie. Maggie, this is my brother Thomas."

Maggie would have hugged him, but he seemed to shy away

from her, She saw that he was a little taller than Joseph, but aside from that, and the scar on Joseph's face, they might have been twins. And yet, she could see that the resemblance was purely physical although perhaps that was only because of what Will had told her.

He said "I guess I'm going to be an Uncle." He smiled and it changed him in some subtle way, from Joseph's damaged brother to just Joseph's older brother. Later, she danced with him and afterward, he told her he hoped that he could come and meet the baby after it was born, and she said "You have to come and see us anytime. You don't have to wait for your nephew to be born."

"How do you know it's a boy? Oh, wait, my Mom told you. She always knows that kind of stuff. Do you believe in that? People being able to tell what's going to happen?"

"Yes, I think I do" she said, remembering the other things Marina had told her.

Jimmy called the following week to tell Maggie that Dan had not changed his mind. He would continue to contest the divorce. That night in bed, she told Joseph. "I'm afraid I'll never be your wife."

"You will be my wife." He said it with such certainty that Maggie thought 'Yes, I will be. Not as soon as we wanted, but some day.'

Chapter 41

For Christmas, Marina knitted scarves for Maggie's children – a very conservative dark blue one for Colin, a red one with a horse worked into the wool for Declan and a delicate lacy pink and lavender creation for Megan.

Joseph picked out the gift for Deco – The Big Book of Horses.

Maggie insisted on buying Megan her first Barbie doll. "She's a little young, but she'll grow into it. I know women today think there's something wrong with Barbie, that she's a bad role model, or she'll make girls feel dissatisfied with their own looks, but I don't think the world will end if Megan dresses up a doll for a few years."

Maggie had no idea what to get for Colin. "He probably won't even open it, but I want him to know we really tried to find something he would like."

In the end, Maggie called Hannah for help. It wasn't only that she didn't know what an almost 15 year old boy would like, but she had to admit that she hardly knew her oldest son.

Hannah told her that Colin had been wanting a camera. "He's

taking a photography class at school. If you're going to get it for him, I'll tell his dad so he doesn't end up getting two."

Christmas Day fell on a Saturday. Maggie had expected Dan to cancel her visitation and she had prepared herself for it, but he called on Thursday to ask her if she planned to drive up on Christmas Day, or if she had other plans.

"No, of course not. I'll come." She hated the tone of subservience she adopted when she talked to Dan. But what choice did she have? He could keep her children from her on Christmas, or entirely, if he wanted to. He could continue to delay the divorce, stop her from marrying Joseph before the baby was born, and for a long time after that. Because he had all the power. He had the children. The children that she loved, turned into weapons to be used against her. She took a breath. She swallowed and tasted fear but she asked anyway. "I would like Joseph to come with me on Christmas. I would like him to see the children."

There was a long silence, an awful silence and then Dan said "Alright. But just this once. I'll do this for you Maggie because it's Christmas."

I should thank him, she thought. But she didn't.

On Christmas day, Maggie and Joseph arrived early. When Maggie told her mother that Dan had agreed to let Joseph see the children, she had asked Maggie if she and Joseph would stay for Christmas dinner.

The knock at the door came early too, at just 1:45 and Maeve answered it to find all three of the children standing with their father. "Merry Christmas, Maeve."

"And to you Dan. You'll be back at 4, I suppose."

"Yes, I'd like them home for dinner with me."

When Maggie saw Colin, she stood for a minute, afraid that if she approached him, he'd turn and run after his father. But then, she thought 'no, I've been afraid long enough.' She crossed the room and hugged him and after a minute, she felt him relax in her arms and then he hugged her back. "You're very fat" he said, then when she laughed, he amended his statement. "I mean, big, very big. I don't remember you being this big before Megan was born."

"I think maybe I was, you've just forgotten."

"Maybe. We all chipped in to get you a present. Hannah

helped pick it out."

Declan went to the porch and came back in with a large flat box.

"May I open it?"

"Sure" Deco said.

She was very careful not to tear the wrapping paper. She folded it neatly along with the bow, to save. Then she lifted the cover. Inside was a hand made quilt. "It's for the baby" Deco explained.

"It's so beautiful" Maggie said. "Joseph, come and see."

She unfolded it and spread it out. "Look at all the colors. Who made it?"

Colin said "A lady that Hannah knows. She thought it would be something you could use. We didn't know if it was a boy or a girl, that's why it's not pink or blue."

Maggie gathered all 3 of them to her. "We have presents for you too."

"Can we open them now?" Deco asked.

"Of course." Joseph said.

"Megan first" Colin said.

Megan tore the paper off and Maggie helped her take the Barbie doll out of the box. "She's pretty" Megan said, touching the doll's blonde hair.

Maeve said "I thought you young women were too liberated to get dolls for your daughters."

Maggie smiled. "I guess I'm not very liberated at all, Mama."

Colin smiled "Deco, you go next."

Deco tore the paper off and looked at the cover. Then he went to Joseph and hugged him before he hugged his mother. When he hugged Maggie, he said "I know who picked it for me."

Finally, Colin opened his gift. Like Maggie, he took the paper off carefully, without tearing it. When he saw the gift, he said simply "Thank you." Then, "Thank you both."

Joseph said "There's film in the box and the instructions."

Colin took his gift to the sofa while the rest of them went to the kitchen for Christmas cookies and hot chocolate. He joined them shortly. "I put in the film. Can we go outside and take some pictures? Maybe down by the beach."

Once everyone had on their coats, boots and gloves, they all walked down to Red Arrow Beach. Megan walked between Maggie and Joseph, holding their hands while the boys ran ahead. Patrick and Maeve trailed along behind. "Too bad" said Maeve to Patrick.

"What's that, Love?"

"That this is only for today."

"These little blessings are all we have. We should be thankful for just this much."

Colin took all of the pictures on his roll of film that day. After Christmas, he took the roll to the drug store to be developed. When he got it back, he looked at the pictures one at a time. When he came to the last one he had taken on Christmas day, he looked at it for a long time. It was a picture of Maggie and

Joseph. They had their arms around each other. They were smiling, not for the camera, but at each other. It was a happy picture, but it made him sad.

Chapter 42

Gabriel Patrick Dodge was born at 10 a.m. on February 7, 1977. Joseph had awakened just after 4 a.m. when the rhythm of Maggie's breathing had changed. He laid his hand on her belly and she said "I'm in labor."

In the hospital, he sat beside the bed, holding her hand and watching her. "Don't look so scared" she said. "I've done this before." But every time the pain came and she began to breathe hard, and her fingers gripped his, he realized he'd never known what fear was before, not even as a child when his father had whipped him.

Then it was time, and they wheeled her into the delivery room and he leaned against a wall and waited until a nurse came and said "Come on. The doctor says you can come and meet your son now."

When he saw Maggie and their baby, he knew that every single cliché he'd ever heard was the absolute truth. He put his hand on her face and she smiled and said "Look what we made."

She didn't stay in the hospital long and Joseph didn't want to ask for favors from the Department so Marina put the useless boy to work in the store and she stayed with Maggie and Gabriel while Joseph worked.

After a few days, Maggie would be up sitting in the rocker in front of the fire with the baby in her arms when Joseph came in from work. Marina said "I can't keep her in bed. In the old days, she would have been one of those women who has a baby and then goes right back to work in the field."

Joseph had expected to be tired but he was too full of joy. He woke up with Maggie in the middle of the night. He got up and took their son from the cradle next to their bed. He changed Gabe's diaper, put him in clean pajamas, brought him to Maggie who sat up against the pillows and took him to her breast. He sat next to her, watching Gabriel nurse, watching his fingers open and close. Maggie would look from the baby to Joseph, smiling, always smiling and later, Joseph would think it was the happiest time of his life.

When Maggie saw Gabriel for the first time, she felt the kind of love she'd felt the first time she'd kissed Joseph's mouth, that night in the hospital after he'd been beaten. The intensity of it was a frightening thing.

Her love for Gabriel, like her love for Joseph, was fierce, unrelenting. Perhaps it was because it was Joseph's child, the child they'd made together. Perhaps it was because she'd all but lost her other children.

In the dead of winter, with snow piling high around the cabin, with her baby at her breast and Joseph beside her, she felt that they were cut off from the rest of the world, but in the best of ways. Nothing can touch us here, she thought. Nothing can take this away from us. She was wrong.

Book Five - Maggie, Megan and John Franco

Choice is everything when freely made. When one is forced to make an impossible decision, it isn't choice at all. But then, women with children have no choices, not really. They can be held hostage, tied to places and situations as if with chains.

Chapter 1

It was mid April and everyone assumed that the worst of winter was over. The storm began during the night with freezing rain. The temperature dropped and by mid morning, it was snowing. Not the kind of snow that melts when it hits the ground, but the kind that comes in winter, piling up by inches until it begins to drift. The plows were out, clearing the main roads, but behind them the snow came down, and it was as though they'd never been there.

When Joseph had first started work as a deputy, every one of his shifts had been 12 hours that Maggie had to get through somehow until he was safely back with her. It had gotten easier as the months had gone by with no serious incidents. She was almost able to convince herself that it was as safe a job as any, that there were even more dangerous things he could be doing, that being a tribal policeman wasn't as dangerous as being a policeman in any major city. Almost.

But the truth was that she still worried, and probably always would. Slick roads were just one more concern so she was happy that he was home on the day of the storm.

They were finishing lunch when the phone rang. Gabriel

began to cry and Maggie went to get him from the cradle while Joseph answered. When she came back from the bedroom with the baby in her arms, Joseph said "It's Dan." Bad news. She knew it from Joseph's face, his voice. He took Gabriel from her.

She picked up the receiver. "What's wrong?"

"It's Megan. She's in the hospital. It's bad, Maggie. You've got to come here."

"I have a baby. He's two months old. I'm nursing him. There's a blizzard." She said it knowing that none of it would matter.

"It's spinal meningitis. She might die."

Maggie sat down. "How long has she been sick?"

"It all just happened. It happened so fast. She was fine. Then right after dinner last night, she was so hot and she was crying. I took her to the E.R. and they admitted her. She's in isolation."

"I have to talk to Joseph. Where are you?"

"At the hospital. You can call the Nurses' Station. They'll come and get me. But, Maggie, you have to hurry."

She hung up. She looked at Joseph where he sat in the rocker with Gabriel. "Megan's in the hospital. Dan says it's spinal meningitis. That's bad, right? He says she might die. I don't know what to do."

"You have to go."

"The baby. I need to nurse the baby. But I can't take him out in this storm. I can't take him to the hospital. He could get sick."

"I'll call my mother."

Maggie took Gabriel. She nursed him. She listened to Joseph's end of the conversation. He hung up and came to her. "She'll come here. She'll bring everything we need to make formula. She'll take care of him for us."

"You can't come with me. You have to stay here with him. One of us has to be with him."

"You can't drive by yourself in this storm."

"I have to call Dan." This time, she held Gabriel in one arm and held the phone in her free hand. When Dan came on the line, she said "I'm coming. Just as soon as Joseph's mother gets here."

"I'm going to come and get you. You can't drive in this storm."

"You can't leave Megan."

"Your parents are here. I can get through this in my car. Just tell me how to find your place."

"Wait. Talk to Joseph. He'll tell you."

When Joseph hung up, he said "If it weren't snowing, he could probably be here in 2 hours. It's probably going to take him twice that long. He says he has a 4 wheel drive car. Is he a good driver?"

"What?"

"Is Dan a good driver, Maggie? I've got to know he'll get you there safe."

"Yes. He's a good driver. Joseph, I don't know if I can do this. How can I just leave?"

"It's Megan."

"What about Gabriel? What about you?"

"We'll be good here. We'll be waiting for you. Here comes Mama. That old diesel truck can get through anything."

Joseph went to let her in. Marina came through the door with packages that she gave to Joseph. "There's more" she said.

"I'll get it."

"No, I'm already bundled up. You unpack this stuff so I can start the formula. I want Maggie to be able to start the baby on the bottle."

Joseph came back with a suitcase and another grocery bag. The suitcase made it real for Maggie. Marina would be staying here because Maggie wouldn't be.

Marina was practical and unemotional. "You can put that up in the loft. I assume you'll want to tend to Gabriel if he wakes up at night. You can give the bottle. I'll show you how. It's easy."

Maggie rocked back and forth, watching Gabriel sleep, watching Marina prepare the formula that would take the place of her breasts.

When Marina was done, she brought a bottle to Maggie. "Let's see if he'll take this."

Maggie guided the nipple into Gabe's mouth. He fastened on it and began to suck with contentment. Marina smiled. "There, you see. He's an adaptable child. He won't starve while you're gone."

She sat down. "Maggie, there's something I want to say to you. I know that Joseph told you about his father. I was not the mother I should have been." When Maggie started to speak, Marina shushed her. "No mother should let fear stop her from protecting her own children. Maybe I was just too young then. But I will take good care of Gabriel for you for as long as you need me. I won't try to be his mother. I'll only be a grandmother. I'll make sure that he knows you."

"I won't be away so long."

"Maggie, I just want you to know that if things should not turn out the way you plan, your son will know you. He and Joseph will be here waiting for you. Remember what I told you the day we sat outside on the bed. Don't lose faith."

She turned toward Joseph. "How long do you suppose it will take him to get here?"

Joseph looked at the clock. "How bad is it out there?"

"They're trying to keep the main roads cleared. It's the County roads that will slow him down."

"Maybe another couple of hours, maybe a little longer than that."

Marina said "Maggie, will you let me take Gabe? You and Joseph should go and be alone while you can." She took Maggie's place in the rocker and she held the sleeping baby against her.

When they were alone, Maggie said "Can we make love?"

He turned down the covers. They watched each other undress and then they lay down and he pulled the covers up over them. "Are you sure you want to? With everything that's happening."

"I want to. I want you to make love to me Joseph, so that I can live on it for as long as we have to be apart."

Their lovemaking that day was unlike any other time. She wanted no foreplay, no teasing, no tenderness, just a joining together with him deep inside her, his weight holding her down, their mouths joined too. She wanted nothing between them, no space at all, just as though they were really one being. They stayed that way until he whispered against her mouth "Maggie. It's time."

Still she clung to him until she realized that she had to have time with the baby too, before everything was taken away from her. She got up and dressed. She refused to bathe, refused to pack a bag.

They went back to the living room and once again, she changed places with Marina, sitting in the rocker with Gabriel close against her. She thought of nursing him, but then realized it would be better if she didn't. It would be easier for him to take the bottle after she was gone, if he hadn't just been at her breast.

Marina prepared a thermos of coffee and a bag of sandwiches. "You won't want to stop anywhere along the way, I know. You'll be going straight to the hospital when you get there."

Joseph brought a chair close to the rocker and he and Maggie sat holding hands and waiting.

Marina heard the car first. She looked out the window. "He's here."

"I can't." Maggie said. But she let Marina take the baby, let Joseph help her put on her boots, her coat, a scarf and hat. "Don't forget to wear your gloves" he said.

There was a knock and Maggie pulled Joseph to her. "Don't come outside with me. Don't say good bye. Don't stand here with the door open, watching me go. I can't look back at you. Do you understand? If I look back at you, I won't be able to leave. I love you with everything I have. If I thought we wouldn't be together again, I would die."

She started to pull away, but he held her. "I'll be both mother and father to him till you're here again. I'll never leave this place. I'll wait for you for as long as it takes. Never forget that. I love you the way you love me." He let her go then. He stood where he was, doing what she asked.

The door closed behind her. After a minute, the car started and then he heard the sound of the tires fade.

Chapter 2

Dan opened the passenger door for her, but when he tried to help her in, she jerked away from him. When he was behind the wheel, Maggie said "How is she?"

"The same. The doctor said she was stable, but that could change at any time. It's bacterial meningitis. If it was viral meningitis, it wouldn't be as serious. They're having trouble bringing the fever down. They're afraid of brain damage." His voice sounded so calm, the way it did in court when he was giving an opening statement. He might have been talking about somebody else's child, not theirs.

He kept talking until Maggie said "Please shut up, Dan."

The County road was bad. The car's rear end felt unstable in spite of the four wheel drive. Maggie's breasts ached. She felt the milk leaking into her shirt. It felt warm.

For weeks after that night, her breasts would ache that way, even after her milk dried up. Even after the milk was gone, the ache persisted. It was then that she realized that the ache was just part of her now. It had nothing to do with her desire to nurse her baby. It was just another sign of what she'd had for a little while and then lost.

The highway was better, the plows had done their job. Still, there were a lot of cars in the ditch and once, when they hit a patch of black ice and spun, Maggie thought 'Maybe we'll go in the ditch like those other cars. Maybe I'll live and Dan will die' and, at the thought of Dan's death, she was filled with a fierce joy.

But they didn't go into the ditch and Dan didn't die, and soon she began to see the familiar landmarks that said they were close to home. They were passing through Peshtigo and she thought '5 miles to Marinette', then Dan turned toward Shore Drive and she said "Where are we going?" It was the first time she'd spoken since she'd told him to shut up.

"She's at Marinette General. There's a doctor there who's a specialist in neurological disease."

When they got to the floor where Megan was in isolation, Maeve and Patrick were sitting in the hall outside the room. They looked very old to Maggie. She'd never noticed it before. Maybe it was just the lighting, or exhaustion from their vigil. They both hugged her at the same time. Patrick said "The doctor's in there with her."

When he came out, Dan introduced her. "Maggie, this is Dr. Sanders. Dr., this is Megan's mother."

"Mrs. Ryan. I'm afraid there's been no change. We're having a problem controlling the fever. We're doing everything we can."

"I want to see her."

"Of course. There are gowns and masks there. And those booties to cover your shoes." He indicated a table against the wall. "There's an area just inside the door, separated from the area where your daughter is where you can take off the gown, mask and booties and dispose of them before you come into the hall again."

Maeve helped Maggie out of her coat and boots and into the gown and mask. The booties wouldn't fit over her boots, so she took off the boots and put the booties on over her socks.

As she stepped into the room where her daughter lay hot and still, it was as though she had stepped into one of those steel jaw traps, the kind that cause animals to gnaw off their own limbs to escape. She felt the teeth of the trap closing around her.

The fever began to come down the next afternoon. Her skin, that had felt on fire under Maggie's hand, began to cool. The day after that, the Doctor said he felt that Megan was going to be alright. Two hours after he said that, the fever spiked again.

It went that way, back and forth, for the first week.. The entire time, one of the nurses, who had a little girl of her own, brought Maggie tea and broth and sat with her to be sure she ate and drank.

Then, one morning, Megan opened her eyes and smiled at her mother. She began to get better. Maggie, afraid to hope, watched for the downturn, but it didn't come. The nurse, whose name was Mrs. Bantle, convinced Maggie it would be alright if she left Megan for just a little while, and took Maggie down to the nurses dressing room so that she could shower and put on the clean clothes Dan had brought her from home, clothes she'd left behind and never expected to wear again.

When she returned to Megan's room and saw that Megan was sitting up and sipping water, Maggie went through her purse for change and then went to one of the pay phones and called Joseph. He was home. "She's off the critical list. I don't know how long it's going to take her to get really well, but maybe I can come home soon. How is Gabriel? How are you?"

"We're doing good, well, not so good without you, but we're okay. Maggie, I know you want to come home, but you need to stay there as long as Megan needs you."

"Oh, I know. But she's so much better. She's sitting up and smiling. My car's there so when it's time, you'll have to come and get me."

"Don't worry. We'll come and get you."

"I'd better get back to Megan. I love you so much, Joseph. Kiss the baby for me. Kiss him and tell him I love him so much."

When she got back to the room, Dr. Sanders was there, along with a man that Maggie didn't know. He introduced her. "Mrs. Ryan, this is a colleague of mine from Rochester Dr. Wiltern. Dr. Wiltern is a pediatric neurologist. I spoke to your husband about him"

"What's going on?"

"Now that Megan is starting to show improvement, we're

going to want to run some tests to see the extent of any cognitive impairment she might have suffered as a result of the meningitis."

"What do you mean 'cognitive impairment'?

"There are some disabilities that are often associated with meningitis."

"What kind of disabilities?"

"Headaches, deafness, loss of balance, learning difficulties, seizures, things of that nature. There's no need to panic. We don't know that Megan is suffering from any of these things. But we need to find out. Even assuming that she is, often they are only temporary."

"But they could be permanent?"

"They could."

"What else? Could there be any other problems, worse problems?"

"Well, at the worst end of the spectrum, cerebral palsy, loss of sight. But there's no indication of that in this case."

"When are you going to be running these tests?"

"We've already begun. There are any number of things we can do here, but as soon as she's able to be moved, your husband indicated that he would like her to be taken over to Rochester. And, of course, that would be best. They can do things there that we just aren't equipped for here."

Dr. Wiltern said "You can come in with us while we do some preliminary tests. It would be good for your daughter to have you with her. Less frightening."

Maggie followed them into the room and watched Megan's face light up at the sight of her, watched Megan's arms open toward her. 'It's because I told Joseph I might be able to come home soon' she thought. 'That's why this is happening. If only I hadn't said it. If only I hadn't even thought it.' But it was too late now, too late to take it back.

Right there at Marinette General, it was determined that Megan had sustained some degree of hearing loss in the right ear. They would be able to pinpoint the percentage with greater accuracy at Mayo Clinic.

There was some partial paralysis in her left leg but it was too soon to tell if it would be permanent. That, of course, could be the reason for her loss of balance.

The good news was that there were no vision problems. And there had been no seizures yet.

Even at Mayo Clinic, due to her age, she was, after all, only 2 years and 4 months old, it was more difficult to assess the extent of cognitive impairment, the kind that would affect her ability to learn. That would become clearer as she approached school age. A private tutor who specialized in cases of this nature would be the way to go until it could be determined whether she would be able to attend a non specialized school.

It was decided that she should begin work with a physical therapist immediately.

Everyone agreed that it was fortunate that the Ryans had the kind of money that would enable them to provide the best care for their child.

And always, there was Megan, at the center of it, a smiling, happy child, who loved no one as much as she loved her mother.

All of this Maggie told Joseph in a very long letter. She told him too, that if she saw him or talked to him at all, she would never be able to do what she had to do, which was to stay and care for her daughter until her daughter was old enough and able to care for herself. She told him that she loved him just as she'd told him when she'd last held him in her arms, and that she knew he loved her the same. She said that he was her only man and she would never be with anyone else no matter how long they were apart. She told him that Marina had known this was coming, but had told her that, in the end, she would come back.

When she mailed the letter to him, she felt something tear inside her. When she laid down at night, in a bed next to her daughter's bed, in her daughter's room, she felt as though someone had placed a great, heavy stone on her chest. Her body ached for him, her longing so intense that she could scarcely draw a breath.

But each morning, she got up and smiled at Megan and they began the routine which Maggie swore would one day allow her daughter to live a normal life, to go to school and have friends and, one day, to find someone of her own to love the way that Maggie loved Joseph.

There had been speculation when Maggie had disappeared, leaving behind her husband and children. The stories had been wide ranging. Some had even contained elements of truth, that she had run off with her lover, that she had had his child.

When she reappeared, in response to Megan's illness, there was a little talk, but it died down quickly, in large part due to the tragedy of the little girl's illness, and the attendant complications. As is often the case in small towns, and close social circles, Maggie's sins were forgiven and she was taken back into the fold. There were always new scandals to entertain and so hers was quickly forgotten.

Chapter 3

On June 1 of the year that Megan turned 8, Patrick Kelly woke early with the idea to take his daughter Maggie and his grand daughter Megan out on the boat. It was a perfect day to be on the Bay.

At breakfast, he told Maeve of the plan and asked if she would like to go along, but she declined and told him she would work the afternoon at Kelly's so they could make a day of it.

He called Maggie just after 9 and she happily agreed to drive over with Megan and meet him at the dock.

Afterward, everyone agreed that it was a good thing it had been a friend on a neighboring boat who had seen him collapse on the deck, a good thing that the rescue squad had come and gone before Maggie arrived, a good thing that she had not been there when he died.

As it was, when she was told by that poor friend on the neighboring boat, she had gone completely to pieces. She had wailed and cried in the man's arms, oblivious to her daughter's hands clutching at her arm, and her daughter's frightened face and brimming eyes.

The poor man who'd known Maggie since she was a child had done his best but by the time Maeve arrived, having been given the news by another friend of the family who had come upon the scene, Maggie had gone to her knees, the man, unable to hold her up, had gone with her.

Megan, forgotten, stood helplessly next to them, wringing her hands together desperately. Maeve had gone straight to Megan, folding the girl against her, then looking down at her daughter, she'd said sharply, "Maggie." Then again "Maggie."

The sound of her mother's voice cut through whatever lost state Maggie was in. She stopped her loud sobbing abruptly as though she'd been slapped and let the man help her to her feet. "Mama. Daddy died."

She sounded even younger than Megan. Maeve said "I know, Darling" and she folded Maggie against her with her free arm, holding them both, her only daughter and her dearest grand daughter.

By the time of her father's death, Maggie had been strong for 6 years. No one should have to be as strong as Maggie had been for that long. Still, her strength continued, getting her through the wake and the funeral, even the grave side service and the funeral dinner in the church basement.

Connor and Sean got into an argument over which one of them Maeve would stay with after the funeral, but they needn't have bothered. Maeve went back to her own house.

When the Ryan's arrived home that evening, all of them, Dan, Maggie, Colin, Deco, Megan and Hannah went into the dining room. The family sat around the table and Hannah brought coffee and brandy and a soft drink for Megan. "I guess we can make an exception today and let Deco join us in a drink." Dan said

After that, Maggie said good night to her sons. Colin was now 21, and living in Milwaukee where he went to Law School. He would go back there in the morning. Deco was 17 and would leave for college in the fall. Like his father and his brother before him, he would attend Marquette. She and Megan got ready for bed. They talked a little about Patrick until Megan drifted off to sleep.

The next morning, Megan was surprised to find her mother still in bed when she woke up. "Mom?" But Maggie didn't answer. Megan touched her shoulder. Her mother was awake. She could see that. But her mother didn't smile at her, didn't respond in any way.

Megan got up and took her cane and went down the stairs, one step at a time, the way she was supposed to so that she wouldn't fall. She found Hannah in the kitchen. Her father had already left for work. "Mom won't get out of bed. She won't talk. She just lays there."

"Honey, sit down here. Here's the cereal and the milk and some orange juice. You stay here and eat your breakfast."

"Where are you going?"

"Up to see your mom. Don't worry. Everything will be okay."

Everything was not okay. Dan insisted on calling the doctor who told him that Maggie was physically fine, but suffering from depression over the loss of her father. He recommended that she be allowed to grieve and that she would probably be back to normal after a few days. The few days turned into a week. Hannah got Maggie up and into the tub for a bath every day. Then she got Maggie into a clean nightgown and saw to it that she ate a little something.

One day, Dan sat down on the edge of her bed and told her it was time for her to pull herself together. He understood her grief, but enough was enough. Megan needed her.

Maggie felt a fierce hatred of him burning inside her, as fierce as her love for Joseph and Gabriel. But she said nothing and she didn't get up. Megan took to sitting on her mother's bed and playing with her dolls or reading. When she got tired, she would lie down next to Maggie.

Chapter 4

One morning 3 weeks after Patrick's funeral, an old truck pulling a horse trailer turned off Route 41. The driver found his way to First Street according to the directions he'd been given. He parked down the block until Dan Ryan drove away, then he started the truck and pulled into the Ryan's driveway and went to the front door and knocked.

Hannah answered and looked over his shoulder at his rig. Then she looked at him. He was a round faced, plump Indian. When he took off his cowboy hat, his hair was cut in a long brush cut. He had a friendly smile. "Is Mrs. Ryan at home?"

"Mrs. Ryan is in bed, ill. Her father died."

"Could you give her this please?" He held out an envelope.

Hannah took it. "You might as well come in" she said.

She climbed the stairs to Megan's room. The door was open. Megan was kneeling on the bed, looking out the window at the Bay. 'Poor thing' Hannah thought "she should be outside on this beautiful summer day.

She walked to the bed and looked down at Maggie. "There's someone here for you. He brought this." She pushed the envelope into Maggie's hand, but Maggie didn't move. 'Ah, what the hell harm could it do' Hannah thought. So she said "It's not him, but it is an Indian. There's a horse trailer in our driveway."

Maggie's face came alive. She sat up and tore open the envelope. Hannah saw how her hands trembled. Maggie read - I bred your mare. This is her baby. I trained him up real good for you and he's ready to ride. The black horse is his buddy. He'll be a good horse for your little girl. We love you.

Maggie got up. "Where is he?"

"Waiting downstairs."

"Get Megan dressed. Hurry."

Maggie went into the bathroom. She brushed her teeth and her hair. She looked in the mirror. She looked 10 years older, but she was smiling. She went to the closet and found a pair of jeans and a tee shirt. She rummaged on the shelves until she found her boots. When she came out, she said "Megan, get your cane. We're going out to the farm."

Megan, happy to see her mother miraculously restored to life, hurried down the stairs after her. She saw the strange man in the hall, holding a cowboy hat in his hands.

Her mother went to him. She put her arms around him and hugged him. "Will. Are you really here?"

The man hugged her mother back and then looked at her over her mother's shoulder and said "You must be Megan."

Megan said "How do you know my name?"

The man said "It's an old Indian trick." And he winked.

They went outside then and there was a trailer with 2 horses in it. Her mother said "Megan, aren't they beautiful?"

Megan thought they were very beautiful and very big.

"What are their names?" her mother asked the Indian and he said "Your's is Laramie and your daughter's is Tally."

Megan said "Mine?" And the Indian nodded.

Then he said to her mother "He said you have a horse farm and that I should stay and take care of them until you can get somebody."

Her mother said "There's somebody living there who will be happy to have 2 more horses to take care of. Can we ride in the truck with you?"

The Indian, whose name was Will, swung Megan up into the high truck and she sat in the middle between Will and her mother.

On the way, her mother asked Will "How is he?" She didn't look so happy any more.

Will said "He's enduring. Stoicism, you know? Our people are used to having things taken away from us."

Years earlier, when she'd first come back and had realized that it would be a long time before she could go back to Joseph, she had driven out to the farm. It had been a rainy, gray day, but even if it had been sunny, it probably wouldn't have been any better. She'd thought that if she went into the bedroom, and laid on the bed, she could conjure him up, bring back memories of the two of them there together. But it had only been cold and lonely and she'd never gone back.

Then 2 years ago, Chuck had come to Maggie with a proposition. He had finished college and gotten a teaching job. He was working on his Master's and he was getting married. Would she be interested in renting the farm to him? Maybe if she ever wanted to sell, he and his wife Debbie could buy it. She was a teacher also. They both liked to ride and wanted to get horses.

Maggie said "What about your writing? Do you still want to be a writer?"

"You remember that? Sure, I do some writing. I'll probably never get published, but I'll keep trying. The farm would be a good place to write, don't you think?"

So Chuck, and Debbie had moved into the farm house. She had never been out to see them, because it was too painful for her to go there, but he called once in awhile and she knew he had horses.

By the time they drove in, it was mid afternoon and she saw that his car was home. When he saw her get out of the truck, he left the corral at a run and came to hug her. "Maggie.

What are you doing here?" He looked at the trailer. "You getting horses?"

"Joseph sent them. One for me and one for my daughter. I wondered if you would keep them here, take care of them."

"Sure I would. Will you be riding? You and your daughter?"

"Maybe we will. Come and meet her."

She introduced Chuck to Will and then helped Megan out of the truck. Megan leaned on her cane and shook Chuck's hand. After that, Megan and Maggie watched as Chuck and Will unloaded the horses and turned them into a separate pasture from Chuck and Debbie's two horses.

"Can't they be together?" Megan asked.

"Eventually, honey. First Chuck will watch them, let them get to know each other across the fence. If they all settle in, then they can be together."

Will came over to her. "Since you don't need me, I'll be getting back."

"Thank you, Will. Chuck can drive Megan and me back to town."

"Maggie, I don't know if this is the right thing to do or not. Joseph doesn't know. I didn't ask him. I know you two have to live by some hard rules to make this work. But you're entitled." He put another envelope into her hand. "This is from me."

Maggie watched him drive away. Then she opened the envelope. She found that her hands were trembling even more than when she'd opened the letter from Joseph. There was a picture in the envelope. It was a school picture. The boy smiled directly into the camera. A big smile. His eyes and hair were black. His face was Joseph's face if Joseph's face hadn't had a scar.

Chapter 5

Maggie had her first real fight with Dan 2 days later at breakfast. She had waited until Megan was outside with Hannah to tell him.

"Are you insane, Maggie?"

"No, I am not, although it's a miracle I'm not."

"She walks with a cane. She has learning disabilities. And you want to put her up on a horse. Are you hoping she'll get killed so you can leave and go back to your lover?"

Maggie stood up and came to stand over his chair. Her hand was raised to slap him, but she pulled it back. "No, Dan, it's you that I wish were dead. But you live on year after year so I guess that wish won't come true."

"I should divorce you. You won't be a wife to me. If Megan didn't need you, I'd throw you out."

"You could let the two of us go."

"Still trying to get away. Well, that will never happen

Maggie. Megan needs special care, care that costs a lot of money. You can't provide for her. I can. It's that simple."

"I talked to her physical therapist. She thinks horseback riding would be good for her. You can talk to her yourself."

"You went behind my back?"

"I wanted to be sure the therapist agreed before I discussed it with you. She says it's becoming a commonly accepted form of therapy. She knows someone who will work with us. The horse we'll be using was very well trained. He's very reliable." She didn't mention that the horse had come from Joseph, had been bred and trained by Joseph.

Finally, after a meeting with the therapist, and with the instructor who would work with Megan, Dan gave in and Megan began to learn to ride.

The lessons were held in the arena at the farm. The therapist suggested that Maggie not watch initially as it might make Megan self conscious. So Maggie began to ride on her own. She took Laramie and followed the trails that she and Joseph had ridden years before. She saw that Chuck and his wife had kept open the trails that they had broken through the woods

When she was riding there, she was almost happy.

Chapter 6

Maggie had been sure that the first years apart from Joseph would be the worst for her. She had expected that the pain would be almost unbearable and then would fade to a dull ache as the years went by. But the first years were so crowded with demands on her that on some days it would be late at night before she could think about him. Thinking about him hurt. Not thinking about him hurt worse.

From the time that the doctors had presented Maggie with their diagnoses of the complications resulting from the meningitis, Maggie had been determined that those complications would not define who Megan was. Megan would not be the girl who was partially deaf, who walked with a limp, who would never go to school with other kids, but instead would be taught by tutors who specialized in children with learning disorders.

Maggie didn't dismiss the physical therapist, the speech therapist or the tutors. She knew she needed them so she worked with them. And every night she and Megan lay awake talking. She told Megan that she would get better because she was strong like her mother. She made Megan believe. There were days when both of them cried with frustration. But the next day, they got up and started over again.

When Megan was 15 years old, she started 9th grade at Menominee High School. She still needed a cane to walk, but the only thing it prevented her from doing was participating in gym class. And Maggie said "I hated gym class so much. You're not missing a thing." Megan, who'd been feeling bad about missing gym, ended up laughing.

She was able to keep up in her classes by working with a tutor every afternoon when she got home from school.

When Maggie told Megan that high school was just a stepping stone to college, she was surprised at Megan's response. "Not for me."

"Why not, Sweetheart?"

"I'm slow. I hear people say that about me."

Maggie supposed she should no longer be surprised by the extent of people's cruelty to other people, but she still was. "People like to hang labels on other people. It makes them feel better about their own shortcomings. But remember, a few years ago, some of the so called specialists said you'd never be able to go to regular high school, but you're there, aren't you?" Megan nodded. "And you're doing fine?"

"Sometimes it's hard."

"Sure, it is. Life is hard. Anything worth having takes hard work. But you're like me. You don't give up. If you want to go to college, you'll go to college. I'd like you to do what I didn't do. I'd like you to get a degree. Just going to college is such a wonderful thing. You'll learn so much about so many things. You'll find out you have all kinds of choices in life that you didn't even know about. I want you to be able to make your own way. It's too easy to just live on Daddy's money. You won't ever know who you are, what you could have been."

"Why didn't you go back? I mean, after you had me. Women have babies and still go to college."

"My life took an unexpected turn."

"What does that mean?'

"Someday I'll tell you all about it."

"Mom, that is so mean. You can't say something like that and then not tell me."

"Even mom's are entitled to a few secrets." And she refused to say anything more although Megan continued to ask.

But now instead of talking into the night with her mother, Megan talked and laughed with her girlfriends who came for sleep overs. It was the beginning of the life that Maggie had wanted Megan to have and the end of Maggie's total immersion in Megan's life. It was as it should be.

Once Megan had passed the crises stage, Maggie had moved into her own bedroom and had asked Hannah to help her push the bed over so that she could look out the windows and see the water. She lay awake at night, alone, looking at the Bay that she'd been looking at all of her life and thought 'just a few more years now.'

When she had moved out of Megan's room, Dan had come knocking. She had thought he might, but then dismissed the thought. Surely he despised her and only tolerated her in his house because of Megan. Still, there he was, opening the door in answer to her "Come in."

He stood just inside the door. It was the year that Megan turned 4. Dan was 59 years old by then but still a handsome man. He'd never gained weight, never lost his hair. He seemed the epitome of the description "aging gracefully." He smiled. Maggie didn't smile back.

"What is it Dan?"

"I thought…" he hesitated which always jolted her, because he was ordinarily so good with words, a typical lawyer. Then he went on "I thought you might be lonely."

"Yes, Dan, I am lonely."

He seemed to take it as an invitation because he stepped further into the room, closing the door. "God, Maggie, I'm lonely too. I miss you so much."

Maggie stared. He took another step and she pulled herself out of the state of disbelief that made her speechless. "Dan, I'm in this house for only one reason and that's Megan. You know that."

"Yes, but I thought…"

"What?"

"Well, it's been years. I assumed it was over, that you'd gotten over it, over him, I mean."

"No, No, Dan, I haven't gotten over him. I am always going to belong to one man and that is Joseph. It doesn't matter how many years we're apart."

"You don't expect him to wait for you?"

"I do."

"You're fooling yourself."

"No, I'm not. Just go, go back to your own room. Nothing is going to change."

"I could divorce you for this."

"But you won't" Maggie said wearily. "You won't because Megan needs me. One day, when Megan doesn't need me anymore, then you can divorce me."

He had turned and left and he'd never been back.

Chapter 7

Maggie rode Laramie every morning. She rode the trails until the cold and ice drove her indoors. Then she rode in the arena. On Saturday mornings, Megan came along and rode Tally. It was no longer painful for Maggie to be at the farm. She could remember all of her times there with Joseph and it was good to remember.

One night near Christmas, Dan said "I thought we could have a party at the Dome for Megan's birthday. Maybe Colin will come up for the weekend and bring his girlfriend." Colin was almost 30 and still not married. He had finished law school and gone to work for a firm in Chicago and had recently called to tell them that he was engaged to an attorney in his office. Her name was Olivia and that was really all they knew. If Dan was disappointed that Colin had chosen not to practice law with him, he never let on. How history repeated itself, Maggie thought, and wondered if Dan ever remembered the years when he had lived in Chicago, choosing not to join his father's firm.

Deco, however, had come back. The sign in front of the law office now read Ryan and Ryan Attorneys at Law. Deco had married a local girl, Sara Morris. She was a nurse at Marinette General. They lived in the apartment above the law office. When he had told his parents that he and Sara would like to live there, Maggie thought of Michael, for the first time in many years. 'So' she thought 'my son and his wife will live the life that Michael and I thought would be ours.'

In addition to the family, Megan had invited her friends to her party, and some of them were bringing dates. This was one of the things that Maggie worried over and couldn't control. Would Megan have a boyfriend one day? She was a pretty girl and made friends easily, but now, halfway through her freshman year, she still had not been asked on any dates. Maggie wondered if there was a boy who wouldn't mind a girlfriend who walked with a limp, carried a cane. 'It shouldn't matter' she thought, but she knew that it did.

Then, the night before the party, Megan came into Maggie's bedroom. "Can we talk?"

Maggie had been reading in bed and she put her book aside and patted the bed. "Come on. Hop in. It's cold."

Megan got under the covers and snuggled against her mother. "I invited somebody to my party tomorrow night. Somebody special."

"Who?"

"His name is Mark, Mark Pedersen but everybody calls him Marco. He's from Menekaunee. I met him when I was with Grama. We went to Pedersen's, you know, where they have the smoked fish and he was working there. His parents own it."

"Is he cute?"

"Yes. No. More than cute. He's got blond hair and the bluest eyes."

"When did you meet him?"

"Last month."

"And I'm just now hearing about him."

"We just met that one time. But then he got my phone number from Grama and he's called a few times. But we talked a long time. We just had so much to talk about. He's got his license and he asked if he could take me out. You know, he just asked me last night for this weekend so I told him I was having a party and I asked if he could come and he said he would."

"I'm happy I'm going to get a chance to meet this more than cute boy. How old is he?"

"He's 16. And now I'll be 16 too. But he's a sophomore."

On Saturday morning, Maggie decided to do something she hadn't done in years. She stopped by Megan's room and said "I'm going shopping for a party dress. Don't you need something new to wear tonight? Something special? We can shop together."

Megan said "I already have a dress. Grama got it for me. You can't see it yet though. It's a surprise."

Maggie drove over to the Style Shop and there was Florence. It was as though time had stopped. Florence hadn't changed, still the perfect lady in a beautifully tailored black dress, her hair artfully arranged in a twist.

"You know, Maggie, I was beginning to think I'd never see you again. I have to say you have really hurt my feelings.

Where are you buying your clothes?"

"No reason for hurt feelings. I haven't shopped anywhere since I was here last and I can't remember the last time I wore a dress."

"So what brings you in?"

"Tonight is Megan's 16th birthday. I thought I should make an effort."

"I shouldn't tell you this, sweetheart, but you could show up at the party in a flour sack and look better than any woman there. Still, I think we can do better than that. Why don't you go on to a dressing room and I'll bring you some things to try on."

Florence went through the racks and selected just 2 dresses. When those dresses had come in, she'd thought of Maggie. Florence had her try on the black dress first. It was sleek, draped across the bodice with a very low back. "That's lovely." Florence said.

"But?"

"Did I say anything?"

"You were thinking something."

"I was thinking that you look very elegant in that dress, but a little too matronly. Try this." She took the 2nd dress off its hanger. It was pink, slim and simple in design. All of what Florence would have described as the excitement of the dress was in the fabric, a sheer layer covered in tiny beading, over a satin shell. She slipped it over Maggie's head and stepped back. "That's it."

Maggie turned and looked at herself in the full length mirror. "I don't know, Florence. Maybe it's a little too young for me, a little too much flash and a little tight."

"You're the only one I know who can carry this off. If you don't buy it, I'm sending it back."

"It's pretty. It reminds me of a prom dress I had once. The prom dress was a lot cheaper."

"No doubt. And you'll need just the right shoes. Check at Haase's. I saw something in the window that would probably work."

Maggie had second thoughts when she got dressed that night. It was Megan's night, and she wondered if the dress would make it look as though she were trying to take attention away from her daughter. She was beginning to wish she'd taken the black dress, when Megan knocked and came in without waiting for an answer.

Maggie stared. Megan suddenly looked like a young woman, not the teenage girl that Maggie was used to seeing. Her dress was the same deep blue as her eyes, It was not at all the type of dress she imagined her mother buying for Megan. The fabric was not unlike Maggie's dress, a sheer beaded fabric over a satin under shell, a rather low neckline and a skirt a little fuller than Maggie's.

"What's wrong? Don't you like it?"

"Nothing's wrong. It's beautiful. You're beautiful. It's just not what I thought Grama would choose for you."

"I know. I almost fell over. I thought she'd get me something all ruffly, like a prom dress. I thought I'd have to make an excuse not to wear it. But she said I was sixteen now so I should look grown up."

When they came downstairs together, Dan smiled and said "You two look like sisters."

On the way to the car, he hung back a little and said to Maggie so that Megan didn't hear "Isn't that dress a little old for her?"

"It must be alright. My mother picked it out. It's just a surprise to see her looking so grown up."

They had the private dining room at the Dome for the party, but there were so many people that they overflowed into the main dining room and the bar.

Megan watched the door and Maggie began to worry that the boy would disappoint her. She decided that it was almost as bad being the mother of a teenager as it was being a teenager. Then Megan's face lit up in a way that Maggie had never seen before.

She followed Megan's gaze. Marco Pedersen looked around in a way that Maggie knew well. It was the way she'd looked when she'd first come here, uncomfortable and out of place. But then he saw Megan and his face lit up to match hers. He was a tall boy with the strong physicality of someone who had grown up working hard, probably, Maggie thought, on a fishing boat in the summers. He was as Megan had described him, blond and blue eyed and more than just cute. He was wearing khaki slacks and an open necked blue dress shirt. He had taken off his winter jacket and was clearly wondering what to do with it.

He and Megan walked toward each other, meeting half way. He took her hand and bent toward her and said something. Megan smiled and said something back, then she looked around and saw her mother and waved her over. When Maggie got there, Megan said "Marco, this is my mother. Can he call you Maggie?"

"Of course he can. It's good to meet you Marco."

He reached out to shake her hand and dropped his jacket. When he had retrieved it and straightened, she saw that he was blushing. 'Not so easy to be young' Maggie thought. She said "Marco, we'd like you to sit at our table, of course. Megan will show you the way. I'll take your jacket to the coat check. I'm going that way." He looked grateful as he followed Megan through the crowd.

Once they had finished dinner and Megan had cut her cake, the disc jockey that Dan had hired set up and the volume of the music made conversation impossible. Maggie went to the bar and ordered a whiskey. She was waiting for the bartender to bring her drink when a voice behind her said "Would you like to dance?"

She turned around. The man standing there was what women described as drop dead gorgeous. Black curly hair, blue eyes, killer smile. "Who are you?"

"My name is John Franco. You'll be in very good hands. I'm a professional, dancer that is. I can tell from the way you move that you're a very good dancer."

Maggie considered. She couldn't remember the last time she'd danced. She stepped into John Franco's open arms and they danced their way from the bar onto the dance floor. By the time they got there, the music changed. Now it was a great seductive Latin rhythm and John Franco segued into a Samba. Maggie found it easy to follow him.

When the song ended, they walked back to the bar where her whiskey waited. He ordered a scotch and said "I was right."

"About what?"

"When I walked in tonight, I looked around and picked out the prettiest woman in the room. Then I watched her walk, and I watched how she moved when she heard music and I said 'she's the one.'"

Maggie laughed. "The one."

"I'm new in town. I really am a professional dancer, or I was until I got too old."

"Too old? What are you 30?"

"Thank you. Thirty-five. Anyway, once you're past 30, you have to grow up. You can't be a chorus boy anymore. Too much competition. Too many younger prettier chorus boys. So I decided to open a dance studio. Not to teach little kids to tap dance, but to teach grown ups. And I figured the best place to locate would be some small town, not too small, and a place where there are some people with money for dance lessons. Less competition, you see. But it's not working out so well."

"Why not?"

"I'm just not getting the business I'd hoped for."

"You aren't doing enough advertising. I didn't even know there was a dance studio for adults in this town and I live here."

"I thought that might have something to do with it. I have an ad in the local paper and I put up some flyers."

Maggie took a sip of her whiskey and considered. "That's not working so well."

"Right. Then I saw you and I said what I need to do is find the right partner and go out and dance, where people can see us and say 'Oh, I'd like to be able to do that.' I think you're the one."

"Lucky me."

"I'm serious. What do you do?"

"I'm a housewife and mother."

"You're kidding."

"No. This party we're having here is for my daughter's 16th birthday. Those 2 handsome gentlemen over there are my sons. One of them is 29 and the other is 25."

"Darling, you must have married when you were 12."

"Thank you."

"I'm serious, you know. I could use a partner. You probably know a lot of people in this town. We can dance up a storm out in public and you can tell all your friends about me."

"I don't have a lot of friends."

"It's a very big party."

"My husband has all the connections in this town. That's him over there with my boys. Come on. I'll introduce you. After he had met Dan, Colin and Declan, she looked around for Megan. "There's my daughter, over there, with her boyfriend. I'd really like you to meet her."

"She looks just like you. Very lovely. Did she have an accident?"

"You mean the cane? No, no accident. She had spinal meningitis when she was 2 years old. It left her with some paralysis in her left leg, also some hearing loss in one ear and what is euphemistically called a learning disorder."

"I'm sorry."

"We try to avoid being sorry about things we can't change. She fought really hard for almost 14 years and now she goes to High School like everybody else. She'll have the kind of life she would have had if she hadn't gotten sick."

"I'm guessing that had a lot to do with you."

"No. I helped her as much as I could, but she's the one who did it."

They worked there way through the crowd to Megan and Marco. "John, this is my daughter Megan and her friend Marco. Guys, this is John Franco. He's a dance instructor. He has a studio in town."

Megan said "That must be a fun job. Teaching people to dance."

"So far, I don't have too many students."

"I'll bet my mom could help you with that. She's really good with people and she knows everybody."

"Well, maybe I can talk her into helping me get started."

"That would be fun for you too Mom cause you don't have enough to do. She rides horses, but she should have more to do than that, right, Mr. Franco?"

"Horses? That sounds like fun."

"I ride too, but not so much cause I'm busy at school. You should go with her some time. You could ride my horse Tally."

"Maybe I'll do that if your mom wants the company."

"You know what else? When you get a lot of students, you could hire my mom to teach. She's the best dancer."

"I'll give that some thought, Megan. Speaking of which" he gestured in the direction of the dance floor "why don't we get back out there."

They said good bye to Megan and Marco and as they walked

onto the dance floor, John draped an arm around Maggie's shoulders. "I hope your husband doesn't mind us dancing together all evening."

Maggie wasn't sure why but she felt comfortable enough with John Franco to say "He's the husband in name only. We stay together for the sake of the children. Child, actually. The boys are out on their own."

"Wow, don't you have any close girlfriends to confide in?"

"Not really. Not for years."

"Well, then, please feel free to consider me your new best girlfriend. I'm very discrete. I never repeat a confidence."

They had a lot more dances that night. As things were winding down and people were starting to leave, Megan came over to tell her mother that Marco would drive her home and would she please make it okay with Dad. Maggie agreed, and said "Marco, drive safely please."

At last, Marco actually said something. He said "I'm a very good driver. I would never take any chances with Megan in the car." He sounded so young and looked at Megan so tenderly, as though he were seeing some kind of vision that no one else could see, that Maggie had to choke back tears. She hugged Megan and then, although she knew it probably embarrassed both of them, she hugged Marco as well.

Chapter 8

Dan was surprised when Maggie suggested that they have drinks and dinner at the Country Club the following Saturday night, but he was agreeable although he suspected she had an ulterior motive. The ulterior motive joined them in the bar as they ordered their first drink. "Dan, you remember John Franco."

"Of course, how are you, Mr. Franco?"

"Fine and yourself?"

"Doing well. It's been awhile since Maggie suggested dinner here. Would you like to join us?"

"Thank you. That would be great."

The club was crowded and after dinner, a few couples started dancing to the juke box in the bar. Maggie and John looked over the selections. John said "There are a couple of things here. But if we're going to impress this crowd, I really wish I could bring in my own music."

"Maybe you can. Let's go order some drinks and talk to

Mitch." Mitch was the bartender at the club and Maggie had now known him for close to 30 years.

When he brought their drinks, Maggie said "Mitch, I don't know if you've met John Franco yet. John is a dance instructor. He has a new studio downtown on First Street near the Harbor. We'd like to see if we can't motivate some of this crowd to take some lessons."

"What are you up to, Maggie?"

"No one's put anything new on this juke box for years. I wondered if we could get away with bringing in a disc jockey, one with some good music to dance to. Then John and I were just going to dance, maybe encourage some other people to dance, no pressure or anything."

"I don't know, Maggie. The membership committee here is kind of old school, you know."

"What if I talked to them?"

"You can try, but I don't know how much influence you'd have. Now your husband, that's a different story."

Dan had been sitting a few seats down talking to another attorney. Maggie sat down next to him, with John on her other side. When he finished talking to the other attorney, he turned to Maggie. "Need a refill?"

"Sure." While they waited for the drinks, she said "Dan, I have an idea." Actually, the idea was taking shape as Maggie talked. She hadn't really thought it out in advance, but now that she'd started, she gained momentum. "I thought maybe we could put together a little fund raiser for the hospital. A dance, maybe, right here at the club. Have everyone pay admission and all proceeds to the hospital."

"I don't know Maggie. If you have to hire a band, you might not end up taking in much for charity."

"We don't need a band. We could hire a D.J. That'll save money. Maybe we can put on a buffet dinner that's included in the ticket price but everybody pays for their own drinks. It'd be fun. You have a lot of influence, so I'm sure you can convince the membership committee. If we really talk it up, we'll get a big turn out and we'll make lots of money for the hospital."

"Not to mention lots of potential clients for Mr. Franco here."

Dan's tone was wry, but not unfriendly. Maggie was reminded for the first time in years that Dan had always known her better than she'd realized.

"Will you do it?"

He took a long drink, then raised his glass to Mitch for a refill. Maggie waited. He made her wait until he had his refill, until he'd taken a swallow. Then he said "Why not?"

So Maggie filled another month of her life with preparations for the fund raiser, including a lot of dance practice with John at his studio. They danced and they planned and Maggie enlisted the assistance of her few friends at the club.

"We're going to need those ladies" she explained. "They'll help us get the ball rolling at the party and they'll probably end up being your first clients."

It had been Maggie's idea that she and John do a flashy Latin number, and then go around and get people out of their chairs and onto the floor for a Conga line. But she knew that they would need some people who would be willing to be first to join in and that was where Maggie's friends came in.

On the night of the fund raiser, Maggie, John and Dan arrived at the club early. The turn out was better than Maggie had hoped for. But when she took off her coat, John looked at her in disbelief. "Why did you wear that dress?"

Maggie looked down at herself. She had worn the pink dress she had bought for Megan's birthday. "Don't I look alright?"

"Spectacular. But you can't do any of the steps we practiced in that tight skirt." He looked around and saw Mitch behind the bar. "Come on." He pulled her along with him. When he got to the bar, he said "Mitch, you must have a knife back there. Something sharp that you use to cut lemons or something."

"Sure."

When Mitch came back and handed the knife to John, he pulled Maggie in the direction of the rest rooms. Maggie was laughing. "What are you going to do? Kill me for wearing a tight dress?"

He opened the ladies room door and seeing no one inside, he pulled Maggie in after him. "How expensive was that dress?"

"Very expensive."

"Well, sorry about that." He knelt down and turned over the skirt, located the side seam and began to cut threads. "Oh, great, it has two layers."

The door opened and Maggie saw Patty Johnson, gaping at them.

John smiled at her. "Just a little wardrobe alteration. We'll be through here in a minute."

Patty backed out and the door closed behind her. John said to Maggie 'Stop laughing. I can't concentrate."

When he finished, he said "There. Now if you get too athletic, the seams are probably going to keep unraveling until you get arrested for indecent exposure. Let's go."

Maggie and John circulated, moving from table to table, as she introduced John to everyone she knew and some people she didn't. Even before people had finished the buffet, the dancing started. At first, it was mostly slow, staid, the kind of thing Maggie had been seeing there for years.

But as the drinks flowed, John went over to the D.J. and they had a brief discussion and the music picked up tempo.

John and Maggie did a few numbers that cleared the floor and had people at their tables standing up so they could see better. Near midnight, Maggie said "I think it's time we pulled out all the stops."

John nodded to the D.J.. They had chosen I Go To Rio by Pablo Cruise for their big number. They had waited until everyone had plenty to drink.

Maggie had told her friends in advance so that when John and Maggie split up and started to pull people up to join the Conga line, they joined in immediately and that encouraged more people to get up and dance, as Maggie had anticipated it would.

Within a week of the hospital fund raiser, John had booked some private lessons, and a lot more group classes. A few months after that, he asked Maggie if she could help him teach as he was too busy to do it alone.

When things hit a lull in the summer, Maggie came up with the idea to advertise Dance as Exercise classes. They took a lot of business away from the Y's Health Club that summer, as word spread that it was a lot more fun to exercise at John's studio.

Every month, through the following winter, Maggie and John held a special dance at The Dome. One month, they did a Disco Revival, the next a Latin for Lovers evening, which brought in some new couples as clients.

When some of the women in the afternoon class confessed to Maggie that they felt self conscious and just couldn't relax enough to move the way she did naturally on the dance floor, she started the Cocktail Class. One day Margaritas, the next Whiskey Sours.

John said "You're going to get us arrested for selling liquor without a license.."

Maggie laughed. "We aren't selling liquor. We're just serving it. And I always make sure nobody has more than one, just enough to get relaxed, not enough to get arrested for drunk driving. By the time they leave here, they've danced themselves sober."

When she and John weren't at the studio, they were out on horseback. He was a good rider, and good company. Maggie sometimes thought that if it weren't for John, she'd never be able to make it through these last few years she had to live through until Megan was independent and no longer needed her.

As Megan's 18th birthday neared, Maggie asked her what kind of party she'd like. She was surprised when Megan said "Just family, and Marco, of course. I thought we could eat at home. And you should invite John, cause he's like family."

When she asked John, he said "That's really sweet of Megan. Am I family?"

Maggie hugged him. "Closest thing to it. You really are my best friend."

They were sitting on the floor in the studio after the last class, drinking beer. "Still, I don't really know anything about you, Maggie. I've known you almost 2 years. I worked with you every day and you cover my ass on Mondays when I don't get back here in time to teach. I know you're estranged from your husband but I don't know why."

That was the truth, Maggie thought. She had never told him anything about herself. Yet, he'd always been completely honest with her. She had known from the start that John was gay. It was something that he kept from everyone but her. On weekends, he disappeared to Green Bay or Milwaukee to as he put it "Be with my own kind." Maggie had asked him once if he didn't want a permanent relationship and he had said "Kind of hard to do in a small town, especially if you want to stay in business." And although she longed to tell him that wasn't necessarily so, she knew there were no guarantees. She felt it was very much his business how he chose to live and whom he chose to tell. And he had never asked her anything about her personal life until that day.

Suddenly she had the strongest desire to tell someone else everything and so she did. She told John. He listened and he watched her face. He saw that when she talked about Joseph, her face was stripped entirely of artifice, naked with love and longing and that her voice was suddenly joyful, just for the excuse to talk about him out loud, to relive some moment she'd shared with him.

When she'd finished, he said "How do you stand it? Being apart from him all of these years?"

"I'm doing penance in a way, I guess. And anyway, soon it will be done and I can go back to him."

"Don't you ever get lonely? Need somebody to hold you?"

"I do, but there isn't anyone."

"There's me, Maggie. It's the best thing about having a gay best friend. I would love to hold you and I would never ask anything of you."

John Franco held Maggie that day and a lot of days thereafter. It was the first comfort she'd had in a very long time.

.

Chapter 9

The end of Megan's senior year came quickly. Time, which had seemed to Maggie to move so slowly, suddenly sped up. It was time for Megan's prom. They shopped for a special dress and discussed the after prom party, but Maggie sensed something wrong. At first she thought that Megan was worried about finishing high school and going on to college. She remembered Megan's words "No college for me. People say I'm slow." She wondered if Megan still thought that way and had only agreed to go to the Center to please her mother.

It rained the day of the prom and Maggie said "I hope it stops. It will ruin the evening."

Dan said "Why? They'll be indoors." She didn't bother to explain the problems of getting from the house to the car into the prom, back to the car, and into the after prom party without ruining hair, dress, and shoes.

Instead she said "I'm going up to check on Megan. Marco will be here soon. Be nice to him when he gets here" she warned, knowing that Dan was less than happy that Megan had dated this boy from Menekaunee, as he described him, throughout high school.

When she knocked on Megan's door, there was no answer. "Honey?" She went in. The bedroom was empty, but the bathroom door was ajar. "Honey?" she said again and looked into the bathroom.

Megan was kneeling on the floor in front of the toilet in her slip. She looked up at Maggie and started to cry. Everything was clear to Maggie in that moment, in the look that passed between mother and daughter.

She wet a washcloth and bent down and wiped Megan's face. "Are you okay now? Ready to get up?" Megan nodded and let Maggie lead her to the bedroom. They sat on the edge of the bed. "How far along are you, Honey?"

"Three months, I think."

"Does Marco know?"

"Yes."

"What does he say?"

"He wants to get married."

"What do you want, Honey."

"I want to marry him."

"Are you sure?"

"Surer than I've ever been about anything. Don't be disappointed Mom. I can still go to college."

"Of course you can, Honey."

"I'm scared to tell Daddy."

"We'll tell him together. Do Marco's parents know?"

"He told them today. They're okay with it. I mean, he wasn't going to college or anything. All their kids married young. They're excited about having another grandchild."

There was a knock on Megan's door. "Honey, it's Dad. Marco's downstairs. Are you ready?"

Maggie went to the door. She said to Dan "Tell him she'll be right down."

When he was gone, she said to Megan "Do you want to go to your prom?"

Megan nodded.

"Feeling better?"

Another nod.

"Alright. I'll help you finish dressing. You go and I'll tell Daddy."

Megan hugged her. "Don't I have to be here when you tell him?"

"I don't see why you should. You know Daddy. He'll probably be upset at first. He can yell at me and then by the time you come home, everything will be okay again. We'll work it all out."

When they came downstairs, Maggie saw that Marco looked miserable trying to make conversation with Dan. She watched carefully to see how he looked at Megan, and she saw the same look she'd seen the night she met him. Satisfied that he loved her daughter, she walked with them to the door and whispered to him "Don't worry. Everything is going to be alright."

It was not alright, of course, when she told Dan. He looked at her and his face turned so red she thought perhaps he'd have a stroke or something and then this ugly scene would be over, but he went and poured a whiskey without asking her if she'd like one.

He swallowed and continued to stare at her. Then he said "She's just like her mother, isn't she? Well, I'll tell you one damn thing. She's not ruining her life by marrying that Menekaunee trash and having his baby."

"I'm from Menekaunee, Dan."

"You left there a long time ago."

"No, I didn't, Dan. I never left. It's always been more home to me than this house. This is not about me, though, Dan, or about you or what you want. This is about Megan and Marco and what they want. They want to get married and have their baby."

"I will not allow it."

"You can't stop it. They're both 18."

"She's still my daughter. She still lives under my roof."

"Not for much longer."

Maggie thought, Not Megan and not me either.

Book 6 - Maggie and Gabriel

If the place we come to in our life at last is the place we want to be, then the road that took us there is the right one, no matter how hard it was to travel.

Chapter 1

Joseph Dodge hated domestic disturbance calls. Some cops got a bad feeling when they made a traffic stop. "You never know" they would say "who's driving that car. You can run a check for Wants and Warrants on the plate and still get blown away by some freak with dope under the seat or some liquored up kid."

Joseph thought those traffic stops couldn't compare to the danger of walking into a situation where two people who used to love each other are right on the edge, in a place where any little thing, a look, an ugly exchange of words, a suspicion of infidelity could trigger a fight ranging from a simple shouting match to bloodletting physical violence, all too often fueled by alcohol or drugs.

He had been a deputy with the tribal police for 15 years and he'd never fired his weapon. He was famous for his ability to bring calm into a room filled with chaos. And he was almost off duty when the radio call came.

The dispatcher said "Hey Joseph, you anywhere near Birch Creek Road?"

Joseph thought about lying, but it just wasn't in his nature so he responded "What's up?"

"Domestic disturbance out at Del LeRoi's place. His wife called it in."

"No. That's not right. His wife took the kids and got out of there 6 months ago."

"Well, maybe she's back" said the dispatcher. "A woman called from out there. She said Del's drunk and she's scared."

"Alright. I'll check it out." The turn off for Birch Creek Road was a few miles ahead of him. While he drove, he thought back through the years he'd known Del.

They'd gone to high school together. Del had graduated, just barely, and never seemed to get it together. He married a local girl and had 2 kids, but he was chronically unemployed, drunk and abusive.

Joseph had answered a few calls out at Del's place until about 6 months earlier when Del's wife had taken the children and left for no one knew where. Joseph thought it was better that way, better for her, better for the kids. Del had looked for her for a couple of months but it had required too much effort and in the end he'd given up.

Joseph hoped she hadn't come back. As far as he could tell, Del was beyond help and that was alright, as long as he didn't take anyone down with him when he went.

He made the turn onto Birch Creek Road and started watching for Del's mailbox, thinking all the while about Maggie. She was always there, inside his head, but there were times, like now, when he really thought about her. He understood how people totally messed up their lives, but there was an undercurrent of resentment in his understanding.

If he had had the good fortune to live with Maggie, he would have been thankful every day. Nothing she said or did could have caused him to love her less than he had loved her at the beginning. If she had hollered because he forgot to pick up milk at the store, if she burned dinner, or was just generally bitchy, he would have kissed away her bad mood, and if he couldn't do that, he'd still be thankful to have her.

Maybe he'd just been living on dreams for so many years that he was being unrealistic, but he didn't really believe that. He laughed out loud just at the unliklihood of Maggie being bitchy, but then he saw Del's driveway coming up on his right and his laughter quieted.

It was that kind of place. It killed laughter. If he and Maggie had to live here, maybe things wouldn't have seemed so perfect to them either. The house was generally run down, with a sagging front porch, The windows were dirty and clouded, no way to see in. He wondered if Del could see out, if he had looked out and seen the cruiser pull in off the highway.

He stopped the car and started to call for back up, then paused. It was real quiet, no sign of trouble, but he had a bad feeling. He almost ignored it, then he remembered a day a long time ago when he'd gone out alone to face 5 armed men who were hunting on Maggie's land. When the dispatcher answered, he said "I'm out here at Del Le Roi's place. It seems quiet, but there's something wrong. I can feel it. You got anybody in the area who can give me some back up?"

After a minute, the dispatcher came back on. "Yeah, Jay Silver's close. I'm sending him over your way. I told him to come in without the siren, unless you want to change that."

"No, quiet's better. I'm going to knock on the door, see if I can talk to him. If it looks dicey, I'll back off till Silver gets here."

He got out of the cruiser slowly, watching the front door, watching the sides of the house for any sign of someone coming around from the back. Del's rusted out truck was parked in front of a shed that looked to be in better shape than the house. The door to the shed was padlocked so Joseph figured no one was going to come at him from there.

He unsnapped his holster and walked up the porch steps slowly. He knocked. From inside, he heard Del's voice. "Yeah, who is it?"

"It's Joseph Dodge, Del."

"Hey, Joseph" Del's voice was friendly. He cracked the door. Joseph could see one blood shot eye. "What you doing out here, Buddy?"

"We got a call from here."

"From who?"

"Don't know, but I've got to check it out."

"Yeah, yeah, sure you do. But there's nothing to check out, nothing going on here."

"Is your wife back, Del?"

"Hell no. Ain't seen that bitch since she took off out of here with my kids."

The wife might not be here, but Joseph was pretty sure somebody besides Del was. "How about you step outside and we'll talk some."

"No way, man, it's cold out there. Why don't you come in?"

Inside with Del was the last place Joseph would voluntarily go. The smart move was to withdraw and wait for Silver, but as he thought it, Del swung the door open and Joseph saw two things. Del was holding a rifle in his right hand, his arm hanging loosely at his side, but he could swing it up real quick and easy. And over Dell's shoulder, Joseph saw the girl, sitting on the sofa. She had a kid in her lap, maybe 2 or 3 years old and she had her hand over his mouth in an attempt to quiet him. She looked terrified. All Joseph noticed about her was that she looked to be about 14, and that her terrified eyes seemed to fill her face. She was just trying to sink into the background, as if she could disappear from Del's shack.

Del looked at Joseph and then turned and looked at the girl, something like comprehension in his face. "Hey did you call the cops?" When she didn't respond, he said louder "Answer me, you cunt, did you call the cops?"

More to shift Del's attention away from the girl than for any other reason, Joseph said "Hey, Del, nobody called. I was just passing by.."

But Del interrupted "Are you fucking with me, Joseph? Because I remember, you said you were answering a call, you had to check it out. Well, CHECK IT OUT" shouting the last 3 words.

Joseph's eyes scanned the room, stopped at the refrigerator. "Hey Del, how about a beer?"

"Yeah, good idea." He started for the fridge, then stopped. "You're on duty. Thought you cops couldn't drink on duty?"

"Hell, you're not going to report me, are you? I thought we were friends."

"Friends, yeah. We go way back." He opened the door of the refrigerator and reached inside for a can.

Joseph took a step forward, thinking he could catch Del from behind while he was bending into the fridge, but Del seemed to read his mind because he straightened and swung in Joseph's direction. He seemed to consider, then he handed the can to Joseph and reached inside for a second can for himself and shut the door, watching Joseph all the while.

The girl exhaled. It came out as a moan. Joseph gave her a warning look, hoping she would stay quiet, hoping Del would forget about her.

Del sat down at the kitchen table, looked at the beer can, said "Fraid you're going to have to pop the top for me, Joseph. Kind of got my hands full." He indicated the rifle in his right hand.

Joseph put down his can, opened Del's, remained standing while Del took a drink. Then he reached for his can, thinking maybe he could throw it at Del before he could react, get him off balance before he could raise the rifle. But he could see that Del was surprisingly focused. 'Don't rush it' he thought. Still he remained standing.

Del said "Remember that good old guy Marty something, used to bring 6 packs to school, pass them out by his locker?" He went on without waiting for an answer. "He was a good old guy, that Marty." He attention seemed to wander, and Joseph took a stop closer, but Del snapped out of his high school reminiscence. "Hey, you got a kid, right? What's his name again?"

Joseph hated to talk about his son in this place, but he said "Gabe."

"Yeah, Gabe, that's right. How's he doing?"

"He's doing fine, Del."

"Gabe, yeah, seen him around some. Didn't his Mama run off when he was just a little kid?"

Joseph felt sick using Maggie but he saw a way to connect with Del and he took it.

"Yeah, she left."

"Women. They're all no good, aren't they? Or good for just one thing, right? At least, she left you with the kid. Mine took the kids, both of them. I miss my kids." Del looked like he was going to cry. Then he cocked his head and said "What was that?"

Joseph had heard it too, maybe a footstep on the porch. He hadn't heard a car, but hoped it was Silver anyway. He said "I didn't hear anything."

Del stood up. Joseph thought he might go to the door in which case Joseph could catch him from behind. Del took a step forward and it looked as though it might go down the way Joseph thought it would, but then the kid in the girl's lap let out a loud cry. Maybe the girl's hand had gotten tired and she had let it slip from the child's mouth.

Everything happened really fast then, but at the same time, it looked like slow motion. Del swung in the direction of the girl and the kid. He raised the rifle. Joseph had no choice. It flashed through his mind that there had been too many of these times in his life, times when he had no choice. He threw himself between Del and the girl with the kid. When he saw the flash from the rifle, he meant to say No, but what he said was "Maggie."

Chapter 2

The morning after the Prom, Maggie attended Mass for the first time in many years. She had come down to breakfast wearing a dress and heels, the sight of which raised Dan's eyebrows. "Where are you going, all dressed up on Sunday morning?"

"I thought I'd go to Mass with you if you don't mind."

"Your reason being?"

"We should talk to Father Reilly about Megan's wedding."

"Megan is too young to get married."

"I married young."

"If I were you, Maggie, I wouldn't use that as an endorsement of early marriage."

"You're right. It's a different situation."

"Not entirely. She is pregnant. But these days, girls don't get married because they're going to have a baby. There are other options."

"Yes?" Maggie waited for him to say it.

"Adoption, abortion, or she could have the baby, keep it, raise it without getting married. I would be willing to provide for her financially. She could go to college."

"You would do all of that as long as she didn't marry Marco? And if she chooses to marry?"

"Then her husband can support her, on a fisherman's salary. That should be quite a change for her."

"You wouldn't help them?"

"I can't condone this marriage. They're too young. It won't last."

"And you think it will end even sooner if she has to go through some difficult times. Well, you're right. They are young. But you don't know that it won't last. And even if it doesn't, they will have had their chance. They deserve that."

"Are you sure that you aren't supporting this marriage

because there will be someone else to take care of Megan. You'll be free finally."

"Dan, Megan is 18. She's not a helpless child. She's ready to live her own life without me, whether or not she marries Marco."

"You're going to leave."

"You knew the day would come."

"I guess I tried not to think about it too much."

"Well, now you do have to think about it. So, may I go to church with you today?"

When he nodded, Maggie knew he was conceding to Megan's marriage and probably to her leaving as well.

After Mass, they joined the line of parishioners waiting to greet the priest on the church steps. When they reached him, Father Reilly said "Good morning, Dan. Mrs. Ryan, it's been awhile. I'm happy to welcome you back."

"Do you have a few minutes before the next Mass?"

"Of course. Why don't we walk a little." As they moved away from the small groups of people still lingering outside the church, Father Reilly pulled a pack of cigarettes out of his pocket and offered it to them. When they declined, he lit one and returned the pack to a pocket under his cassock. Then he said "I'm happy to see the two of you together."

Maggie realized the priest thought they were there to request marital counseling. She wondered what Dan had told him, how much he had confided or confessed over the years. "It's about our daughter Megan. She and her boyfriend Mark Pedersen are getting married. We'd like you to perform the ceremony."

"Surely little Megan can't be old enough to marry?"

"She and her boyfriend are 18. They're graduating high school this week."

"She's pregnant" Dan broke in.

Father Reilly looked from Dan to Maggie. "Does she want to get married?"

Maggie said "Yes" and Dan said "She thinks so."

Maggie was surprised by the priest's response. "There are other options these days. It's no disgrace to have a baby out of wedlock. Plenty are doing it."

"I thought that the Church would be more supportive of marrying." Maggie said.

"We are indeed supportive of marriages that last a lifetime, as they were intended to. That's why we counsel couples to be sure before they go ahead. So many young people today think that till death do us part means or until we get tired of each other." Maggie wondered whether she was being paranoid or whether Father Reilly was addressing his remarks to her.

"Megan and Marco are sure."

"Yes, well, that's fine, Mrs. Ryan. Why don't we set a time for the two of them to come and meet with me?"

When they left the church, Maggie saw that Dan appeared pleased by the way things had gone, clearly hoping that Father Reilly would convince Megan not to marry.

When they got home, she went upstairs and found Megan still in bed. "How are you, Honey?"

"I'm okay. I was hiding. Did you tell Daddy?"

"I did."

"What did he say? Is he very mad?"

"He was a little mad at first, but he'll get over it. We talked to Father Reilly today. He'd like to meet with you and Marco."

"Why?"

"He wants to be sure you and Marco really want to get married."

"We do. Why do we have to talk to him?"

"Because he's the one doing the marrying. If you're sure, you'll convince him and that will be that. I thought we might go over to the Pedersen's today. I haven't even met them and we're having a grandchild together."

"I'll call Marco and see." She sat up and reached for the phone. Maggie watched her face get flushed and happy while she talked to Marco.

Maybe they were too young, but as far as Maggie could see, they loved each other. In that moment, she decided that no one was going to interfere with her daughter's happiness. If Megan and Marco wanted to marry, they would marry.

She knew there would be those who would criticize her, who would judge her harshly for encouraging her daughter's early marriage. But she was long past worrying about the judgments of other people. Because she knew something more. The right to choose had been taken away from her when she was Megan's age. And 15 years ago, she had been forced to make a choice that no one should have to make, a choice between two children, and between a child and the man she loved. Megan would make her own choice. If it was the wrong one, at least it would be hers.

In response to Megan's call, the Pedersens invited the Ryans to lunch that day. Dan declined to go and shut himself up in the den. Megan thought of going in to ask him again, but he didn't answer her knock.

On the drive over, Maggie said "When we leave the Pedersens, we should stop and tell Grama your news before she hears it in the neighborhood."

"She likes Marco" Megan said, comfortable in her belief that her grama would back her up.

Once the introductions were made, Marco's mother suggested they sit outside. She had set up a lunch table under a big shade tree and there was a breeze off the bay that carried a faintly salty smell of smoked fish from the Pedersen's smoke house. It was a smell that Maggie had grown up with and associated with her neighborhood and it made her instantly at ease there.

She could see that Marco and his father, whose name was Carl, were close. There was an easy camaraderie between them that she had never observed between Dan and the boys.

"Marco's the baby" Sue Pedersen told Maggie. "I guess by the time he came along, Carl got the hang of fathering. Marco has two older brothers and one older sister. The boys all work on the boats, and my daughter's husband does too."

As they talked, Sue and Maggie discovered that they'd been in the same class at Marinette High. "Funny we never knew each other with both of us from Menekaunee and all."

Maggie said "I wasn't around much. I dated a boy from

Menominee High all through school."

"Not Dan Ryan" Sue said. "He'd be too old." Then she flushed and said "Sorry. That's me. Open mouth, insert foot."

Maggie laughed. "No, you're honest. I like that. It was someone else I dated." She didn't tell Sue it had been Dan's brother.

When Maggie and Megan had left, Sue told her husband she had been expecting Mrs. Dan Ryan but had gotten Maggie Kelly who'd grown up just around the corner. "She's real nice, isn't she? Just like she never left the neighborhood." Carl nodded agreement and went back to his Sunday paper.

Marco had asked Megan if he could go along to Maeve's but she told him no. "I'll call you later. Don't look so worried. She's not going to be upset with you. Everything will be fine."

Marco looked at Maggie. "Mr. Ryan, he's pretty upset though, right?"

Maggie hugged him. "He'll get over it."

When they got to Maeve's, she was sitting outside on the front steps. Megan sat down next to her. "Hi Grama, what's going on?"

"Nothing. I just got home from Kellys and it was too nice outside to go indoors. What are you two doing down here?"

"Aren't you glad to see us, Mama?"

"Of course I am. But you don't just drop by for no reason."

Megan said "Marco and I are getting married."

"When's the baby due?"

"Grama!"

"Did you think I'd be shocked? There's no disgrace in it. Connor was born a little early, you know."

"I didn't know" Maggie said.

Maeve shaded her eyes from the late afternoon sun. "Isn't that the boy himself lurking down the block?"

Megan stood up. "He wanted to come along. He was so worried you were going to be mad at him. I'll go get him."

Maeve and Maggie watched her go. "She hardly needs her cane when that boy's around" Maeve said. "I don't suppose Dan is too happy about this?"

"Well, you know Dan. He'll come around. He has no choice. She's 18."

"You'll be leaving now."

"As soon as they're settled."

"Have they any idea where they'll live? I assume they won't want to stay with Dan."

"No, I think that would be a bad idea."

"I suppose he'll work for his dad, fishing summers, and find something to tide them over winters. Will Dan help them financially?"

"He says no, but he'll probably give in. He won't want Megan to do without."

"Marco won't like that. They're a proud family. He won't want to be under Dan's thumb."

"No, he won't." Maggie thought of Joseph refusing his pay for work on her farm because it came from Dan.

Maeve watched Megan and Marco walking toward the beach. As they passed, they both waved.

"Maggie, it's lonesome in this house without your father, you know. They could live here if they didn't mind the company of an old woman. If it didn't work out, they could always find their own place. What do you think?"

"I think you should ask them."

"What would you think if I left this house to them? It's not so grand as what Megan's is used to."

"Oh, Ma, I don't think Megan cares much for grand things. She's always loved it down here."

"Well, then I'll talk to them when they come back from their walk."

Chapter 3

On Monday, after Megan and Marco's graduation rehearsal, Maggie went with them to see Father Reilly. She waited outside without being asked. After an hour that seemed like two or three, he came out with them and said "I think we can dispense with the Banns given the circumstances" and Maggie knew that at least one other person believed as she did.

She lingered with Father Reilly while Megan and Marco walked to the car. He said "They're very young, but they impressed me with their sincerity. We'll hope for the best."

"Yes, we will. Thank you, Father."

When she got to the studio, John greeted her impatiently. "You missed 2 classes, Maggie. I can't handle this place without you."

"John, I love you, you know I do, but you're going to have to learn to get along without me now. Megan is getting married and I'm going away."

"When did all of this happen?"

When she finished telling him everything, he hugged her. "I don't know how I'm going to live without you, Maggie. But I'm happy for you. Even though I don't know how I'll run the studio by myself."

"Maybe it's time you moved on too, John. Didn't you tell me that you met somebody who you really care about?"

"Greg. He's been trying to talk me into moving down to Chicago with him. Right back where I started from."

"Yes, but not alone. Maybe you should think about it, John. Wouldn't you like to be with him all the time, not just on weekends?"

"How can you be so sure about things? What if I give up everything here and it doesn't work out?"

"Sometimes you just have to take a chance, John. You can always come back here if it doesn't work out."

"That's easy for you to say, Maggie. You know Joseph loves you."

"And you're not sure Greg loves you as much as you love

him?"

"How can I be sure?"

"I guess you can't. Sometimes you just have to take that leap of faith."

"Once you're gone, there's really nothing to hold me here."

"Well, there you go, John. You might as well take the chance. You know, I'll miss you holding me."

"But you'll have Joseph to hold you. Am I invited to the wedding?"

"Of course you are. This is going to be a really busy week for me. I don't think you're going to see much of me here."

"As the mother of the bride, you're forgiven." He hugged her tight. "God, Maggie, I hope I'll still be able to see you once we're living so far apart."

"It's not that far." But she was surprised at how sad it made her to think about not seeing John every day. He had been so much a part of her life for over 2 years. He had gotten her through so many bad days, had given her something to fill long empty hours, had made her laugh when she felt like crying.

After that, she didn't have a lot of time to think about missing John. Graduation was the next day. Dan had planned to take the family to dinner after the ceremony but then Sue Pedersen called Maggie. "We always have a big family party for the kids and their friends after graduations and of course, we would like Megan to be here, and your family."

Maggie accepted without discussing it with Dan. He was about as upset as she'd expected him to be when she told him. "Are we going to be spending every major event in our lives with these people now?"

"In about a week, we're going to be in laws and you haven't even met them. And Megan would rather be there with Marco than out to dinner with her family."

Dan grudgingly gave in, realizing that he was losing every major battle where Megan was concerned. He left work early on graduation day, but when he got to the house, it was empty. Hannah had left a note on the counter to let him know that she, Maggie and Maeve had gone to the Pedersen's to help with the party preparations and would be home in time to get ready to leave for the ceremony.

Megan got home before her mother. Dan saw her get out of Marco's car, carrying her graduation gown. She leaned in through the open driver's window and kissed him goodbye, then watched as he drove away.

When she came in, she said "Hi Daddy. You're home early. "I wanted to have plenty of time to get ready. Mom and Hannah are still at Pedersen's, but they'll be home pretty soon. I have to go and shower."

"Honey, are you sure about all of this?"

Megan looked at him straight on, the way that Maggie did. She looked so much like her mother at that moment that Dan blinked in surprise, wondering that he'd never really noticed it before. She answered directly, not pretending that she didn't know what he was really asking. "I'm sure I want to marry Marco and have this baby."

"How can you be sure? You're so young."

"I just know what I want. Don't worry, daddy. Everything

will be alright." She stepped forward and kissed his cheek. He couldn't remember the last time she'd done that.

He had no words to answer her certainty, so he just watched her go up the stairs, wondering why they'd never thought that the stairs must be hard for her. She took one step at a time, right foot, then left, then the next step, right foot first, then left.

Maggie would have said 'Of course it's hard for her. Life is hard, but if she wants to live a normal life, she'll have to learn to do it.' Had Maggie really said that, years earlier when Megan was just a little girl, or was he only imagining it, knowing it was the kind of thing Maggie would say?

He thought he might start to cry, so he went in and poured a glass of scotch and before he had finished it, he heard the car and then Maggie and Hannah came through the front door and there was no time for a show of emotion.

His nostalgia continued unabated throughout the graduation ceremony, not so different from his own. Could that really have been 55 years ago? He looked at Maggie, sitting next to him. Only 18 when he married her, she would turn 50 in just a few weeks, yet she still looked almost like a girl to him.

After the ceremony, Megan rode to the Pedersen's with Marco, while he, Maggie, Hannah and Maeve rode together.

It was the kind of party he would have expected. Dozens of people he didn't know and couldn't keep straight, a long table loaded with a variety of home made food, tubs of ice water filled with beer and soda and a make shift bar with bottles of hard liquor.

There were tables and chairs set up in the yard, and the trees were strung with Christmas lights. There was loud conversation and even louder music and most everyone was up and dancing.

He realized as he watched Maggie move through the crowd, talking to everyone, that she had been right when she told him she'd never left this neighborhood. It would always be more home to her than his house had been.

Declan and his wife seemed to know everyone and he wondered how that could be. Megan had undoubtedly spent more time here than he'd been aware of, but how was it that Deco seemed equally at home?

"Feeling a little overwhelmed?" He turned to see Sue

Pedersen smiling up at him. She was Maggie' age, he knew, but looked a little more faded, a little older, but still a pretty woman, blonde and a little overweight. He supposed that most people would have described her as down to earth.

"I've always been pretty good at remembering names, but I'll admit I'm not doing so well at it tonight."

"Yeah, there are an awful lot of people here. Once the kids are married, you'll have plenty of time to get to know everyone. It'll be easier then." He was aware that she was studying his face, watching for what?

"I suppose you're right."

"Look, Dan, is it alright if I call you Dan?"

"Of course."

"I know this is not what you would have chosen for your daughter. I'm sure you feel she could have done better than my son. But she loves him, and believe me, Megan is his whole life. He'll take good care of her and he'll be a good husband and father. It's the way he was raised. You probably don't believe me now, but you'll see that I'm right as the years go by."

"Maggie seems to agree with you."

"Maggie is a good woman."

"You think so?"

"You don't?"

"She's leaving me, you know. Just as soon as the children are married." He had no idea why he was confiding this to a woman he'd just met.

"I didn't know. I'm sorry."

"You can be sorry for me, but there's no need for you to be sorry for her. You see, I've kept her from the man she loves for a long time now, more than 16 years. I used Megan to do it. Some women might have resented the child for tethering them to a place they didn't want to be, but Maggie never did."

"No, Maggie wouldn't do that."

"I don't know why I'm telling you these things. I guess I've had too much to drink and I need to confess to someone other than my priest. Maybe I'm afraid he'll refuse me absolution."

"Do you think your sins are that terrible?"

"I don't know anymore. There was a time when I blamed Maggie for everything, but now I see that wasn't fair. Do you have any more of this fine Scotch?"

He expected her to tell him he'd had enough, but she said "I'm sure we do. Come on."

He followed her to the makeshift bar where she scanned the bottles until she found what she was looking for. He expected her to fill his glass, but she took the bottle in one hand and beckoned him to follow her.

They walked away from the lights down to where the back yard met the water. She sat down on the ground and he sat next to her. "I didn't realize you lived right on the Bay. Just like we do."

Sue's laugh was warm. It seemed to come easily and he thought she probably laughed a lot. "Not quite the same as you do. This is the poor end of town."

"It's actually very nice here. All these years I've been coming down here with Maggie and I guess I never noticed."

He was silent again, staring out at the water.

Sue said gently, carefully "You spoke of sins so terrible that the priest would refuse you absolution. You don't need to tell me, but if you feel it would unburden you, it's like a confessional here."

"I didn't just keep Maggie from the man she loves. I separated her from her son. The son she had with the man she loves. He must be 16 now. She hasn't seen him since he was a baby just two months old. He was at her breast when I called to tell her that Megan was so very ill and she would have to come home.

But, of course, it didn't start there. It started a few years earlier. Maggie didn't want another baby. She'd gone back to college and she had one more year to go. I could feel her slipping away from me, more and more. I made sure she'd get pregnant, even though I told her we'd be careful. I told her what I told myself, that she could go back to school. A lot of women had babies and finished college.

After Megan was born, Maggie was depressed. More than that. It was as though all of the life went out of her. I started to be afraid that she wouldn't get better.

One night, I came into the living room and she was watching something on T.V., some PBS Special about horses. Her face was all lit up. She was smiling. I saw a way to make her happy again.

I went out and bought the farm, out on River Road. Then I asked around until I heard about some horses for sale. I drove up in the County and bought the horses. The man who sold them to me asked who would be taking care of them and I realized I hadn't even thought about it.

He told me he had a man working for him who was good with horses. The man was an Indian."

"Native American" Sue said softly. "They're called Native American now."

"Are they? It seems I'm always a little behind these days. I talked to him and, even though I knew nothing about horses, I could see that he did. I hired him to bring the horses and live on the farm, take care of the horses and the place, teach

Maggie to ride if she wanted to learn. Ironic, isn't it?" His tone was bitter. "I brought him into our lives.

From the first day, Maggie was in love, with the horses, the farm, probably with him as well. She spent hours there every day. I saw less and less of her. When she was at home, she wasn't really there. I could see it in her face. She didn't even try to hide it.

I don't know when they became lovers, whether it was right away, or some time later. But about a little less than a year and a half later, Maggie came home and stood in the doorway of my den. I knew before she spoke what she was going to say.

She told me she was leaving. I told her not to say anything she couldn't take back. I told her she could have it all, everything, home, family and her lover, as long as she was discreet.

She said she couldn't do that. She started talking about how much she loved him, how she would die without him. Every word she said was like a knife. I hit her. I was going to hit her again until she told me she was pregnant.

After that, I told her she would have to go away. I sent her to pack, only her clothes, nothing else. She thought I would let her take the children but she didn't make a scene when I refused. Megan and Declan were crying, I remember that. But Maggie held it together, for them.

When we went to court for the first hearing, the Judge was a friend of mine. He'd been a friend of Maggie's as well but he looked at her with such contempt. It was obvious by then that she was pregnant. We took everything from her. She wasn't even allowed visitation. I couldn't look at her face.

A week later, I called and told her she could see the children for two hours every Saturday. The only restriction I put on the visitation was that he couldn't be there. Every Saturday, she drove up from Keshena where they were living.

Colin only went the first time. He hadn't realized she was pregnant and it upset him badly. I should have warned him. When I dropped off the kids and picked them up, I would see her, her belly getting bigger each week with that man's child. Until then, I'd tried to tell myself that she'd come back, but once I saw that, I knew she never would.

She had the baby in February. In April, Megan contracted

spinal meningitis. I called Maggie and I drove down to get her. She put her baby into his father's arms and she came out to the car through the snow.

I'm sure Maggie believed that, when the crisis was over, she would go back to them. But by then, Megan clung to her day and night. And there were the complications of the illness. It would take a long time for Megan to get better.

I told myself it was the right thing to do. Megan came first. Megan needed her. And Maggie needed my money to take care of Megan. She needed specialists, and tutors, things that Maggie and that man couldn't provide. They had nothing, you see, except each other.

Maggie ached for her baby all of the time. Megan was too young to remember that her mother had had another baby. And the boys were just happy to have their mother back. They noticed nothing wrong.

But I knew. I saw the pain that was always there in her face. When she was with Megan, she would smooth it away. If you didn't know any better, you might not see it. But I did. I saw it.

Is there any forgiveness for me, do you think?"

"It's not for me to judge you. We all do desperate things sometimes. I'm not a priest but I will pour you another whiskey and we'll drink to the hope of forgiveness."

He touched his glass to hers and they were quiet until Sue said "Megan and Marco would have been welcome to live here. We have the room but I guess they've decided to stay at Maeve's. They can always get their own place if they find they want more privacy." After a pause, she added "You didn't know?" He wondered how she could read his face so well in the dark.

"I seem to be uninformed about most things these days. They could live with me if they wanted to. The house is big. It will seem really empty once Maggie goes." He realized he probably sounded pathetic, and he felt a need to explain himself. "I wouldn't interfere in their life. I suppose that sounds hard to believe given my past behavior, but I mean it."

"Maybe they feel that Maeve needs their company more, being older."

"Maybe it's just that Megan feels she belongs here. She's like her mother in so many ways. Maggie always believed it was somehow better to be poor than to have too much money. Nothing I ever gave her meant as much to her as that locket she wears all the time. You've seen her locket? She told me she bought it at an Art Fair but I know he made it for her."

Sue refilled their glasses. They sat silently side by side looking out at the Bay. Finally he said "I'd like to take care of the reception, if that would be alright."

"Of course. Your daughter is the bride. That's as it should be. I'll get you a list of guests so you and Maggie can plan."

"I guess we should get back. It's late."

He stood and offered his hand to pull her up. She looked up at him. "I would never repeat anything you told me. If you ever need someone to talk to, I'm here. We'll be family soon."

Chapter 4

Dan broached the subject of the wedding reception to Maggie the next morning at breakfast. "I would like to help you and Megan plan the wedding and reception if that would be alright."

"Of course. That would make Megan really happy. Why don't we wait till she comes down and we can see where she want to have the reception. It's pretty short notice so she may not get her first choice."

Megan's first choice was The Flying Dutchman at The Dome. Dan was skeptical. "It's an awfully small room, Honey. I think by the time we add up the guests, it'll be really crowded."

Maggie said "The dining room is small, but in this weather, we can have tables outside, And we'll probably have a better chance of booking it last minute than we would with someplace bigger."

Dan called and confirmed the room was available and put Maggie on the phone to discuss the menu. When she finished, she said "Megan and I are going over to see Florence about a dress, then we have to go to the florist. Can you and Hannah work on a guest list for our family and then call Sue for her list?"

Dan found that Hannah had already begun. He poured himself a second cup of coffee and sat down with her at the kitchen table.

Hannah said "Our list is probably going to be shorter than Sue's. They've got 4 kids, 3 of them married with children and I suppose Marco has some friends."

Dan said "On our side, it will be Maggie, Declan and his wife, Maeve and me. I'll call Colin. I'm sure he'll want to be here and he'll probably bring Olivia."

"Maggie will want to invite John Franco and Chuck and Debbie Schmitt. Have you called Erin?"

"I didn't think of it. Everything's happening so fast."

"It will all work out, Dan."

"Surely Megan has some girlfriends. Someone to be Maid of Honor and Bridesmaids."

"Megan wants Maggie to be her Maid of Honor."

"The Bride's mother can't be the Maid of Honor."

Hannah gave him the look he'd been getting from her for years every time he said something that she considered ridiculous. "Of course she can. The Maid of Honor can be anyone the Bride chooses. And Megan chose Maggie."

Dan stood up slowly. He felt a hundred years old. "I'll call Erin."

******

At The Style Shop, Florence told Megan "I dressed your mother for her wedding, you know. And you are going to be as beautiful a Bride as she was."

"I don't want a big fancy dress. I thought something simple, maybe not floor length. And no veil."

"Are you sure, sweetheart? It's your special day. You can wear anything you like, but your dress should be memorable."

Maggie smiled and then started to laugh. Megan looked surprised. "What's funny?"

"A long time ago, I took your Grandmother's wedding dress out of the trunk where she kept it, all wrapped in tissue. I was about 8 years old. I put it on and paraded down the street. I thought I looked just lovely."

"What happened?"

"She caught me, of course. I still remember how she looked. You know, when she got really mad, her face would get very red, so you couldn't even see her freckles. Then she'd go all white and the freckles would reappear, like magic."

"What did she do, Mom? Did she hit you?"

"Oh, my no. No hitting in our house. It was almost worse than a spanking. She just had this look, like I'd stabbed her right through the heart."

"What happened?"

"My Da came home and saw me crying so he took me fishing. He told Grama it was only a dress. He didn't understand, you see. It is important that you have the right dress. Don't settle, Honey. Let Florence find you something wonderful to wear.""

While Megan tried on dresses, Maggie told Florence about Megan's decision to have Maggie as her Maid of Honor. "Maybe once she makes her choice, you can help me find something appropriate for a 49 year old Maid of Honor. And I hope you're going to be able to come to the wedding and the reception."

"I was there for your wedding, Honey, and I'll be there for your daughter's. Now let me go and look, I think I have just the dress for you."

When they finished dress shopping, Maggie and Megan had lunch at Mickey Lu's. Then they met Marco at the Courthouse to get the marriage license. Afterwards, Maggie asked Marco if he could take Megan home on his way back to work.

From the courthouse, she drove to Jimmy Faller's office to keep an appointment she'd made on Monday. There was no one at his secretary's desk, but his office door was open so she called hello.

He came out to meet her, tie askew, shirt rumpled, without a suit jacket. He had a sandwich in one hand and waved her inside. She thought how different he looked from Dan, who always presented himself as the ultimate businesslike attorney, impeccably dressed and groomed. It was one of the many things she liked about Jimmy. He had always been honest with her and done his best for her at one of the most difficult times of her life and had remained her attorney when she returned from Keshena

"Sorry, Court ran late, right through lunch. Would you like half of this?" He held up the sandwich.

"No, thanks, Jimmy. Megan and I ate at Mickey Lu's."

"Lucky you. If I'd known, I would have asked you to bring me a couple of burgers. So, what's going on?"

"Megan's getting married Saturday."

"Congratulations. Who's the lucky boy?"

"Marco Pedersen from down in Menkaunee. A nice boy, nice family."

"The Pedersen's who have the smokehouse? Yeah, I know them. They're good people. I didn't realize Megan was old enough to get married."

"She's 18. I'd like you and your wife to come to the wedding. You would have gotten a formal invitation, but there weren't any. Everything happened pretty quickly."

"I'm sure we're free on Saturday and we'd like to come. But I'm guessing that you're not here just to deliver a wedding invitation."

"That's right. I'd like you to file divorce papers for me as soon as you can get them drafted. I don't want anything from Dan except my freedom."

"Well, you can refuse spousal support, Maggie, but you've been married a long time and I'm going to advise you strongly to accept a financial settlement. You're entitled."

"You know the circumstances under which I came back here, Jimmy. I haven't slept with Dan since I left here for Keshena. I've had a separate bedroom since I came back. I have a child outside of my marriage. Do you still think I'm entitled?"

"Maggie, no one is more aware than I am of why you came back here and why you stayed. Regardless of everything that happened back then, Dan has not played fair with you so yes, I still say you're entitled."

"Ask for what you think is fair then. But if he wants to fight us, I want you to drop it."

"You'll need help getting started Forgive me, but we're none of us so young anymore and you've never worked."

"Do what you think is best but let me know if Dan puts up a fight. I'd rather just forget about all of it."

"Are you moving out of the house?"

"As soon as the wedding is over, I'm going to spend the night at The Dome. I'm leaving Sunday morning for good."

"You're going back to Keshena." It wasn't a question. She nodded. "Have you contacted Joseph?"

"No. I want to finish with this life. I want to know that all of my duties here are done. But I know he'll be waiting for me."

"You have great faith."

"There's no reason for me not to have faith in him. He told me he'd wait for me and he knows I'll come back.. There's something else I want you to do for me. And it's important to me that we get it accomplished right away. I don't care if you have to bribe the County Recorder."

"'I'll just pretend I didn't hear that. What is it you want me to do?"

Chapter 5

Jimmy Faller called Maggie just before 2 the next day to tell her that he'd accomplished what she'd asked. "It wasn't easy, believe me. I don't have Dan Ryan's pull, but I'm not above using the Ryan name when I have to, so your document is ready."

School was out for the Summer so Maggie took a chance and drove out to the farm without calling first. Chuck was in the corral. When he saw her drive in, he jumped the fence and came to meet her. "Where have you been all week? Your horses miss you."

"I miss them too, but it's been a busy week. First, I want to invite you and your wife to Megan's wedding on Saturday. I know it's short notice."

"We don't have any plans we wouldn't change to see Megan married."

"The ceremony is at Lourdes at 2 and the reception's at The Dutchman. So you can come?"

"Absolutely."

"Good. It's mostly family, but you're family to me so I'm glad you can come. Bring your folks too."

Maggie took a breath. The more she talked about it, the more real it became to her. "I'm leaving here for good, Chuck. On Sunday morning. Once I get settled, I'll come back and get the horses."

"Of course. Unless you'd like us to haul them down to you. I assume you're going to Keshena. Joseph must be happy."

"He doesn't know yet. I know it seems strange but I just feel as though I have to take care of everything here first so that I can start over with no obligations. Do you understand?"

"I think I do. I'm happy for you Maggie, you and Joseph. You've waited long enough to have your life. Things shouldn't have had to be this way."

"If I can live the rest of my life with him, I'll be thankful. Now, there's one last thing. Can we go in and sit down and talk?"

Chuck led the way. "My wife's out for a couple of hours. Her mom's in the hospital."

"Nothing serious, I hope."

"They're running tests. Can I get you something to drink?"

"You have any beer?"

"Still like Bud?" She laughed and he brought out two bottles and handed one to her and sat down across from her.

Maggie opened her purse and pulled out the document she'd picked up at Jimmy's office. She handed it to Chuck.

He looked mystified, unfolded it and read, then put it down on the table. "I don't understand."

"It's the Deed to this place."

"I see that. But it's in my name."

"You always said you wanted to buy this place from me."

"I still do, if you're ready to sell."

"I want you to have it. You and your wife."

"You can't just give it to us."

"I can and I have."

"I can't accept it. It's worth too much money."

"Let me tell you something, Chuck. This was the place I was the happiest once. And I still love it. But I'll never live here again. I know you love it as much as I do. That's why I want you to have it."

"We can have it. We can buy it from you. We can swing a mortgage. We both work."

"Please don't refuse me. I've known for a long time that I want to do this. And there's one thing you can do for me in return that would mean more than you making mortgage payments to me. I want you to write your book and when it's published, you can put my name on that page where authors thank people in their lives. Just add my name to that list. Now, I have to go. There's still a lot of work to do. I'll see you on Saturday."

Maggie met Chuck's wife's car on River Road, heading home as Maggie was driving back to town. They waved at each other in passing.

Chapter 6

Erin arrived on Friday night. Megan ran into her arms. "Auntie Erin, you came."

"Did you think I'd miss your wedding?" She looked past Megan at Dan, sitting in the living room with a drink in his hand. "Well, some things never change." Then she said "Megan, Honey, do you want to come up and visit while I unpack?"

Megan said "I can't. Marco's picking me up. We're going out for pizza with some friends."

"What happened to those traditions? Like rehearsal dinners and the bride not seeing the groom the night before the wedding."

Megan giggled. "We're very unconventional, up here in the U.P. You've probably forgotten, living in New York and all." The bell rang and she ran to answer it. "That's Marco. You can meet him."

Once Marco and Megan were gone, Erin went in to see Dan. "You look like hell, big brother. What's going on?"

"My baby is getting married and my wife is leaving me."

He got up and poured another drink. Erin said "Could I have one of those?"

He poured her a scotch and refilled his glass. "Aren't you going to express shock, or at least surprise?"

"About Maggie, no."

"No, I suppose not."

"Where is she?"

"I believe she and the mother of the groom are seeing to some last minute details. She'll be back soon. She served me with divorce papers this week. She didn't even wait until after the wedding. She told me she won't be coming back to the house after the reception. She's driving to Keshena Sunday morning."

"Are you surprised?"

"No." He took a long swallow of his drink.

Erin was shocked at how ravaged he looked. She realized that he was 73. She had never thought of him as old and she felt a surge of unexpected sympathy at the thought of him living alone in this big empty house. "You're still working?"

"Yes. Declan's working with me at the firm. It's Ryan and Ryan. Funny, I always thought it would be Colin, but he's just like I was at his age, up and coming in that big Chicago firm."

"Are you very disappointed about Megan marrying?"

"It's not what I would have wanted for her. She's too young."

"Maggie married at 18."

His laughter had a bitter edge. "Maggie said the same thing and I'll tell you what I told her - I hope you didn't mean that as an endorsement. You see how well that's worked out."

She bit back her response, that Megan loved Marco, perhaps the way that Maggie had loved Michael, that if Maggie had married Michael, things might have been different. What point now in making him feel worse. He was her brother after all.

She was on her way upstairs when Maggie came home. "Want to watch me unpack? We can catch up."

When they were in Erin's room, sitting side by side on the bed, unpacking forgotten, Erin said "Dan says you're leaving."

"Yes, I am. I'm going at last."

"You look happy just at the thought."

"I am. I've waited a long time. I don't begrudge a minute of the time I spent with Megan, but there were times when I thought I'd die from missing Joseph and my son. If I hadn't told myself I'd be with them again someday, I couldn't have done it."

"What have you told Megan?"

"Nothing, yet. I'm hoping to talk to her tonight. I meant to do it earlier but there was so much to do. Everything's happening so fast."

"Dan doesn't look good."

"He drinks too much. And he's not young anymore."

"And he's losing you."

"You can't lose what you never had."

"You should have married Michael, but then I guess Michael shouldn't have run away."

"Dan told me years ago that he knew where Michael was all along. He thought that Michael wanted to be found."

"But he kept that from you. And he never contacted Michael. Jesus, Maggie, how did you stay with him all these years?"

"I haven't really been with him. And you know I stayed because of Megan."

"Did I hear my name?" Megan came into the room, flushed, smiling, happy looking.

Erin got up to hug her. "You look like a blushing bride." Megan started to sit down but Erin, with a look at Maggie, said "Don't get too comfortable, Honey. I'm exhausted from the flight and the drive up from Green Bay. We'll have time to visit in the morning."

Megan said good night to Erin and she and Maggie went down the hall to Megan's room. "Are you very tired, Sweetheart?" Maggie asked.

"No, I'm too excited to sleep. Will you come in and talk to me for awhile?"

"I'd like to do that." They sat side by side on a love seat in front of the window that overlooked the Bay. "Megan, do you remember a few years ago you asked me why I didn't go back to college and I told you my life had taken a turn?"

Megan nodded.

"You asked me to tell you about it and I told you that someday I would. And it's time. This is not an easy story for me to tell. You have to remember that what I tell you will be my story, the way it was for me. Your father would tell it differently and your brothers would remember it in their own way. And you, Sweetheart, you are too young to remember any of it."

Just after you were born, your father bought the horse farm and four horses for me. The horses were Beauty, Rio, Hank and Sugar. Laramie is Sugar's baby. A man named Joseph Dodge brought those horses to us and he stayed on to take care of them and the farm too."

Megan looked wide eyed, remembering something. "There was something about his face."

"He has a scar, just a thin line."

"I used to put my hand on his face."

"Yes, you did, whenever you saw him. Do you remember anything else?"

Megan shook her head. As she talked, Maggie wondered what Megan was feeling about these revelations. She realized that at some point, Megan had taken her mother's hand and was holding it between her own. It seemed to take a long time to tell but at last Maggie finished.

Megan said "How could you never see your baby?"

"At the time, I thought it would be easier, not just for me, but for him, not to have me moving in and out of his life. And I knew that Joseph would be so good at raising him."

"Mama, why didn't you just take me and go, get a divorce?"

"It was a difficult time" Maggie said quickly. "Anyway, now you know why I'm going and where. And I hope you and Marco will come and see us often, and that we can come here to you."

Megan hugged her mother. "Yes, I want us to do that."

Maggie started to stand. "You need to sleep now, Honey. It's late."

Megan's eyes got wide again. She looked as though she were somewhere else.

Maggie sat back down. "What's wrong, Sweetie?"

"I remember."

"What?"

"We tried to leave, you and me. I remember that part. It was just after Grampa died. You had been so sad. And then a man came and brought the horses."

"Will, his name is Will."

Megan went on as though Maggie hadn't spoken. "We found out the tutor was going to be late. She used to be there before Daddy left for work, but that day she was going to be late. You told me we were going on a trip but I couldn't tell anybody, not even Hannah. We didn't pack anything, but you let me bring my Barbie. We were in the car and we were leaving and then Daddy was there. He was so mad. He took me out of the car and carried me back into the house. I said 'I'm too old to be carried' and you were crying. He said awful, terrible things to you."

"He told me if I ever tried to take you away, I'd never see you again."

"He said other things, worse things."

"Megan, it's best forgotten now. It was a long time ago."

"God, Mama, I hate him for what he did to you."

"Megan, remember when I told you that this was my story and that your father would have his own? Your father loved you then and he loves you now. He thought he was doing what was best for you and maybe he was."

"And maybe he did it to punish you."

"Maybe I deserved punishment. You're getting married to Marco and that means something. I'm not an innocent victim. I betrayed your father. I betrayed our wedding vows."

"You were in love, you're still in love."

"Does that excuse all my mistakes? We could have done things differently, honestly. It's what Joseph wanted. But I didn't listen to him. Maybe we wouldn't have caused so much hurt to so many people, ourselves included."

"Everybody makes mistakes, Mama, everybody."

"Once you have children, you can't afford to make mistakes. The cost is too great."

"I love you Mama. I love you the most and I always will, no matter what. You could have stayed away, or you could have left anytime, but you never did. You must love me a lot, more than I can imagine. So now you go and be happy and I'll come real soon to see you and meet my brother."

When she got to her bedroom, Maggie got out the picture of Gabe that Will had brought her and studied his face. She wondered if he would be as forgiving as Megan, if he would understand how much she loved him, if he would welcome her back into his life.

Chapter 7

Dan ordered a scotch and, while he waited for the bartender to bring it, turned and looked around the room at the crowd celebrating his daughter's wedding. He saw Maggie standing at the bank of windows that looked out on the Bay, and it was as though 32 years slipped away in that moment, taking him back to New Year's Eve 1961. He saw Maggie in her pink prom dress, 17 years old. He saw himself standing just behind her in this room that had been dark and empty because the party was upstairs. He remembered what it had been like to kiss her, to feel that he had a chance to take his brother's place with her. The memory should have been bitter, but it made him happy just for a moment.

They had driven to the church for the wedding as a family, he and Erin in the front seat, Maggie and Hannah in the back seat with Megan. Declan and Sara had brought Maeve. Colin and Olivia had driven up from Chicago and arrived late, coming straight to the church.

When it was time, Megan standing beside him at the back of the church, she had suddenly turned toward him and whispered "Daddy, I don't want to use my cane. For once, I want to walk to Marco without it. I can do it if you help me.

And on the way back, Marco can hold me up."

So small and slight she seemed next to him that he barely felt the extra weight she put on him. He wished that walk could have taken longer. It seemed over before it began and she was standing next to Marco, Dan placing her hand in Marco's hand and she seemed to already have forgotten that her father was there, her flushed and lovely face, Maggie's face, turned up to the boy who would be her husband.

It was only natural, he told himself, to be remembering his own wedding in that same church. He had had a brief absurd hope that Maggie would be reminded as well, and would come to him after the ceremony and say 'Remember that day, Dan. We were so happy then.' And he would say 'We could be happy like that again. Remember that night, on the boat, Remember when I showed you that I'd renamed her the Maggie Ryan.' But no matter what he had told himself 32 years ago, he guessed he'd known even then that she had not been happy on her wedding day. Perhaps she'd been thinking of Michael and everything she'd lost. He knew then that if he didn't stop thinking about Maggie, he would break down and cry in front of all of these people. He finished the scotch and ordered another.

Although Dan would never know it, Megan's wedding day had brought a flood of memories to Maggie as well. She remembered that New Year's Eve. She had known how Dan felt about her that night, and she saw now that she might have changed the course of both of their lives if only she'd been wise enough to realize that she had turned to Dan only because she thought that she had lost Michael.

She thought of her own wedding day, when she'd been so young and so sure that she was doing the right thing, doing what was best for her baby. Still, what good was regret now? Perhaps life simply had to follow a certain course. And if she'd made different choices, would she still have found Joseph? In the end, if the life she'd lived was the price she had to pay for having him, she'd pay it gladly.

She saw that Megan and Marco were alone for a moment, outside on the terrace, not surrounded by friends and family wishing them well. She moved quickly to speak to them while she had the chance. As she approached them, for the first time she almost agreed with Dan. They looked far too young to be married, like children playing grown up.

For once, it was Marco, shy Marco, who spoke first. "I want to thank you for everything, Maggie. For helping us, for the wedding and the reception."

"Well, you can thank Dan for the reception. Megan picked the spot, but the rest was all his doing. Now, I have something for you. I known you didn't make any honeymoon plans."

"Daddy offered us the Maggie Ryan. He thought we might want to go over to Door County for a few days."

"Did he?" Maggie wondered if he'd been thinking of their own honeymoon when he'd made the offer. "So is that what you'd like to do?"

"Marco works on a boat. I know it's different, but it's kind of the same too. Do you know what I mean?"

Maggie smiled. "I guess I should have talked to your father before I made any arrangements, but I thought the two of you might enjoy a week up at the Grand Hotel."

Megan looked delighted and Marco just looked surprised. "Mackinac Island. I haven't been there since I was a little girl. And Marco's never been. We talked about going some day."

"How about tomorrow? You could spend the night here at

The Dome or on the Maggie Ryan if you want to and then drive up and take the ferry over in the morning."

"Mama, did you really make us a reservation?"

"Everything's all taken care of. I think it's a wonderful place for a honeymoon."

Megan hugged her and pulled Marco into the embrace so that the three of them stood with their arms around each other. When they stepped apart, Maggie said "Just one more thing. Are the two of you really sure that you want to live at Maeve's? It isn't just a financial decision, is it? Because I think a young couple might want to be alone. I know that you don't want to accept help from us, Marco, but I want both of you to be sure about what you want."

Marco spoke up again and he suddenly sounded very grown up. "Megan's real close to her grandmother and I like her too. It's really home for both of us. She'll be a lot of help to Megan when I'm working. And if we ever think it isn't working out, well, I hope I wouldn't have to ask for any help, but I'd do whatever is best for Megan and the baby."

Any doubts Maggie might have had vanished. She had a

strong certainty that, young as they were, these two would have a good life together.

When she left Megan and Marco, she searched the crowd for Declan and when she found him, she beckoned him to her. "Could I take you away from Sara for just a little bit?"

"For as long as you like, Mom. What's going on?"

"Why don't we walk outside a little, away from all this noise?"

They found a bench to sit on, facing the water. Maggie said "I'm leaving here tomorrow."

"I wondered how soon you'd go now that Megan's married. Have you told Joseph yet that you're ooming??"

"No. I'm just going to drive down in the morning and tell him in person."

"I'm happy for you, for both of you. And you'll finally get to know your son, my brother. Do you think Sara and I could come down and visit someday soon?"

"You know how much I want that, for all of you, Colin, and Megan and you, to know Gabriel and Joseph."

"Mom, I wouldn't count on Colin too much. Not now anyway. Maybe after some time goes by. He's always sided with dad. He won't be happy to hear that you're leaving."

"Perhaps he'll understand one day, even if he can't forgive me."

"From your lips to God's ear. Remember the day you said that. We were driving away from the farm. I told you I wished we could live there."

"I remember. Deco, you're my darling. Promise to bring Sara down to see us real soon."

"We'll just give you a few weeks to get settled. You call me with your number when you get there."

Her most difficult encounter was ahead. She considered whether it might be better not to simply let some time pass, as Deco had suggested, but felt it would be wrong to talk to everyone about her plans, everyone except her oldest son. She saw him at the bar and made her way through the crowd to where he stood. "Colin, we haven't really had a chance to talk."

"Don't bother. Dad told me. He told me you're leaving. You found someone else to take over Megan's care and now you're free to go."

"Megan married freely. She married the boy she loves. They're going to have a baby."

"You rushed her into it even though she's too young, just so that you can run out on everybody, the way you always do. You know, you're like a stranger to me. Living with you all those years was like living with a ghost. You were never really here. You lived inside your head, with him, as if the rest of us didn't exist."

"Is that how it seemed to you?"

"That's how it was."

"I'm so sorry that it was that way for you. I love you all so much."

"Yes, well, perhaps in your own way, you do. All of us but

Dad, of course. And, none of us as much as your bastard."

"Colin.." But he was moving away from her. She started after him, but he put his arm around Olivia and said something to her and they went toward the exit. Maggie realized that she'd never even had a real conversation with Olivia, knew nothing about her other than the fact that she was from Lake Forest, the wealthy suburb north of Chicago and that she was a partner in Colin's law firm.

She was sorry now that she hadn't listened to Deco. It seemed she had been a far worse mother to Colin than she'd imagined. She'd always believed that the distance between them arose from his closeness to Dan. She could no longer deny to herself that it was her own failure that had allowed this gulf to open and widen over the years. Still, she couldn't let go of her hope that in the coming years, he might forgive her.

Maggie was surprised to find that Dan had arranged for music for dancing after dinner. It seemed somehow unlike something he would think to do. It was the same disc jockey that had played for Megan's birthday party and the music was a good mix, a little of everything.

She found John in the crowd and said "Dance with me. It might be the last time we get to dance together."

"That would make me very sad, Maggie. I still can't believe you're leaving me."

"You know that one of these days you would have gone off with someone and broken my heart into tiny pieces."

"So you had to break my heart first. Maggie, you are cruel to me. But still the best partner I've ever had, on the dance floor anyway. See how everybody watches us."

"John, stop trying to avoid the subject. What are you going to do after I'm gone? Have you thought at all about what I said?"

"I've been thinking about it all week. Ever since we talked. I called Greg last night. I told him what you said, about it being time for me to move away from here, make a commitment. He was thrilled, of course. Because he's been hounding me for weeks to move to Chicago. He says a city is a more hospitable atmosphere for people of our persuasion."

"Sad to say, he's probably right. What will you do?"

"Not go back to professional dancing, that's for sure. I'm too old anyway. Greg thinks I should go back to school. Finish up the credits for my degree. Get a teaching job."

"Greg's got some good ideas."

"You think so? You think I should do it?"

"What have you got to lose, John?"

"What if it doesn't work out? What if he breaks my heart? First you, then him."

"You're not a very trusting person, are you?"

"Maggie, I don't know where you get your trust, after everything you've been through. You've never once in 16 years thought that Joseph wouldn't be waiting for you."

"He'll be there, John."

John held her close to him, then drew back to look at her face. "You are absolutely radiant. I've never seen you look more beautiful than you do right now. You make me believe in love."

Chapter 8

Maggie left a wake up call, never thinking she'd need it. When the ringing phone jarred her awake, it was a moment before she remembered where she was. She picked up the receiver to hear the night operator at The Dome say "Mrs. Ryan? It's 6 a.m."

She thanked him and hung up. It had been past midnight when she'd last looked at the clock and she'd been sure she wouldn't sleep at all. She showered and dressed and was in the car by 7 a.m. She was too excited to eat or drink anything. As she left the city limits of Marinette behind, she said aloud "Just two more hours."

She had always liked music while she drove and had put in a tape before she left, but she felt a sudden desire for silence and turned it off. She had imagined that when this day came the drive would be unbearably long but almost before she knew it, she was passing through Keshena. Then she was on the county road, watching for the driveway. When she saw the mailbox with Dodge painted on it, her heart began to pound. She could hear it and she thought that if she looked down, she would see its movement in her chest.

She turned in and slowed for the curve that she remembered. Then she saw the cabin ahead and off to the right, the horse corral. Beyond it, there was a big new riding ring that hadn't been there when she left.

There was no truck in the driveway. She parked and walked up on the porch. The screens had been put up for summer but the door was closed. She knocked, knowing there wouldn't be an answer. There was no one here.

She walked back to the corral. Four horses came to greet her. Two of them were strangers to her, but she recognized Beauty and Sugar. They came to her at once, nickering softly and Sugar pushed her nose into Maggie's hand. Maggie' s eyes filled with tears. "Sugar, my mare, my Sugar. I'm home. And I'm going to bring your baby back to you." Sugar and Beauty had to be in their 20's. Rio and Hank must have passed on by now. The other two looked to be fine quarter horses and once they saw that Sugar and Beauty accepted her, they joined the greeting committee.

After awhile, she walked back to the cabin and sat down on the steps. She wondered how long she'd have to wait for someone to come home. The morning sun was warm and she felt sleepy.

She must have dozed off because she came awake suddenly when she heard a truck coming along the drive. She thought she would stand up, but suddenly felt that if she tried to get to her feet, her legs would give out.

The truck stopped, the driver's door opened, and a dog jumped out ahead of the driver and ran toward her. When he got close, she saw that it wasn't Moses. It wouldn't be, she realized. Too many years had gone by.

She looked up as the driver came toward her. The sun was in her eyes but she was certain it was him and she said "Joseph." Then he was closer and she could see his face, Joseph's face, but so much younger than she'd ever seen him, and there was no scar.

"No" he said. "I'm Gabe."

As many times as she'd imagined this meeting, she'd never known what she would say. Then, before she could speak, he bent down, studying her face and he said "Maggie? Is it really you?"

Her voice shaking, she said "It's me."

He sat down next to her, never taking his eyes off her face. "You look just like he said. Just like your pictures."

She put her arms around him. She held on to him, wondering if he'd push her away. Why shouldn't he? How could he understand the choices forced on her? But he didn't push her away. He put his arms around her and he held her as tightly as she held him. 'Of course' she thought. 'Joseph would have made him understand everything.'

She had a sudden sense that she'd come too late. Afraid to ask, afraid to know, she stayed as she was, leaning into her son, waiting, waiting for him to tell her. He kept holding her like that, even after he started to talk. He said "You just missed him. I took him up river with the canoe. He'll be back in a couple of hours. Right down there, below the cabin. He usually canoes on Sunday morning.."

She laughed and it came out shaky so that he pulled back and looked at her face. "I was afraid" she said "all of a sudden. Afraid that I had come too late."

"No, oh no" he reassured her. "He's fine now."

"Now?" Suddenly afraid again.

"He got shot last year" Gabe said. "On a domestic disturbance call. It was really scary. If Silver hadn't showed up when he did, he might have bled to death. Silver is another deputy. Do you know him?"

She shook her head. She thought she might be sick. She saw that for Gabe, it had all happened long enough ago that it had become a story to tell. But not for her. She could see it. Joseph lying somewhere bleeding, close to death, while she, unknowing, went on with her life, doing what – dancing with John at the studio, shopping. He could have died without her knowing.

"Why didn't anyone call me?"

"He wouldn't let us. Grama and I wanted to, but he said he was going to be fine."

"Tell me about it."

"He was on the way home when he got the call. This crazy guy named Del who Dad knew since high school had some girl and her little boy at his place. He was drinking and threatening her with a rifle. Dad called for back up and then he went in because he didn't think it was safe to wait. Dad was a hero. Del went to shoot that girl and the little kid and Dad saw it coming and he threw himself in front of them. He was shot in the leg. The bullet just missed the femoral artery. It shattered the femur. The doctor wanted to take off his leg, but Dad said no. They put it back together with all these pins. Then he got an infection and they started talking amputation again. But you know Dad. Then they had to take out the pins and start all over again. But finally, he got better.

He needs a cane, but he gets around real well. He's on permanent disability. No more police work. He teaches piano and guitar. He still rides and works with horses. I help him out when he gets a horse that's a little hard to handle. We put that ring in a couple of years ago to teach riding.

You know, he never would have told anybody how it happened. But the girl told everybody how he saved them. He was a real hero." Gabe said it proudly. He laughed. "That girl, with the little boy? She wanted to marry Dad. Dad said, Thanks, Honey, but I already have a woman."

Something must have shown in her face, because Gabe said "He meant you, Maggie."

She had to have breathing room, had to have time to think

about everything he'd told her. "Moses died?"

"Yeah, years ago. He was pretty old. This is Mister. He never took to the canoe like Moses or he'd be out with Dad."

"When will he be back?"

Gabe looked at his watch. "Maybe an hour and a half or so. I usually meet him down there and help him get the canoe out of the water. It's hard for him to do that by himself."

"Tell me about you. You must be a junior in high school now."

"I graduated." At her look of surprise, he laughed. "Dad told me you skipped a grade so he thought I should be able to do that at least. I skipped two. I'm starting college in the fall."

"I missed everything. What do you want to study?"

"Medicine, maybe. I do okay in science."

"A doctor."

"Maybe some day. It's a long way off."

"The years go by fast."

"Are you home now? Home for good?"

"I am."

"He said you'd come back as soon as you could. He told me about Megan. How is she?"

"She just got married. She's going to have a baby. My first grandchild. She's going to come here soon. She wants to meet you." She wondered how he would feel about the sister she'd chosen over him.

He seemed to know what she was thinking because he said "Dad told me you had no choice. Megan was really sick. She might have died without you. You were all she had and I had Dad so you could do what you had to do even though it was almost too painful to live with. He said you were forced to make an impossible choice and that you were the strongest person he'd ever known because not many people could have done something that hurt so much."

"You understand a lot for someone so young."

"Did you ever doubt my father when he told you anything?"

"Never."

"Did you ever think he wouldn't be here waiting for you when you came back?"

"No. I always knew he'd wait for me."

"Then you know how it is for me. He said you loved us both with all your heart and you would be with us if you could and that someday you would come home. And you did." He looked at her closely. "You look really pale, really tired. Why don't we go inside? I'll get you something to drink. Are you hungry?" She shook her head. "Maybe you want to lie down until it's time to go down and meet him."

"I can't. I can't lie down."

"Alright. We'll just get something to drink then. Some lemonade?"

"That would be nice." He helped her up and they went inside. She looked around. "It's all the same. Nothing's changed."

"Not for as long as I can remember. Your clothes are even still in the closet."

He poured the lemonade and they sat down at the table. "Tell me more about you. Do you have a girlfriend?"

"Yes. Her name is Nettie. Antoinette LaChappelle. She's 18. We grew up together. I've always loved her. I think she always loved me too, but she used to say I was too young for her. Then I caught up to her in school and she stopped saying that. We're going to the same college in the fall."

"What does she want to study?"

"She's an artist. Painting, sculpture. She's very talented."

"Is she pretty?"

"Here, here's her picture." He got up and took a framed picture from one of the bookshelves. The girl was smiling. She had great round dark eyes and long shining black hair. The same high cheekbones as Gabe.

"She's beautiful. I can't wait to meet her."

"You will. We're both working at the recreation center for the summer."

"What are you doing?"

"A little bit of everything. Lifeguarding, teaching tennis, coaching baseball. We can head down to the river pretty soon and watch for him."

Maggie stood up. Her hands were shaking. Gabe looked at her and smiled. "Maybe you should go on down by yourself. I can come down and help with the canoe after you guys get a chance to say hello."

"You know, I was pulling that canoe out of the river down there when I was pregnant with you."

"Then you two can probably handle it by yourselves."

She touched his face, kissed his cheek. "You're so much like him."

As she went through the door to the porch, the phone rang. She paused on her way out, heard him answer. Then he said "Nettie, my mom came home today." She stopped to listen, thinking she should be ashamed to be eavesdropping, but needing to know how it felt to him, meeting his mother after 16 years. After a pause for Nettie's response, he went on "She looks exactly the way he described her, just like her pictures. It's like time stood still all these years. But the best thing is it isn't just the way she looks. It's the way she is. I mean, I knew he would tell me the truth about her, but it would be his truth, you know and he loves her so much, he would see her like she was perfect. But she is everything he said she is. And she wants to meet you."

Maggie didn't wait to hear more. All she could think was 'Thank you, Joseph, for teaching our son to love me even though I left him before he could remember me.'

She took the familiar path down through the trees to the river bank. When she got there, she took off her shoes and stepped into the water. It was colder than she remembered and the rocks under her feet were mossy close to the shore so that she had to step carefully to avoid slipping. When the water got a little deeper, the current kept the rocks clear of moss, but some of the rocks here were sharp. She began to make her way upstream, slowly, holding her arms out for balance.

She knew it was foolish, but she couldn't just sit on the shore waiting for the canoe to appear. She wanted to shorten the time now so she continued on her way, the current causing her to feel disoriented and a little dizzy.

She never heard a sound. He had always paddled so quietly, efficiently. She had been looking down, watching where she stepped, and when she looked up, she saw the bow of the canoe rounding the bend in the River just ahead of her. He had turned his head to look at something on the opposite shoreline so that she saw him just before he saw her.

She thought 'He looks the same, as though no time has passed at all.' She said his name so softly that she was surprised he heard. But he did and he turned his head and saw her. She watched the paddle slip from his fingers. She tried to run, knowing she couldn't, couldn't run against the current, on the rocks, but she tried anyway and slipped and went down, sitting in the water up to her waist, while he, even though he knew better, began to stand in the canoe. As it began to tip, she struggled upright and reached out for him.

The canoe turned over, dumping him into the water, close enough for her to touch, to grab hold of. They were holding onto each other, holding tight, then pulling back to look at each other's faces. She was crying and laughing and saw that he was too. She was kissing him over and over on his mouth, his eyes, hearing him say her name, asking 'Are you really here?' And she said "I really am, I'm here. I'll never, never leave you again."

Then she said "I'll get the paddle. I think it's caught on those rocks."

He said "We've got lots of extra paddles. Help me get the canoe out."

They had some trouble turning the boat over in the current. After a couple of tries, Joseph let go of the canoe and pulled Maggie against him. She could feel his heart beating, hear every breath he took. She thought she could never be close enough to him.

The current was stronger than she remembered. It buffeted their legs. If he hadn't been holding her, she thought it might have knocked her down, but maybe that was only because her legs felt so weak. It caught the canoe, spun it around, pushing it toward an outcropping of rock just past the place they usually beached. "The canoe." She pointed.

"The hell with it. We'll buy another one."

"No, no Joseph, that's our canoe. We have to get it."

He let her go then and they waded to within reach. He caught and held the bow end while Maggie moved to the stern. Then he said "On 3. Are you ready?" She nodded and watched his face while he counted. On 3, they turned it easily and pulled it back to the shoreline. Maggie pulled her end out of the water first and once it was on the sand, Joseph pushed it the rest of the way out of the water.

She saw that he stood uncertainly, looking around. "What's wrong?"

"My cane was in the bottom of the canoe."

She waded back in until she was about where she thought the canoe had gone over. The water was so clear that she could see to the bottom and after a minute she saw the cane. It was heavy enough that the water didn't move it. She bent down and retrieved it and waded back to him.

He took it from her. "Do you know about this?"

"Gabe told me, but I want to hear it from you one day."

"I'm a wreck of a man, Maggie and you don't look a day older."

"You see me that way because you love me. We need to get out of here before our feet freeze off"

"I can't use the cane here." He indicated the rocks. "Can you help me to the shore? I'll try not to put too much weight on you."

"Please put all your weight on me." He put an arm over her shoulder and she put an arm around his waist. She moved slowly, conscious of her own unsteadiness. It wasn't so far, but it took them longer than she had expected. When they were on solid ground, she said "Don't let go of me." As they started up the little rise that led to the cabin, she said "We need to bring the canoe up to the shed."

He laughed. "We'll get it later."

The dog didn't run to greet them and the truck was gone. "Where's Gabe gone to? You don't think he left because of me? We talked, everything was so good."

"Maggie, you don't need to worry about Gabe." As they came

up the steps to the screened porch, she saw a piece of cardboard tacked on the post next to the door. "He always leaves a note when he goes somewhere" Joseph told her.

They read it together. It said "Dear Mom and Dad, Nettie and I are going to a movie. We're having dinner at Grama's and I'm sleeping over there tonight. Sixteen years! Don't think I want to be around while you two are getting to know each other again.

I'll be home tomorrow after work. If you need the truck, call Grama but you've got Mom's car if you want to go anywhere. I'm sure you won't. Love, Gabe P. S. Mister came with me so all you have to do is feed the horses."

Maggie said "When I got here, he was just driving in. The sun was in my eyes and I thought it was you for a minute. He knew me right away. All the while we were talking, he called me Maggie."

"Well, it looks like you're Mom now. We have to get out of these wet clothes."

"Can we undress out here? So we don't drip water all over the floor inside." She was having trouble catching her breath and her words were so low, she thought he might not have heard, but he reached out and started to unbutton her shirt.

"We still don't have any close neighbors and I'm not expecting anybody to show up." He slipped the shirt from her shoulders and it fell to the floor. He said "This opens in the front" as he unclasped her bra. He held her breasts in his hands and closed his eyes. "They feel the same."

She unbuttoned his shirt and pushed it off, then she drew him against her. The chill she had felt from the cold water and wet shirt was gone instantly at the touch of his skin against hers. She heard his cane when it fell from his hand and hit the floor.

She was already barefoot. He stepped out of his deck shoes and they unfastened each other's jeans and finished undressing each other. "I want to look at you for a long time" he said. "When did you stop eating? You're so thin."

"I'll gain it back now that I'm here. Let's look at each other in the bedroom. I want us to make love in our bed. If I look at you here, we'll make love on the porch floor."

He bent down to retrieve the cane, but she stopped him. "I'm here" she said. When they got into the bedroom she said "It's all just the same."

"After you left, I took the sheets from our bed and I put them in the dresser drawer. Every night, I pressed my face against them. At first, I could smell you when I did that, but after a few days I knew that it was just in my head. I still kept them there though. And the nightgown you were wearing."

They walked to the bed. She realized she could hardly feel his weight against her. They sat down side by side. She said "For sixteen years, I've slept alone. I've ached for you and pretended you were with me. You are the only man I've been with here" she touched her head "and here" and then touched her heart. " I lay alone at night and I lived on memories of the two of us. I haven't made love since the last day we were together."

"It was the same for me, Maggie. I lived on dreams of you. I never wanted anyone else. We have a lot of lost years to make up."

"I'm afraid I've forgotten how to make love to you."

He reached for her, laid her down, then lay beside her. "You haven't forgotten anything, Maggie. It will all come back to you." He held her face between his hands and kissed her mouth. He cupped her breasts in his hands. His fingers traced small circles on her skin and where his hands moved, his lips followed. From her breasts, he moved to her stomach, then lower. He parted her legs and kissed the inside of her thighs, pressed his face into her, immersing himself in her fragrance, her taste.

She was drowning in desire, reaching down to take his face between her hands, moving his mouth higher, back to her stomach, her breasts. Then his mouth was on hers again and she said "I can't wait for you. Come inside me."

When he did, she wrapped her legs around him. He held her head between his hands and they watched each other's faces. Then he said "Let go, Maggie, let go now. Give up everything to me and I'll come with you. I'll follow wherever you lead."

She had no words but his name and she said it over and over, obeying his sweet command, giving up everything to him.

Chapter 9

They lay silent in each other's arms until he said "I knew you hadn't forgotten."

Her laughter rang out in the stillness. "You brought it all back."

"Talk to me, Maggie. There's so much to tell it will take us a long time, but you can make a start."

"Megan was married yesterday to a boy she loves very much. His name is Marco and they're going to have a baby. He's a fisherman from Menekaunee. They're going to live with Maeve."

"Your father?"

"He died when Megan was 8 years old. We were going to go out on the boat for the day, the 3 of us. He had a heart attack. It was very fast and it came out of nowhere. I thought you must have known somehow because after it happened, I couldn't get out of bed for the longest time, even though I knew Megan needed me. I remember she would sit on my bed for hours, playing with her dolls. Then Will came with the horses. And I came back to life. Will brought me a picture of Gabe."

"I'm sorry I couldn't be there with you."

"Oh, you were always there with me. Every minute of every day."

"And your boys, Declan, Colin?"

"Declan is an attorney now. He works with his father. He's married to a woman named Sara. No children yet."

"And Colin?"

"He's an attorney too. He lives in Chicago. He's engaged. He hates me."

"He doesn't hate you."

"Perhaps not, but he doesn't love me. At Megan's wedding reception, he told me that he knew I would run out on him again, like I always did, all of his life. He said that living with me was like living with a ghost, that I lived inside my head with you. And he was right."

"Let some time go by. As he gets older, he'll see that he's judged you too harshly."

"Have you ever softened toward your father?"

"My father was cruel. That's something no one could accuse you of."

"Perhaps not physically, but if I wasn't there for him emotionally, isn't that as bad?"

"He turned away from you early on, turned to his father."

"It's always been strange to me that Colin is Dan's favorite. There's no question. And yet Colin is Michael's child. And Dan always knew that."

Joseph wondered if the day would ever come when Maggie's happiness wasn't touched by some kind of sadness. There would be time later to talk more about Colin, but now he wanted to bring back her smile. "What have you done all these years besides care for Megan? Did you ever go back to school?"

"I never did. When Megan was young, there was no time.

Then when she went to high school and really started to have a life of her own, I met a man named John Franco. He's a dancer and we met at a party we had for Megan's birthday. I ended up working with him at his studio, teaching people to dance. He was my best friend. I guess he still is. I hope you'll meet him one day. He's moving to Chicago with his lover. He told me I made him believe in love enough to give up his fear of getting hurt."

"I'm afraid our dancing days are over, Maggie."

"Oh, Joseph, I think I'm all danced out. Now you tell me everything about you, about Gabe."

"Aren't you hungry?"

"Are you trying to avoid telling me something?"

"No, I'll tell you everything. But I need food. I haven't been this hungry in years."

They got up. He pulled on his jeans, quickly she thought, before she could see his leg.

She put on the shirt he'd been wearing, loving the feel and

smell of it and followed him to the kitchen.

He opened the fridge and they stood side by side looking at the shelves. "There's a lot of leftovers in here. What looks good to you?"

"Everything" she laughed. "All of a sudden I'm starving too."

"Good, because you're too damn skinny. I'm going to put 20 pounds on you." He started pulling containers out. "Spaghetti and marinara sauce. Pizza. Which?"

"Both. Is there beer?"

"There's Bud." He put the food on the counter and opened two bottles. "Sit down and drink your beer while I heat stuff up."

She insisted on helping him. Once the food was on the table and they were sitting across from each other, he began to talk. He knew she wanted to know it all, all the details of their years apart, the raising of their son, all of the things he wanted to tell her without breaking her heart for what she had missed.

She cried in the beginning, when he told her how he had sat in the rocking chair in front of the fire on long winter nights, holding Gabriel, rocking him while the wind blew outside, making it seem even more lonely than he would have imagined.

On days that he worked, he bundled the baby up and drove to Marina's. And there Gabe spent the day, in the company of his grandmother, and all of her customers so that in no time, Gabe was known by everyone in the village. There were plenty of doting adults, and children to play with so that he was never a lonely child.

On Joseph's days off, Gabe was with his father, at home and wherever Joseph went. As he grew, Joseph taught him to swim and to fish, took him canoeing, hiking with the dog, and when he was old enough, Joseph taught him to ride the horses. He was riding bareback before he started school

In school, he excelled, skipping two grades as Maggie already knew. He did well at sports and Joseph taught him to play piano and guitar.

And always, Joseph talked to him about his mother, who wanted to be there but couldn't, but who loved him, loved them both with all her heart. Gabe knew the music she listened to, knew how she danced and laughed and loved books and lighted up the rooms she came into.

When Joseph had finished his story, Maggie said "Thank you for raising him to be a good man and for teaching him to love me."

"It was all easy Maggie, except for being without you. Having Gabe was like having a part of you here with me. If it hadn't been for that, I don't know that I could have gotten through these years." He looked at her plate. "You were starving but you've hardly eaten anything."

"My mother always said my eyes were bigger than my stomach. I guess I'm just too emotional to have much of an appetite."

He looked at his own plate. "I didn't do much better than you, but I was doing all the talking."

They stood up together and cleared the table. Joseph went out to check the horses while Maggie rinsed the dishes. When he came back, she said "Can we call Gabe to say good night?"

He called Marina and held the phone out to Maggie. "She

wants to say hello."

Maggie took the phone. Marina said "Welcome home, Maggie. Gabe hasn't stopped talking about you. We are so happy to have you back."

"And I'm happy to be back."

"How is your little girl?"

"Not so little anymore. She was married yesterday. She's going to have a baby."

"Will we see her soon?"

"Really soon. She wants to meet her brother."

"Good. It's time the family comes together. I'm going to put Gabe on now, Maggie."

Then Gabe said "Hi Mom."

"You didn't have to leave."

"Yeah, well, I figure you guys could use some alone time. I'll be back tomorrow after work."

"You'll be here for dinner?"

"Sure."

"Why don't you bring Nettie? I want to meet her. And bring Marina too. Oh, and could you pick up a couple of things for me at the store?"

When she hung up, Joseph said "Aren't you tired?"

Maggie laughed. "You're just trying to get me back into bed. But I need a bath first. Will you come and get in the tub with me the way we used to?"

While the tub filled, they brushed their teeth, side by side at the sink. Then they sank down into the hot water, the weight of both their bodies raising the water level almost to the top of the tub. She lay back against him. She remembered the first time they'd sat in a tub like this, the morning after they'd made love for the first time. The thought filled her with desire and she stood, pulling him up with her, stepping from the tub. They dried each other and moved to the bedroom, making love as though it had been years instead of hours. Before they fell asleep, she turned on the light and studied the scars on his leg. "Will you tell me all about this?"

And he said "Some day soon. Not just yet. But there is something I want you to tell me right now. When are you going to marry me, Maggie?"

Chapter 10

She turned off the County Road into the driveway. It seemed so much longer than the last time she'd driven it. She didn't remember there being so many curves before the cabin came into view.

It was dark by the time she got there. What had become of the day? She'd left early and yet inexplicably it was night. In June, there would be light until almost nine at night so it had to be later than that.

She stopped the car and got out. At first, she thought she must be in the wrong place. There was nothing there. Then the moon broke through the clouds and by its light, she saw the cabin. A great relief washed over her.

But as she walked forward, she saw that it was deserted. The windows stared blankly at her. No light shown from within and the porch screens were torn in places. She went to the steps and saw that the front door stood open, but uninviting.

She forced herself to enter. Inside, the furniture looked the same, but, upon closer inspection, stuffing had come through the fabric of the couch and the chairs from the burrowing of small animals. A layer of dust covered the tables and the floor under her feet was covered with twigs and dry leaves.

"Joseph" she called although she knew there was no one there. Then she heard a sound outside, perhaps his voice answering hers. She ran back to the porch, but it had only been the wind, sighing through the branches of the trees.

She noticed for the first time that the horse corral stood empty.

She could hear the sound of the River as it ran over the rocks.

"Joseph" she called again, knowing he was gone. She had waited too long, come too late and there was nowhere that she could go to find him.

Her face was wet with tears, a sob escaped her and became a wail, the kind of wild keening she remembered from Irish wakes.

Then the most amazing and wonderful thing happened. She could hear his voice saying her name over and over "Maggie, Maggie" and his lips were on her face, kissing away her tears. His arms were around her and he was rocking her, saying "It's just a dream, baby, just a terrible bad dream."

She came fully awake then, clinging to him, still sobbing. "Oh, oh, you're here, really here. I dreamed I came too late. The cabin was empty and I knew I'd never find you."

He shushed her with his lips. "We're here together now. We'll never be apart again. Don't be afraid. Go back to sleep.:" He soothed her until she quieted, but even after she slept, she held onto him desperately all night long.

In the morning, Maggie pushed the dream from her mind, but for the next few nights, she was almost afraid to fall asleep. She never had the dream again, but for a very long time after that, she slept holding tightly to him and woke instantly at any change in the pattern of his breathing or any movement of his body.

Chapter 11

On the day after Maggie's return, while they waited for Gabe, Nettie and Marina, Joseph told Maggie about Nettie. "Her father was French Canadian and her mother is pure Menominee. Nettie was the only child. He worked as a logger and got killed in an accident when a chain broke and spilled a load they were putting on a truck. Nettie's mom about died of grief. Then she remarried. This time to a Menominee, like her. They had a son and then another daughter. He calls Nettie the little half breed. He's tough on her . She spends a lot of time with us."

"Is there a lot of talk like that? Is there prejudice?"

"There are people who feel as though our existence as a people is threatened when the blood line is diluted, people who think that we've been decimated in so many ways that we have an obligation not to intermarry."

"I never thought about it. I should have thought about it. Has it been a problem for Gabe?"

"No. Most people around here don't hold those views. I understand why some people see the world that way. The problem is that it doesn't take real people into account. People fall in love. They want to be with the person they love. When Nettie started having problems at home, she didn't want to tell Gabe at first. She thought it would hurt his feelings. When she finally told him, he just said 'You're a half breed, I'm a half breed, put us together, we're a whole breed.' I like to think he sees the world the way you and I do."

"I used to think I was really tolerant. But as I got older, I began to realize that I actually just didn't care all that much what people thought or what they did, as long as they didn't hurt anybody else."

"Well, maybe that's what tolerance is all about."

"Or maybe I'm just apathetic." Maggie flushed. "Intellectually lazy or something. I just want to be left alone to live my own life, with you. Nothing else matters to me very much anymore."

"There's nothing wrong with feeling that way. You just live and let everybody else live. That's not something to apologize for, Maggie."

When the truck pulled in just after 5, Maggie went outside to meet them and was surprised to see only Gabe and Nettie, more surprised when Gabe got out and Nettie remained in the truck. "What's going on? Where's Marina?"

"She's driving her truck" Gabe said. "Can I talk to you guys?" He was looking past Maggie at Joseph who had followed her down the porch steps.

"Trouble at Nettie's." Maggie noticed that Joseph stated it as a fact, not a question.

"Can she stay here till we leave for school? She can have the loft. I'll sleep on the couch. We brought all her stuff. She can't go back there so please don't say no."

Joseph looked at Maggie. She said "Gabe, why don't you get Nettie and we'll sit down and you can tell us everything." While Gabe walked back to the truck, Maggie said "Has this happened before?"

"She's stayed over once or twice but she always went back after a day or so." Joseph looked over her shoulder and drew in his breath. As she turned, Maggie saw that Nettie had turned her face slightly so that she wasn't quite facing them, but Maggie could still see the bruise that purpled her jaw.

When she reached them, she said "I'm sorry. I didn't want to create problems for you, but Gabe insisted on bringing me here."

Maggie stepped forward and put her arm around Nettie. "You don't have to be sorry for anything. Come on." They went up the steps and sat on the porch,.

"Tell me about it" Joseph said. His voice was low and even, but Maggie heard the undercurrent of something more than anger.

Nettie heard it too and tried to counterbalance it by making less of her situation. "I mouthed off at him and he slapped me. That's all."

Joseph was undeterred. "How long has he been hitting you?"

Nettie seemed to consider carefully before she said "A few months now, mostly not so it would show."

"Anything else? Has he done anything else to hurt you?"

"He hasn't tried to molest me. Nothing like that. Just slapping. But that's getting worse. More often, and harder.

This is the first time it left a real mark. Otherwise I wouldn't have let Gabe talk me into this. I don't want to make any trouble for you."

"You're 18 now. He can't make you come back home." Joseph turned to Maggie, waiting, she realized, for her to make a decision.

"Of course you're welcome here, Nettie. Why don't we bring in your suitcases and whatever else you brought along?"

While Gabe and Nettie carried things up to the loft, Joseph took advantage of their few minutes alone. "I guess it will be awhile before we get to live that nice, quiet life you were envisioning."

"How can I complain? I've got you and our son and now our son's girlfriend. That's our family. Speaking of which, I think your mother just arrived. Is she still driving that same old truck?"

"We tend to drive them till they won't go anymore. I think she brought along a couple of extra mouths to feed." Maggie followed his gaze and recognized both of the men with Marina. One was cousin Will, the other Joseph's brother

Thomas. "Your brother's back?"

"For awhile now. He's been doing pretty well, has a regular job driving a tow truck, has a girlfriend he sees pretty regularly."

"And Will?"

"Will is Will. Never married, but always has some woman who's willing to put up with him."

Thomas looked older, greeting her with reserve. But Will was unchanged and charged in to pick her up and swing her around. "Finally, somebody to dance with. You've got to get Joseph to bring you over to the tavern."

"I can't wait" she laughed. "Do they still have the good Seger on the jukebox or are you dancing to something else nowadays?"

"Same old, same old. This new stuff can't compare." Then, to Gabe, who had joined them, "Your mother is the best dancer around. Did you know that?"

"No. I have a lot to learn about her."

"Well, you'll have plenty of time to do that now" Marina said. "Welcome home, Maggie."

Their first family dinner was a picnic on the porch. Joseph set up the barbeque and grilled salmon and foil wrapped corn on the cob. Marina had brought potato salad. After dinner, Gabe asked "What are we going to do with the stuff you had me buy?"

"Make dessert" Maggie said. And to Joseph, "You never made S'mores with him when he was growing up?"

"I was waiting for you to come home."

After dinner, Maggie had a sense that Nettie wanted to talk to her alone and suggested that the two of them do the dishes together, leaving everyone else to visit on the porch. Maggie waited to see if Nettie would take the first step. When she didn't, Maggie said "I want to tell you something, Nettie. When Joseph asked you if your stepfather had done anything else to hurt you, you said he didn't. I know you might not want to talk in front of Gabe or Joseph, but if he did, you can talk to me. A man tried to force himself on me once and I never forgot what that felt like. I was lucky. A friend of mine came along in time, before anything happened. If there is anything, it's better to talk about it. I wouldn't tell anyone if you didn't want me to."

"No, Maggie. It's the truth. He never has done anything like that. He has very strict rules – for himself, for my mom, and the other kids. He thinks it's his mission in life to somehow rebuild the purity of the race. That's what he says. And I'm the only one in the family who doesn't fit in with that plan. I'm an embarrassment to him. He thinks it reflects badly on him, having a daughter whose blood isn't pure. I just couldn't listen to him anymore."

"How does he treat your mother?"

"You mean because she married outside the tribe? Oh, he's forgiven her. He sees it as a youthful indiscretion. Listen, I know you just got back and you have such a little time to get to know Gabe before he goes away to college. It's not fair to drop all of this on you. I can stay with Marina till school starts."

"Nettie, I can't imagine why I can't get to know my son just as well with you here. You've been part of his life a lot longer than I have so maybe you can help me get to know him. Gabe told me he's been in love with you since you were kids, but that you always said you were too old for him till he caught up to you in school."

"That's true. I loved him too, but I got teased a lot because he was a little kid. Then all of a sudden, he was just so grown up, more grown up than the boys my own age, and people quit kidding me." Nettie looked levelly at Maggie. "Are you wondering if we're having sex?"

"I thought about it."

"Well, I won't lie and tell you that all we do is hug and kiss, but we haven't slept together. We'd like to and if Gabe was my age, we probably would. But I don't feel right about it, not yet. He's mature but he's still only 16."

Maggie's relief was charged with a feeling of hypocrisy, remembering that she had been a few months younger than Gabe when she began making love with Michael. She had never felt guilt about it and never regretted it but she didn't tell Nettie any of that.

Chapter 12

In those first weeks, Joseph fell asleep at night still inside her, then later, somewhere between sleep and waking, they would make love again so that in the morning, it would be impossible to be sure if it had really happened or if they had only dreamed it. When they woke in the morning, she had usually spooned herself against him and he would laugh softly and tell her that she had the most luscious bottom. Their lovemaking soundless so as not to wake their son who slept on the sofa or Nettie who slept upstairs in his bed.

But in the morning, at the breakfast table, while Maggie in her chaste white cotton nightgown sliced peaches onto cereal, and Joseph watched her smiling, anyone who saw then would know how it was.

Gabe saw that his mother's love for his father was an overwhelming thing, both carnal and worshipful. She looked at him the way that one might gaze upon an unexpected miracle and he looked back the way that a man dying of thirst in the desert would look upon an oasis.

Gabe saw now that his vision of his mother, his knowledge of her, was second hand, colored entirely by his father's perception of her. He wanted to know her first hand, the way that a son knows the mother who raised him. But how to do that when he was nearly an adult, 16 years lost forever.

She had brought little with her. A few suitcases of clothes and he soon saw that she favored jeans and tee shirts or cast off shirts of his father's and bare feet unless she was outside working with the horses when she would wear boots.

The only mementos of their years apart were boxes of books and music that she'd brought along. So he asked her if he could read some of her books, listen to her music. And she'd smiled, knowing what he was looking for, and said "Of course you can." They sorted through the books together. Some he had read, others he knew of.

"You like mysteries a lot" he said. He held up a book. "Rebecca, I've heard of this one, but I don't remember what it's about."

"It's what is euphemistically referred to as a woman's book, but it's actually wonderfully written. It's the story of a poor, unsophisticated, un-named young woman who meets a mysterious, handsome reclusive widower in the south of France. He married her and takes her to his family estate

Manderly where she's haunted, not literally, by the ghost of his dead wife, the fabled Rebecca."

"What happens?"

"You should read it for yourself. Have you read Wuthering Heights? In school or something?"

"That one I have read. Catherine and Heathcliff. It reminds me of you and Dad. The love that transcends everything part of it, anyway."

Her music, he supposed, would be described as eclectic. As they played tapes, she would say "That's Oh What a Night by The Dells. It's the greatest doo-wop love song of the 50's when I was young.."

Then, "I was in college when I first heard these – Jimi Hendrix, Janis Joplin, the Grateful Dead. I saw them live once. It was amazing."

All smiles now. "That's Dream Baby by Roy Orbison. It's the first song I danced to with your father.

She liked classical music as well and sat beside his father on the piano bench at night while he played. And she sat beside him on the porch steps while he played the guitar.

One night when he and Nettie came back from a ride, and finished putting away the horses, he saw them on the porch, saw them as clearly as if they were on a stage set, the soft light from the porch, against the black night. He stopped walking, and put a hand on Nettie's arm to stop her as well.

The song playing was one he couldn't remember having heard before. Maggie was singing along, some words about a gun that didn't make any noise.

The melody haunted, the rhythm bringing Maggie to her feet to dance while Joseph watched her. Those lyrics, Gabe thought, must have some special meaning for his mother, maybe because Joseph had been shot. He was so sure that this was the key to really knowing her that he almost held his breath, waiting for the music to end, waiting to see what she would say.

But when the song ended, she went back and sat down with his father, rested her head on his shoulder and all she said was "Low Spark of High Heeled Boys. That's my favorite Traffic song."

Gabe almost laughed out loud, not at her words, but at himself for thinking that a song from her past would be the way to know her. It was just a song after all.

The next day, alone with his father while they waited for a riding student to arrive, Gabe said "I've been trying to know my mother, know her for myself, not just through you."

Joseph said "How have you been going about doing that?"

"Reading some of her books, listening to her music."

"Well, that might tell you a little about her, but mostly it will just tell you that she likes music she can dance to, and that she likes mysteries and fiction in general more than she likes non fiction. What else have you learned since she's been back?"

"She hates housework, but she's not lazy. She'll work all day, mucking out turnouts, and grooming horses and cleaning tack. And she's not a very good cook. But don't tell her I said that. I don't want to hurt her feelings."

"She'll be the first to tell you she's not a good cook. But that's pretty superficial. What do you really know about her? Think about it."

"Everybody likes her. She's fun to be with. She's kind. She gets all emotional whenever she thinks anybody is hurt or feeling bad. And she has a way of looking at you that makes you feel special."

"Yeah, I know what you mean. It sounds like you know her pretty well, maybe better than you thought you did."

"I just feel like I'm missing something."

"Maggie has serenity. You can see it in her eyes and in her smile. It's as though she knows the secret and if you know her, then you'll know it too. But really, it's just that Maggie loves being alive. Every day, no matter how ordinary, brings her joy and that quality she has makes you want to melt into her."

"You were apart for years but I think you probably know her better than anyone."

"Megan and Deco are coming to visit. Maybe they'll fill in some of the gaps for you."

Chapter 13

They arrived early on a Saturday morning, all together. Megan and her husband Marco, Deco and his wife Sara, and Maeve, the grandmother he'd never met. She was still slender, freckled and red haired, at 78. She held him at arms length, said "You look just like your father" then hugged him tightly and stepped aside so that he could be hugged by Megan.

Megan looked so much like their mother that it sent a little shock through him, like seeing Maggie at 18 and pregnant. She held onto him a long time, then introduced him to her husband, and finally said "Gabe, meet Deco."

Deco looked a little like Maggie, same blue eyes and dark hair. He started to shake Gabe's hand, then hugged him instead and introduced his wife, a strong looking young woman, with soft curly blonde hair and brown eyes, who hugged him as well. Deco said "She's a nurse" as if that explained something about her, perhaps her solid presence.

Megan turned next to Joseph, saying "I remember you. I always remembered you." Then looking down at his cane, she brandished hers, and said "Lucky we're gimpy on opposite legs, we can hang onto each other" before handing her cane to Marco and throwing her arms around Joseph.

Once the introductions were over, they sat on the porch, Sara exclaiming over the beauty of the setting. Nettie came out of the house then and Gabe realized that in the excitement of the arrival, he hadn't realized that she wasn't beside him. He stood and went to meet her, taking her hand, walking her from one to the next, introducing her as his girlfriend.

The conversation flowed easily, first as they brought Maggie up to date on what was happening back in Marinette and Menominee, then as they discussed Megan's pregnancy and Sara's work at the hospital which segued into Gabe's starting college in just a few months with a pre-med major.

After lunch, Megan asked Gabe if he would walk her out to the corral to see the horses. "I ride you know" she said. "When I'm not pregnant, anyway. I guess I'll start again after the baby comes."

After the horses, they walked down by the river and he helped her to sit down. She said "I'm sorry, Gabe."

"Why are you sorry?"

"I'm sorry that you didn't have her with you when you were growing up. I hope you won't blame me. I didn't know about you. I guess that's not an excuse but anyway…I especially hope that you never blame her."

"I don't blame you. I don't blame anyone, especially her. My dad told me why she couldn't be with us."

"It was my father, Gabe. He said everything he did was for me, but I know that he really wanted to punish her for loving your father and for having you. When I was little, maybe 8 years old, and I was getting better, she and I were going to leave. Just run away. We were going to come here. But he found out and stopped her. After that, she never had a chance. But I know she loves you so much, that she always loved you."

"Thank you, Megan."

"For what?"

"For telling me that. I know she loves me. I know she didn't have a choice. But it's nice to hear it from you." He looked up toward the cabin. "What about your other brother?"

"Colin? Colin's close to Daddy." She hesitated, then went on. "He remembers when Mom left, when she came here with your dad. When she was pregnant with you. He never forgave her."

"But you and Deco did."

"I was so little I can't even remember her being gone. But Deco always loved her best, and he loves your dad too. He told me on the way here that he used to wish that he could live with her and your dad. Your dad taught Deco to ride. He used to go out to Mom's horse farm. Me too. I always remembered your father's face. Even when I didn't remember anything else, I remembered that."

Marina arrived just after 5 with fish fries from the Wolf River Tavern. Shortly after dinner, Deco announced that they should be starting for home. Maggie made them promise to come back soon and stood in the driveway in the circle of Joseph's arm watching as the car pulled away.

"Don't look so sad, honey" he said. "We can always drive up and see them anytime you like."

"I'm not sad. It was a wonderful day. Megan is really

showing, isn't she? I'm going to be a grandma. Will you still think I'm sexy when I'm a grandma?"

As for Gabe, the visit had filled in a few more pieces of the puzzle that was his mother. He could picture her now caring for Megan but missing him.

Chapter 14

The following week, Gabe said "I hear a lot of big talk about what a great dancer Mom is. So when am I going to see that?"

Joseph said "Tonight. Let's go over to the Wolf."

When they walked through the door, Will stood up and came to meet them. Gabe watched as his mother and cousin Will hugged each other warmly. Then Will said "Seger's still on the juke box. Are you ready?" When Maggie nodded, Will said "Come on. Let's show the youngsters how it's done."

Will and Maggie danced to Nutbush City Limits just as they had years earlier. Nettie said "Your mom can really dance."

"Yeah, she worked in a dance studio for a few years."

"Maybe she could teach us. We could use a little help."

When they asked her, Maggie said "I would love to. Come on, we'll play something just a little slower to start with." She chose Dream Baby and danced with Gabe while Will danced with Nettie. After a few steps, she said "Look how fast you pick it up. Next song, you dance with Nettie."

When they came back to the booth, and Maggie slid in next to Joseph, he said "I love to watch you dance. Don't ever say your dancing days are over because of me."

Will said "You've always got me, Honey."

That night was the first time since her arrival that Gabe turned his attention from his study of his mother. He had thought that he knew his father as well as he possibly could and had wanted to feel that he knew his mother that way.

His earliest memories were of his father, the only parent he had had. He realized with a shock for the first time that night, crowded into that booth, that his father had been a lonely man, a man filled with a deep sadness, a man who had hidden his feelings so well that, if Maggie hadn't returned, he, Gabe, would never have known.

The evidence was in the change in him since her return. It wasn't as if, in all of the years of her absence, he had been depressed or self absorbed. He had been a loving and a giving father, and although given to long silences at times, he had talked and smiled, and laughed. Gabe suddenly realized his father knew everyone, but had no close friends. He had been a man alone, but for his son.

With the return of Maggie, it was as though his father had awakened from a long sleep. He had lost the look of introspection, the demeanor that Gabe now recognized for what it was, a sense of being disconnected from the world.

His father was fully alive for the first time and that made Gabe wonder if Maggie too had been lonely and sad for all those years they had been apart. He supposed she must have been as well, and wondered if her children had been oblivious to her suffering as he had been to his father's.

Chapter 15

A hot day at the end of July, peaceful, lazy, Maggie and Joseph lying together in the hammock on the porch. He was reading, but she had abandoned any pretense and her book had dropped to the floor. She lay with her eyes closed, listening to the sound of the River running over the rocks, and from the kitchen, the even more musical sound of the voices of Gabe and Nettie as they prepared a picnic lunch to take with them in the canoe.

She didn't have to open her eyes to see him, tall and strong, black hair that fell past his shoulders, just like his fathers. When she had first talked about him to Joseph, she'd said "He is the picture of you. It's as though I had nothing to do with making him."

But Joseph had said "Look again. He has your mouth, your smile."

However he was described, one thing she knew. He was a beautiful boy, their son and she loved to watch him. It was like seeing Joseph at 16, untouched by any of the violence that had marked his childhood.

In the weeks since she had returned, she had been unreasonably frightened to let Joseph out of her sight. When he gave riding lessons in the ring, she could sit on the porch steps and watch, or even be inside the cabin where she could hear his voice, patient and kind, as he taught some child or some nervous adult coming to riding later in life.

But when he had to drive to town, to the community center to teach piano and guitar, she rode along, bringing a book and sitting outside waiting for him. She sat, not really able to focus on the words on the page, thinking instead of how grateful she was that he could no longer be a policeman. She felt guilty for being thankful for his shattered leg. For her, it was a small price to pay for his no longer having to do a dangerous job.

Finally, one night, unable to keep anything a secret from him, she told him how she felt "And I know it's wrong, selfish of me to feel that way. But you're safe now and I don't know if I could stand for you to go off every day, not knowing if you'd come home at night. I'm so sorry. It's not that I'm happy that you were hurt, that you endured so much pain, that you'll have a reminder every single day for the rest of your life. Will you tell me about it now? Gabe told me, but it's not the same as you telling me."

And so he told her, just the way it happened. He thought about not telling her everything, but in the end, he told her that when the rifle went off, he had called out her name.

But now that nightmare was behind them, along with all of the other nightmares, and she felt the greatest contentment of her life.

She heard the phone ring inside, heard Gabe say hello? And was surprised when he came to the door and said "Mom. It's for you."

She opened her eyes, but didn't move. What came into her mind in that moment was the phone ringing on a long ago winter night while she sat with her baby at her breast sure that nothing could disturb their contentment.

"Who is it" Maggie asked. Gabe shrugged. "Ask who it is" she said.

In a moment, he was back. "She says it's Hannah."

Maggie sat up and swung her feet to the floor. When she stood, she felt unaccountably dizzy. She supposed it was anxiety. She went in and took the phone from Gabe.

"Hannah? How are you?"

"I'm fine, Maggie. Megan says she and Marco had a wonderful visit with you. She told me all about Gabe. She says he's wonderful."

"He felt the same way about her. I'm glad they got along so well."

"Yes, well, Maggie, I'm calling to ask a favor. I know it's a lot to ask, but Dan would like to see you."

"No."

"He would have called you himself but he knew you wouldn't talk to him. He's very sick, Maggie."

"What do you mean?"

"He's dying.."

"What's wrong with him?"

"It's the same illness that his mother had."

"How long has he known?"

"I don't know exactly. I think he knew back when Megan got married, but he didn't tell anyone."

"Do the children know?"

"Colin does. He's coming home."

"What about Deco and Megan?"

"Not yet."

"Why does he want to see me?."

"He didn't confide the details to me, but I believe he wants to try to make amends."

"It's too late for that. It's too late to change anything that happened."

"Maggie, you know that I've never taken Dan's side. I've never been close to him. But I'm sorry for him now. He told me to tell you that, if you come, he would like you to bring Joseph and your son with you."

"Why? Why would he want to see them?"

"He didn't tell me. Could you perhaps find it in your heart to come?"

"Hannah, do you know what this reminds me of? It reminds me of the last time Dan called here and told me to come home. He kept me there for 16 years. Sixteen years while my son grew up without me." Maggie saw that Gabe was watching her. She tried to smile at him, but tears were filling her eyes. "I can't come back there again."

"That's up to you. I told him I would ask you and I have. If you would just think about it before making a final decision…"

"You're making me feel that I'm letting you down."

"Maggie, this has nothing to do with me. It's between you and Dan. You have every right to hate him and no reason at all to forgive him."

"I'll talk to Joseph and Gabe about it. I'll call you back." She hung up.

Gabe asked "Are you alright?"

"I know you and Nettie want to get out on your canoe ride, but I'd like to talk to you and your father."

Nettie said "I can go outside."

But Maggie said "No, you stay. You're part of this family, Nettie."

They went out to the porch and Maggie got back into the hammock with Joseph while Gabe and Nettie sat side by side on the swing. "That was Hannah. You remember her, Joseph, our housekeeper in Menominee." He nodded and waited for her to go on.

"Dan asked her to call because he knew I wouldn't talk to him. He's ill. Dying, she says. He wants us to come there to see him."

"Us" Joseph said slowly.

"You, me and Gabe. She doesn't know why. She thinks he wants to try to make amends."

"How do you feel about that?"

"There isn't anything he can do to make amends. My first thought was that I wouldn't go."

"And your second thought?"

"Ah, you know me so well. Perhaps we should go. Maybe I need to face him, to put it all behind me, make an end to it. But at the same time, when I look back on all of those years we lost because of him, I can't imagine any kind of forgiveness. What do you think we should do?"

"Let's hear from Gabe."

Gabe answered his father. "You were always a good teacher. You taught me not to hate. You said that when we hate, we end up hurting ourselves more than the person we hate. When Del shot you, I wanted him to die."

Gabe turned to Maggie. "So I understand how you must feel. But he's just a sick, old man now. And he's Megan's father. I'll bet you never tried to make her hate him no matter what he did."

Maggie nodded. "That's right He's father to three of my children and they love him. It will hurt them to lose him. So Gabe thinks we should go. And you?" She looked at Joseph.

"I say we go. There's nothing more he can do to hurt us. We're all together again and we'll go together. Staying away won't give us back anything we lost."

Maggie sat up and got out of the hammock. "Can you get off work, Gabe? Because I think there might be some urgency to this visit."

"I'll call. It's a family emergency."

Joseph said "I have to cancel a few lessons. How long do you think we'll be gone?"

"We could do it in one day but I think it would be nice if we spent a few days there. We can stay at my mothers. We can have a visit with Megan and Deco." She knew that Colin might be in Menominee when they got there, but didn't hold out much hope for an amicable meeting of her oldest and youngest sons.

She called Hannah back that night after dinner and told her

that they would leave early the next day and be there just after lunch. Hannah suggested that she could have lunch ready for them, but Maggie couldn't imagine sitting down to a meal at the Ryan house with Joseph and Gabe so she said "No. I want to go to Mickey Lu's. I haven't been there in awhile and Gabe's never been."

Chapter 16

The next morning, they dropped Nettie and Mister off at Marina's and she promised that she and Will would look after the horses. After some debate, they had decided to take the truck. Maggie felt secure sitting in the middle, Joseph in the driver's seat and Gabe next to the passenger door.

When they got to Marinette, they had lunch at Mickey Lu's where Gabe agreed the hamburgers were the best he'd ever eaten. Then they drove across the Interstate Bridge into upper Michigan. When they got to the house, Gabe said "Wow. It's big."

"Yes, it is." Maggie agreed. "But somehow it never seemed like home to me. When we get to Menekaunee, you'll see where I grew up. And where your people came from."

"What?"

"Didn't your father ever tell you that the Menominee tribe originally came from Menekaunee, long before they settled where they are now?" Gabe shook his head. "He told me the first time I took him there. I thought it was fate that we were together. Both coming from the same place."

"Well, yes, except your mother's people actually came from Ireland, not Menekaunee" Joseph teased.

Maggie said "I guess we've procrastinated long enough. Let's go." When they got to the front door, Hannah opened it before she could knock.

Maggie and Hannah embraced. Then Maggie said "You remember Joseph. And this is our son Gabe."

Gabe shook her hand. Hannah said "You have your mother's smile."

Maggie said "Not too many people notice that. He looks so much like Joseph."

"I've been seeing your smile for a long time, Maggie. Come in, please." Then she said "Dan is in the den. He asked if he could talk to you and Joseph alone first. Then he'd like to have Gabe join you."

When Maggie agreed, Hannah said "Gabe, come on. I'll get you something cold to drink and then we can go out and take a look at the Bay."

When she stood before the den door, Maggie reached for Joseph's hand and held it so tightly that it hurt, but he smiled and said "It's going to be alright." She knocked and Dan said "Come in."

Her first thought was that, if she'd seen him on the street, she might not have recognized him. How could someone change so completely in less than 2 months? His hair had thinned so that she could see his scalp. The bones of his face were prominent. His skin had a waxy yellowish pallor and looked as though it were stretched too tight. He had lost weight and sat slumped in his chair. He reached for a glass of whiskey that sat on the table beside him and took a long swallow.

"You look shocked Maggie. I'm sorry. Hannah should have prepared you better." He took another swallow of his drink "I guess it's too early for you." Maggie nodded.

"Please sit down." He indicated the couch, the same one that he'd pushed her into the day she'd told him she was leaving him. She was relieved to sit down. Her legs were unsteady and she continued to cling to Joseph's hand, thankful to feel him sitting close beside her.

"Thank you for coming. I know it's not easy for you to be

here. I considered putting all of this into a letter, but then I decided it would be too easy that way, for me, I mean. I'm really not doing this to hurt you, Maggie. There's been enough of that in our life. I'd like to start at the beginning if you don't mind. Would that be alright? Please say something Maggie."

"Yes, Dan, that would be alright. Start at the beginning."

"I'm sure you remember when I came home from Chicago, just before my parents' death. I confided in you then that I believed my parents had committed suicide because of my mother's illness. Now it seems I have the same illness, but I'm not really brave enough to drown myself. Perhaps if I had someone who didn't want to go on living without me, but that's not the case.

My parents left this house and the law firm to me. The rest of their estate was divided equally among myself, Michael and Erin. As you know, Erin and I did very well with our shares. Michael is another matter. He should have had his own construction business by now, but apparently he ran through all of the money and he's still working for a builder out in Portland. I tell you this only because it has bearing on the division of my estate. Erin doesn't need my money and

Michael would only waste it therefore I haven't provided for them.

I've set up trusts for each of the children in equal shares. Colin and Declan could do without it but they are, after all, my children. Megan will need it given her marriage to the poor fisherman. Don't look so offended Maggie. That's what he is and I don't really care, as long as he makes Megan happy. But at least I'll know when I die that she'll not have to go without because of who she married.

I've taken care of Hannah as well. She gave her entire life to this family.

I intended to sell this house, but when I spoke to Declan he surprised me by saying that he would like to live here. It seems the prospect of seeing a For Sale sign on the lawn made him realize that this place has some meaning for him. So the house is going to him and Sara.

And that brings me to you."

"To me? You don't owe me anything."

"Please let me finish. It's the least you can do for a dying man. I loved you dearly Maggie. Too much. It's no excuse but it's the reason I did the things I did. I can't forgive you for not loving me, for loving another man, but I can understand it because I know what it is to want someone so much.

I know you won't take anything from me. Joseph, Maggie has always believed that poor is better than rich, more noble or something and I guess you're pretty much the same. I know about your disability. I know that the two of you don't have money. And I know that you think it doesn't matter. But you have a son. He's in high school. College is next."

Joseph spoke. "Gabe graduated this year. He starts college in the fall."

Dan smiled. "A bright boy, then, skipped grades, like his mother. What does he hope to study eventually?"

"Medicine."

"That will be very costly. I have set up a trust for Gabe as well as the other children. He's Maggie's son after all. Please allow him to accept. It will ensure his education."

Joseph said "We can't do that."

Dan took another drink. Maggie saw his hand shake. "Listen to me, both of you. I told you that I could not forgive Maggie and that's the truth. But the one thing I regret in all of this is depriving that boy of his mother for 16 years. I will probably burn in hell for that. This is the only way that I can make amends. Perhaps it will save me. I am begging you to see to it that your son takes this money and uses it for his education."

Joseph shook his head.

Dan watched him, then asked "Doesn't Maggie have any say in her son's future?"

"She does."

"But you haven't let her speak."

Maggie said "Joseph is right. We can't take your money."

"Not even if it means your son will become the doctor he wants to be?"

Maggie looked to Joseph. Joseph said "Shall we leave it up to Gabe?"

Dan looked astounded. "You would leave a decision of this magnitude up to a 16 year old boy?" Joseph nodded. Dan said "Well, then perhaps it's time I met him."

Maggie stood. She felt stronger than she'd felt when she'd entered this room. She went out and found Gabe sitting on the terrace with Hannah. She said "Dan would like to meet you."

When they got back to the den, Gabe stepped forward and shook Dan's hand. "It's good to meet you, Sir."

"Well, you certainly look like your father, Gabe. It's hard to believe that Maggie is your mother."

"Most people say I have her smile."

Dan looked more closely and said "Perhaps. Gabe, I asked you and your parents to come here today to talk about the future. Your future. I have no future. I set up trusts for Colin, Declan and Megan. I offered to do the same for you, for your education. I understand that you want to be a doctor. It costs a lot of money to go to medical school. I'm sure you know that. Your parents are willing to let you make the decision as to whether or not to accept my offer."

Gabe looked at his father, and then at Maggie. He said "I'm sure it's a very generous offer Sir, but I'm afraid I can't accept."

"Why is that, Gabe? It would mean a great deal to me if you would accept. I'm trying to make amends for depriving you of your mother. If it weren't for me, you would have grown up with her. I know this is a poor substitute. But it's the best I can do."

"It's a kind offer. I know you mean well. But you can't make up all those years with money."

"You want to be a doctor. That comes at a very high price. You'll have to sacrifice a lot. I think you're probably up to the challenge. But how will you manage financially?"

"We'll find a way. I'll work. There are scholarships and grants."

"You're all being naïve. Please let me help you."

But in the end, they said goodbye without accepting his gift, as he'd known they would.

He watched through the window as they got into that ridiculous old truck, the same truck Joseph had been driving when he arrived with the horses many years before.

As they drove away, Dan called his attorney. "You were wrong. They didn't take the money." He listened, then said "Yes, well, I know Maggie better than you do. Here's what I'd like you to do. Set up the Scholarship Fund for the Menominee Tribe. It has to be absolutely anonymous, untraceable. It is to benefit good students who have an interest in pursuing a career in medicine. The first Scholarship goes to Gabriel Dodge. He's a very bright young man. There will be no question that he deserves it. He has all of the best qualities. After that, I will have no more input into the selection process."

Chapter 17

As they drove away from the Ryan house, Joseph said "Maybe we should have let you talk to Mr. Ryan alone, Gabe."

"Why?"

"Because I would be more sure that turning down his offer was really your decision. That you didn't do it because you thought it was what I would have wanted you to do."

"It wouldn't have made a difference. I would have told him the same thing whether you were there or not. You can't buy back time. And it didn't feel right. Even if it would have made it easier for you and Mom."

Maggie took his hand. "Don't worry. Rich people aren't the only ones who go to medical school."

"I know. I'm not worried. Anyway, I have to get through college first. So, when do we get to Menekaunee?"

"We're about to. Just as soon as your dad drives across this bridge. Right now, we're still in Michigan." She listened to the sound of the metal drawbridge under the truck and then said "And now we're in Wisconsin. This is Menekaunee. Right down the street is Kelly's, my parents' bar. And in two minutes, we'll be at the house where I grew up."

When they turned onto the street leading to the beach, Maggie said "Oh, Glory be, what's all this?"

Joseph and Gabe looked at her in astonishment. Joseph said "Glory Be? Where did that come from?"

"Well, just look." There were a number of cars parked along the road in front of Maeve's house. There were picnic tables set up in the yard and a barbeque grill. And there were a lot of people.

Megan came out to greet them before they had the truck parked. When Gabe stepped down, she threw her arms around him. "I hope you don't mind. Everybody's here to meet you." She took his hand and led him along to the yard while Maggie and Joseph trailed behind.

Megan made the introductions. "Gabe, these are Marco's parents Sue and Carl. This is my uncle Sean and his wife Annie, my uncle Connor and his wife Paula. Oh, here come Declan and Sara. And then there are all the bratty kids."

Deco said "Megan, you're really getting big. But I guess it comes naturally. Mama was as big as a house when she was pregnant with Gabe."

Gabe looked at Maggie and laughed "Were you really?"

"So they say."

Maeve put her arm through Gabe's and said "Will you help me bring some things out from the kitchen? It will give us a chance to talk."

Declan suggested making one long table out of two so that everyone could sit together. Maeve had put ears of foil wrapped corn on the grill to roast. She and Gabe carried out bowls of potato salad and condiments while Sean and Connor grilled the brats she had soaked in beer, and hamburgers and hot dogs that they served up in buns toasted on the grill. There were pitchers of lemonade and a tub of ice water filled with bottles of beer.

When everyone was seated with a full plate in front of them, Maeve raised her beer bottle and said "Gabe, welcome to our family at last. It's been too long in coming, but we have many years to make it up."

They lingered around the table as evening came on. Maeve said "Everyone has to fix their own dessert."

Maggie said "S'mores? Oh, Mama, you are perfect."

Maeve, handing out marshmallows, graham crackers and squares of chocolate, said "This is all I had to do to become the perfect mother? Well, if I'd known, I would have done it years ago."

After the table was cleared, everyone lingered, drinking beer and talking. When her brothers began to reminisce about Patrick, Maggie's eyes filled with tears. To change the subject, she said "Look at the fireflies. Remember when we used to catch them in a jar. They made such a bright light."

"Yeah" Connor laughed. "Right before they died from lack of air."

Maeve said "You all sit and visit. I'm going in to do the dishes." Gabe stood and said "I'll help you."

It was a warm night, not even a breeze off the Bay. Maggie sat leaning against Joseph, thinking how many years it had been since she'd sat around a table with her brothers. It felt good to be with family. She heard the phone ringing in the house and after a minute Maeve calling "Maggie? It's for you."

She rose reluctantly. How long, she wondered, before she stopped hearing every ringing phone as a threat to her happiness? As she stepped away from Joseph, she bent and kissed the top of his head.

When she went inside, her mother said softly "It's Dan."

Maggie picked up the phone warily. "Yes?"

"Maggie, there's something I want to discuss with you that we didn't get around to today. I'd really like to talk to you alone."

"You can talk to me now."

"No. I'd like to talk to you face to face."

"Dan, you could have done that this afternoon."

"I intended to, but you left so abruptly. Are you going to be in town for a few days?"

"We're going home tomorrow."

"Could you come by before you leave? Joseph and your son can come along and wait while we talk."

"Dan…" she began.

"Maggie, it's important. It's a decision that I can't make without you. Please. I promise you I'm not playing games."

Maggie felt incredibly weary suddenly. "Alright. Is ten o'clock okay?"

"Ten is fine. I'll look forward to it."

Maggie thought, I won't.

When she got back outside, her brothers and their wives were saying goodnight. Declan and Sara were next to leave, then Sue and Carl. Maeve said "Maggie, you and Joseph can take my room. Gabe can have the boys' old room and I'll sleep in the sewing room. I still have the bed in there." Gabe insisted the sewing room would be fine for him and Maggie left them to argue it out. She went in and got a blanket from the linen closet in the hall and came back out with it over her arm. She took Joseph's hand and said "Come on. Let's walk down to the beach."

When they got to the beach, they walked toward the lighthouse pier. There was no one around. They spread the blanket and sat down side by side. She said "Tell me."

"What?"

"Tell me what you're feeling. You've been so quiet since we left Dan's this afternoon. I think I know but I want to hear it from you."

He was silent as though thinking about how to put it, then he said "It was a generous offer. At first, I almost thought about accepting it. After all, he's right. Medical school is expensive. Do I want my son to have to struggle, maybe not be able to go at all because I don't have the resources? It made me think about years ago when I told you that we would be poor people and you said it didn't matter.

I've never believed that money is important, beyond what little you need to live a good life, a decent home, good food to eat, enough to take care of your family. I guess, compared to Dan, I've never really had ambition for more. I thought my life was a good one. Then, suddenly, today, I saw that perhaps that was selfish. Dan said that you and I were alike, that we saw poor as being more noble than rich. That's fine for us. But what about Gabe? What about his education? What if he doesn't get a scholarship?

And I thought that the children you had with Dan would never have to worry about things like that. They were provided for. And I couldn't provide for Gabe that way. It made me feel like a failure for the first time in my life."

"I hate him more for making you feel that way than I do for anything he ever did to me. You're a better person than he is, a better father than he ever was. Look at Gabe. Look at what a good person he is because of the way you raised him. The more I think about it, the more I think the real reason he offered the trust for Gabe was to do just this, to make us feel bad, as though we were deluded for thinking that money isn't important."

"I don't think so, Maggie. It's just what he believes. And it's the only way he knows to try to make amends."

"Well, aside from everything else, it's so typically Catholic. Trying to buy his way into heaven." Joseph laughed for the first time that night. "It's true, you know. Catholics just do the most God awful things, then they go to confession, or, if they have real money, they buy a new stained glass window for the church or something and then they're forgiven. Let's not think about him anymore tonight."

She decided to wait to tell him about Dan's request for another meeting. "I have the most tremendous desire to make out with you right here on this blanket just like we were teenagers instead of 50 year olds. Do you think you might want to do that?"

His answer was to pull her down into his arms and kiss her, while he unbuttoned her blouse.

Chapter 18

Gabe elected to stay at his grandmother's house the next morning while Maggie and Joseph drove over to Menominee. "It'll give me a chance to talk to her without a crowd around" he explained.

When they were in the car, Maggie said "He seems to have taken to my mother."

"You sound surprised."

"I always favored my father so much. Maybe I still do even though he's been gone for more than 10 years now. I'm sad that Gabe never knew him. I never found my mother very likeable. I love her, but I've never felt close to her. Except the one time. The first time she and my father brought Deco and Megan to us in Keshena, behind Dan's back. But even after my father died, she didn't fill his place for me. So I can't wait to hear what Gabe has to say about her."

When they pulled into the driveway, Joseph said "Are you sure you want to talk to him alone?"

"No, I'm not sure at all. But he asked and I said I would. So here we are. I'm sure Hannah will keep you company or you can sit outside on the terrace."

Hannah let them in and told Maggie that Dan was in the den. "Does he ever come out of there?" Maggie asked.

"He sleeps there now, on the couch, when he sleeps at all. I think he's afraid to sleep, Maggie."

Maggie felt a sharp unexpected pang of sympathy, a hot rush of quickly blinked back tears as she knocked on the den door. "Dan, it's me."

He opened the door for her. Standing up, he looked even worse than he had the day before. He had always been so tall, stood so straight. Now he was hunched over, almost folded in on himself. He stepped back to let her enter and returned to his chair. She saw that his usual glass of whiskey sat beside him on the table although it was barely 10 a.m.

She almost asked him how he was and then realized how inappropriate that question would be. She wondered if he was taking anything for pain, and whether he should be mixing it with alcohol, but she supposed it didn't matter anymore.

She wanted to say something to fill the quiet, but couldn't think of anything. He saved her from the awkwardness with a question of his own. "You haven't changed your mind about my offer, have you?"

On the verge of telling him that his offer, even if it had been well meant, had caused hurt to Joseph, she suddenly felt that that fact should remain between her and Joseph. It was not something to share with Dan. So she simply shook her head no and waited to see what he would say next.

"Very well then. I asked you to come to talk about Colin, Colin and Michael."

"What about them?"

"Erin called Michael to tell him about my illness. He's decided to come home for a visit. I guess he wants to see me before I die. Do you realize he hasn't been back since the summer after Colin was born?" He didn't wait for her answer. "Maggie, I'm thinking that Colin should know the truth. He has a right to know who his father is."

"No." Maggie had answered without conscious thought and saw that Dan was surprised, not only at her response, but also at her tone.

"You didn't even have to think about it. I always thought that someday you would want him to know."

"I might have thought so years ago, but no longer. Colin isn't close to me, Dan. I'm not even sure he loves me at all. But he does love you. You're the foundation that his entire life is built on. Can you even begin to imagine the damage it would do to him to hear that you aren't his father?"

"Some people would say that he is entitled to the truth. He could find out someday and feel even worse."

"You and I are the only people who really know the truth. It was so many years ago I don't think anyone who even suspected would remember anymore."

"You seem very sure."

"There are only a few things in my life that I am sure about and this is one of them. This is not something you need to confess to clear your conscience. He'd never be able to trust in anything again. You'd destroy everything he believes in."

"You don't think Michael will tell him, do you?"

"You said it yourself. Michael hasn't come back here in all of these years. Michael may have suspected at one time, but he has no way of knowing, not for sure. I don't think he would say anything based on speculation."

"If he does, after I'm gone, can you handle it? Can you promise me that Colin will go on believing that I was his father? Because I wouldn't want him to find out from someone else when I wasn't here to explain why I didn't tell him." He reached out and caught hold of her hand. His fingers were cold and thin, but so strong that her hand ached.

She didn't pull away. She said "I promise."

Chapter 19

Exactly two weeks later to the day, Dan was dead.

On the day he died, Maggie had awakened early, not really knowing why. It was barely daylight and the only sound was the trilling of some early rising birds. She lay still feeling Joseph's deep even breathing against her back. Then he said "What woke you?"

"I don't know. I was dreaming, but I don't remember the dream I need to tell you something. You're a better person than I am, Joseph."

"Why do you say that?"

"Because I thought about accepting that money. Please, let me tell you why. It has nothing to do with you and everything to do with me. All of these years, I never contributed anything to the raising of our son. You did it all. And now I've come to you with nothing again. No money, no job. Not only do I have nothing to help with expenses, I'll just cost you more money. I think I should try to find work to help out, at least while Gabe is in school."

He turned her to face him. "I don't want you to work. We've been apart so long. I don't want to give up one hour with you. We're not that poor. This place is paid off. We have enough coming in. If Gabe doesn't get a scholarship or some kind of financial aid, we'll find a way to help him. You just stay with me."

"Let's sleep in a little. Maybe we can take a ride after breakfast."

She was drifting off again, enjoying the feel of the breeze that ruffled the curtains when the phone rang. Just past six, so she knew it would be bad news even before she heard Megan's voice.

"Mama, Daddy died."

"When, Honey?"

"About an hour ago. He wasn't doing so well last night so Marco and I stayed over. I'm glad I was here. I got up to check on him and he was awake. I said 'Daddy, do you need anything?' and he shook his head no. Then he smiled at me and he closed his eyes and I didn't realize right away. I thought he just went back to sleep. But he was gone."

Maggie hadn't expected to cry, but she felt a hot rush of tears. "I'm so sorry Honey. Are you alright?"

"I'm okay. Everybody's here – Michael and Aunt Erin, Colin and Olivia and Deco and Sara, but I want you. Can you come?"

"Of course. We'll leave as soon as we can."

Joseph was already in the kitchen making coffee. She told Megan she would call back later that morning and hung up.

She poured orange juice for them both and took a box of cereal and two bowls from the cupboard. Joseph got cups and milk and watched while she peeled and sliced a peach for their cereal. "That was Megan. Dan died about an hour ago."

"I thought it would be the only reason for such an early call. He went fast."

"I think he wanted it to be over. He was always so strong willed. He probably made it happen. Megan wants me to come there. Today if I can."

"You need to go."

"Not without you."

"Maggie, I'll drive you there and I'll wait for you. But you have to go the wake and the funeral with your children. It would be deeply offensive to a lot of people for you and me to be there together."

"You and I belong together. I don't care what the people in that town think."

"This is not the time to let people know that. You need to honor Dan's memory for the sake of the ones who are still here, Megan, and Declan and Colin."

"It seems so hypocritical. Everyone knows the truth, or at least some of the truth."

"Sometimes the only thing that matters is appearance."

"That doesn't sound like something you'd believe, let alone say out loud."

"I only mean that this is something you'll want to do for your children. This is Dan's funeral, not a place for you and me to make a statement."

"What are you guys talking about?" Gabe got up from the couch where he slept and came to the table, with Mister at his side.

"Dan died last night. Maggie's going to the funeral."

"What about you?"

"I'll drive her and I'll wait for her at Maeve's till it's all over."

"You aren't going to the funeral?"

Joseph shook his head.

"I guess this is something Maggie has to do for Megan and Deco and Colin. You think it might not look right for the two of you to be there together?"

Maggie said "Come here and let me hug you good morning. How'd you get so smart?"

"I guess I take after my mother. What's for breakfast?"

Maggie stood up. "I'll slice some peaches for your cereal. That's what we had."

Joseph said "I'm going to make some toast. Do you two want some?"

Gabe nodded yes, but Maggie said "Get that bread away from me. Do you know that I can hardly get into the jeans I was wearing when I got here? It's only been a few weeks and I'm gaining weight like crazy."

Gabe chortled. "Maybe you're pregnant."

"Sorry to disappoint you, but I'm past my child bearing years."

"Too bad. A baby brother or sister might have been kind of neat."

"Neat? Joseph, what kind of outdated slang have you been teaching my son?"

"If you'd been doing the teaching, he'd probably be going around saying groovy."

Maggie started to giggle. "When have you ever heard me say 'Groovy'"?

"I think it was while you were listening to Hendrix the other day."

Gabe said "You guys are crazy. Can I shower first today so I can get to work?" He started out of the room, then said "I guess Nettie and I'll take Mister and go stay at Grams while you're gone. That way I won't have to miss more work."

"And you won't have to miss Nettie either" Maggie teased.

"Seriously, it would have been okay if you guys did have another baby."

Maggie said "You'll just have to settle for being Uncle Gabe to Megan's baby in a few months."

"Hey, that's right. I'll be Uncle Gabe. That's kind of groovy." As he walked away, he started singing "Purple Haze" under his breath.

Maggie and Joseph looked at each other and she said "See, that's what I mean. You raised him to be that way. He's so different from my other kids. He's smart and funny and he already knows exactly who he is and that's all because of you. You think money can compare to that?"

"Ah, Maggie, you Irish are so full of, what's the word?"

"Bull?"

"No, Blarney. You're full of Irish charm."

Maggie and Joseph were packing when she said "I'll be right back. I have to call Hannah."

When Hannah answered, Maggie said "Did Colin get there to see Dan before he died?"

"Oh, sure, Maggie. He's been here since just after you left. Do you want to talk to him?"

"No, it's better if I do that when I get there. I'm really calling to see if any of my clothes are still there."

"Sure. Everything's in your closet, just like always."

"I'll need a dress for the funeral. I'll come by to get it when we get there this afternoon."

"Just so you know, Michael's here."

"Megan told me."

"He showed up last week. I think Erin called him. She's here too."

"How's everybody doing?"

"Erin's handling things pretty well. Michael seems more broken up than you'd expect. Megan and Deco are taking it about as you'd expect. When all's said and done, he was their father. But Colin, it's worse for him. I think he's feeling like he should have stayed here, like he shouldn't have gone off to Chicago."

"I never really understood why he did that, as close as he was to Dan."

"I have no idea, Maggie. He never confided in me."

"He never confided in me either, Hannah. I don't expect he'll start now. We had a bad exchange at Megan's reception and I don't suppose he feels any differently about me now."

"Well, perhaps he'll turn to you now that Dan's gone."

"How are they all going to feel when I show up there?"

"I don't have to tell you about Megan and Deco. They always loved you best. Erin will be glad to see you. She was closer to you than she was to Dan. I can't say about Michael."

"Did he ever marry? He was with a woman in Oregon when we last saw him, but that was 30 years ago."

"He never said. He's here alone. That's all I know."

"Is Colin's fiancée with him?"

"Wife. She's his wife now."

"When did they get married?"

"Just before they came home. Dan was pleased. He liked her."

"But he got married without telling any of us, not even Dan?"

"Apparently. I thought I should tell you, that you should know before you walk in here. May I ask you something?"

"Of course."

"Is Joseph coming with you?"

"He's driving with me, but he plans to stay at Maeve's. We both know this is something I have to do alone."

"None of the others would mind if he were with you, but Colin is a different story. I thought you should know that too."

"Thank you, Hannah. You've always been honest with me and I appreciate that. We're going to leave here in an hour or so. I should probably be there by 2."

"The wake will be tomorrow and the funeral the day after. There's something else. Dan said he told you that Deco decided that he and Sara would like to keep this house. They've asked me to stay on with them and I think I'll do that. I used to think I'd be happy to be on my own one day, but I guess I've gotten too old and too used to my nest."

"I'm glad you're going to be there for them, the way you were for me. I expect they'll start having babies one of these years and you can help raise another crop of Ryans."

"Before you hang up, I just want you to know that I really like your son, your Gabriel, very much. I hope I'll have the opportunity to know him better. It seems his father did a fine job of raising him."

Chapter 20

Gabe, Nettie and Mister took the truck and Maggie and Joseph drove to Menekaunee in her car. There was no one at Maeve's when they got there, so they went to Kelly's. Maeve was behind the bar and Joseph told Maggie he'd keep her company and they'd walk home together, while Maggie went to the Ryan's to pick up her dress.

Hannah let her in. "Colin's in the den, if you'd like to talk to him."

Maggie saw that the door was open and she went and stood in the doorway. Colin was sitting in Dan's chair. There was a glass of whiskey on the table beside him. She wondered how he could look so much like Dan. She saw it in the way he carried himself, his expressions, his gestures.

Colin didn't greet her. He said "Is he with you?"

She didn't have to ask who he meant. "No, he's at your Grama's."

"At least he had the decency not to show up here. He isn't coming to the funeral, is he?"

"No. We thought it would be better if he didn't."

"You're starting to show some class."

"Colin" she began but he interrupted her.

"Look, you're my mother so I suppose I love you, for giving birth to me and all that crap but I always loved my father best and that's just the way it is. That isn't going to change now that he's gone, if that's what you were hoping."

"I never meant to shut you out. Do you remember those summers before Megan was born when we used to go to the beach at Henes Park?"

"I remember I babysat Deco while you spent hours with your friend, what was his name?"

"Paul."

"Yes, Paul. Tell me, was he your lover too?"

"There was never anyone but Joseph."

"There was John Franco."

"John is a friend. John is gay."

"I guess he was your lover in a purely figurative sense."

"Colin, that's enough." The voice came from behind Maggie. Colin looked startled and Maggie turned around. Olivia was standing there, a tall, slim young woman with her blond hair pulled into a pony tail. She wore no make up and her horn rimmed glasse would have made some people miss the fact that she was pretty. Her clothes were casual and expensive, making Maggie suddenly aware of her own faded, too tight jeans and the sleeveless tee shirt she wore, one that had shrunk too small for Joseph, emblazoned with the words Wolf River Tavern. She was conscious of her lack of make up, her hair piled carelessly up on her head, starting to come loose.

It was easy to see that Olivia came from money, but there was more to her than that. She had dignity, class, whatever you wanted to call it. She came to Maggie and took her arm. "Why don't we get some fresh air, maybe something cold to drink." She looked disapprovingly at Colin. "You shouldn't talk to her that way."

Colin's voice was cold. "Oh right. We should be polite, never speak the truth, keep everything civil, the way your family does."

As Maggie and Olivia left the den, Colin said "Livy, I didn't mean that. I'm sorry." But he didn't get up, didn't follow them.

They went to the kitchen, which was empty, and got soft drinks from the fridge, then went and sat on the terrace. Olivia said "I'm sorry. Colin isn't like that, not really. It's just so difficult for him, losing his father."

Maggie thought 'But that's exactly what he's like. It's the way he's always been, cold, disapproving, judgmental.' She wondered that Olivia couldn't see that.

Olivia didn't wait for Maggie to respond. "I'm sorry too that we got married without telling anyone. We didn't tell my parents either. My mom was pretty upset. She was looking forward to putting on a big wedding, just like hers. Colin and I didn't really want that. We've been living together so long, it just seemed ridiculous, you know?"

"I understand" Maggie said, although she really didn't. "So you and Colin are both partners in the firm. Do you enjoy practicing law?"

"I do. I'd like more trial work, but I guess that will come in time. Colin told me that you considered going to law school."

"It was a long time ago. I actually never finished college."

"You could always go back. Lots of older people are doing that. Not that you're old. God, I can't seem to say the right thing today."

"Don't worry, Olivia. It's a stressful time for everyone." She saw a man, walking along the shoreline toward them, something about him so familiar it made her ache. So changed, but she would have known him even if he hadn't been within the context of this place.

Olivia said "Oh, there's Dan's brother. Colin said he hadn't been home for more than 30 years. I can't imagine staying away from my family that long, even though we're far from ideal. I'll leave you two to talk. I'm going to go in and see if I can settle Colin down. Will you be here for dinner?"

"No. I'm staying at my mother's house. I thought I'd have dinner with her."

"Well, then, we'll see you tomorrow for the wake."

Maggie stayed seated, not trusting her legs suddenly. Michael came across the lawn, shading his eyes, seeming not to recognize her until he got close. Then he said "Maggie, it's you. How is it you haven't changed when everyone else has?"

She laughed, accepted his kiss on her cheek, watched him sit down next to her where Olivia had been. "I think you're full of that old Irish Blarney" she said, remembering Joseph saying that about her just hours ago.

But he continued to study her until she felt uncomfortable at his scrutiny. To distract him, she asked "Did you ever marry, Michael?"

"I married the woman in Portland, the one with 2 children. You remember me telling you about her?" He didn't wait for an answer. "We're currently separated. We might get back together though. I thought this trip would help, give us a little breathing room."

"Did the two of you have children?"

"We never did. We talked about it, but the two she had pretty much wore her out. We decided to wait and then it just got too late. She's 12 years older than I am."

"I hope it works out for you, Michael."

"Dan told me everything." For a minute, Maggie felt a rush of panic. Had Dan decided to confide in Michael about Colin, without telling her, some kind of deathbed confession?

But then, Michael went on "I'm sorry for everything you went through all of these years. Dan could be a vindictive man. His excuse for everything was always that he loved you so much. Anyway, I understand that you're back with the man you love so, I guess it's better late than never. Maybe I'll get lucky too. I don't really want to be alone at my age."

"Go back to her then, Michael. Let her know how you feel about her."

He sat in silence, as if considering. Then he said "Maggie, there's something I want to talk to you about. Do you remember that summer, when Colin was a baby? It was the last time I saw you." Maggie nodded, not trusting her voice, waiting to see what he would say next.

"I was pretty sure then that Colin was my child. I've wondered all of these years. Now you're the only one left to tell me the truth. By the time I saw Dan, he was so sick, I didn't want to confront him. Will you tell me the truth, Maggie?"

"Colin is Dan's child, Michael. I'm sorry if that's painful for you to accept."

"But that night, the last night we were together, you remember. I didn't use protection. I wanted you to be pregnant. How can you be sure?"

"Because I was already pregnant with Colin then, Michael, pregnant by Dan."

"You slept with me, knowing that?"

"It was my intention to try to comfort you. I never meant to hurt you. I had wanted to be the one to tell you and then Dan spoke to you first."

"Look me in the face, Maggie. Are you telling me the truth?"

She stared straight into his eyes. She said "It's the truth, Michael."

"Are you ever sorry, Maggie, for the way that things turned

out?"

"Things turned out as they were meant to be."

"How can you be so sure?"

"Because I'm with the man I was meant to be with, always."

"I wish I were so sure, Maggie."

"Ah, Michael, let the past go. It's over. It can't be changed. Go back to Oregon, to your woman, if that's what you want. And if not, then try to find out what it is that you do want."

"Do you remember Ma's?"

Maggie nodded, not sure she could trust her voice.

"I went looking for it. But it was gone. I drove in over the weeds and the gravel down to the River. I thought there'd be something, a falling down building maybe. But there was nothing. It was as though it never existed. I loved you so much, Maggie."

Maggie felt a great sadness descend on her. She laid her hand over his mouth. "Don't break your heart like this, Michael."

He stood up and walked away. She remained where she was, staring out at the Bay through eyes suddenly full of tears. Then she felt him, close beside her. He bent down and whispered against her face. "I'll never believe you slept with Dan while I was away at school. I remember our last night together."

That night, in bed, she said to Joseph "I'll never be sure that I did the right thing. It isn't just that I promised Dan. He was considering telling Colin the truth and I told him not to. I thought it would be better if Colin didn't know. Now I wonder if I had the right to keep such a thing from Colin, and from Michael. Maybe Colin should have the right to know who his father is. And shouldn't Michael know that he has a child? All I could think about was how painful it would be for Colin to find out that Dan wasn't his father."

"It's done now Maggie. You did what you thought was best for your son. Now you have to let it go."

When he saw her tears, Joseph said "I know that you're sad. He was your first love. It's something you never forget."

"But you are my last love, Joseph. You are my true love, my real love. The rest was just a dream"

Chapter 21

Life settled back into a routine once they returned from the funeral. The day of Gabe and Nettie's departure for college was getting closer and they were excited, already starting to pack, deciding what to take along, what to leave behind.

It was a hot still August day, too hot to ride. Since Joseph had no lessons scheduled, he and Maggie caught a ride up river with Will and floated the canoe downstream. They paddled just enough to stay away from the shore, letting the current carry them. In a quiet place not far from home, they went into the water and swam to cool off.

When they got back to the cabin, and hauled the canoe out of the water, they saw that Gabe was already home. "He's early" she said unnecessarily, as if Joseph wouldn't realize that.

Joseph said "Every little change in routine doesn't mean something's wrong." And she knew he was right. But she couldn't seem to shake a sense of foreboding, every time the phone rang at an unexpected time, or anytime a strange car turned up their drive.

"I know, it's just that every time I think that the bad times are behind us and that we can finally be happy, something happens."

Gabe and Nettie came through the screen door and down the porch steps to meet them, and her apprehension disappeared.

Both of them were smiling and Maggie knew at once that there was some news they couldn't wait to share. Maggie thought 'please don't let it be a baby, not yet.'

Gabe said "What'd you two do, tip the canoe over? Your clothes are all wet."

"We jumped in on purpose" she said. It's so hot. What are you two doing home early?"

"Tell them, Gabe" Nettie said. "If you don't, I will."

"Okay. Remember I was up for that scholarship?"

"You got it?" Joseph smiled.

"Even better. My counselor came and found me at work this afternoon. A couple of weeks ago, he brought me in some papers to fill out for a different scholarship, a better one. It's for Native Americans, actually for the Menominee, and it's a full scholarship for students who want to study medicine. I didn't tell you guys at the time because I wasn't sure I'd get it, and I didn't want to disappoint you. But I got it. It covers everything, college and medical school, tuition, books, housing, everything. All I have to do is maintain my grades and get into medical school. I mean, that's a lot, but I can do that. And now, you don't have to worry about how we're going to pay for it." The words had come out in a rush, almost too fast to follow.

Maggie and Joseph didn't look at each other. Maggie waited. Gabe said "Well, are you in shock or what? Aren't you happy?"

Joseph stepped forward and pulled Gabe to him. Then he reached out one arm and pulled Maggie into a three way hug. "Come on, Mama, hug this son of ours. He's going to be a doctor."

Gabe laughed and said "Well, some day anyway."

Maggie said "Come here, Nettie" and pulled Nettie into the circle. "What do you want to do to celebrate?"

Gabe said "I don't know. Pizza maybe."

Joseph said "I think this calls for something a little more festive than pizza. Everybody go in and get ready."

He didn't tell them where they were going, but when they turned off Highway 32, Gabe said "Maiden Lake."

"Where?" Maggie asked.

"You grew up here and you've never been to Maiden Lake?" Joseph's tone was unbelieving.

"I didn't really grow up here. I grew up in Marinette."

"Everybody comes here, even people from Marinette. Isn't that right, Gabe?"

"I can't believe you're just bringing Mom here for the first time."

They parked and Joseph led the way through the bar and dining room. "There are tables outside by the lake. I thought we'd have drinks there before dinner."

The hostess showed them to a table and Joseph ordered Champagne from the outdoor bar, and sodas for Gabe and Nettie. When the drinks came, he raised his glass. "To Gabe, who will one day ease suffering and bring comfort and to Nettie, whose art will make the world a more beautiful place."

They clinked glasses and drank. Joseph looked at Maggie. "Are you going to cry?"

"No. Well, maybe a little. This is such a happy time. It's a beautiful place and we're all together. But before you know it, these two will be gone."

"We're not going that far, Mom. And we'll be back every Holiday. Besides, aren't you just a little bit happy about having the house to yourselves? You can get rowdy if you want to, run around without your clothes, make love on the kitchen table. Look, Nettie, Mom's blushing."

"Hush now" Maggie said. "Here comes the waitress to take our dinner order." As she watched the waitress approach, she saw 2 couples get up to go inside to the dining room. They looked familiar and one of the women looked directly at her, but before she could place them, they were gone.

When Maggie saw the menu, she said "Ooh, lobster."

Both Gabe and Joseph said "No, Walleye. You have to have the Walleye."

"Why? Fish is fish. And lobster is heavenly."

"First time, try the Walleye" Joseph said. "If you don't like it, I'll bring you back here for lobster next Saturday."

Maggie and Joseph drank more Champagne until the hostess came over to tell them their table was ready.

In the dining room, they feasted on Walleye and when they finished, and the three of them looked expectantly at Maggie, she readily admitted they had been right. "I can't believe I lived here my whole life and never ate Walleye before. It was always Perch and Trout when I was growing up."

On the way out, Joseph suggested that they stop in the bar for after dinner drinks. He greeted the bartender and said "4 Brandy Alexanders, 2 without the brandy for the kids". Gabe made a face at being referred to as a kid. Maggie had a sudden vision of sitting with Michael and his parents in the Bar at Graby's, drinking Brandy Alexanders when they'd been younger that Gabe and Nettie. She guessed that times had changed.

Maggie said "I have to go to the Ladies Room.

"Me too" Nettie said.

Joseph said "This is a lesson for you, Son, the ladies always pee in pairs."

Maggie slapped his arm good naturedly as she got up.

The Ladies Room was small and when Maggie heard voices from inside, she and Nettie stopped to wait in the vestibule. The voices from inside were familiar and in a minute she had it, putting the names with the faces of the women she'd seen outside before dinner. Vi Hancock and Lydia Hedge, two of her acquaintances from long ago, when Dan had begun bringing her to the Country Club.

As the recollection came to her, Vi said "Well, I guess all those rumors were true after all. We always heard she had a baby back when she went away the first time. But then she came back and the talk died down."

Maggie could imagine Lydia's smug expression as she said "We were all willing to forgive and forget. After all, who hasn't had a little indiscretion at one time or another. Although this is really going too far. She ran out on him when he was dying and then had the nerve to show up at the funeral. Probably thought she could cash in on the Estate."

"It could be worse. Imagine if she had somehow got hold of the house and moved back with her boyfriend? Can you imagine them at the Country Club?"

Vi laughed. "I assume that's the son. Although it's hard to tell. He's the right age, but he looks pure Indian. Can't really see any Menekaunee Irish there."

"You're just awful" Lydia said, but her tone was approving, and she clearly meant it as a compliment.

Maggie pushed the door and it banged off the wall. Both women jumped and Maggie was pleased to see that Vi had a smear of lipstick on her cheek from the open tube in her hand. "Hello, ladies."

"Maggie, what a surprise. I thought that was you outside. I said to Vi 'Doesn't that look like Maggie Ryan?' But then our table was ready so I didn't have a chance to come by and say hello."

Vi was dabbing ineffectually at the lipstick, spreading the smear across her face. She said nervously "So, Maggie, what are you doing all the way out here?"

"We're celebrating. Our son is starting Pre-Med this fall. He's only 16."

"Well" Lydia said "That's quite an accomplishment."

Maggie stepped past them toward the stalls. She had almost forgotten Nettie was there until she heard her voice. "You two aren't good enough to be in the same Rest Room with her." Her voice was low and incensed. "Come on, Maggie, let's go."

Maggie said "But I have to pee." Nettie looked so surprised that Maggie started laughing. In a minute Nettie joined in. Vi and Lydia vanished, letting the door bang shut behind them.

When Maggie and Nettie rejoined Joseph and Gabe, they were still laughing. Joseph said "What's funny?"

"Life is funny." Maggie sang.

"What's that" Gabe asked.

"A song" Maggie said. "It's a song, a song from my youth. Well, not my youth exactly. A song that was popular when I was in College. A friend of mine would play the drums and we'd sing along. I'm sure I still have a tape. Maybe I'll play it for you one day."

They got home late, but Maggie said "Joseph, I need to walk off some of that dinner." They walked past the corral, checked on the horses and then went down to the River and sat on the bank, listening to the sounds of frogs and night birds. Finally, she said "We'll never know for sure. He would have set it up so that there was no way to trace it back to him."

"I figured that."

"Still, it wasn't easy for you."

"I know it's time for me to step back, swallow my pride. Our son wants to be a doctor. Now he's one step closer. He won't have to waste his energy trying to work his way through. I just realized I didn't have the right to make it harder for him just to make myself feel better."

"You did good, Daddy. You did the right thing. And you'll always know that when Dan gave Gabe the choice, he turned it down. He wasn't looking for the easy way. And, there's something else. It makes me feel as if those sixteen years without you, everything I missed, everything I lost, were more than a penance I had to do. Maybe in some part, because of that, I contributed somehow to our son's future. The money came from Dan, but it was his penance for separating Gabe from his mother. Does that make any sense to you?"

"You're a wise woman, Maggie. Wiser than me in so many ways. I'm glad you're home."

Chapter 22

"You know I always spend Labor Day weekend at Lake Geneva. And this year, for the first time, we were going to do it together."

"It's not as if it's Lake Geneva, Switzerland. It's just Lake Geneva, Wisconsin. And we'll do it next year, I promise."

"Please tell me why I'd willingly give up a reservation at a sublime lakeside resort for a weekend at a real Reservation?"

"For me. You'd do it for me. I moved to Chicago for you. I went back to school for you."

"It's for you and you know it. I swear if I didn't know you were gay, I'd think you were in love with this woman. Are you sure you are gay? Maybe you're bi and you just don't know it."

"Are you jealous?"

"Probably just a little. You talk about her all the time."

"Wait until you meet her. You'll fall in love with her too."

"I sincerely doubt that, but I can't say no to you."

"Just remember, she's the reason I'm here. She made me believe."

"In what?"

"In love, in you, all that corny romance novel stuff."

Chapter 23

"My Mom is going to be so excited when she finds out about the baby."

"I don't think we should tell everybody this weekend. It's a wedding, not a baby shower. I'd feel like we were trying to get too much attention when it's really all about your Mom and Joseph."

"Hannah, what do you think? Sara thinks we shouldn't tell anybody because we don't want to take anything away from the wedding."

"I think your mother won't mind sharing the spotlight for such happy news."

"What about you, Hannah?" Deco teased. "Are you happy? You're going to help raise another Ryan."

"It seems that was my purpose in life, helping to raise Ryans. First Michael and Erin, then you, Colin and Megan."

"Do you think Colin and Livy will have kids?"

"Deco, your brother is one Ryan that I helped raise and can't read. As close as he was to your father, he chose not to come back and practice law with him. But I guess that made him just like your father. Your father did the same to his father."

Deco looked thoughtful, then sad. "Hannah, is he ever going to forgive Mom? He's not close to any of us, not me or Megan or Grama. And he doesn't like Livy's family either. Livy's all he's got. And sometimes I wonder why she puts up with him. He isn't even very nice to her."

"She loves him even with all his moodiness and bitter feelings. Who's to say why one person loves another, when love can cause so much unhappiness."

"Because" Sara said "love doesn't just cause unhappiness. Sometimes it comes with the greatest joy and so most of us are eternally optimistic about love. Look at your Mother and Joseph. They were apart for so many years. They never stopped loving each other. They never stopped believing that they'd be together again. Aren't they a reason to believe?"

"That kind of love is rare. And look how much unhappiness they had before they got where they are now."

"I think your Mother would say it was worth it. What do you think, Hannah?"

"I think that Maggie endured whatever she had to because she believed that in the end she would be with Joseph again. Maggie is a great believer in love."

Chapter 24

"Marco, look at me.. How can I be the Maid of Honor?"

"Because your Mama wanted you to be. She doesn't care if you're kind of large. You look real pretty anyway, Honey."

"I look like a giant wedding cake in this dress. What was I thinking?"

Maeve said "You do look kind of like a wedding cake, but that's fitting, don't you think? Now, come on, it's a two hour drive and we don't want to be late."

Once they were in the car, Maeve said "Oh, Sweethearts, just one moment. I forgot something."

When she got back inside the house, Maeve went into the bedroom and looked through her top dresser drawer until she found what she was looking for. It was her own wedding picture taken so many years before. She studied their young faces, hers and Patricks. She said out loud "I wish you could be here today, Darling, to see your favorite daughter married to the man you called her one true love. You know, I was wrong all those years ago. It was you who were my one true love. It took me such a long time to realize it and I never told you. I hope that somehow you knew. I miss you so." She decided to carry the picture along and give it to Maggie.

Chapter 25

"Do you think she'll like it?"

"She'll love it. This place was so important to her. Now that everything's turned out so well, it won't hurt her to look at it every day."

"It's a beautiful painting. And it's where she met Joseph. Look, you can see the corral, and the house, and even down to the River."

"I don't think we can ever thank her enough, Chuck, for making this our home."

"She told me she wanted someone who loved the place like she did to have it and we love it that way."

"Do you think our boys will grow up feeling the way we do?"

"I hope they will, but if they don't, they have to live their own lives. Anyway, we'll be here for a long time before it'll be time to pass this place along to someone else."

Chapter 26

The horses gathered at the fence and watched as the guests arrived. By 2 o'clock everyone was in place. Maggie thought how lovely it would have been if her father could have been there to give her away. It made her just a little sad, as did the fact that Colin had refused to attend.

She sat at the dressing table. Outside she could hear voices and laughter, friends and family. She looked at her reflection, at the locket that she had worn all of these years. It was worn smooth from the touch of her fingers. The night before, Joseph had said "I can hardly see the outline of the horses anymore. You should let me recarve it for you one of these days."

But she had refused. "Oh, no. It has to be this way. Every time I look at it, I think of all the years we were apart, when I touched it to feel closer to you. Seeing it worn smooth will always remind me of how precious our time together is."

There was a knock and Marina came in. "It's time. The day came just the way I told you it would all those years ago."

"Marina. Can you tell me something more?"

She didn't need to ask what Maggie wanted to know. "The two of you will be together for many, many years, Maggie. You've earned your happiness."

Maggie walked onto the porch and down the steps to the grass. Megan was there, her Maid of Honor, just a few months away from motherhood. And Gabe stood next to her as his father's Best Man.

Joseph waited and as she walked to him, he reached out his hand to her.

On a beautiful warm day, Saturday September 4, 1993, Maggie Ryan at last became Maggie Dodge. She and Joseph were married on the banks of the Wolf River, outside their cabin. Afterward, everyone drove to the Wolf River Tavern for the reception.

When it came time for dancing, Joseph told Maggie to dance with his cousin Will and with John Franco because, even if he could not dance himself, he still loved to watch her. But Megan said "Joseph, I've walked with a cane for as long as I can remember, almost my whole life and I can dance. If I can dance, so can you. You just have to go slow."

So they took the floor, and Joseph held Maggie in his arms, and they danced. It was their first dance as husband and wife, but only the first of many. They would dance for the rest of their life together and that would be a very long time.

Epilogue

"I love the Spring, don't you?"

"You love every season, Maggie."

"I do, but Spring especially."

"Time to feed the horses."

"Wait for me and I'll help you. I'm going to walk down to the mailbox and get the mail first."

"How about we drive over to the Wolf for a fish fry for dinner when we're done?"

"That sounds good. I'll be right back." She said to the dog "Come on, Mister, walk with me." Then, "I think he misses Gabe as much as we do. I thought we'd have 2 years together before he went away to school."

"He'll come home for awhile before summer school starts."

He watched her go, Mister walking by her side and in a few minutes, watched the two of them come back toward him.

She was carrying a thick package wrapped in brown paper.

"What have you got there?"

"I don't know." She sat down next to him and removed the wrapping. "Look, Joseph. It's Chuck's book." The cover scene looked familiar. She realized it was the same as the painting that Chuck and Debbie had given them as a wedding gift, the painting that hung over their fireplace. The book's title was On River Road.

She opened the book. "I asked him once to include me among the people he thanked. You know how authors do that. But I'm not there."

Then she turned a page. She found the dedication. It said

        For Maggie, Who Inspired Me

Made in the USA
Lexington, KY
13 April 2015